RUNNING ON EMPTY
AN LCR ELITE NOVEL

BY CHRISTY REECE

Running On Empty
An LCR Elite Novel
Published by Christy Reece
Cover Art by Patricia Schmitt/Pickyme
Copyright 2014 by Christy Reece
ISBN: 978-0-9916584-3-5

PROLOGUE

Paris, France

Sabrina Fox stood at the window of her apartment and looked down at the bustling street below. Since she lived on the thirty-sixth floor, recognizing anyone from this distance should be almost impossible. But she would know him…she would recognize him from any distance. From the moment she had met Declan Steele, she had *known* him.

Not that it had been love at first sight. A smile tugged at her mouth as she thought about those early days. She had hated Declan with a passion unrivaled since the fury she had known as a kid. He had infuriated her, challenged her…made her see things in ways she had never considered before. She had wanted to succeed in everything he taught her, but at the same time had resisted him with every fiber of her being. Even then she had realized her hatred for him was different. He had been her trainer and harder on her than anyone else in the class, but even in their darkest moments with each other, she'd felt as if an invisible force had been drawing her to him.

Still, there were many days she'd left her training sessions plotting his excruciatingly painful death. Dangerous, since he had been teaching her how to kill.

Having been born into the very definition of a dysfunctional family, she had endured a childhood of sheer hell. She had been rescued from that hell by Albert Marks, who had offered her a job, bringing her into the dangerous world of covert ops. The job had saved her life.

The Agency, EDJE (Eagle Defense Justice Enforcers), was known to only a few, including the president and his closet advisers. When assassinating terrorists and dictators, the fewer people who knew about such things, the better.

When Albert had told her about the Agency, she'd laughed in his face, sure that it was just another gimmick or trick. In her world, adults did one of three things—lied to you, abused you, or drugged you. They didn't offer you an escape.

Albert's patience, sincerity, and sheer determination had convinced her. She would always be grateful to him, not only for saving her life but also for introducing her to Declan.

Because of Albert and the Agency, she had learned to believe in herself, to realize there was more to Sabrina Fox than being a victim to beat, demean, or rape. She had worth.

And Declan? He had taught her many things, but the most important was that she deserved to be loved.

Leaving EDJE hadn't been an easy decision to make. She still believed that what she had done for them was right and just. She admired what the Agency stood for. But it had taken its toll. With each new assignment, she had felt as if she lost a little part of her soul. She would have hung on, doing the job even as it destroyed her, but Declan had seen the damage, too. He had been the one to introduce her to Jordan Montgomery, who had left the Agency years ago to become an operative for Last Chance Rescue.

Even though she'd known about LCR, Sabrina had never encountered any of their operatives. Jordan had met with her, told her a little about the organization and then arranged a meeting with Noah McCall, LCR's leader. From that first meeting, she had been hooked. Rescuing victims as opposed to killing? Doing good without taking lives? The chance to work for LCR had felt like a gift from heaven. So she'd joined the Last Chance Rescue team and never regretted it for a second.

The emerald and diamond band on her left hand captured the sunlight, creating a colorful prism on the window. It felt strange to be wearing it. Unless she was on an undercover assignment, she rarely wore jewelry. No one at LCR, other than her boss, knew she was married. She kept her personal life private for many reasons, but one of the biggest was her concern for Declan. As one of EDJE's top agents, his life was in constant danger—she refused to add to it by revealing her connection to him.

Just over a year ago, she and Declan had exchanged vows in the sanctuary of a small church. Other than the minister and his wife, there had been no witnesses. Then, for five glorious days and even more glorious nights, Declan had been hers and no one else's. No calls, texts, or email warnings of dire events and impending doom.

Breath caught in her throat. There he was, getting out of a cab. As if he knew she would be watching, he looked up. She couldn't see his face from here, but his image was etched in her memory. Square chin, stubborn and implacable, but the hint of a dimple in the center gave it a slight softening. His cheekbones, as if carved from stone, were the kind a camera would love to capture. Unfortunately, with his job, photos of any kind weren't possible. He had a high, intelligent forehead and a slash of thick black brows that he often arched when he was expressing himself passionately about something. And beneath those expressive brows were startling, deep-blue eyes that could glint like a sapphire flame when he was angry or sparkle like jewels when he was amused. His nose was a noble blade that she had once teased him would look perfect on a Roman coin. And his mouth…oh, Declan's mouth would make angels weep. Full, sensuous, delectable. Firm and hard when he was in a mood, but soft and delicious when he was kissing her.

If that wasn't enough, all of that masculine beauty was surrounded by ink black hair so thick that it took a strong wind to even ruffle a strand. And his body—six feet, five inches of masculine perfection. Broad shoulders, muscular arms, a sprinkling of hair on his well-defined chest led down to granite-hard abs. Long, powerfully built legs that could run for hours without tiring. To make it doubly unfair, he possessed a keen, intelligent mind, a quick wit, and a good heart. When God had been passing out special favors, Declan had been standing at the front of the line.

She turned at the sound of the door opening, and there he stood, looking even more wonderful than she remembered. He barely took one step inside before she was across the room. The door closed behind him, his luggage dropped with a thud, and then she was in his arms.

"I've missed you." She spoke against his neck and inhaled, loving the fragrance of her man. He smelled of the aftershave she'd given him the last time they were together and clean male musk. Pulling slightly away from him, she gazed up into those deep-blue eyes and her insides melted.

"I missed you, too, Little Fox."

Little fox. She smiled at the nickname he had given her when he'd first started training her. At first it had infuriated her. She'd come from a family who called her derogatory names more often then they'd used her given name. She had been sure it was an insult. And her? Little? Okay, she was smaller than Declan, but at five feet, eleven inches in her bare feet, she was far from little. She was sure he had meant to demean her. But then, after she had come to know him better, she had heard the affection behind the name.

Her fingers traced a slight crease beside his mouth, one she swore hadn't been there the last time they were together. "You're well? No new bumps, bruises, abrasions?"

"Nothing to speak of. And you?"

"Not a scratch."

The relief in his eyes was a reflection of her own feelings. This was the life they'd chosen but that didn't lessen the worry.

"And now that you're in my arms, I'm perfect."

"I couldn't agree more," she said softly.

Lowering his head, his smiling mouth covered hers and time disappeared. His taste deliciously familiar, heady, sexy, rocketed her from simmering need straight to full arousal. Declan's big hands, callused and urgent, roamed over her body. She was so immersed in him, lost in her desire, it took a moment or two to register cool air washing over her.

Pulling away slightly, she laughed breathlessly against his lips. "What's so funny?"

"You're the only man I know who can strip a woman without any effort."

He looked down at her black skirt and aqua blue cashmere sweater lying on the floor. A lacy black bra and bikini panties lay several feet away as if flung by impatient hands.

His grin was wicked. "Be warned, this is how I intend to have you all weekend."

"You'll get no complaints from me, but how about you?" She took a step back. "Think you can undress yourself as quickly as you did me?"

In seconds, he showed her how he could be even faster. Ripping his shirt open, they both ignored the buttons that fell to the floor. He toed his shoes off and pulled his pants, underwear and socks down in one determined move. And he stood before her, gloriously aroused, gloriously hers.

He pulled her back into his arms and growled, "Ready, wife?"

"Always," she answered softly. Melting into his embrace, she allowed him to possess her body, just as he possessed her heart. Everything she had, everything she was, belonged to him. Her husband, her lover, her life.

Hours later, Declan stood beside their bed and gazed down at his sleeping wife—the woman who had become the beat of his heart. She was everything he'd ever dreamed of having in a mate and was the biggest reason he fought against the shit he faced daily. How she had become so vital for his survival still surprised him.

Having lost his entire family years ago, he had never planned on loving or having deep feelings for anyone again. And now here he was today, incredibly, undeniably, and fiercely in love. Every ounce of tender emotion he possessed was tied up with this beautiful, intelligent, courageous woman.

Everything else in his life was duty, but Sabrina was his purpose, his reason to exist.

Holding back a heavy sigh, he strode over to the reading chair across the room and dropped into it with an uncharacteristic lack of grace.

All the plans he'd had were now shot to hell. Would she hate him when she learned the truth or would she understand? She had been in the game a long time, too. She knew better than anyone that you did the job no matter how objectionable. If you let emotions get in the way, people died.

The ache in his chest might be shame. It had been a long time since he'd felt this way, so he wasn't sure he would recognize the emotion. Didn't matter. He had a job to do and would do it to the best of his ability.

When the assignment was over, he would tell her everything. Didn't mean she wouldn't be hurt or royally pissed. When they married, he had recited vows—ones he had written himself. At that time, he had meant every single one. In those vows, he had promised to never willingly hurt her. What a stupid, idiotic thing to have said. In one way or another, he'd been hurting people all of his life. Why would he think Sabrina was any different?

He had known from the beginning that their marriage wouldn't be like others. His job as a top commander of EDJE didn't allow for normal. Maybe if he were still just an agent, still in the field, it could have been semi-normal. But when his pay grade had been upped, the danger had increased, and semi-normal had gone to hell.

Regretting his decisions would do no good. He believed in what he did, what EDJE stood for. Protecting his adopted country, one that he loved as much as he loved his homeland of Scotland, meant sacrifice. He just damn well hated certain parts of it.

"For a man who recently gave his wife ten orgasms, you're looking awfully serious."

Throwing aside his dire thoughts for the moment, he glanced over at her. "You're keeping count?"

"Hell yeah. If I don't, how will I know when you're slipping?"

"So is ten better or worse than the last time?"

"Better." She beamed at him. "Thank you very much!"

He chuckled and shook his head. Only Sabrina could pull him from the darkness. "I ordered a meal for us…that little Italian place down the street you like so much. Should be here in about twenty minutes."

Her movements graceful as a dancer, she rose from the bed. "Just enough time for me to shower." Her naked body seductive, enticing, she held out her hand. "Join me?"

Declan followed her into the bathroom. All the worrying in the world wouldn't stop the inevitable, but for a few hours more he could hold back the sense of impending doom that shadowed his every step. Reality would come soon enough.

Placing her fork onto her empty plate, Sabrina leaned back in her chair with a satisfied sigh. Nothing like incredible, mind-blowing sex to increase her appetite. "That was wonderful."

"More wine?"

"No, thanks. Good choice, though. It was fabulous with the risotto."

"I was surprised the restaurant had a bottle. It's sometimes hard to get."

What she knew about wine or the finer things of life, she had learned from Declan and her Agency training. Odd that knowing such things as the correct wine or proper fork were important, but when infiltrating certain organizations to get close to the leader, that knowledge could be paramount. Men and women who perpetrated some of the most heinous acts on mankind often cloaked their evil ways behind wealth and privilege. Blending in had been vital to her success.

Working for LCR was a refreshing change in many ways, but more than once she'd had cause to be grateful for her earlier training. Though she now rescued kidnap victims instead of assassinating evil leaders, she occasionally went deep cover. Her skills had come in handy.

She eyed the beautiful man across from her. Though Declan could hide any emotion or thought behind a cool, implacable facade, she had known him for twelve years, loved him almost that long. Making a career of being someone else enabled him to hide behind a mask, but she knew every nuance and expression… something was bothering him.

Their time together was so limited that neither of them liked to bring the outside world in, but she knew that was about to happen. And if it was bothering him, then she definitely wanted to know.

"You want to talk about it now or do you want to wait till later?"

She appreciated that he didn't bother to pretend he didn't know what she was talking about.

He swallowed as if what he was about to say was difficult and gave an odd, twisted smile. "I've been giving a lot of thought to our marriage. What I want out of life."

She wanted to tease him and say she was glad he'd been thinking about her. The darkness in his eyes prevented that. "You want out?"

He jerked slightly. "No…hell no."

Relief flooded through her. "Well, then…what? If you don't tell me quickly, I'm going to imagine all sorts of terrible things."

"I want more than this…clandestine, too dangerous life. I want a family, a house with a yard, I want pets…maybe a kid or two."

Frozen in dismay, she could only stare. Never had he indicated that he wanted something like that. The nature of their careers made those things almost impossible to carry off. "I…uh…"

He grinned. "Damn, I love seeing you speechless."

"But, Declan, the Agency is your life. You've been with them for years."

An intense light entered his eyes. "The Agency is not my life, Sabrina. You are. Never forget that." Then, as if pulling himself back from the force of those words, his body relaxed and his expression cleared. "I'm proud of what I've accomplished. But I want to be with you more than a few days out of the year. I was fooling myself thinking I could have both. I don't want both. I only want you."

Happiness burst within her. To have him out of danger. To not worry while watching news of bombs exploding and people dying in war-torn countries if he was there in the midst of it all, trying to stop the chaos. To not worry about that middle-of-the-night phone call telling her he'd been killed or injured. Yes, yes, yes!

"So you're leaving the Agency? I mean, really, seriously leaving it?"

"Yes. I talked to Albert about it already. He was surprised, to say the least, but he understands. I have just a couple of minor issues I need to rectify. Nothing major. Won't take more than a month or so to finalize everything, and then I'm all yours."

"So…you want to, uh, like…get a regular job? Nine to five, the whole deal?"

"I've got some money saved up, so I don't have to make a decision right away."

She bit her lip. While she was thrilled that Declan would be out of the dark, gritty, and dangerous world of covert ops, she wasn't sure how he felt about LCR. She loved her job, and though it was dangerous, often just as much as his was, she didn't want to leave it.

A thought flashed across her mind like a meteor. "I have an idea. How would you feel about working with me? I'm sure that No—"

His fingers covered her mouth. "Let me get this out of the way, and then we'll see. Okay?"

Even though she was a little disappointed at the lack of enthusiasm for her suggestion, she told herself it was understandable. Here he was finally giving up a dangerous job, and she was asking him to jump right back into the fire.

"So the things you're finalizing. Is it an op or—"

He leaned forward and grabbed her hand, squeezing it gently. "Don't ask, darling, and I won't have to say no."

Even though she understood, it still hurt. It wasn't because he didn't trust her—she knew without a doubt he did. His reticence to share was always about one thing—protecting her. And that scared her most of all.

"I love you." She didn't know why, but she felt the need to say it once more.

His face softened. "I know. Believe me, sometimes it's the only thing that keeps me alive."

"Don't say that."

"For now, it's the job."

She nodded. They'd had this discussion before. Either of them could be killed on any mission. They'd agreed to make the most out of their lives, their marriage. Soak in as much as they could. But that conversation hadn't seemed as grim as it did now.

"You've got that look on your face that I don't like. I can't tell you what I'm finishing up, but I will say that it's much less dangerous than usual. Very routine. Mostly paperwork and assignment shifts. Absolutely nothing covert."

Why did she suddenly feel as though they were talking about two different things? She shook away her disquiet. His news had just thrown her off-kilter, that's all.

Realizing their discussion had changed the atmosphere of their time together and wanting to get back to enjoying themselves, she asked one last question, "When do you need to leave?"

"Tomorrow."

"Tomorrow? But we—" She held her tongue. This was the job, too. Missions rarely came at convenient times. If he could've delayed it, he would have.

She drew in a silent breath. Okay. All right. Complaining about it would do no good and only spoil their last few hours together. No way was she going to let that happen. And once he was finished, he'd be back with her permanently.

"Then let's not waste time we don't have."

His smile of appreciation washed away the taut atmosphere. Still seated, he pulled her into his arms, onto his lap. *"Tha gaol agam ort."*

She smiled her delight. Other than some sexy time when he was seducing her or turning her on in bed, Declan's Scottish heritage rarely showed itself anymore. Occasionally, she'd catch a hint of brogue, but for the most part he sounded as American as she did. However, he knew she loved it when he spoke Gaelic to her. His words, *Tha gaol agam ort* meant *I love you.*

Surprising her even further, he did something incredibly odd, something he had never done before. He drew her closer, cupped his hand around her ear and said in an almost soundless whisper, "You're my everything, Little Fox. Never ever forget that."

Last Chance Rescue Headquarters
Paris

"For right now, I'm offering the job only to those with special ops or covert experience."

Sabrina sat before Noah McCall, her boss and the leader of Last Chance Rescue. Even though she'd been with LCR for four years, she had not yet learned how to read him. A few months back, he had hinted that there were going to be some changes for LCR. She had never anticipated this. Not only was Noah moving the main headquarters to the States, he was creating another branch, LCR Elite.

She loved being an LCR operative, but this sounded even more exciting. And with her background and training, a natural fit for her. Rescuing victims from the most dangerous places in the world. Totally unsanctioned and off the grid. Every mission a high-stakes risk. Her blood pumped with excitement.

"So. You interested?"

His black eyes coolly assessing, Noah asked the question with no emotion, not a hint of coercion. Not that the LCR leader would ever try to persuade an operative to take on an assignment. That was not his style. However, the question he'd asked her wasn't as easy to answer as it might have once been. With the changes Declan wanted to make in his life, how would this new job mesh with it? If only he would come back so they could discuss this together.

"I actually don't know yet."

Black eyes flickered with compassion. "Still no word from your husband?"

She shook her head. "He said he'd be gone for no more than a month…it's been almost two."

"He ever been gone this long before?"

"Yes, but for some reason, this feels different." She wasn't much for psychic premonitions, but she did trust her gut. Something wasn't quite right.

Aware that Noah was waiting for her answer, she said, "How soon do you need to know?"

"You've got some time. I've commissioned the building of a training camp outside Tucson, Arizona. Three former Navy SEALs are designing it. Once it's done, they'll be chomping at the bit to put us through their own version of Hell Week."

Adrenaline surged within her. She loved challenging her physical and mental skills, pushing herself to do more. Hopefully, Declan would be back before she had to give Noah her final answer.

"I saw Aidan leaving when I arrived. I'm assuming you offered him a spot, too?"

"Yeah. With his Special Forces background, Thorne is a natural fit. If you join, you can continue as partners. You work too well together to mess with that."

That was another reason she'd hate to turn down this offer. She'd be losing Aidan Thorne as a partner. They'd been watching each other's backs for a long time. She'd miss the man she considered a friend.

"Just a warning. He's already expecting that you'll be on the team. And since he doesn't know you're married, he might be a little confused if you turn it down without explaining."

She inwardly winced. She had been putting off that conversation for too long. Her brutal childhood had trained her to keep her mouth shut about private matters. And her Agency training had only reinforced her reticence to share personal information. Breaking a thirty-one-year-old habit was damned hard, but she owed her partner the truth.

"It's time I told him."

"Any reason why you haven't? I know it's not because you don't trust him."

"No, trust isn't an issue." She shrugged, unable to explain what probably was a defect in her personality. Getting the hell beaten out of you for telling personal details created an adult who had trouble opening up to others. She'd fought with all her might to overcome her past but still carried scars, both physical and mental. Declan had been the only person she'd ever been able to be completely open with, allowing him to see the real Sabrina.

"Aidan's like a brother to me." She'd never had a real brother, but her stepbrother had been a monster, so that was probably not the best description of their relationship. "Outside of you and Declan, there's no one I trust more."

"Good to know. I—"

The ring tone on her phone played Rod Stewart's *Purple Heather*. Declan! Heart leaping to her throat, she jumped to her feet and barely took the time to throw Noah a look of apology before she dashed out the door. The amused glint in his eyes told her he understood completely.

The instant she was out of Noah's office, she read the short text: *Meet me in Florence tomorrow at 3:00. Salvatore's Café. Have a surprise for you. DS*

Her feet flew to the elevator, thinking about all the things she needed to do to get to Florence by three tomorrow. Didn't matter what she had to do. She would not miss this opportunity.

Florence, Italy

Sabrina rushed out of the airport. Flying commercial and getting somewhere at a specific time rarely meshed anymore.

Why hadn't Declan given her more notice? She was going to be at least fifteen minutes late, if not more.

Waving madly at a taxi, she caught the attention of the driver. Barely waiting for it to stop before she opened the door, she threw herself into the backseat.

Giving the driver the location and street address, she sat back into the seat and tried to make herself relax. Silly. She didn't know why she was so anxious about being late. It wasn't as if he'd leave without seeing her. In fact, she was a little surprised he hadn't already called to check on her. She'd called his cell phone to let him know she was running late and gotten his voice mail.

She tried not to be disappointed that it was just going to be a quick visit. If he were through with his assignment, he would have come to Paris. She'd already given Noah notice that once Declan was finished for good, she would be taking several days off. Her boss was a happily married man and understood.

The taxi driver slammed on his brakes as a gridlock of traffic loomed ahead. Cursing softly, Sabrina spoke in rapid Italian, "I'll just walk from here." She dropped several euro into his outstretched hand and jumped out of the car.

She stood in the middle of the stopped traffic to get her bearings. Up ahead was a traffic jam of massive proportions. Horns were blaring, people were getting out of their vehicles and shouting. Any other time she might have enjoyed the entertainment of drivers spouting colorful and inventive curses. Today, she was too focused on her target—getting to Declan.

She spotted a street sign and realized she was within three blocks of the café. Even though she'd worn heels and a dress, she didn't let that stop her. Weaving in and out of stopped cars, she got to the sidewalk and then started hoofing it toward her destination.

She stopped at a street corner and caught a glimpse of the café in the distance. Squinting against the afternoon sun, she focused on a man standing beneath the canopy in the doorway. That was Declan, or was it? He was the right height and coloring. She waved and was glad to see he waved back.

Traffic had picked up again, and she was going to have to either wait until the light turned red to cross the street or take her life into her own hands. She assessed her chances of making it across the busy street without getting hit—not good. Shrugging slightly, she waited. She'd rather arrive alive.

The instant the light turned red and pedestrian traffic was allowed, Sabrina crossed the street at a run. Declan was still there. Odd, but he looked as though he'd put on some weight. She grinned at the thought of teasing him about secretly hiding away and stuffing himself.

She took another step and barely registered the jolt and massive noise before her feet flew out from under her, and she was propelled backward. As she landed with a hard slam onto her back, her breath left her body. She lay for several long seconds as her mind scrambled to comprehend what had happened. Pain radiated throughout her body. What in the world…?

Breath finally returned, and gritting her teeth, Sabrina sat up. Horror washed over her. The restaurant was gone. Flattened. Demolished. The remains were heaps of ravaged brick and burning wood. The building had exploded.

Declan? Declan!

Darkness threatened, and she fought against its comforting pull. She went to her knees, and then stood, wavering. Her head swam, and blackness skirted the outer edges of her vision. An odd numbness swept up her right arm. Absently, as if she was looking down at a stranger, she noticed a large piece of wood sticking out of her shoulder. Blood dripped down her arm to the ground.

Sabrina tried to hold on to reality, to the fierce need to get to Declan. He couldn't be dead. He was trained for things like this. He would have heard the beginnings of the blast and flung himself away from the building. Yes, he might be injured, but he wasn't dead. She refused to even consider the possibility.

She took a step, felt a vague, distant pain on the bottom of her feet. Odd, but she was barefoot. Her shoes were gone. Ignoring the smoldering wood that scorched her skin and the broken glass that shredded her feet, she weaved and hobbled her way closer to the demolished building.

Declan was fine, she continued to reassure herself. Still, she needed to find him so they could help others. She jerked to a stop. A few feet from where the café had stood lay an arm beneath the rubble. Her heart stalled, her breath halted. It was tanned, large, obviously male, and on the hand was a wedding ring identical to Declan's.

Shaking her head, mumbling, "No, no, no," she pushed the debris out of the way and pulled on the hand. It came loose. She stood among the ruins of the destroyed building, holding an arm. No body was attached. Her mind screamed in denial, black mist swirled around her, and she fell forward into a blessed, mind-numbing darkness.

CHAPTER ONE

Republic of Congo
Central Africa
Eleven months later

A whomp-whomping noise woke him. His mind, though dulled from malnutrition and brutal beatings, could still recognize the unmistakable sound of a helicopter. He touched his eyes, felt them blink—the only way he knew they were open. How long had he been inside the tank this time? A week? More?

They'd dumped him here after his last interrogation. Not because he had refused to give them information. He'd been here a long time and hadn't given them shit. Would never give them shit. No, this time the punishment had come from managing to break free for a few seconds and slamming his fist into his torturer's gut. For the first time in forever, he had felt a spark of triumph...of life. Yeah, it'd gotten him a more severe beating and then thrown into this dark, dank hellhole, but damn, it'd felt good.

He didn't even think about when they'd let him go back to his regular cell. He preferred being able to see sunlight instead of pitch-dark nothingness, but it was all relative. Hell was hell. At least in here, myriad insects weren't sucking out the last of his blood.

The helicopter noise grew louder, like it was hovering overhead. New prisoners coming in? When he'd first arrived here, he'd glimpsed a few. But that'd been a long time ago. Months? Maybe years? He had no concept of how long he'd been here. Since he heard the occasional pain-filled scream, he knew some were still here. Had they given up all hope? Did they exist in a state of dull mindlessness, waiting and hoping to be killed, thinking that only death would give the final release of pain?

Odd how he could wonder about them but feel not one ounce of sympathy. Torture did that. Turned a normal, caring human being into an empty shell—hollowed out and lifeless. No heart, no soul, no humanity.

Gunfire erupted. Sounded like military grade. M4s, maybe? AK-47s? Whoever and whatever, there were several of them. Had someone tried to escape?

He noticed that his heart rate had picked up. That hadn't happened in a while. He mentally shrugged. Whatever the reason for the fireworks, the speculation had given him a brief reprieve from misery.

A loud clanging noise sounded outside his cell. Apparently, it was time for another interrogation. Or would he be taken back to the hole he called home, where the endless sounds of her treachery whispered in his ears? Wouldn't his torturers get a kick out of knowing that he'd rather take a beating than listen to that soft, soothing voice of betrayal?

Hurried footsteps came closer. He didn't bother to raise his head. They'd get here soon enough.

Piercing light penetrated his sight. He squinted his eyes shut. Damn, that hurt. Covering his face with his arm, he lay still. Waited to be hauled out, for an attack…more pain. Coercion, more voices of betrayal. No point in getting to his feet. Why make it easy for them? Besides, if he tried to stand, he'd just fall.

Then he heard a voice. One he hadn't heard in a very long time. "My God, it is you. It's really you!"

Was he dreaming? No, he no longer did that. Dreams were for those with hope. So if this wasn't a dream, was this reality? After all this time…after all the shouting, cursing and praying. After giving up completely, had someone actually come for him?

Seven days later
Somewhere above the Atlantic Ocean

Declan Steele returned from the dead a changed man. Eyes that had once been vibrant blue and glinting with life were now dark, murky…empty. The strong, muscular body that had once carried a comrade ten miles through a sizzling-hot desert was unrecognizable. Thick, dark-as-midnight hair had been replaced with a dull, wild mane that reached well past his thin shoulders. An emaciated wraith, more than thirty pounds underweight, with a bitter twist to his sensuous male lips, stood in his place.

His appearance wasn't the only change. Hatred seethed and burned within him. He was a hardened, embittered, heartless creature, determined to achieve only one goal—vengeance.

After his rescue, he had been taken to a large private home, where he had been allowed to shower, alone and with clean water. Fresh clothes had been provided, and food that wasn't covered in maggots or mold had been set before him.

A doctor had given him a physical, declaring him malnourished and anemic but in good shape considering what his body had endured. The doctor had remarked that his captors had been amazingly humane in allowing aid workers to attend to him from time to time. Declan had stared blankly at him. Humane?

The word apparently had a different meaning for the physician, because he'd seen no humanity in any of the bastards who'd tortured him daily.

The health aid workers had been beneficial in one aspect, though. Apparently, one of the physicians from the group had told of a tall, dark-haired prisoner with a slight Scottish accent and predilection for quoting Robert Burns. And that had gotten the attention of his former fellow EDJE agent Jackson Sands.

"We've been working like mad to get you out. The minute I heard the description of the prisoner, I knew it had to be you." Jackson shook his head. "Still can't believe it…we thought you were dead, man. Everyone thought you were dead. That you'd been killed in that explosion in Florence. But then I heard about…" He lifted a broad shoulder. "I just had to make sure. We worked around the clock to save you."

Jackson had been repeating these words since his rescue. Damning himself for asking, Declan said, "Who?"

The other man's eyes widened. Was it the shock of Declan finally speaking or the rough gravel of his damaged voice?

"Who what?"

"Who's been working like mad?"

"Oh…sorry…my team. I have my own security business now." He jerked his head toward the two large, silent men across from him. "Meet Neil Erickson and Kyle Ames. I couldn't have done it without them. Took us a couple of months to pull this off."

The men remained silent, watching. Declan gave them a nod of acknowledgment and returned his attention to Jackson. "The Agency wasn't involved?"

"They don't know we found you. I'll leave it up to you, when you're ready, to let them know you're alive. Sabrina doesn't know, either. I haven't been in touch with her since…well, since we thought you were killed. I—"

At the mention of that name, Declan turned away. Discussing the woman and his plans for her was out of the question. This was between the two of them and no one else.

Jackson blew out an explosive sigh and shut up. Declan could tell he made the man uneasy. At one time, he'd been the type to go out of his way to put people at ease. It had been one of his gifts. Those kinds of talents weren't worth shit anymore.

He had worked with Jackson, had once thought of him as a friend. Even though he had no feelings left in him for anyone, he respected that the man had possessed the balls to carry off a rescue op. A soft emotion like gratitude didn't fit him anymore, but he owed the three men, Sands, Erickson, and Ames. They'd risked their lives for him. He wouldn't forget it.

The blue sky and puffy white clouds outside the airplane window were invisible to him as he thought about his next move. He was headed back to the States. He hadn't asked about their destination. Where he went, where he lived, all of that was meaningless. His heart pumped for one reason only now. To repay the scheming, red-haired witch who'd put him in that hellhole. Sabrina Fox would pay with everything she had. And when he finally put a bullet between her lovely, lying green eyes, she would know exactly how it felt to have your heart ripped out by the one person you loved and trusted above all else.

And then it would be over for both of them.

CHAPTER TWO

Las Rios, Honduras
Four months later

The dance was on.

Lucia St. Martine lifted her long, auburn hair and, with a twist of her wrist, created a sexy, elegant updo. Securing it with a diamond-studded hair clip, she stepped back to take in her appearance. Yes, her game face was officially in place. Looking in the mirror was a little like watching a familiar play. She knew the cast, the script, and the lines she would deliver. The only question was how the other cast members would respond. Fortunately, she was prepared for every possible scenario. And, like any good actor, she knew when to make her exit.

Once the play ended, she would go back to being Sabrina Fox. For the past month, she had been Lucia, and tonight was the culmination of all of her hard work and preparation. In a few moments, Lucia would be auditioning to become the mistress of Reuben Pierce, part-time terrorist, part-time human trafficker, full-time cold-hearted, sadistic bastard.

Not that a real audition would take place. She had lured more than one man with promises of ecstasy and left him waiting, wanting...and occasionally in the hospital. She had played this scenario out only a few times for LCR. In her previous job, acting the femme fatale had been one of her primary roles.

Lucia St. Martine had always been one of her favorite covers. Early in her career with EDJE, Sabrina had created the character, and though she'd availed herself of the role only twice before, she had enjoyed the mystique as well as the luxury that came with the woman's background. Hard not to enjoy fabulously expensive clothes, an elegant residence in Tuscany, and a pearl-white Maserati GranTurismo convertible that would make a race-car driver weep with envy.

Lucia had earned her wealth the old-fashioned way. Her number one priority was pleasure—taking and giving. She was discreet in her sexual liaisons—helpful, since there weren't any real ones—but if necessary, she could produce half a dozen men who would vouch for her as the most satisfying mistress they'd ever had.

When she had left the Agency, she had taken her covers with her. Without her, there was no need for the Agency to maintain them, so Sabrina had been able to fall back into her role as Lucia with no glitches.

Reuben Pierce had been on the government's radar for years. His elusiveness had been both infuriating and costly. Sabrina had been on several task forces to bring Pierce down, and each time he had evaded capture. Now she was going to be able to achieve a goal she had never been able to obtain in her previous job.

Declan would be so pleased to know that Pierce was about to go down. How many nights had they sat around and planned his demise only to have him evade them once again? Wouldn't Declan be...

Shit. How had he gotten into Lucia's head? Those totally out-of-place thoughts rattled her.

A soft, melodic chime sounded outside her door. Show time. Spine straight, shoulders back, the too-vulnerable, brokenhearted Sabrina Fox disappeared. Lucia was back in place.

With one more glance to make sure her game face was set, she turned from the mirror and exited her room. Her sleeveless black evening gown floated around her long legs, creating a fluttering subtle wave of femininity and elegance. Snuggly hugging her body just enough to outline her slender frame, the gown left much to the imagination. She would be accepted in any high-society dinner party and would likely be one of the most conservatively dressed women in attendance.

There was little reason to blatantly flaunt herself. Pierce could have her stripped with one look. Not that she planned to allow that, but advertising her body wasn't her intent, either. Mystery and allure would hook the man, not overt sexuality. With Reuben Pierce's money and influence, he could have some of the most beautiful women in the world with a curl of his short, stubby finger. Though men found her attractive, Sabrina knew she was no great beauty. What she lacked in looks, she made up for in many other ways—talents that would appeal to Pierce.

A tall, gaunt man stood at the entrance to the room Sabrina had been told to come to at the sound of the chime. Slightly bugged eyes dragged down her body, and then he gave what sounded like a disapproving sniff. Extending his wrinkled, scrawny neck only slightly, the man intoned in a pretentious and laughably fake British accent, "Mr. Pierce will see you now."

The Igor-like man pushed the door open, and Sabrina stepped into another world.

"Welcome, Lucia."

Her smile as seductive as the viper tempting Adam and Eve in the Garden, she glided toward Reuben Pierce. He sat at a low table, leaning back against a long couch. Sabrina didn't even let herself think about the times he had probably shoved the table away and used the couch for more than just sitting. She made a vow to herself that it would never be used in such a way again.

"I am pleased you accepted my invitation."

"How could I not? It was uniquely intriguing."

The invitation had been delivered by one of Pierce's men. Not the usual discreet white card with a request for her to dine with him. Instead, the package had included a financial portfolio, photographs of his many houses, and a short but explicit list of expectations.

She had to hand it to the guy, the financial offer was a generous one. Or so it would seem. She knew more than most people about his past liaisons. Many were no longer living, and the man responsible for their deaths reclined indolently against the sofa as if he hadn't a care in the world. Before she left him, she planned to give him something to care about.

Extending his hand, he waved at the straight-back chair on the other side of the table. "Come. Don't be shy."

Relieved she wouldn't have to submit to being on the sofa with him just yet, she gracefully made her way to the chair and seated herself.

As if her sitting had been a signal, servants holding trays with a variety of delicacies scurried around them. Sabrina knew better than to look at them to see if she recognized any of the young faces. Giving away her interest in anyone other than the man in front of her would have caused suspicion she couldn't afford.

"I selected a wide array of Spanish dishes I thought might please your palate."

Sabrina took in the variety and smiled her delight. He was definitely trying to tempt her. Lucia St. Martine had been raised in a small convent on the outskirts of Madrid. The fact that she had no family was likely a mark in her favor. No pesky relatives to bother him when he tired of her and she disappeared.

In actuality, Sabrina Fox was born and raised in the hills of North Carolina and was as all-American as they came. The only thing she had in common with Lucia was the lack of relatives to mourn if something happened to her. She pushed away the pointless self-pity.

"How thoughtful you are, Reuben. Everything looks delicious."

"I hope you understand that my thoughtfulness extends well beyond ordering your favorite foods."

Her smile slow and coy, she asked, "May I?" and held her hand toward a small, flaky, meat-filled pastry. The flavorful spices wafting through the air created a pleasing culinary fragrance.

His mouth tilted in a pleased smile. He gave a nod of approval.

Biting into the delicacy, she closed her eyes and groaned at the flavor, only halfway acting—it really was delicious.

"I'm glad you're pleased."

Her eyes opened. Undisguised lust had turned Reuben's semi-attractive features into something revoltingly evil. Satisfaction gave her a small inner glow. Using food to turn a man on was such a simple, easy technique. Declan had once teased her that she could make him come just by watching her consume a meal.

Sabrina jerked her mind away from wherever it'd been headed. Declan again? What the hell? She had trained herself never to think of him during a mission. With several children's lives on the line, this certainly wasn't the time to loosen her restrictions. Becoming mired in the hellish memory of her past was best done at a time when she had a sparring partner close by. Grief could bring a surge of anger that only physical activity could assuage.

Her thoughts solely in the present once more, she threw Pierce a look of approval. "It's delicious."

"Tell me more about yourself."

She raised a shoulder in a feminine, careless shrug. "There's not much to say. I grew up in a convent far from the city. I left when I was eighteen."

"And though you don't look much older than eighteen, I know your age, so tell me what you've been doing for the past seven years."

Nice that her age wasn't showing. Pierce thought her to be twenty-five. She had turned thirty-two on her last birthday. "I worked in various fields. Retail, secretarial, restaurants. Nothing really appealed to me."

"And when did you decide to leave those careers and concentrate on pleasure?"

A smile, knowing and confident, tilted her full, lush lips. "When I realized how good I am."

"I would accuse you of boastfulness, but I have heard too much to discount your words. You have a reputation unlike any I've known before."

That was because her cover was damn good. "I was trained well."

"Ah yes, I did hear that you were trained by the sensual mystic Arood Mendalmo in the art of bringing pleasure."

Delight bloomed within her. Arood Mendalmo didn't exist outside an impressive website and a phone number that when called went straight to an LCR facility. The receptionist who answered the phone was prepared to handle just one caller—Reuben Pierce. Pierce had called, inquiring about her training, and had been told that Lucia St. Martine had been one of Mendalmo's most gifted students.

Admittedly, Sabrina did have some talents in that direction, as her previous job had required knowledge of sensual arts and pleasing a lover. The man across from her would never have the chance to discover them. Being touched by this creature wasn't something she could stomach. She once had the kind of physical relationship that most people could only fantasize about, never believing it could come true. That experience had spoiled her for anything less—another reason her personal life was a barren landscape.

She gave Reuben a look of slight arrogance and extreme confidence. "I was my instructor's top student."

Reuben leaned forward and nabbed a green olive off a platter. Placing the olive at his lips, he wrapped his tongue around it and sucked noisily. Sabrina couldn't decide if he thought such a thing was seductive or if he just didn't know how to eat in polite company. Either way, he couldn't know how disgusting he looked or sounded.

"After you have been here awhile, I would like you to train others."

"That wasn't in our agreement."

"I can be extra generous to those who go the extra mile for me."

She hesitated as if to consider his offer and then gave an elegant nod of her head. "Then I would be happy to teach others."

Looking as though he had expected nothing else, he pushed a plate toward her. "Have another pastry."

Though tension wasn't something she normally noticed, she could feel her nerves tightening. By this time, she had expected Reuben to make his move. Chatting with her as if this was a semi-normal date wasn't something she had anticipated. She wanted to get on with the show.

With that thought in mind, Sabrina lifted her right leg and slowly dropped it over her left knee in a sensual display no man could misinterpret. Her well-toned legs were, in her opinion, her best assets. Impossibly long and sleek, most men who got close enough never realized how much danger they were in until it was too late. She could wrap them around a man and literally squeeze the life from him. That wasn't something she'd done in a while, but once she had learned how, the technique had become one of her favorite ways to subdue her prey.

Reuben's eyes flared with desire, and his breath became slightly erratic.

Satisfied, Sabrina took a small tubular pastry from the plate, ran her tongue lightly over the length of it and then leaned forward, offering it to Reuben. He opened his mouth, and she placed it between his lips.

He closed his mouth and chewed slowly. Patting the empty space beside him, he gave her what she was sure he meant to be a sexy smile. Unfortunately, he had a large piece of chicken stuck between his front teeth.

Accepting the unspoken invitation, Sabrina slowly stood. Every movement a graceful dance of seduction, she went to him. Reuben scooted over to give her room. Sabrina lowered herself beside him and slid her long leg in a slow, sensual glide across Reuben's. Looking as though torn between ripping her clothes off and continuing this slow seduction, Reuben made the surprising choice to continue their meal.

He leaned back against the cushions. "Feed me."

As Sabrina reached for another pastry, she continued to rub her leg against Reuben's. And just in case his eyes wanted to wander to her hands, she bent closer, allowing him to get a glimpse of her second-best physical assets—her generous, creamy breasts. Assured that his eyes were focused on her cleavage, she unwrapped the pastry. Deftly unlocking the clasp on her ring, she emptied the contents into the mixture. The color of cumin, the powder would blend perfectly with the food. She'd tasted it once. From what she'd remembered before she passed out, it had a lovely smoky flavor. It was also one of the most potent sleeping powders ever created. One-eighth of a teaspoon would put out a two-hundred-pound man for at least six hours, sometimes longer.

Quickly rewrapping the pastry, she turned to Reuben and held it to his lips.

"You first," he said.

Like hell. "This one is for you. I'll make another for me."

He grasped her wrist and pushed her hand toward her mouth. "We'll share."

Shit. "If you insist."

Holding the pastry carefully, Sabrina took a delicate nibble. She'd been trained to withstand a variety of torture, both physical and mental, and though she had enough self-discipline to maintain control of her senses under extreme circumstances, at some point biology would prevail. If she ingested too much, it didn't matter how much willpower she had, she would fall flat on her face and this mission would fail. Just this small bite was going to make her ability to rescue Catie incredibly hard.

As she swallowed, her taste buds noted the minute smoky flavor, telling her that she had indeed consumed some of the drug. She reminded herself that she had been through worse. She had once rescued a young couple from Kent, England, who had been abducted on their honeymoon. The rescue had gone perfectly, and as far as she knew, the couple was still happily wed. Sabrina, however, still had the scar from the gunshot to her side, and the bullet was still inside her. If she could rescue two people on her own with a gaping, bleeding hole in her side, she could damn well stay awake and save Catie Conaway.

Thankfully, Reuben had a healthy appetite and practically stuffed the entire pastry in his mouth. Turning, she took his glass of wine and raised it to his lips. The drug would act fast, faster still with alcohol. She watched him take a healthy swallow and then another.

Reuben turned to grab another delicacy and knocked a serving spoon onto the floor. Throwing her a goofy grin, he leaned forward to pick up the spoon and kept going, collapsing with a solid thud.

She would have to be quick. Even though the drug would keep him out for a sufficient amount of time, she had no guarantee that his servants wouldn't return to clear the table. She went to her feet and then just as swiftly sat back down. Crap, even though she'd taken only a tiny bite, the drug was already inhibiting her motor skills.

She gave a vigorous shake of her head and rose again. This time, she stayed up. She didn't bother wasting precious time to try to move Reuben. If anyone walked in, whether he was lying on the floor or on the sofa wouldn't matter. An alarm would sound, and the search would be on for her.

Her focus was as clear as it was going to get. She slipped out of her heels and pushed them under the table. Running barefoot would be a lot easier than moving around in four-inch heels. With only a slight wobble, she made her way to the door. Twisting the knob, she eased it open, hoping to avoid any sound. Sabrina peeked out. Only one guard to her right, looking down at his hands. She closed the door behind her and then, feet silent, she stealthily moved toward him. He should have seen her out of the corner of his eye…why hadn't he noticed her yet? As she drew closer, a snuffling snore gave her the answer.

Sabrina gave the sleeping guard a not-so-gentle tap to his head. The man slumped forward, and she repositioned him so he would look as though he were still snoozing. And he was, only a little deeper than he had been before.

She scanned the broad hallway and located the door to the third-floor staircase. Even though LCR hadn't been able to get inside the mansion until now, they had been able to access the mansion's floor plan. After careful study, the majority opinion had been that Reuben would keep his captives on the third floor. It was out of sight of the many guests the mansion often hosted, but would give him easy access when he wanted them.

She was about to take a step when a wave of dizziness swept over her. Pulling in a deep breath, Sabrina blinked away the lightheadedness and dashed to the door. The quicker she got this done, the better for everyone.

She twisted the doorknob and tugged it open. Fellow operatives Aidan Thorne and Justin Kelly would handle the guards surrounding the mansion. Both former military snipers, the two men would have no problem taking out the seven guards on duty.

She entered a small foyer that led to a stairway to the third floor. Another wave of vertigo attacked. Taking a moment, she leaned against the wall and breathed in deep, cleansing breaths. Feeling slightly better, she forced her legs to run up the stairway. The faster she moved, the better her chances of staying awake. She reached the top of the steps, and before a fresh wave of dizziness could attack, she gave her face a stinging slap, then another. The pain reenergized her—refocusing her thoughts.

From the plans they had obtained, there were four rooms on this floor. She headed down the hallway. All doors were closed, but a window had been added to each door, much like a mental hospital. She ignored the shiver of a memory.

Peeking in one window, she saw what she expected—two beds and two small lumps, one on each bed. Children. Oh, how she looked forward to taking this bastard down. Sabrina made fast work of checking each room and found the same in each. Two beds, two lumps. That meant at least eight children they could rescue. If this went down as they'd planned, this would be her most successful rescue.

She twisted the doorknob, unsurprised that it was locked. A locked door had never stopped her before. Taking a small tool she had sewn into her demi bra, she knelt on the floor and inserted it into the lock. A little slide, a click, and it was done. She pushed the door open. She didn't worry about cameras. Days ago, Deacon Greenaway, LCR's newest computer genius, had hacked into the mansion's security cameras. Now when a guard looked into the monitors, they saw the lumps in the bed and nothing more. LCR had been working on the operation for well over a month, with every detail planned out.

Shaking a small shoulder gently, she looked down into the angelic face of a child—maybe six years old. There was a part of her that wanted to hold the little boy close and sob at what he had endured. A stronger, less emotional part told her to get the job done. She was here to save these children, not commiserate with them.

"Hi there, my name is Sabrina. Would you like to go home?"

A desperate hope gleaming in his eyes, he whispered, "The mean man said I had to stay here."

"You don't have to worry about that man again."

He shot a look over to the other bed. "Can Lucy come, too?"

"Absolutely. Everyone gets to go home today."

He sat up in the bed and threw the blanket off. "Okay."

"Can you do me a favor?"

Eyes solemn and much too old for a six-year-old gazed up at her solemnly as he nodded.

"Will you wake Lucy up and tell her that she's going home? I need to let all the other children out."

"Okay."

Resisting the urge to hug the little guy for his bravery, Sabrina turned and ran from the room. Each door she opened, she made the same promise. The children's ages ranged from six to maybe thirteen. The last room she came to, she found Catie Conaway. The ten-year-old had gone missing from her front yard in Cincinnati, Ohio, two months ago. Her parents had approached LCR a week after the abduction when police leads had dried up. Though it could have been just another filthy pedophile who had abducted Catie, there had been enough chatter to know that Reuben Pierce's people had been in the area. Sabrina was thrilled their investigation had been correct.

At one time, Pierce had been a small-arms dealer and then expanded his business to terrorism, selling his expertise to the highest bidder. He had no political agenda or religious conviction—old-fashioned greed was his primary motive. A few years ago, he had learned the profitability of human trafficking. Concentrating solely on children, Reuben had quickly become one of the most wanted criminals in the world. Unfortunately, with his contacts and wealth, he had also been one of the most elusive.

Now looking down at Catie Conaway's bruised, pale face, Sabrina wished she had been able to do more to the bastard than just give him a nice sleep. Anyone who hurt a child was lower than pond scum.

"Catie, my name is Sabrina. Your mama and daddy sent me to bring you home."

Tears filled the little girl's eyes. Even without the bruises, the limp blond hair and malnourished appearance told Sabrina the child had suffered. Healing would take time, but at least now she had a chance.

She instructed Catie and her roommate to grab their shoes and come with her. Within ten minutes of leaving an unconscious Reuben lying on the floor, Sabrina had gathered all eight children in the hallway. Now to alert her fellow operatives.

Going to the room that faced the north side of the estate, Sabrina flipped the light switch three times in quick succession. Her go signal. Aidan and Justin Kelly would have the guards neutralized by the time she and the children made it downstairs. She turned to Catie and assessed her. The little girl wasn't the oldest, but from what she had learned from Catie's parents, she was more mature than most.

"Catie, do you feel up to leading the group?"

"What do you mean?"

"I'll go ahead of you. If anyone tries to stop us, I'll have to stay behind and deal with them. I want you to go to the back door and see that everyone goes with you. Run as fast as you can away from the house to the back of the property. A woman named Riley will be waiting for you. She'll lead you out."

"But what about you?"

"You don't worry about me. I'll be fine. Okay?"

Her face much too serious for a ten-year-old, she gave a swift nod. "I'll take care of everyone."

"Thank you." Sabrina turned and headed to the door that led downstairs. When she reached it, she turned and nodded approvingly. All the children were in single file, right behind Catie. They had probably practiced fire drills like this at school.

She opened the door and peeked out. All clear. Motioning Catie with her hand, she said, "That's great, everyone. Just follow Catie, single file like you're doing. Don't stop for anything. No matter what happens, keep moving."

Taking the stairs softly, she made frequent checks over her shoulder to ensure everyone was able to keep up. So far, so good. Eight little faces looked up at her with trust and hope. She would not let them down.

She reached the small foyer and stopped, waiting for everyone to gather with her. "Okay, we're going out the back door on the first floor. Follow Catie. And, Catie, you follow me. Stay quiet. No talking until we're away from the house. Okay?"

Eight solemn nods.

Sabrina opened the door to the second-floor landing and looked out. Still clear. Leaving the door open, she walked down the landing, barely hearing the patter of feet behind her. When she reached the top of the stairway that led downstairs, she stopped and turned. Still single file and still following Catie. This would be their biggest challenge. She had wanted to get the children first. Neutralizing the guards beforehand would have taken too much time. She anticipated there would be at least three of them, if not more, on the first floor. She hoped to avoid them, but if she didn't, she trusted Catie to follow her directions.

She whispered a warning again. "Okay, everyone. Stay together and do not stop for anything."

Turning, she crept down the stairs, aware of the small feet behind her and keeping her eyes and ears open for anyone who might try to stop them. They made it to the first floor without any trouble, and Sabrina breathed out a long, silent sigh. Almost home free. They were in the middle of the giant foyer, headed to the kitchen and back door when their first obstacle, in the guise of a short, thick, brutish-looking guard, appeared at her right.

"What the hell!" he shouted.

Swift and silent, Sabrina reached the guard in seconds before he could draw his gun. Trusting the children to continue on, she concentrated on taking care of the giant. As he fumbled for his weapon, she kicked it from his hand, then followed with a roundhouse kick to his head and a hard jab to his neck. He fell to the floor with a nice, solid *thunk*.

Turning, she ran toward the door, relieved that the children were nowhere in sight. She was almost to the door when two men, one on either side of her, appeared.

"Stop right there," one growled.

Not allowing him to draw a weapon, she punched his face and then followed up with targeted kicks to his stomach then his groin. He crumpled before her. Hands grabbed her shoulders and whirled her around. A meaty fist slammed into her face.

Adrenaline covering the pain, Sabrina planted her feet to the floor and refused to give in to the need to collapse. Hands fisted together, she slammed them upward into the man's nose. A satisfying crunch followed, but he remained on his feet. Grabbing her hair, he brutally threw her forward, his intent to slam her against the wall. She moved along willingly, but then broke his hold with her arms and jabbed her fist deep into his soft belly and followed quickly with another one to his groin. Before he could retaliate, she slammed a fist into his nose once more. His eyes rolled back into his head, and he toppled.

Sabrina took off. When she reached the kitchen, she was relieved to see the door standing wide open. Catie and the children were outside. Riley would be waiting for them. She dashed through the door. Cool air washed over her and kept her on her feet. The combination of the sleeping powder along with the hit to her face tempted her to keel over where she stood. Collapse would have to wait for a more appropriate time. Or at least until she was on the other side of the gate with all eight children safe, as well as her team.

"Over here!"

Sabrina whirled and saw a grinning Aidan standing at the gate where he had created an opening. She ran toward him, reaching for his outstretched hand.

"Everyone safe?" she asked.

Aidan nodded. "All eight accounted for. Riley and Justin have them. I came to see what was taking you so long."

She threw him a grin as she ran beside him. "Stopped to chat with a couple of fellows."

"Hope they're not too bad off. I can't wait to see these assholes in jail."

Once the children were safe, the police would take over, and everyone would be taken into custody. It was never LCR's wish to gain media attention or credit. As long as the rescue was successful and the culprits put away, Last Chance Rescue was satisfied. Tonight, Reuben Pierce would sleep in a very uncomfortable bed and have a hangover from hell in the morning.

Yeah, this had been a damned good rescue.

CHAPTER THREE

"How's the eye?"

Sabrina lowered the ice pack she'd been holding against her face to allow Aidan to see the bruise. When he sucked in a breath and winced, she knew it wasn't good.

Applying the ice pack again, she shrugged philosophically. "At least the guy who did it is in more pain than I am. With that kick to his balls, he'll be singing soprano for months."

Both Aidan and Justin grimaced and shifted uncomfortably. Typical guy reaction. Mention anything about damaging a man's testicles, and there was always a show of sympathy, even if the guy in this case was a slimy weasel.

"Did everything inside go as planned?" Riley asked.

"Almost but not quite. Pierce insisted I eat a little of the pastry I prepared for him, which unfortunately held the sleeping powder."

"Shit. How the hell did you function?" Aidan asked.

Sabrina shook her head. She didn't really have an answer. Having been trained to ignore pain or discomfort, it was second nature to her. But she could still feel the drug weighing her down. Once their debrief was over, she planned a serious, uninterrupted snoozefest.

The children were all being seen to and treated by health care professionals. Only minutes after their escape, they had been loaded onto a waiting bus headed to a small medical facility where doctors, nurses, and counselors had taken over their care.

It grieved her to see their little faces filled with shock and fear. Children should know nothing about horrible creatures like Reuben Pierce and his associates. She had learned about these kinds of monsters in her childhood, too. She hoped full recovery was possible for all of them. It had taken her years to overcome her abuse. Of course, it would have helped if anyone had believed her.

She shook off the painful memories. Nothing good ever came from reliving the past.

After they'd surrendered the children, she and the other operatives had headed for their debriefing. Javier's Hideaway was a dive that attracted some of the most dangerous and seediest people imaginable. It was also a haven for LCR operatives. Years ago, Javier's thirteen-year-old niece had run away from home. LCR had found her and brought her home. Since then, whenever a meeting place in Las Rios was needed, this was where they went.

"Okay, we ready?" Riley asked.

Sabrina nodded. She and Riley had worked together on at least a dozen missions. The young operative was one of the most serious people she'd ever met. Professional at all times, Riley rarely cracked a smile and never joined in the gentle ribbing or sometimes off-color conversations that often took place after a successful mission.

Justin Kelly leaned forward, his expression going from relaxed to blank in a second. Sabrina thought Justin and Riley had the oddest partnership. There was never any kind of banter or even pleasant conversation between the two. If they talked to each other at all, it was always about the op. Yet on a mission, they acted as one, almost as if they shared the same brain. It was weird and freaky but definitely worked for them.

Sabrina shot a look at Aidan and couldn't help but grin. Her too-gorgeous-for-his-own-good partner was throwing peanuts up in the air and catching them with his mouth. When she'd met Aidan for the first time, she had been thrown off by his incredible good looks and easygoing charm and had inaccurately judged him. Even though she knew Noah McCall would never hire an operative who wasn't both intelligent and tough as nails, Aidan's man-candy looks had made her doubt that knowledge. She had soon learned that a rapier-sharp wit, off-the-wall intelligence and supreme fighting skills could actually come wrapped in a pretty package.

In their time as partners, she had come to appreciate Aidan for who he was. It wasn't his fault that he could body slam a three-hundred-pound gorilla and look good doing it. He'd saved her ass more times than she could count, and she not only trusted him, she liked him immensely.

"Hey, Peanut Man, want to join in the debrief?"

His smile good-natured, Aidan caught one last peanut, munched and swallowed. "Missed my midnight feeding. Gotta keep my strength up." The man had the appetite of a seventeen-year-old boy.

"Then let's get this done so you can feed and I can sleep."

"Roger that." All business now, he said, "I arrived at my designated spot at eight forty-five. Spotted two guards on top of the mansion—like a freaking embassy or something. Two more walked the perimeter. Since the shift changed at nine thirty, our timing worked great."

Sabrina nodded. They had agreed to wait until close to the end of a shift before acting. A sleepy guard, ready to be relieved of his post, would be less diligent and more likely to ignore an odd noise or small disturbance.

"Ingram and I observed Thorne from our perch on the hill," Justin said. "We split up, with me going north and Ingram going south. I arrived at my shooting destination within five minutes."

Riley Ingram picked up where her partner left off. "Two minutes from the gate, I double-clicked my mic to alert Thorne."

"And that was our signal to shoot tranquilizers into the guards' asses," Aidan said, and then added with his famous grin, "Which, by the way, I thoroughly enjoyed."

"Three minutes after the guards went down, I had welded an escape hole," Riley said. "I then backed away and hid in the trees while we waited for your signal."

Sabrina nodded. "I received the summons from Pierce at eight thirty. As soon as I went in, servants arrived with platters of food. I didn't chance looking at them, but from peripheral observation, they were in their mid to late teens.

"We chatted for a few minutes as we cleared up a few things in the contract. At nine eighteen, I fed Pierce the powder. He went down within two minutes. On the way to find the children, I neutralized one guard. The kids were on the third floor, as we'd figured. I set about waking them and then gave the light signal to let you know we were coming out. On the way out of the mansion, I took out three more guards." She added, "Catie was a great help in leading the children out of the house."

"And the instant we spotted the children," Riley said, "Kelly and I went through the escape hole and pulled them outside to safety."

"And at nine forty-three, I saved your ass," Aidan added.

Sabrina snorted. "You wish."

"Gotta say, this went a helluva lot smoother than I anticipated."

Sabrina had worried about it, too. There had been too many "what ifs" to be completely sure that the mission would go off without a hitch. Other than the small amount of sleeping powder she'd had to endure, along with the punch to her face, it couldn't have gone any better.

Aidan glanced at his watch. "Should be hearing from McCall soon."

Their team would have no direct contact with the authorities that raided the compound after the rescue. Even though local police would get all the credit, city officials sometimes had inflated or fragile egos. It was easier and cleaner to pretend that LCR hadn't been involved.

Everyone went silent as they waited for the call from their boss with the news that Pierce and his minions had been apprehended. Secondary to that was the knowledge that the mansion held other victims. The teens who had served their meal couldn't all have been there by choice. Rescuing everyone wasn't always possible, but it was something LCR strived for in every operation.

The cell phone Aidan had placed in the middle of the table buzzed. Pressing the answer key and then the speakerphone, Sabrina gave the information she knew her boss would want to know first. "We're all here and in good shape, Noah."

"Excellent. Great job tonight, guys. In addition to the eight children you all rescued, the authorities found three older ones in the kitchen on the first floor. To sweeten the pot, eleven assholes will be rotting in a jail cell for a long time. You've all got a lot to be proud of."

She knew her boss too well not to recognize there was a huge "but" coming. Even though Noah was thousands of miles away, she heard the grimness in his tone.

"What's wrong?"

"Pierce was nowhere to be found."

Sabrina shot an incredulous look at Aidan. "That's not possible. The man was unconscious. He swallowed enough of the powder to put him out for at least ten hours."

"Someone must've gotten him out," Aidan said.

"Igor," Sabrina snarled the name.

"Who?" McCall asked.

Cursing herself for not taking out the ugly-assed man, Sabrina explained, "He's Pierce's shadow. I should've stayed long enough to take him down. I didn't see him during the rescue and stupidly assumed he'd gone to bed."

"There's no way you could've prevented it, Fox. Don't beat yourself up."

Yes, there was. She should have made sure. Aidan, Riley and Justin would have taken care of the children. She should have stayed and finished the job.

She shelved the self-anger for later. "How about Catie and the other children?"

"Catie's already seen her mom and dad. They were waiting at the clinic when the bus arrived. They wanted me to make sure you all knew how grateful they are. The other kids are being identified as we speak."

"McCall, what about Pierce?" Justin asked. "We going after him?"

"He'll go to ground. Take comfort in the fact that we've greatly impeded his ability to do business. No point in going after him until he resurfaces. We'll be ready for him when he does."

"So what's next?" Riley asked.

"You and Kelly report back here tomorrow afternoon for a new assignment. Thorne, I've got you cleared for a couple of days off."

"What about me?" Sabrina asked.

"Fox, you didn't ask for it, but you've got at least a week of downtime coming. Just because you said everyone's okay doesn't mean I don't know about the slug you took to your face."

"Not to mention the sleeping powder she ingested with Pierce," Aidan added.

"I won't even ask you how you stayed upright," Noah said. "Grab that sleep you've been putting off for too long."

She knew better than to argue. Stupid to have ordered a beer. She'd only taken a half dozen sips, but that small amount, along with the drug, was pulling at her like nobody's business. If she didn't get horizontal soon, she'd keel over.

"Will do," Sabrina agreed.

"And I mean it, Fox, do not even think about going after Pierce yourself. Understand?"

Since she was about five minutes from losing consciousness, she had no problems making a promise…at least for now. "Not a problem," she assured him.

The call ended. As if her body had been waiting for that signal, she swayed in her chair.

Aidan grabbed her upper arm and righted her. "Whoa, you okay?"

Shaking herself from her stupor, Sabrina pushed up from the table and stood. "I don't know about you guys, but I'm wiped." She nodded vaguely at the table. "G'night. See you in a few days."

Standing, Aidan threw some money on the table for their drinks. "I'll walk you to the hotel."

"Don't be silly. I'm fine."

"You're sure?"

"Absolutely. It's a two-minute walk, tops. I can stay awake that long."

She headed toward the door. The instant she was outside, she drew in a deep breath, sure that the fresh air would rejuvenate her. A wave of dizziness followed. Crap. Maybe it would be a good idea if Aidan walked her back to the hotel. She wanted a soft pillow beneath her head, not Javier's graveled parking lot.

She made a half turn to go back inside. Something covered her head, and her vision went dark. She felt the prick of a needle at her neck. Comprehension came quick. She managed to connect with what felt like a hard jaw before her mind blanked into unconsciousness.

CHAPTER FOUR

"What do you mean you can't find her?" Jordan Montgomery's sharp voice came through the phone like a whip.

"Just what I said." Phone to his ear, Aidan stomped around Javier's parking lot, looking for a clue, anything, that would tell him what had happened to his partner. "Her bed wasn't slept in last night. I let her sleep in because I figured she'd be out for at least eight hours. When she didn't answer the door, I had management let me in her room. Her luggage is still there, but there's no evidence that she made it back to her room last night."

"Shit."

That was just one of the many curses Aidan had uttered over the last half hour. He'd been about to sound the alarm to McCall when Jordan had phoned from LCR's Paris office to congratulate them on a successful mission. The words "Sabrina is missing" had been Aidan's first words to Montgomery.

Dammit, why the hell hadn't he walked her back to her room? She had been groggy, almost asleep on her feet. Any other time, if anyone had accosted her, he had no doubt who would've won. Sabrina was the most capable person he knew, male or female. Having that drug in her system had made her vulnerable. Aidan cursed himself for not watching her back.

The voice of Eden St. Claire, Jordan's partner and wife, broke into his dire thoughts. "When's the last time you saw her?"

"She left Javier's Hideaway around one thirty. Said she was going back to her room for a long sleep."

"I know Javier doesn't have surveillance cameras in his parking lot," Montgomery said, "but what about the hotel?"

"Ingram is checking it right now, but so far, nothing is showing up. Looks like she might have been taken in Javier's parking lot."

The silence on the other end of the phone was telling. Both Montgomery and Eden were probably thinking the very same thing Aidan was. With no surveillance and no witnesses, how the hell were they going to find her?

"I was about to give McCall the news when you called."

"We'll alert him," Montgomery said. "You, Ingram, and Kelly shake down all known contacts of Reuben Pierce until there's nothing left for them to talk about. If he's the asshole who took her, he can't have gone far with her."

"This makes no sense, guys," Eden said. "There's an all-points bulletin out for Pierce. Why would he risk getting caught to go after Sabrina? Any sane criminal would go to ground and wait it out."

"And how the hell would he even know where to find her?" Aidan said. "It can't be Pierce."

"I'm not disagreeing with either of you," Montgomery said. "However, let's get the question of whether it's Reuben Pierce or not out of the way so we can concentrate on who else it could be."

"Agreed," Aidan said.

Disconnecting the call, Aidan's eyes roamed over the parking lot. There wasn't much of one—mostly a small graveled area that could hold only perhaps four to five small cars. Since this was a small town, most people walked to where they wanted to go. The entire city limits could be covered on foot in twenty minutes or less.

He headed to the back of the building for one more look. There had to be something…some kind of a clue. His peripheral vision caught the glint of something. Turning, he strode to a drainage ditch on the far side of the property and knelt. A cell phone, identical to Sabrina's, lay in a puddle. The screen was shattered, as if someone had stomped it. Dammit, that confirmed his fears.

Not one to feel helpless or hopeless, Aidan surged to his feet and determinedly set his mind to finding out who the hell had taken his partner. And when he found them, he would make damn sure they regretted it. Kidnapping an LCR operative wasn't a good move for anyone. One that could prove to be a fatal mistake.

LCR Headquarters
Alexandria, Virginia

His thoughts grim, Noah ended the call from Eden and Jordan. Even though he knew what he had to do, he didn't immediately act.

Since moving the main LCR facility to Virginia, he had spent way too many hours with government officials. When he had developed the concept of LCR Elite, he had accepted that as a necessary, if unpleasant, side effect. With its focus of extracting hostages from war torn and terrorist-ridden countries throughout the world, the intel often provided by these officials could make the difference between a successful and failed rescue op. However, involving any government, even his own, in LCR business would never be something he took lightly.

The transition from France to the US had been smooth. He had expected nothing less. His people were the best. He had hired them, trained most of them, and trusted all of them with his life. LCR operatives knew better than anyone how to adjust to change.

Samara and the kids were settling in nicely, too. He had made the change for them. Samara came from a large family, and with her busy schedule as LCR's main counselor, she'd managed to see her folks only a couple of times each year. And it hadn't been fair to their kids, Micah and Evie, to deprive them of their grandparents, along with all the aunts, uncles and cousins. Noah might shudder at the sheer number of in-laws, but seeing his wife's and children's happiness and contentment more than made up for his discomfort.

The changes within LCR had been numerous but all good. Thanks to LCR operative Lucas Kane, who had donated a substantial amount of money to the organization, Last Chance Rescue had been able to expand beyond Noah's wildest dreams. LCR branch offices spread all over the globe, with trusted informants throughout the world on alert and ready to help, the most up-to-date technology at their fingertips. Most important, LCR had the toughest and bravest operatives imaginable. Last Chance Rescue was thriving.

LCR Elite, now with ten operatives, had gotten off to a good start with several successful rescues under their belt. Sometimes working in conjunction with other agencies but most of the time on their own, LCR Elite was a force to be reckoned with.

But now, one of their own had been taken. Anyone who knew Noah McCall and LCR had to be aware that they would upend hell to recover a fellow operative. And because of the identity of this particular operative, Noah's gut told him her disappearance had nothing to do with Sabrina's job as an LCR operative. This went back to her previous job, before LCR. Which meant he had no choice but to contact those government types again.

Noah opened his desk drawer and withdrew Sabrina Fox's personnel folder. Opening it, he pulled a sealed envelope from the side pouch.

The day Sabrina had accepted his offer to work with LCR, she had presented him with this envelope and the instructions that if she were ever taken and they had no clear idea of her abductor or her location, he was to open the envelope and follow the instructions.

He ripped open the envelope, withdrew a single sheet of paper, and took in the contents—a code, consisting of numbers and letters, along with a phone number with a DC area code.

Noah punched the number into his phone, heard one ring and then an androgynous voice stated, "Code verification."

Not knowing if he was supposed to speak the code or punch it in, Noah tried entering it first and received nothing but silence. He then spoke the code and almost immediately heard a clicking noise and then an older male voice said, "State time and location of the last time Ms. Fox was seen."

"I don't think so," Noah said mildly.

"Excuse me?"

Noah got the feeling this man wasn't used to being challenged. There was not only surprise in the gruff voice but also amusement.

He wasn't one to get into a pissing contest, especially when one of his own people's lives was at stake, but he damn well wasn't going to give information to some unknown person and then just back away. Sabrina was no longer a government agent. She was one of his, and he took care of his own.

"If we're going to find Ms. Fox," Noah stated baldly, "then we're going to work together."

"We don't work with others."

"Make an exception or you won't get the information you requested."

"You would put her life on the line?"

"Absolutely not. But neither will I kowtow to some secret government entity. We work together and we'll find her."

"You don't know who you're dealing with."

"Feel free to tell me."

There was a long, silent pause. He wondered if the guy was even breathing. Finally, he said, "Very well, Mr. McCall. Meet me at the Lincoln Memorial in an hour."

"How will I know you?"

"Don't worry. I know you."

Noah clicked the key to end the call and then sat back in his chair. Why did he suddenly feel as if he'd just made a date with the devil?

Coley Springs, Idaho

Fury bubbling within him, Declan's hands fisted at his sides. The unconscious woman before him had starred in every recent nightmare. Limp and lifeless on the cot, her black cotton T-shirt was a startling contrast to the bleached paleness of her face. Except for one jarring exception.

"Dammit, Sabrina, where the hell did you get that bruise? I know I didn't hit you. I couldn't—"

No, of course he hadn't hit her. The rage he felt at the vivid bruises on her soft, fair skin conflicted with the bitter hatred he had for this woman. Just how damn stupid could he get? He was planning to kill her...why did it matter that she was bruised?

Was that why she was still unconscious? He'd given her only enough of the drug to disorient her. She'd rarely taken drugs, said they made her feel stupid and slow. But when she had taken them, there had been no adverse effects. So why had one small dose knocked her on her ass?

He touched his fingers to the pulse on her neck, telling himself to ignore her petal-soft skin. Her pulse was strong. Her breathing shallow, not erratic or fast. She was asleep, nothing more. Ignoring the surge of relief, he removed his fingers before he did something asinine like trail his fingers down her creamy skin to that tender hollow place at her neck.

How many times had he kissed her there, relishing the warmth of her skin, the erratic beat of her pulse throbbing against his tongue as arousal had taken over? How many nights had he lain awake and watched her sleep? When she was awake and aware, her face was lively and animated. Asleep, she looked as innocent and serene as the Madonna.

She had said more than once that she was no great beauty. Declan used to argue with her but had soon realized her inability to see herself as beautiful had been one of the ways she dealt with her past. As a teenager, she had been both sexually and physically abused by her stepbrother. One of the defenses the bastard had used against her was her looks—constantly drumming into her head that her beauty caused him to do the vile things he did. It had taken her years to overcome the psychological mind-fuck. Denying her beauty became one of her ways to deal. Declan hadn't argued. Having his own demons to contend with, who was he to criticize her methods?

He pressed his fingers to the pounding in his skull. Why the devil was he even thinking about that time anyway? What they had shared had been a lie of epic proportions. Maybe she'd made the whole abuse thing up. She was an accomplished liar—something he had once appreciated. He'd just never figured she'd use her lies on him.

But lying there, unconscious and vulnerable, made her look as helpless and defenseless as a kitten—a slender, beautiful woman with the face of an angel. She didn't look as though she could step on a spider, much less kill a man with her bare hands. He had watched her do the latter more than once. The woman was one of the most dangerous people he had ever known.

Without a backward glance, he went out the door. He'd let her stew for a few hours. When the time was right, they were going to have a long, uninterrupted discussion. Neither of them would survive it.

CHAPTER FIVE

Consciousness returned in slow increments. First, she was aware of a hard surface beneath her body—not a bed—more like a thinly padded slab of concrete. The complete absence of noise was her next awareness. Shouldn't there be street noise? Sabrina lay still and quiet for several minutes, carefully assessing. Her mind felt thick, unwieldy. Drowsiness tempted her to go back to sleep. An inner voice whispered an urgent message that all was not right.

She struggled to hold on to thoughts that seemed as wispy and insubstantial as a spider web. Why? What had happened? Why was alarm replacing the dull lassitude? Her eyes fluttered, tried to open. She managed to lift one eyelid to a slit. What she saw forced both her eyes open in a blinding flash of realization and comprehension. Fury followed. Grogginess evaporated. She had been abducted. Who and why didn't matter. There were probably thousands of people who would like to see her dead. Admittedly, only a fraction of those people would have the guts to actually kidnap her, but the number of those who would was still quite high.

She didn't bother to question how she'd been taken. She didn't remember anything after leaving Javier's. Didn't really matter. The only thing she needed to concentrate on was getting the hell out of here in one piece.

"You're awake." The mechanically distorted voice exploded into the silence.

Refusing to carry on a conversation with the disembodied voice while lying flat on her back, she sat up and put on the face she had perfected long ago. The one that said the instant she freed herself, heads would roll.

Her surroundings were as harsh and austere as the bed had been. Her eyes roamed the small area, looking for the weakest point where she could make that escape happen.

"Don't bother looking around. There's nothing for you to see."

Those words were true. She was in a square cinderblock room. Its contents: a cot, sink, and toilet. Nothing more.

"And no way to escape," the voice continued.

She'd just see about that. "Why am I here?"

"All in good time."

The voice was coming from the small speaker in the corner. She noted a camera as well. Everything she did, every move she made, could be seen. "Who are you? What do you want?"

Silence.

She pushed herself to her feet, cursing softly when her knees buckled and she fell back to the bed. She was as weak as a day-old kitten. Even if the door in front of her had been wide open, she honestly didn't know if she would have been able to walk through it.

Whatever drug they'd given her, on top of the sleeping powder she had ingested, had temporarily disabled her. The instant she regained her strength, she would show them why her code name had once been Red Death.

Teeth gritted with determination, she went to her feet again. With slow, halting steps, she shuffled to the sink. Ignoring the filth and grime, she turned the faucet on and was relieved to see clear water. Though it was only a trickle, it was enough. She cupped her hands to gather the liquid, drank her fill and then splashed her face and neck.

Hydrated and much more alert, she turned back around and faced the room. With bullet-like speed, it hit her. She was in a cell. Locked up. No way out. Escape was impossible. Panic raced through her. Black spots appeared before her eyes.

Cursing the weakness, she pushed the fear into a little box, just as she'd been taught. It didn't exist outside that compartment. This was nothing like when she was a kid, unable to fight back. She could and would defend herself against anything…anyone. She was bigger, stronger than she had been back then. She had proved that she could survive anything.

Breathing in and out slowly, she felt the fear wash away. Fury returned, and she welcomed it as an old friend. White-hot wrath had saved her life more than once. It would save her now.

"You seem…upset."

The voice returned. And even though it was digitally altered to sound asexual and emotionless, she detected a hint of emotion. Amusement maybe? Damned if she'd let herself fall prey to this test. They wanted her to lose control. And once that happened, they'd try to extract information. Whoever it was didn't know her well. She had been trained by the best. She would die before she gave anything up.

Every facial expression and movement were being studied and analyzed. Sabrina faked a bored yawn and returned to her cot. She lay on her side, facing the camera. If she turned her back, it would make her look weak, as if she were hiding. They needed to see she had no weaknesses.

Her eyes closed, she regulated her breathing. She had learned this relaxation technique when she first started at the Agency. By concentrating on an object or a pleasurable memory, non-threatening and soothing, she could lower her pulse and blood pressure. Many times she had willed herself to sleep this way. During those dark, horrible days after Declan's death, when grief had almost destroyed her, this technique had saved her. Otherwise, she wasn't sure she would have survived.

She slipped into a peaceful sleep, her last conscious thought of the time she and Declan had been lying on the beach in Costa Rica and he had leaned over and whispered he loved her. It had been the first time he had confessed his feelings. The memory soothed her, and a smile tilted her lips as she fell into a soft, easy slumber.

Declan backed away from the screen. He had been within seconds of going to her. When she'd turned from the sink and he'd seen the stark terror in her eyes, he'd almost walked to the door and into the cell. He had almost revealed everything.

He shoved a trembling hand through his hair and turned away from the woman who was now lying peacefully on the bed, a slight smile curving her full, lush mouth. He told himself that his reaction to her fear meant nothing. It was merely a byproduct of his own experience in captivity. He would feel empathy for anyone who felt trapped and hopeless. It was nothing more than that. Their past life together was dead and buried—he had nothing but hatred for this woman.

He went out the door and stalked up the path to the house. This location was perfect for his plans. In the middle of the woods, deep in a valley between two mountains with no other house within fifty miles. Plenty of privacy. In a way, the land reminded him of his boyhood in Scotland where some of his happiest moments were spent.

Built more than fifty years ago, the main house had needed work. In between regaining his health and his strength, he'd concentrated on making it livable. Though small, with only a kitchen/living room/bedroom combo and a bathroom, it was fifty times more spacious than his prison cell and a helluva lot cleaner.

He went through the front door just as a chime from the cell phone in his shirt pocket alerted him to a text message. Withdrawing the phone, he clicked on the message icon: *Any luck?*

He had refused Jackson's assistance in finding Sabrina. It had been impossible to say that he wasn't looking for her. No one would have bought that lie. But that didn't mean anyone needed to know what would happen once he found her location. Telling anyone his plans, even one of the few people he still trusted, was out of the question. His plans for Sabrina were between him and her, no one else. Jackson would most definitely not approve.

He gave a quick reply: *Not yet.*

Another chime sounded. *How are you feeling? How're the nightmares?*

Declan shrugged off the irritation. It'd been a long time since he'd had someone care about his welfare, and while he knew Jackson's concern was well meant, he didn't like the questions. He had been questioned daily for months. He hadn't answered his interrogators under severe torture, so he wasn't about to let a polite request for information sway him.

The terse reply of *I'm good* was the best he could do.

Switching the phone off, he dropped it into a kitchen drawer and walked away. Contact with the outside world still felt strange.

In his previous life, before everything had gone to shit, he'd been less of an introvert than he was now but still not much of a social animal. In the small amount of free time he'd been able to carve out, he had preferred quiet evenings at home. How many nights had he sat in front of a fire, sipping a good bourbon and reading? Probably sounded boring to most people, but it had been his way to decompress.

While imprisoned, he'd had no rights and little privacy. Showers had been infrequent and medical care even less so. Food had been scarce and tasteless. The daily inquisitions and frequent beatings almost more than he could bear. However, it had been the lack of reading material that had almost driven him insane. From the time he could read, he had devoured books like an alcoholic devours booze. Out of everything that had been done to him, it had been lack of words that had almost made him crazy.

He stood in the middle of the room and waited for peace to settle over him. This was his new sanctuary. The one place where he could surround himself with everything he had missed. In one corner he had placed two floor-to-ceiling bookshelves. In front of the shelves were boxes filled with some of his favorite classics—their number only a fraction of his once extensive library. But it was a beginning.

He didn't wonder what Sabrina had done with his belongings. Made sense that she would have sold everything. His book collection alone would have brought a small fortune, which she would have pocketed, along with the money she made from her betrayal. It was just one more reason to hate her.

The room's remaining contents were simplistic, basic. A king-size bed, perfect for his large frame, was covered in bedding that smelled clean and fresh. In the corner, some free weights, a weight bench, and a boxing bag. After several months of intensive training, he was stronger and fitter than ever.

His gaze moved to the kitchen area, which housed a small fridge, a microwave, a two-eyed stove, and a toaster. Gallons of spring water sat on the countertop. And in the bathroom, he had a running toilet, a sink, and an enclosed shower with clean, plentiful water.

Instead of the peace he expected, bitterness, like a dark, evil entity, swirled within him. *This* was what he had been reduced to? A box of books, a toilet that flushed, and clean water? This was supposed to make him happy? After what she had done to him? After she had taken everything from him? He was supposed to settle for this?

He turned his back on his small oasis and walked out the door. He had planned to give her some time to worry about why she had been taken. Suddenly, he didn't give a damn about the psychological torture he had planned. He wanted answers, he wanted an explanation, and then he wanted vengeance. Her death was the only thing that would give him peace.

CHAPTER SIX

Washington, DC

"Hello, Mr. McCall," a cheerful, male voice said.

The man who stood before Noah looked about as dangerous as the rescued black Lab puppy he and Samara had picked out for their kids last week. With iron-gray hair, a wrinkled, craggy face and twinkling, light blue eyes, he was the picture of non-threatening. In fact, if he put on about fifty pounds, he might make a convincing Santa Claus. No way was he involved in the dangerous world of covert ops.

"And you are?" Noah asked.

"Albert Marks." He held out his hand. "You can call me Al."

The friendly, low-key demeanor made Noah more wary than ever. As he shook the older man's hand, Noah noted the firm, solid grip along with the calluses on his trigger finger.

"And I assume you are Sabrina's former employer?"

"Something like that." He gazed around as he spoke. To a casual observer, it looked as though he was taking in the view, but the keen alertness in that sharp gaze made Noah reevaluate his first impression. This wasn't a man who did anything without a reason.

"Why don't we walk and talk?" Albert said.

Setting his gait to the slower pace of the older man, Noah waited for him to start. He had come to this meeting with almost no knowledge of what he would learn. When he hired Sabrina, it had been on the recommendation of Jordan Montgomery, who had, at one time, worked for the same agency.

Noah knew enough about Sabrina to trust her implicitly, but some things he had taken on faith. Though he usually liked to know as much about his operatives as possible in order to assess their strengths and weaknesses, he had accepted not knowing everything about Sabrina. Recommendations from one of his most trusted operatives, along with the knowledge that she had worked for the ultrasecretive EDJE had gone a long way in his hiring decision. He had never regretted his decision. For the years she had been an LCR operative, her job performance had been exemplary.

"Sabrina was once our most valued female agent," Marks said. "I oversaw her training. Watched her grow from a wary, damaged young woman to a mature, finely tuned, lethal agent. There's not a finer or more dedicated professional alive. Working for you, Mr. McCall, may have saved her sanity."

"I didn't come here to be convinced of my operative's professionalism or strength. I'm aware of that. I came here because you seemed to have a means to find her. If that's not the case, then you're no help to me or her."

A dry chuckle emerged. "Forgive me, son. I have a tendency to go down memory lane a little too often these days." He nodded. "Yes, I do have the means to find Sabrina. In fact, I'm waiting on a call about her location any moment."

"You know who took her?"

"There are numerous people who would like to get their hands on her, so the suspect list is quite long. However, I don't know who has her or why."

"Then how can you pinpoint her location?"

"She has a locating device in her arm."

"You tagged her?"

"With her permission, of course. We tag all EDJE employees for their protection. When she left, I offered to remove it, as we always do for departing agents. However, Sabrina knew she would always be a high-value target. She trusted me enough to keep the locator device active. I'm the only person who knows that she still has hers. Official records indicate that it was removed."

"That's why she gave me your phone number and code."

"Yes." He smiled. "We've always had a good relationship. Most Agency employees called me Albert, but Sabrina always called me Uncle Al.

"I retired last year, but Sabrina and I still chat from time to time. Even though it pained me to no end when she left us, I understood her reasoning. Taking lives can destroy a person's soul, no matter how rotten that life might have been. Of course, Declan saw the damage long before I did." He shook his head. "Never seen anything like those two. They could read each other better than most people can read books."

Albert's gaze went unfocused as he reminisced. "Sabrina was twenty, but in many ways still just a child when she came to us. And though we have numerous female agents, Sabrina was like a daughter to me. And, of course, Declan was as dear to me as my own children. When they fell in love...it just seemed like it was a perfect match.

"Did you ever meet Declan, Mr. McCall?"

"No," Noah said. "Never had the privilege."

"Finest man I knew. Losing him was like losing a part of my family. In fact, he—"

Hoping to divert Albert's journey down memory lane again, Noah opened his mouth to suggest that the man call his people again to see if they had a location on Sabrina. A cell phone chimed in Albert's pocket, stopping him.

The friendly, charming smile disappeared, and a cold, deadly look entered Albert's eyes. As he answered the phone with a clipped "Yes," the older man's expression went rock hard. *This* was the man who had trained assassins and been in charge of deadly operations.

Albert listened for a full minute before speaking. Noah was transfixed by the incredible transformation in the man's demeanor. No doubt about it, in his younger years, Albert Marks would have been a helluva an agent.

The older man pocketed his phone. "We have her location. Now, let me ask you, Mr. McCall, do your people have what it takes to rescue Sabrina?"

"Without a doubt."

"And the people who took her…can you capture them?"

"Of course."

"Excellent. I'd like to have them brought to me. I'll text you a location." The affable, charming smile reappeared. "I'll handle it from there."

Having seen both sides of Albert Marks, Noah realized every expression he had revealed and each word he had uttered had all been chosen for a reason. This man, whoever the hell he was, was both impressive as all get-out and scary as hell.

Coley Spring, Idaho

Strong, hard hands bit into her shoulders and shook her awake. Sabrina blinked her heavy eyelids and gazed blearily up at the tall figure above her. A black ski mask covered his face, and even his eyes stayed hidden behind reflective sunglasses. All she saw was her reflection—ratty hair, pale face, hideous bruise on her cheek and tired, glazed eyes.

Whoever the man was, he wanted his identity to stay hidden, which meant she knew him. And by hiding his face, she assumed he didn't intend to kill her. At least not yet.

He pulled her to her feet, and she realized that he had bound her hands behind her. The thought that she hadn't wakened when that happened infuriated her. Allowing that fury to envelop her, she managed to jerk away from his hands and stand on her own. Though she swayed like a drunk, she was pleased that her legs held.

Shoulders straight, she ignored the knowledge that she looked like three-day-old roadkill and glared up at her abductor.

The man took several steps back and just looked at her through those damn glasses. While he looked, she took the time to assess him. He was tall. Maybe about six-foot-five and muscular. Not just muscular—strong, hard, seemingly indestructible. The hands that shook her had been large, unyielding. His strength didn't intimidate her. She had taken down men just as large and brutal. Every man had his weakness...she would find his.

As she regarded him unblinkingly, he backed away further. Her heart lightened. He had to know what she could do to him. A worldwide reputation of lethal legwork commanded respect.

Still, he continued his silence. Would taunting him bring him closer? It was worth a try. She smiled up at him, challenge in her eyes. "What are you so afraid of? I'm all tied up, barely able to move."

Silence.

Fine, she would wait him out. They continued to stare at each other for what felt like an eternity. At last, when she was to the point of screaming at him, he huffed out a long, heavy breath and said, "Do you have any idea how very much I want to…kill you?"

Every sense went on alert. She knew that voice…didn't she? Though it was raspy, gravelly, it was a voice she'd heard before. Or was it? Years ago she had been able to not only identify voices within a sea of chatter but also accents and dialects. And once she had even ID'd a man on a recording from an explosive sigh he had given just before he'd shot an EDJE agent.

This man's voice was familiar and not. It sounded damaged or not right, as if his vocal cords had been strained beyond endurance. Yet the timbre or tone called to her. An outbreak of chills swept through, and goose bumps covered her entire body. That was damn strange. The voice didn't incite fear or even anger. Instead, it was causing some sort of odd excitement in her bloodstream.

Holy hell, was she getting turned on by a stranger who had brutally abducted her? That was freaking sick. Not only was it too early to consider Stockholm syndrome, her reaction didn't compute to that kind of feeling. She actually felt a rush of arousal zooming through her.

Admittedly, it had been a long time since she'd been with a man. Still…this was all wrong. Sabrina Fox didn't get turned on easily. The few men she had allowed to get close enough to find that information out would attest to that. Only one man had ever been able to move her like that.

"You don't seem disturbed that I want to kill you."

Shaking off the odd feelings his voice evoked, Sabrina shrugged. "You're not the first, won't be the last."

"If I succeed, I will be the last."

"You won't succeed."

"You seem sure of that. Why?"

"Bigger men than you have tried and failed."

"You've killed many men, haven't you?"

"Enough."

"How many?"

"Sorry, asshole. I don't kill and tell."

"Estimate," he barked.

She had truly never counted...never wanted to know. But still, she couldn't resist his taunt. "Twenty...twenty-five. After a while, you just lose count...you know."

"Have you ever killed anyone you cared about?"

That was a damn strange thing to ask.

"Answer my question." The harsh words snapped like a whip.

"No, I've never killed anyone I cared about."

"Ever betrayed anyone you loved?"

"Look, can we just get on with—"

"Answer. The. Fucking. Question." His voice had gone soft but held an unmistakable lethal edge.

"No, I have never betrayed anyone I loved. Satisfied?"

Call her crazy, but she got the idea that her answer disturbed him. He continued to stare silently at her, but she could swear his shoulders drooped a little. Seconds later, he recovered and said in that harsh, ravaged voice, "Have you ever cared about anyone?"

"Okay, this is getting ridiculous. Either tell me what you want to know or let me go."

Sabrina snapped her mouth shut and hurled silent curses at herself. She had been trained to endure torture and hardships.

Instead, she had allowed him to draw her out with little more than a couple of taunts. Damned if he'd get another rise out of her. Her reflection in his sunglasses was pitifully humiliating. She looked like a mutinous five-year-old refusing to eat her spinach.

Straightening her lips into a thin, hard line, she gave him her best death stare.

Despite the torrential rage whirling through him, Declan felt a swell of emotion. The infamous death stare. They had been in Italy and Sabrina had still been in training. He had spent hours teaching her how to freeze her features into a cold, emotionless mask and blank her gaze as if her eyes could pierce a soul. Even though the lessons had been serious, more than once she had laughed at how uncomfortable it had been to stare without blinking.

Declan had an advantage few could claim—he knew how to get under her skin. Her insecurities, her doubts, her fears…what made her tick. She might have lied about a lot of things, but he knew the truth about many. He had the information to break her.

"You say you've killed twenty-five men. Did you enjoy it? Did they have families? Children? Did you deprive children of their fathers? Deprive mothers of their sons? What did it feel like to hear them take that last breath? Hear the death rattle and know you were responsible?"

Silence.

"You're nothing but a killing machine. No redeeming values or qualities. No better than the men and women you killed." He paused for several seconds, then continued, "Do you have a conscience? Morals?" He repeated the questions, the insults, the taunts…drilling into her insecurities. Five, ten, fifteen minutes, he was relentless in his need to make her suffer.

She swayed, caught herself and straightened. Her face was paler than death, but she continued her silence. The stare continued. Not by even a flicker did she indicate his words made any impact.

What was the point of this? If he planned to kill her, then he damn well needed to get on with it. Still, there was one last question he had to ask: "In your entire, miserable existence have you ever loved anyone?"

A lone tear drizzled down her pale cheek.

Finally, he had penetrated that frozen composure. Impacted her rotten, black heart. Why didn't he feel triumphant? Why didn't he laugh at her pain and tell her she was going to die? Why instead did he feel a rip so deep in his chest, it felt as if a hand was clawing at his heart?

Before he did something stupidly asinine, like wipe the tear from her cheek, he did an about-face and headed for the door. As he walked out, a question popped from his mouth. "Do you still eat your peas with a knife?"

Shock kept her eyes glued to the door long after he had gone. As comprehension swept through her brain, dizziness washed over her. Uncaring of her hands, which were still tied behind her back, she collapsed onto the bed. No. It couldn't be. It just could not be. He was gone...dead. He had been blown up right before her eyes. She had seen his ravaged, mangled body. There was no way he was alive. But the question he'd asked... No one but Declan knew that about her.

She had been in training for just a few months...hadn't even started training with Declan yet. Uncle Al had invited her to have dinner with him, and Declan had been there. Just as they'd sat down to eat, Albert had gotten a phone call and left the table.

She had been nervous to be left alone with Declan. Not only was he still mostly a stranger, she had never been that close to anyone so incredibly gorgeous. It was also before she'd had her etiquette training and still had the manners of a pig. Without giving any thought that she should wait on Albert to return, she had picked up her knife, scooped up some peas and slid them into her mouth. While she munched, she'd caught Declan grinning at her. He'd told her later that, silly as it seemed, it was one of the first things he loved about her.

She had stopped the bad habit immediately, but it was something she and Declan had laughed about over the years.

He couldn't be alive, could he? No, how was that even possible? He was dead…she knew he was dead. Declan had probably just told someone about the peas, and somehow this man had learned this innocuous but private information.

Even as she had that thought, she dismissed it. Declan didn't tell personal stuff…didn't talk, period. It was just not his way. So if this man hadn't learned it secondhand, that could only mean one thing…

An unmistakable noise caught her attention. A helicopter. Voices shouting. Heavy boots running. Her shocked brain acknowledged what was happening—the locator in her arm had done its job. Noah had contacted Uncle Al, and they'd traced the signal. LCR had come to rescue her.

The door burst open. The man was still wearing a ski mask and sunglasses, but he had something else he hadn't brought with him before—a gun. "Obviously, we're not going to be able to continue our discussions as I'd hoped." He raised the gun and pointed it at her head. His other hand went to the ski mask.

She reached out a hand toward him. "No…Declan. Don't."

The door burst open. Aidan flew through the air and tackled the man, throwing him off his feet. Sabrina watched in horror as the two men rolled around on the floor. Fists slammed into each other's bodies in a furious fight. Aidan's hits were pure rage, but then Declan did something extraordinary. He dropped his hand to his sides and stopped fighting, stopped hitting back. It was as if he didn't care...as if he didn't want to live.

"Stop it, Aidan!" She tugged violently on the chains around her wrists. Aidan was going to kill him. "Dammit, stop!" she bellowed.

Finally, Aidan pinned the other man to the floor and looked over at her. "You okay?"

"I'm fine."

He turned his attention back to the man he'd beaten. "Let's see who this bastard is." He ripped off the mask.

A gasp of horror, followed by a whimper, escaped Sabrina. Her distress wasn't caused by the fact that it was Declan. Unbelievable as it was, her brain had already acknowledged he was alive. But this wasn't the Declan she remembered. His face was the same but not. Harsh, unforgiving, brutal. His beautiful eyes, once as blue as the ocean, were dark, murky...dead. This wasn't the beautiful, charming man she had loved. This man looked as though he'd crawled through hell and had left his soul behind.

"Who are you?" Aidan snarled.

When Declan didn't answer, Aidan raised his fist, ready to deal him a knockout blow. "No!" Sabrina screamed. "Don't!"

Aidan held his punch and looked up at her. "You know this guy?"

Her entire body trembling with shock and sorrow, she nodded.

"Who the hell is he?"

Finally finding her voice, she managed a hoarse whisper, "Declan Steele…my husband."

Chapter Seven

LCR medical facility
Alexandria, Virginia

Legs curled beneath her, Sabrina sat on a sofa in the small waiting room and sipped hot, soothing herbal tea. Declan was in the next room being examined by one of LCR's doctors.

The second after she'd whispered that Declan was her husband, he'd started fighting like a fiend. Aidan had ended up having to knock him out to subdue him. On the flight back, he had regained consciousness but refused to look at her. She had tried talking to him, but he'd just stared past her as if she didn't exist.

Aidan had zip-tied his wrists. When Declan had woken, he'd glanced down at his bound hands and hadn't flinched. He had been worryingly docile. No emotion, not even anger, appeared on his face.

This wasn't the Declan she knew. Her Declan would have been cursing and hurling insults while he fought like a demon to be set free. This Declan acted as if he wasn't even human.

There wasn't a place on her body that didn't ache. She was worn out, physically and mentally. The residual effects from the drugs continued to weigh her down, along with the shock of her abduction. However, nothing had shocked her system quite so much as finding out that her husband was alive. The man she had watched blown to bits before her eyes hadn't been Declan. The closed casket carrying his remains that she had held on to, sobbing, hadn't been her husband's. The hand she'd found with an identical wedding ring hadn't been Declan's. Who had that man been? And who had set it up to make it appear that Declan was dead?

She had seen the DNA reports confirming that the body was Declan's. There had been no doubt that the man she'd seen blown up had been Declan Steele. So who the hell had created this elaborate hoax?

Where had Declan been? The dark, bleak look in his eyes told a tale of unspeakable horror. What had he endured? And why did he seem to hate her?

The cell phone lying on the coffee table in front of her chirped. She took a shaky breath, already knowing the identity of the caller. She just wasn't sure if she wanted to talk to him. Had he been the one to betray them? It hurt to even have that thought. He had been a father figure and her mentor. Could the man who had saved her from hell been responsible for sending her to another one?

Albert had been in charge of the Agency when this went down. If nothing else, she held him responsible for allowing something like this to happen on his watch. And as much as it hurt to consider her mentor and friend as dirty, she refused to bury her head in the sand and blindly trust him as she once had.

She would have to talk to him eventually. She pressed the answer key. "Hey, Uncle Al."

"You okay?"

"I'm fine. Guess you've heard."

"Yes. I don't know what to say other than we'll find out the truth, my dear."

"Yes, we will."

"I wanted him brought to me, but your boss refused."

Even though she couldn't smile...wasn't sure she ever would again, she felt amusement at the insult in Al's tone. No one turned down Albert Marks. Kind to many, he was also a wolf in sheep's clothing. Few crossed him. Those who did lived to regret it. And she had heard rumors that some hadn't lived afterward.

"That was at my request."

"He's one of ours. I may be retired, but that doesn't mean I can't ensure he gets the help he needs. We could—"

"He's my husband. My responsibility."

"And he's obviously damaged. He needs help."

"And he'll get whatever he needs, but only from people I can completely trust."

The silence was painful. Sabrina inwardly winced but refused to apologize. He had to know where she stood.

"You're right, my dear. I'm sorry. I will find out who did this, and they will be dealt with accordingly."

"If you find out, I want to know. And if I find out first, I'll let you know."

"That seems fair, but I would like to talk with Declan myself."

"I'll ask him. If he says yes, I'll contact you."

Albert huffed a harsh breath into the phone. "I know you hold me responsible...as you should. He's one of mine, and I failed him." In the hard voice she'd heard only a few times, he added, "Someone will pay, I promise."

"Good-bye, Uncle Al." Sabrina ended the call before she said anything she would regret. She was no closer to knowing Al's innocence or guilt than she had been before, but she agreed with him on one thing. Whoever had done this to Declan would pay. She would make sure of it.

Declan lay on the bed. Not just any bed, though. This one he was handcuffed to, on both sides. A man with coal-black eyes and an even darker expression had told him he would stay this way until he could be trusted.

How laughable. No way in hell were they going to release him. He had exchanged one prison cell for another. Admittedly, this one smelled a lot cleaner, but prison was prison.

He should've killed her when he'd had the chance. He had intended to. That had been his only goal when he was being beaten and interrogated. He had seen her in his mind's eye and had held on to that goal of one day taking his revenge. He'd had her in his grasp, could have taken her out at anytime he liked. But then old, useless memories had stalled his plan. When he escaped, he wouldn't make the same mistake again.

For now, he would stay put. He had spent thirteen months in a hellish prison without talking. Anything these people did to him here would be a picnic.

The door clicked open, and she stood there. He didn't have to look to know it was her. There was just something about Sabrina. If he'd been blindfolded and a hundred women walked through those doors, one at a time, he would have had no trouble picking her out. He used to think it was some sort of psychic connection—something mystical. What a crock.

"Declan?" she said softly, tentatively.

He did nothing to acknowledge her presence.

She came to stand beside the bed, and he had no choice but to see her. She still looked exhausted, and that hideous bruise on her face had darkened to a blue green. Despite all of that, she was still the most beautiful woman he'd ever known. That thought confirmed just how screwed up he really was.

She sat in the chair beside the bed and lightly touched his hand, which was attached to the railing by handcuffs. "I don't know what happened. It's obvious you're furious with me." The laugh she released held a definite sob. "I know I'm a slow study sometimes, but kidnapping me and threatening to shoot me was a good clue."

When he said nothing, she whispered, "Please, Declan, tell me what happened…where you've been."

Tears glistened in her beautiful eyes, and Declan ground his teeth together to keep from saying something to comfort her. It had once been his job—one that he'd taken with utmost seriousness. These tears were obviously fake. She was an excellent liar… he had trained her well. They used to practice on each other. A game they'd played for fun and to keep their skills sharp.

A sigh came from her lips, and warm breath rushed over his face. Despite his best attempt to stop it, blood rushed to his groin, and Declan felt himself harden. Well, so the hell what? It had been a long time since he'd had sex. Any woman would turn him on. His reaction was a normal, physical response. It meant nothing.

"All right." She continued to caress his hand as if she couldn't stop touching him. "You can keep silent as long as you feel the need. Let me tell you what I know, and then hopefully by then you'll be willing to share."

Her voice was thick, husky. "I watched you die, Declan. I was standing maybe fifty yards from you when the bomb went off. I found…" She swallowed and continued, "I found only pieces of you."

Did she honestly think he was going to believe her? How much bullshit was she willing to feed him? Yeah, he knew all about the supposed bomb. Jackson had told him everyone believed he had died. But not this woman—she knew it wasn't the truth.

"What I found...was barely recognizable, but we found your identification. Your wedding ring was on the hand I found. They did DNA testing. Which you know is standard procedure for the Agency. The results came back as an exact match to yours." She breathed out another shaky breath. "I had no reason not to believe it was you."

She swallowed and added, "I buried you in Scotland...beside your parents and sister."

So some nameless stranger was buried in his place? Or was that even the truth? How was he to separate the truth from the lies? He couldn't. All he could do was disbelieve everything.

"I'm telling you the truth, Declan."

He was tired of this bullshit. His jaw so tight with anger he thought it might crack, he managed to grind out, "You set me up."

Her eyes went wide with shock, and her already pale face went a sickly yellow. "You...I... What the hell are you talking about?"

"You know exactly what I'm talking about. Don't try to deny it."

She was shaking her head before he finished his words. "How did I set you up?"

He turned his gaze away from her. "There's no reason to talk with you. Whatever comes out of your mouth is a lie."

"The least you can do is tell me why you think I set you up."

He closed his eyes as pain speared through his head.

"Declan? What's wrong? Are you in pain?"

Despite the searing agony in his head, he sent her a glare that had her gasping and jerking back. Good. The sooner they got past the lies, the quicker the truth would come out.

A knock on the door sent her to her feet. "Got a minute, Fox?" a deep male voice asked.

"Yes. I'll... Yes." Looking rattled, she turned to walk away from the bed. Declan cursed himself for watching her leave. She stopped at the door, and showing him that as usual she recovered fast, she threw over her shoulder, "We'll get to the bottom of this, but one thing you need to know, I never betrayed you.

She walked out the door before he could call her a liar again.

Sabrina leaned against the door and worked to stay upright. Of all the things she had thought Declan would say to her, never had she dreamed that he'd think she betrayed him. Which was stupid, really. Why else had he abducted her, tried to kill her? Her brain was running on nothing but adrenaline. She could barely hold a coherent thought in her head, much less figure out what the hell had happened.

Noah stood a few feet away and studied her. "You okay?"

The answer was a definitive no. She didn't know if she would ever be okay again. "He thinks that I betrayed him...set him up. He hates me."

"Sounds like someone might've betrayed you both."

"I have to find out who and why." She shook her head. "I don't know who to trust anymore."

"Yes, you do."

She lifted her gaze to the man across from her. Integrity, compassion, and character were stamped on his handsome face. He was right. She did know whom to trust.

Noah continued, "This might not be our usual type of op, but you're one of ours. You need help, you've got it."

Sabrina wanted to hug her boss. She wasn't a demonstrative person. That kind of carefree act had been strangled out of her at an early age, but that he'd offered his help meant so much. He was the leader of an organization responsible for rescuing victims all over the world. He had to negotiate with presidents, heads of state, and law enforcement. He had more responsibilities than the leaders of some small countries.

"Thank you, Noah. I could use your expertise and an objective perspective."

"Why don't you get something to eat, grab a nap, and then come to my office at four."

She nodded her thanks and then took in a breath to settle herself. A brightness appeared in her thoughts. Despite the knowledge that he wouldn't welcome her, she said with an odd sense of contentment, "I think I'll grab some sandwiches and have lunch with my husband."

The food was good, he couldn't deny it. How many nights had he longed for something as simple and basic as a cheeseburger and fries? Though he wanted to wolf down the entire meal with one swallow, he forced himself to take his time. His appetite had improved in the last few months, but it still wasn't as large as it had been. Eating an entire cheeseburger, along with large fries and a soda, was almost more than he could manage. But still, it was damn good.

"Remember that dive in Luxembourg where we found those incredible bratwursts?"

They'd been sitting in the outdoor picnic area for over ten minutes, and Sabrina had tried one "remember..." story after another. At one time, it had usually taken a word or just a glance for them to get into a lengthy conversation. He'd always found her take on life and its peculiarities fascinating.

The meal he'd been enjoying turned to cement as his gut twisted. The wrinkle in her normally smooth brow and the sadness in her eyes made him want to reach out and reassure her. How in the hell could he hate her for betraying him and still want to soothe her? Damning himself for his weakness, he said, "I remember you ate three."

Delight brightened her eyes, and her smile took his breath. "And you told the waiter that I was the world champion hot dog eater."

"And he asked for your autograph."

She grinned and said, "Remember when we—"

"Stop it, Sabrina. It's not going to work."

"What's not going to work?"

"Reminding me of good times. They were all fucking lies."

She flinched at his profanity. Yeah, he'd never been much for cursing before, but he'd learned that certain crass words belonged to certain situations. This one definitely qualified.

Instead of proclaiming her innocence again, she said, "Declan...where have you been?"

"In hell, darling, where you put me."

Her mouth tightened slightly, but she continued with her questions. "How did you get out...escape?"

"You think I'm going to rat out the people who had the balls to save me?"

"How long have you been...out?"

"Four months."

"How did you find me?"

"Took awhile. I figured at some point you'd use one of your old covers."

Knowledge entered her eyes. "You found Lucia St. Martine."

"Yeah. Thought about taking you as soon as I found you."

"Why didn't you?" Sabrina didn't doubt that he could have pulled it off any time he liked. As much as she prided herself on her abilities, Declan had been better. He'd been a master strategist.

His response was a careless shoulder lift. Sabrina didn't pursue it. She wanted to think that he hadn't taken her until after her mission was complete because he hadn't wanted to ruin a rescue operation. Even though she feared she was giving him credit for qualities he no longer possessed, she chose to believe that was the reason for his delay.

"Where have you been?"

"You know exactly where I've been, Sabrina."

"Dammit, pretend I don't for a moment. Where were you?"

With his jaw clenched, the word ground from his mouth, "Africa."

"Where in Africa?"

"Dolisie."

"That's…where?"

"Republic of Congo. Central Africa."

"What happened to you there?"

"You know what happened."

She pursed her lips and just glared at him. No way was she going to give him the satisfaction of once again hearing her deny involvement in his abduction.

Apparently seeing he hadn't gotten the rise out of her as he'd hoped, he shrugged. "I was interrogated."

"About what?"

"Now who's being silly? If I didn't tell them anything, why would I tell you?"

"Because I'm your wife."

A harsh, jagged sound erupted from his throat. "You are a piece of work. But know this. *That marriage certificate? It means nothing. You mean nothing.* As soon as I escape this new hell you've put me in, I'll be making sure our so-called marriage is dissolved."

"Like hell you will."

It took everything Sabrina had to keep from upending her soda on top of his head. Of all the insulting, infuriating things he could have said, this was the worst. Like she was going to just step back and let him end their marriage when two days ago she hadn't even known she still had a husband.

He arched a black brow in that arrogant fashion she used to love. "What's wrong? Surely you can't still want to be married to me."

"Right now, the only thing I want is to find out who did this to us. After that's settled, we'll discuss the rest of our lives."

He sat back in his chair. She noted he'd eaten only three-quarters of his burger and about half his fries. Yes, she knew he should be eating more-nutritious food, but she had wanted to treat him to one of his favorite meals.

"Is your burger not to your liking?"

"It's fine. Just can't eat it all."

The old Declan would have eaten two burgers, plus the rest of hers. Stupid, silly tears filled her eyes, and she dropped her gaze back to her own half-eaten meal. How ridiculous. After all that had happened and she hadn't broken down once. Now here she was, about to start sobbing because Declan couldn't finish his burger.

"So tell me—let's just say, for the sake of argument, that you had nothing to do with my capture—who do you think is responsible?"

"Since I don't know what they did to you or the questions they asked, it makes it a little harder to come up with viable suspects."

"Try," he snapped.

She held back her exasperation. "Declan, you have enemies all over the world. How the hell should I know?" She shook her head. "Wait, don't answer that. I already know why you think I should know."

He stared at her for so long she feared he wouldn't speak again. After several long minutes, he finally relented enough to say, "They tortured me."

The stark, unadorned words slashed a bloody crease across her heart. "For what?"

"Information."

"What kind of information?"

"Are you really that stupid?"

Sabrina put her napkin down and stood. "I'm suddenly not hungry anymore. Andre will take you back to your room. Don't bother to fight him." She withdrew the cuffs she'd taken off of him earlier and said, "Hands behind your back."

He didn't move, but the fury in his eyes said it all. Surprising her, he complied, and she snapped on the cuffs.

"Andre, please return Mr. Steele to his room."

As soon as she said this, Andre came to stand beside Declan's chair. Several inches over six feet and well over two hundred pounds, the orderly should have had no trouble handling anyone. Declan wasn't just anyone. Showing what a smart man Andre was, he didn't try to pull Declan up, but waited.

Though his eyes flashed with rage, Declan didn't speak. Sabrina needed to get away from him before she said or did something she would later regret. Haunting, mocking words followed her out the door: That marriage certificate? It means nothing. You mean nothing.

And she knew that was true.

CHAPTER EIGHT

LCR Headquarters

Sabrina arrived for her meeting with Noah feeling only slightly more alert. After her disastrous meal with Declan, she had made use of one of LCR's apartments. After a long, hot shower, she'd barely been upright. Since she felt she could sleep well into next week, she had set the alarm for two hours and fallen into bed, sure that she would be unconscious in seconds. Fifteen minutes later, she'd gotten out of bed. Her body might feel half-past dead, but her mind would not shut down.

She'd put her clothes back on and headed back to the clinic. Declan had been asleep, and she'd sat beside his bed and just looked at him. Despite all the hurt she felt at his cruel words, she still marveled that he was actually alive. No matter how much she might personally want to smack him, she couldn't be anything other than glad that he still lived.

Even in sleep, he couldn't rest easy. His body moved restlessly, and he grimaced as if he were in pain. He was still a beautiful man, but in a much harsher way. Lines of suffering around his eyes and mouth told of unspeakable agony. Calling herself all sorts of stupid didn't stop her from kissing him on the forehead before she walked out the door.

And now she was here to spill her guts to her boss. Noah had taken a lot on faith when he hired her, and though he knew more about her than anyone else at LCR, there were still things he didn't know. Things she needed to reveal. Not only because he had offered to help her, but because he deserved to know the truth.

She practically fell into the chair in front of his desk and released a weary sigh.

"You get any sleep?" Noah asked.

"I tried. Didn't work."

He nodded as though he understood. "You want anyone else here with you?"

"No. Just you for now."

"Very well. You want to start?"

She took a breath. "When I was twenty, Albert Marks found me at a psychiatric hospital for the criminally insane. I had been incarcerated there for three years."

"For?"

"Killing my stepbrother."

One thing she'd always appreciated about Noah was his non-judgmental attitude. He didn't even look surprised.

"No need to go into a lot of detail…since it's not really relevant, but my stepbrother began raping me when I was twelve. When I finally worked up the courage to tell my mother and stepfather, they accused me of lying. I was too ashamed to tell my teachers or counselors at school. I endured until the day I couldn't."

She no longer became nauseated or dizzy when talking about that day. She really didn't know what had caused her to snap at that precise moment. Maybe hundreds of rapes had accumulated into that monumental moment of rage. After Albert rescued her from the institution, she'd gone through extensive counseling.

She'd learned to deal with her anger and to understand that what had happened that day wasn't all that unusual. She'd just finally had enough.

"Since I was seventeen, they wanted to try me as an adult." Her mouth twisted with a bitter smile. "You see…after a few years, he stopped having to beat me to rape me. I was conditioned to lie there, accept what he did. Other than my parents, I had told no one what was going on. I was this weak, timid creature who let everyone take advantage of her. There was no evidence of force…so no one believed me."

"How did you kill your abuser?"

"After he raped me that last time, he went back to his room and fell asleep. My mother and stepfather were out for the evening. I cleaned myself up, went to the kitchen to make a sandwich. I remember slicing some cheese. The next thing I know, I'm standing over the bastard's bed and blood's dripping from the knife. I'd stabbed him multiple times."

She rarely thought about that poor, ravaged creature she'd once been. So weak and malleable…only wanting someone to believe in her. And until Albert, no one ever had.

She appreciated that Noah made no sounds, sympathy or otherwise. Sympathy never solved a damned thing.

"I called the police. They came, and I confessed. I had a crappy, court-appointed public defender. My parents refused to pay for a defense attorney." She shrugged. "Not to draw it out, I got a reduced sentence if I agreed to go to a psychiatric hospital. I didn't think I'd care. After all, I'd been in hell in one way or another much of my life. What was one more?

"Turns out, I did care. The minute I was locked up, I went berserk. Certifiably crazed. I guess killing Tony finally released all that anger that had been building up inside me. They drugged me every damn day. Even when I was halfway coherent, they still wouldn't believe my claims of abuse."

She remembered crying, pleading, begging. Hours of rocking back and forth in her bed, mumbling details of Tony's rapes. Reliving the horror. She had thought no one paid attention…no one heard her. But someone had.

"Albert had a relative who worked at the hospital. She told him about me. He came to visit. We would talk for hours. One day, he asked me if I'd like to leave. I said yes, and it was done."

"And he started training you for EDJE?"

"Not right away. Had to do a lot of psych evals." She smiled without humor. "Turns out, I wasn't crazy. Once I got off the meds and could articulate without trying to beat someone up, I actually felt like a human being. And behaved like one.

"I was at the EDJE facility about a year before I started my training. Lived in an apartment there. Went to a small private school. Found myself, you might say. Then Albert approached me, gave me a choice. Said I could leave, go out in the world, get a regular job, be normal. Or I could work for EDJE. It was nice to have a choice, but it wasn't a hard one to make. The thought of actually doing something worthwhile and useful was a powerful motivator."

"And you felt as if you owed your benefactor."

"Albert never coerced me." She grimaced as she admitted to Noah what she'd only realized herself several years after her Agency career began. "But you're right, I did feel as though I owed him."

Gauging Noah's expression wasn't easy, but she wanted him to know everything. "I became an assassin."

Again, no surprise flickered in his face. Just a nod and, "I've seen your fighting skills. And I know some of what EDJE does."

"Declan became my main trainer, my partner, and then my husband."

"And Albert Marks...do you still trust him?"

For the first time since she'd started talking, she hesitated. "I don't know. My heart says yes, of course I do. He saved my life, and he was more of a parent to me than any other person I've ever known. But that doesn't mean he didn't betray us. He was in charge when Declan was taken. As much as I love Albert, I know there's a cold, calculating side to him." She shook her head. "I just don't know."

"Then we'll leave him out of this for the time being. Any clue who would do this?"

"Any number of people. You don't work for the Agency without collecting a lot of enemies."

"What about your mother and stepfather?"

"My stepfather died a few years ago of prostate cancer. My mother, the last time I heard, was about to marry her fourth husband. We don't keep in touch."

"Any reason to think she might have something to do with this?"

"No. Not only would she have no idea where to find me or Declan, she wouldn't have the funds to pull it off, much less the intelligence."

"And Declan's family?"

Sadness pulled at her already tender emotions. "His mother, father, and sister were killed in a terrorist bombing in London while on holiday. Declan was in college here in the States, and instead of joining them there, chose to go on a trip with some of his friends. He never forgave himself."

"Major incentive for a young man to join an agency that fights terrorism."

"Yes."

"What was Declan's job?"

"He started off in ops, then did part training, part ops. The last year, before he disappeared, he was taking on less ops and became even more secretive. The last time we were together, he told me he wanted to quit the Agency. Said he wanted to have a normal life, normal marriage, but he had some loose ends to tie up first. Said they weren't dangerous. Then he disappeared."

"And he believes you were involved in his abduction?"

"I don't know how they convinced him of that or why. What's the purpose?"

"Breaking him down...making him more vulnerable. If he believed the one person he trusted most in the world had betrayed him, that might've made him weaker."

She shook her head. "Then they didn't know Declan. It might have pissed him off and he might hate me, but it still wouldn't get him to talk."

"He's going to have to talk to someone. My money's on you."

After her discussion with Noah, she should have been exhausted enough to sleep. She wasn't. Instead of doing the sensible thing, like going back to the apartment to rest, she'd crossed the hallway to the LCR gym and massacred a punching bag. Sweat poured down her body, saturating the mat. She had no concept of time or discomfort. At some point, she was aware of an audience of one, her partner. She paid no attention to Aidan. Her total focus was on the bag in front of her and her need to beat it into submission. Her fists slammed into the bag repeatedly, and with each hit, she cursed the bastards who had hurt Declan. And then cursed Declan for believing she could hurt him like that.

Just how crazy was it to be deliriously happy that he was alive but want to beat the hell out of him, too?

With one final roundhouse kick that she felt all the way up to her shoulder, she stopped. She bent over, put her hands on her knees, and heaved out harsh breaths. Every part of her body ached, but not enough to give her peace. Standing, she raised her fists, ready to go at the bag once more.

"Killing yourself won't solve the problem."

Her eyes on the swinging bag in front of her and not on her partner at the door, she said, "No, but at least if I'm hitting a bag, I'm not scratching Declan's eyes out."

Aidan snorted. "A few hours ago, you were thrilled to have found him, and now you want to scratch his eyes out. Yeah, you're definitely married."

Not for much longer. Declan had been clear about that.

"You up for a walk down memory lane?"

She turned to face the man she thought of as a brother as well as a partner, but there were certain things even a brother didn't need to know.

"I appreciate the offer, but reliving it won't solve the problem."

"Let me know when you're ready to talk." Grabbing a fresh towel from the stack at the door, he threw it to her. "But that's not what I meant. Noah's got some new intel about an old case. You're going to want to be there. We're meeting in fifteen minutes in the large conference room."

Sabrina wiped her face down, then the rest of her body. Even though she longed to go in the steam room for a good muscle-easing soak, and then take an invigorating shower, she headed to the shower instead. "Be there in ten."

Seven minutes later, Sabrina entered the conference room. Her hair was in a haphazard ponytail, she wore no makeup, and the clothes she'd found in her locker were ones she'd worn on a messy op a year ago. She'd been shot. Just a flesh wound, but stopping to patch herself up with bullets whizzing by hadn't exactly been wise. An impoverished childhood had created an adult who couldn't throw things away until they had disintegrated. Though freshly laundered, no amount of bleach was going to get the bloodstains out of the shirt.

Several steps inside the room, she stumbled to a stop. This wasn't just a meeting. This was a full-fledged LCR briefing. Her gaze took in the six operatives present, but it was the man at the end of the table where her eyes stuttered, then stopped. And why was Declan here?

Sabrina was the only woman who could look elegant and beautiful in blood-stained, worn-out clothes and a messy ponytail. Her lovely face and gorgeous body were a plus, but it was the grace and confidence with which she carried herself that made anything she wore look good. If she had wanted, she could have graced the covers of magazines or walked down the runways of Milan and Paris. Instead, she had chosen a dangerous, high-adrenaline occupation that could get her killed. The stains on her shirt were a testament to that fact. And despite his anger and distrust, Declan's gut twisted to know that she had been injured.

"What's going on?" she asked.

Her green eyes targeted McCall, and Declan had to give the LCR leader his due. He shot a glance at Declan, allowing him to explain. "Mr. McCall convinced me that there could be some advantages to my cooperation."

"Such as?" Sabrina asked.

He raised his handcuffed hand as far as he was able. "I might be able to walk around as a free man."

Before Sabrina could respond, McCall's cold, black eyes shot him a hard look. "Since you tried to kill one of my operatives, I think you're damn lucky you're not still unconscious."

Declan gave a nod to the man, acknowledging his point.

Sabrina settled into a chair beside him and said under her breath, "I'll have you unlocked as soon as we leave here."

Dammit, he didn't want any concessions from her. As if she hadn't spoken, he turned his gaze on the rest of the people in the room. They looked as pissed as McCall, telling him there would be no quick forgiveness from them, either.

"So, how can I help?" Declan asked with obvious fake politeness.

McCall turned to a screen behind him that showed the lone photo of a middle age man. "This is Barry Tyndall from Tulsa, Oklahoma. He disappeared eight months ago while traveling with his family in London. Three months after his disappearance, his wife came to LCR asking for help. The US State Department had been working with Scotland Yard, but all leads had dried up. Mrs. Tyndall was desperate. She had no idea by whom or why he had been kidnapped. There has never been a ransom demand."

Turning back to face the room, McCall continued, "By the time we got the case, the authorities were close to the end of their investigation with no real idea who or why the man had been taken."

As McCall continued his briefing of the Tyndall case, Declan observed the faces of the operatives around the table. Even though Sabrina had worked for LCR before they were married, Declan had never met any of them but Jordan Montgomery. Sabrina had told him enough about McCall to expect a hard-assed, no-bullshit kind of leader. Looked like, at least in that description, she'd told the truth.

He'd been introduced to the other people in the room but paid little attention to them. Once the meeting was over and the bullshit was said, he'd find a way to get out of these cuffs and disappear.

"Are we boring you, Mr. Steele?" McCall's harsh voice blasted through the room.

"As a matter of a fact, you are. If you would be so kind as to unlock the cuffs, I'll be on my way, and you can continue your little meeting."

"Declan!"

He told himself that Sabrina's horrified whisper didn't bother him. She was looking at him as if he'd grown another head.

"What?" He threw an amused look around the room. "I'm supposed to care about some clueless bloke from Oklahoma?"

Any remaining doubts that Declan's experience in captivity had changed him were forever gone from Sabrina's mind. He had been the planner…the strategist. The most focused and toughest man she'd ever known, but those talents had been tempered with compassion. Where she could be hotheaded, impulsive, and sometimes coldly calculating, Declan had been her compass, guiding her. What had they done to her wonderful, caring husband to make him so calloused and heartless?

Refusing to be embarrassed for him, she stood and addressed the room. "Declan and I will get updated later."

Noah tossed her the key to Declan's handcuffs, his expression unreadable.

Sabrina unlocked the cuff that bound Declan to the table. She didn't wait to see if he would follow. She knew he would.

Once they were both out of the room and the door closed behind them, she turned to him and unlocked the remaining cuff. Then she headed to the door leading outside.

"Where are you going?"

"I'm leading you out of here. There are people who might try to stop you. I'll stop them. Then you can go."

His lips curled into a disdainful snarl. "So I'm like some stray dog you rescued, and now that you realize it isn't the warm, loving creature you want, you're letting it go."

Her heart was literally ripping in two. "No," she answered shakily. "I'm giving you a choice."

"And that is?"

"Your new reality. Accept that I didn't betray you. That we were both set up."

"And if I do?"

"Then we work together to find out who did this to us and we make them pay."

"Or?"

She took another breath. "You're free to walk out of here."

"If you think that's going to convince me you're innocent, then you're not as bright as you used to be. No way in hell am I ever going to believe that you weren't involved."

Her heart ripped completely apart. "Why, Declan?"

"Because hating you was the only thing that kept me alive. Without that, I've got nothing."

And with those words, he passed her and walked out the door.

CHAPTER NINE

Declan stood on the sidewalk. The sun beat down on his head, and a warm breeze washed over his face. He was in Alexandria, Virginia...he knew that much. Sabrina had told him. On the flight here, she had held his hand and reassured him. She had apparently thought telling him everything that was happening and where they were going would soothe him, like he was some kind of child who needed comfort. Since he'd been handcuffed to the armrests, he couldn't keep her from holding his hand. He told himself that if he had been able to, he would have pulled away from her.

And now she had let him go. Like a lost child, he stood on the sidewalk without any idea where he was supposed to go, what he was supposed to do. He had never felt so directionless in his life. Who the hell was Declan Steele?

What he had told Sabrina was true. He had stayed alive for one reason only—to make Sabrina pay for her betrayal. When the leather whip had seared his skin, tearing strips of hide from his flesh till his feet were standing in a pool of blood, he'd screamed curses at Sabrina. When his head had been held under water so icy cold it had seared his lungs like fire, he had seen her face behind his closed lids, taunting him, keeping him alive. Vengeance had been his solace, his goal. Without that, what did he have?

Declan took a step, then another. With each one, his stride increased in speed until he was running down the sidewalk. Where was he going? Hell, he didn't know.

Passing small businesses, then residences, he kept moving in a straight path. Fortunately, he wore running shoes, but the jeans and heavy shirt that had felt comfortable in the mountains of Idaho were stifling. He stopped long enough to rip off his shirt and tie it around his waist. A few people stared, most likely wondering why this large, scarred, wild-eyed man was stumbling down the sidewalk. He didn't care. He had to keep going. If he stopped, he'd have to face the awful truth.

What if she was telling the truth? What if Sabrina hadn't betrayed him? What if this had been some elaborate hoax designed to get him to give up the secrets in his head? What if she was innocent? He told himself he should be happy that the woman he had loved hadn't betrayed him. Unfortunately, there was no happiness or relief. Without his hatred, he had nothing...he was nothing. A cold, dead heart, a conscienceless bastard, an empty shell. That's all he could ever be again.

Agony speared through his head. No, she was guilty. He knew she was. How the hell did she do that? Make him question what he knew to be the truth. She was screwing with his mind again. Maybe that was her new torture.

With an unnamed fear clutching at his gut and shards of agony zooming through his head, what else could he do but keep running until he could no longer breathe?

"Where could he have gone?"
"He's a grown man. He can take care of himself."

Standing at the window in Noah's office, Sabrina shook her head at her boss's words. The old Declan would've had no problem. This wasn't the same man, and she cursed herself for not accepting that sooner. She had been treating him as if he was still the man she married. As if he could just flip a switch and be the same Declan Steele she'd fallen head over heels for years ago. As if he could forget about all the hell he'd been through. And she still didn't know what he had endured. He had said that hating her was the only thing that kept him alive. If that were true, then she thanked God for his hatred. Whatever he'd had to do, she was just glad he had survived.

The LCR doctor who had examined him had called, asking to meet with her. Though she wanted to go and discuss the doctor's findings, she hadn't wanted to leave yet. Not until she knew Declan was safe. What if he didn't come back? What if he just disappeared from her life again?

She gave herself a mental ass-kick. She was a trained operative—an expert in finding missing people. He wouldn't disappear from her life. Now that she knew he was alive, she would hunt to the ends of the earth. But she prayed she wouldn't have to—that he would come back on his own.

"I shouldn't have tried to treat him as if nothing had changed. Everything has changed." She threw a pleading look over her shoulder. "That man in the conference room—that wasn't Declan."

"I know that, Sabrina. I shouldn't have brought him into the meeting. We haven't had a new lead on the Tyndall case in so long, my enthusiasm got the better of me."

"What new lead?"

Noah motioned her over to his desk. She had missed the rest of the briefing about Tyndall. After Declan had walked out, she had stayed close to the door, hoping he would just turn around and come back. A useless hope.

Tearing her gaze away from the window, she made herself go to Noah's desk, where he had an open file and notes, maps, and photos spread across the entire surface.

"After Mrs. Tyndall came to LCR to request our help, we delved deeper into his life. Cole Mathison was the lead on this op and uncovered some inconsistencies in Mr. Tyndall's life."

"Like what?"

"He's supposed to be a mid-level manager in a large consulting firm, and the people who work there back up his claim. However, his travel dossier reads like a Robert Ludlum novel. In the last ten years, he's been in every political hot spot."

Sabrina looked at the world map with at least a dozen red circles of every volatile location from Russia to Syria. "Why would a middle-management consulting firm employee need to travel to these places?"

"Exactly. When Cole pressed Tyndall's company for answers, he received a visit from two suits who encouraged him to stop asking questions."

She almost smiled. She had worked with Cole Mathison on a couple of missions before she'd changed over to the Elite team. For any LCR operative, being told to back off was the equivalent of waving a red flag at a bull. To Cole, who was one of the most tenacious investigators she'd ever known, he'd probably viewed the warning as an invitation.

"So is mild-mannered Mr. Tyndall a secret government spy or something else?"

"We think he's a courier for an as-yet-unnamed government agency, but we have no proof. What information we've been able to obtain was shut down completely when we started digging deeper."

"So whoever he was working for is just going to pretend he never existed."

"Exactly."

Fury washed through her. That was an all-too-common occurrence. EDJE had the same philosophy—one she whole-heartedly disliked. Yet she didn't for a moment believe they had known about Declan's captivity. If they had, the Agency would have done something. Not necessarily a rescue. They might have tried one, but if it hadn't been possible, they'd have found a way to kill him. Declan knew too much to allow him to stay alive.

"Here's the reason I brought your husband into the meeting." He pointed to a map of the Republic of Congo. "Here's Dolisie, which is the area your husband said he was held captive. Though Tyndall's last known location was in London, a man fitting his description was seen in Sibiti, the region's capital, about four months after he disappeared."

"I'm assuming an LCR crew went to Sibiti?"

"Yes. We scoured the area. Concluded Tyndall had been there but not any longer. Dolisie and Sibiti aren't next door to each other by any means. I know it's a long shot, but Steele said there were other prisoners where he was held. If there's a chance Tyndall is in the same prison, we need to check it out."

"I haven't been able to get him to talk about his imprisonment. Did he see any other prisoners?"

"I don't know," Noah said. "I managed to get him to tell me he heard other prisoners. When I asked for more information, he shut down. I had hoped if we brought him in and treated him as a member of the team, he might be more cooperative."

"By handcuffing him to the table?"

Noah raised his brow. "Wouldn't have done that except when Thorne went in to get him, your husband decked him."

She winced. No wonder Aidan had looked so pissed earlier. "Declan needs help. We can't keep treating him as if nothing has happened to him."

Noah nodded. "That's another thing I wanted to talk to you about. Since we might have a lead on Tyndall, Cole's headed this way. I'd like for him to spend some time with your husband."

"Why?"

"A few years back, Cole had something similar happen to him. We thought he was dead. Turns out, he'd been abducted, drugged daily, and tortured. He went through hell, and though it took him awhile, he came out of it even stronger than before."

The only things Sabrina knew about Cole's personal life were that he had twin daughters and a one-year-old son. He and his family lived in East Tennessee, close to an LCR branch office.

"Talking to a man who's gone through a similar experience might help." Her eyes went back to the window. "If Declan comes back," she murmured.

"You're all he's got. He'll come back."

Declan sat on a park bench in the shade, enjoying a vanilla ice cream cone he'd purchased from a street vendor. For the first time in forever, he felt almost normal. Laughter and the occasional excited scream surrounded him as kids played in the little playground. Moms and dads sat on benches and watched over them. Birds twittered and tweeted, butterflies fluttered, bumblebees buzzed. Dogs barked in the distance. All so peaceful, all so normal. Sounds he had once taken for granted and knew he never would again.

Africa could have been a lifetime away—a nightmare that had never materialized.

But it had been real. It wasn't a nightmare he'd dreamed in the safety of a comfortable bed. He had lived through that hell. Adapting to surviving was harder than he'd anticipated.

"Want a cracker?"

Declan glanced at the man beside him. He was dressed in a loose-fitting T-shirt and khakis, both of which had seen better days. With a full beard, wire-rimmed glasses and three front teeth missing, he had the appearance of a down-on-his-luck street bum. There was a kind twinkle in his eyes and a tilt to his lips that said he hadn't lost his sense of humor, no matter his circumstances.

"How's that?" Declan asked.

The man shoved a paper towel filled with saltine crackers toward him. "The shelter throws these out after a few days 'cause they're stale, but the pigeons, they don't mind."

Declan looked at the pigeons surrounding the bench. They were looking expectantly up at the man beside him.

"I come here every day and feed them." He shoved a cracker toward Declan. "Go ahead. They won't bite."

It'd been years, maybe decades, since he'd done something as simple as feeding pigeons in a park. Taking one of the proffered crackers, Declan pinched off a bit and threw it toward the birds. A couple of them dipped their heads for it, ate quickly, and then stared up at him with the same expectant look. Declan threw another crumb.

"There's something so elemental about animals, don't you think?"

"In what way?" Declan asked.

The man lifted a boney shoulder in a shrug. "They don't look for hidden agendas. And though they're wary of strangers, once you earn their trust, they rarely go back to distrusting you, no matter what happens." Another shrug. "People, on the other hand, seems like you have to keep earning their trust, over and over."

"That's because everyone's out for their own selfish interest."

"I'd say these pigeons are out for their own selfish interest, too."

"Yeah, but they don't stab each other in the back to get a bite."

The man nodded. "Yep, there's the difference. It's a sad fact of life, but these here pigeons…they miss something only humans can enjoy."

"What's that?"

"They'll never have more than this. Survival is their only motivation."

"Isn't that what we all try to do, especially humans? Survive?"

"Maybe, but they'll never know the depths of despair nor the peaks of happiness."

Now it was Declan's turn to shrug. "Seems like a more peaceful way to live."

"Somebody's hurt you, son."

Getting into a philosophical discussion with a stranger was one thing—he enjoyed the sharing of ideas. Spilling his guts was another.

Declan stood. "Nice chatting with you."

"Sorry, didn't mean to pry."

"That's no problem. Need to get going."

"One thing you might want to remember. Those despairing moments of life sometimes make those highs even greater."

Since he didn't anticipate ever experiencing any kind of high again, Declan nodded vaguely and took a few steps away. He stopped abruptly and, for no reason whatsoever, called out, "What's your name?"

"Jack."

Declan nodded. "Nice talking to you, Jack. Thanks for sharing your crackers."

"Anytime."

Turning away, Declan headed back the way he'd come. He still had no clear path, but putting off the inevitable was pointless. He and Sabrina needed to talk. Hiding behind his bitterness was getting him nowhere.

Sabrina sat across the desk from Dr. Anson Lamar. The tall, lanky physician had laugh lines bracketing his mouth and light green eyes brimming with intelligence. Though not an official LCR physician, Dr. Lamar offered his services to the organization gratis. Years ago, his wife and son had been kidnapped. LCR rescued the doctor's family, returning them unharmed. Now retired, the doctor gave back as much as he could to the organization that had saved his loved ones.

"I wanted to talk with you before releasing the medical profile I developed on your husband."

Declan had yet to return to the LCR office, but Noah had promised to call her the instant he did. She prayed fervently that he would come back. Perhaps talking with Dr. Lamar would provide her with some answers or guidance on how to deal with him when he did return.

"Has your husband talked with you about what happened to him while he was in captivity?"

"He hasn't said much of anything. I know he was tortured. I don't know how or why. And I know he thinks I'm responsible."

"Have you seen his body?"

Dread swept through her, followed by a quick rush of nausea. "No."

"I wanted to talk with you, to prepare you. He has scarring over most of his body. His back took the most abuse. Some of the worst I've seen."

Steely, hard discipline was the only thing that kept her from springing from her chair and running out of the doctor's office to find Declan. She had known he'd been tortured but had forced herself not to think about just how badly. Not one who usually buried her head in the sand, she had been uncharacteristically reticent in learning everything she could about Declan's ordeal.

"Did he tell you anything?" Sabrina barely recognized the shaky, weak voice as hers.

"No. He was silent during the entire exam."

She nodded numbly. If she got in Declan's face and demanded answers, would she be treated to the same stony silence?

"I know little of his background—only what you provided when he arrived. And even though I don't know the details of his experiences, the ordeal he's endured would have broken most men."

"He's trained to endure and survive extensive torture."

"I've seen many people survive hideous things, but beneath the surface, they're never the same."

Odd and incredibly sad that EDJE taught their agents to endure and survive hell, but there had been few discussions on how to deal with the other side. Once you've gone through it, how do you come out on the other side and be a functional human being, much less the same person you were before?

"What can I do to help?"

"Based on Declan's resistance—something I've seen all too many times in dealing with LCR operatives—suggesting counseling won't go over well."

She agreed with him. Even before this, the old Declan would have refused treatment. Not because he didn't believe in it, but because spilling his guts went against his very nature.

"And without his cooperation," the doctor continued, "it would be pointless to even try."

"Noah mentioned that Cole Mathison had gone through something similar. He's hoping Declan might open up to him."

"That's an excellent idea. Much of Cole's ordeal involved mental torture, and I have a feeling Declan could relate to Mathison quite well."

"Any suggestions on how I should deal with him?"

"I'm assuming that before this happened you two were happy together?"

They'd had the kind of relationship that defied reason—a closeness of mind, heart, body, and soul. With utter confidence, she replied, "Yes, we were."

"Then treat him as you once did. Just be aware, he may not see you the same way."

Since he believed she was responsible for his abduction and torture, that was a no-brainer.

Suddenly, the need to see Declan overwhelmed her. She went to the edge of her chair, indicating her desire to leave. "Anything else?"

"No, other than that patience will be required. Being thrown back into the world after what he's gone through will be, in a way, another kind of torture. He'll want to be normal when normal isn't possible anymore."

She thanked the doctor for his help and turned to leave. Her hand was on the door when Dr. Lamar stopped her by saying, "Don't expect too much."

Her throat closed at the dire warning. There was a part of her that wanted to find a dark corner and howl out her grief and bitterness. How many times had she wished for Declan to be alive? Even believing that wasn't possible, she had occasionally had those silly, foolish dreams of do-overs and what ifs. And now that wish had come true. Only, he wasn't her Declan anymore.

She jerked herself out of her self-pity. Just what the hell was wrong with her? Her husband was alive. Life meant hope. Even if things could never be the same. And, yes, even if Declan never believed her or decided he no longer wanted her, she'd damn well be happy for what she had been given. Declan was still in this world. That was all she needed to concentrate on.

That and the little issue of who the hell had done this to them.

Declan walked back into the door he'd walked out of three hours earlier. With no sign on the structure and a distinctly run-down appearance, the building was unattractive and uninviting.

He remembered Sabrina mentioning that the LCR building in Paris was a bland, nondescript building, too. She said it was that way to deter passersby. Apparently, that philosophy had been adopted here, too.

When had she moved to the States? And why? And why the hell did he even want to know?

The receptionist, a young, petite blonde, gave him a bright smile, a wink, and then clicked open a door to her left. "Welcome back, Mr. Steele."

Her cheerful welcome gave him an idea that she had been asked more than once if he had returned yet. Sabrina no doubt wondered if he had gotten lost or if he was returning at all. They had unfinished business. After that, who knew what would happen?

She met him in the hallway. Though she wore a serene expression, he saw the worry in her eyes. "I'm glad you came back. We need to talk."

"Yes, we do."

"You look like you could use a cold drink." She jangled some change in her hand. "How about a soda?"

He nodded and followed her into what was apparently a break room. Vending machines, a microwave, a fridge, and a sink all looked like normal break-room fixtures. The only anomaly was the large gun cabinet in the corner.

"You guys have much need to grab a snack and a gun at the same time?"

She flashed him a brilliant smile, and Declan ignored the gut-punch reaction.

"The square footage is smaller here than our Paris office. This was the only place they could fit the cabinet."

She handed him a soda and then sat down with one of her own. Declan took a long swallow from his, appreciating the cool bite of sweet carbonation as it hit his tongue and slid down his parched throat.

"Why are you here now, instead of Paris?"

"Noah's wife's family lives here in Virginia. He decided to move the main headquarters here so they could be closer to them."

When he didn't respond, she took a nervous sip of her drink and swallowed. "So here's what I'd like us to do. I want to go over not only the day of the bombing, but also the days leading up to it. Maybe together we can figure out what happened and who's responsible."

Declan opened his mouth to refuse her request and then closed it. Sabrina had been on her feet for more than twenty-four hours. Before that, she had been belted in the face, drugged, and kidnapped. And if he were to believe her—which he didn't—she had learned that the husband she'd thought dead was alive. That was a helluva lot for a lifetime, much less a forty-eight hour time-span.

Knowing her well, he didn't mention any of this. Sabrina would force herself to go on, no matter how exhausted she was. "I think I'd do better after some sleep."

The relief in her eyes almost made him smile. She pushed her chair back and stood. "My place is about an hour from here, so I'm using one of LCR's apartments."

Before he could protest that he could find his own room, she added, "It's a two-bedroom, two-bath. Plenty of privacy."

"Sounds good."

Her response was that brilliant smile again. Before they walked out the door, he needed to make sure she knew one thing. "Even if you're telling the truth—if you had nothing to do with what happened to me—I've got nothing left for you, Sabrina. The quicker you accept that, the better off we'll both be."

The smile disappeared, which is what he told himself he wanted.

"Don't worry, Declan. You've been gone for a long time…I've moved on."

She turned her back and strode out of the room. Declan gripped the back of the chair in front of him to keep from going after her. If she had believed he was dead, then she mostly likely had a new man in her life. He didn't know what disturbed him most, the fact that she might have taken a lover or that it bothered him to think of her in another man's arms.

Cursing his stupidity, Declan left the room and then stopped abruptly when he spotted the asshole who'd punched him out—Aidan Thorne—talking to Sabrina. He had his hand on her arm, was leaning into her so close his mouth was almost touching her ear as he talked in a low murmur. Was he her lover?

Pushing aside the fact that he had nothing to give her and she'd had every right to move on, he glowered at the couple. "I can find my own place for the night." He turned and walked away. If she didn't follow him, then so be it. Damned if he'd stand there and watch his wife and her current lover.

Seconds later, he heard her behind him. Saying nothing about his boorish behavior, they walked out of the building together. Declan sneaked a quick glance down at her and didn't feel the least bit better. A small smile was tugging at her mouth. Whatever the prick had said to her, she had liked it.

CHAPTER TEN

Sabrina opened the apartment door, a silent Declan beside her. He'd barely said a word on the ride over. That was fine with her. If she talked anymore tonight, she'd be a basket case for sure. His undeniably cruel remarks earlier had barely dented her tough exterior, but his blunt statement that he had nothing for her had almost brought her to her knees. Even though she had accepted he was no longer the Declan she had known, his words had made it clear that he was no longer her Declan, either.

She was relieved to note the clean, fresh smell of the apartment. It had smelled decidedly musty earlier. Housekeeping had come by and freshened up the place. Hopefully, that also meant they'd brought the supplies she had requested.

"The fridge should be fully stocked. Help yourself to whatever you want."

"You're not eating?" Declan asked.

After the day she'd had, food was the last thing on her mind. "I have two goals: hot shower, ten hours' sleep, in that order." Giving him a brief, curt nod, she headed to one of the bedrooms.

Once inside, she leaned against the door and tried with all her might to pull her emotions in. Breaking down would be pointless. Besides, if one looked at today's events objectively, the good outweighed the bad. Her husband was alive. On a scale of one to ten in life events, that was a mind-blowing, life-altering, phenomenal one trillion. How could she not be thrilled and grateful?

He had been tortured, believed she was responsible, had tried to kill her, didn't want to be married to her anymore, and hated her.

Okay, but there was a downside to every good thing, right?

Tears filled her eyes, and sobs clogged in her throat. She ripped off her clothes and headed to the shower seconds ahead of her well-deserved meltdown.

An odd, inconvenient ache had developed in his gut as he'd watched Sabrina walk to the bedroom. Her body had literally drooped with every step as exhaustion dragged her down. And her expression. He'd seen that look on her face a thousand times. Years ago, before his soul had been devoured by pitiless demons, he would have followed her into the bedroom, showered with her, and then held her while she cried.

Declan turned away from the closed door and went into the second bedroom. He wasn't surprised to see clothes on the bed—underwear, jeans, shirts, slacks, socks and shoes, along with various toiletries. That would be Sabrina's doing. Even now, after all he had done and said to her, she was still trying to take care of him.

He huffed out an exasperated breath, turned around, and headed to her bedroom. Calling himself a fool, he twisted the doorknob and went inside. He heard the shower running and knew exactly what he'd find when he entered the bathroom.

A naked Sabrina sat on the floor of the shower. Hot water sprayed over her bowed head as her body heaved and convulsed with sobs. Declan grabbed the towel hanging from the hook beside the shower and opened the door.

Sabrina's head popped up. Her eyes, brilliant green and swimming with tears, glared up at him. "What are you doing here?"

Instead of answering, he turned off the water and then held out his hand. The instant she placed her hand in his, he pulled her to her feet and then wrapped the towel around her soaking body.

Sabrina told herself to reject his offer…she didn't need or want his pity. But from the moment she'd met him, Declan had been her biggest weakness and greatest strength. Saying no to him just wasn't in her. As he lifted her from the floor and wrapped the fluffy towel around her body, she pushed aside all the reservations and allowed herself to savor the moment.

Once he had covered her with the towel, he snagged another one for her hair. Then doing what he had done a hundred times in the past, he lifted her in his arms and carried her to the bedroom.

As if nothing had changed and they'd never been separated, he settled back against the headboard of the bed and just held her. With this part of the ritual complete, Sabrina did what she had always done—burying her face against his chest, she allowed the emotions to overtake her.

The soft loving words didn't come as before, nor did the tender kisses on her head. Silly, but that made her cry all the harder. Someone had taken a wonderfully caring, loving man and replaced him with this damaged, injured, hollowed-out person. She wanted to howl in grief, roar in pain. And she wanted to make them pay.

Pulling in an exhausted but much calmer breath, she pressed a kiss to his beard-stubbled cheek. "Thank you."

"Get some sleep." His gruff voice rumbled, the vibration beneath her cheek a comforting and familiar memory.

Sabrina closed her eyes and let herself drift away.

Declan closed his eyes, this time to fight his own tears. This was a memory he hadn't allowed himself to have. Sabrina was one of the strongest people he knew. She'd endured a hellish childhood and had escaped that hell only to be imprisoned in a mental institution. When she'd come to EDJE as a new recruit, he had watched her develop into the savviest and most dedicated operative in the Agency.

He had been her trainer. Seeing her potential and raw talent, he had been tougher on her than most new recruits. He had known her background and had done everything within his power to break her. Not because he didn't want her to succeed. He had put her through the tough training for one reason only—if she could survive what he did to her, no one could bring her down.

During that grueling, intense training, not once had she shown any emotion other than fury and anger with him. She had fought him, snapped at him, and cursed him, but never had she shown the hurt she should have felt. So he had continued to push hard, and then harder still.

One day after a particularly difficult session, he noticed she'd left her gun behind. At first, he'd been infuriated at her unprofessionalism. He'd gone to her room, ready to rail at her for being so careless. And then everything had changed. Instead of the tough-as-nails trainee who fought and spit at him with every breath, he'd found a fragile, sobbing woman in the shower.

Declan had wanted to pick her up and comfort her, believing he had finally broken her. Instead, he'd stepped back into her room, and when she'd come out of the bathroom, he'd been in the process of cleaning her gun.

At first, she'd looked both startled and worried, but he'd just started talking to her, telling her about his family and his reasons for joining the Agency. He hadn't really meant to tell her anything so personal, but she'd looked so lost and empty, and he had wanted to share something of himself.

He had left her with a soft but stern warning that if she ever left her gun behind again, there would be consequences. He hadn't really known what he meant by that, mostly because he had assumed that he had broken her and she would quit. Once again, she had surprised him and returned to training the next day as if nothing had happened. He'd been even tougher on her that day, certain that she was on the edge, about to snap. Certain that she wouldn't be able to handle all the shit he threw at her. She had proved him wrong.

After that training session, he'd again gone to her room, telling himself he was going to talk some sense into her. Once again, he found her in the shower. This time, he had broken all the rules, picked her up, held her, comforted her till she fell asleep. The same ritual went on for over a week until he finally got it through his thick skull. Sabrina could endure anything and everything that came at her, but she needed the catharsis of tears to survive. Some people drink, some take up other unhealthy vices. Tears were Sabrina's escape.

When that realization came, he had known he was falling in love with her. Declan had never believed in a happy ever after, but Sabrina, strong, independent, tempestuous, and vulnerable, had made him a believer.

But it had all been a lie.

Sabrina pulled a tray of biscuits from the oven and set it on the stove. She wasn't much of a domestic goddess, but having been responsible for all her family's cooking and cleaning from the time she was strong enough to open the oven door, she knew her way around the kitchen well enough to cook up a decent meal. When she and Declan had been together, they'd traveled so much that when they'd had the chance to be home together, cooking had not been one of her priorities.

Since coming back to the States, she'd found herself enjoying playing house. LCR provided her with an excellent salary, so instead of renting an apartment like most of the other operatives, she'd opted for a house in a small rural area on the other side of Remington. It was a kindness to call it a fixer-upper. Every spare moment she had outside work, she spent inside the house. She would probably be old and gray before she had it exactly as she wanted, but it was home. Sabrina hadn't realized just how much she had missed having one.

If Declan hadn't been taken from her. If things had worked out and he had left the Agency as he'd told her he wanted, what would life have looked like now? He could have had a vegetable garden in the backyard the way he said his father had when he was growing up. And when she came home from an op, she could have played around in the kitchen. Maybe had a couple of fur-kids at her feet.

This morning she had woken in his arms. Had lain quietly, not wanting to disturb him, and had listened to him breathe, relished his warmth, the beat of his heart. Treasures she'd thought lost to her forever.

Her movements methodical and practiced, she cracked eggs into the skillet, stirred the fried potatoes, double-checked the bacon in the microwave. Declan liked his bacon crisp.

She wanted to please him, make him smile. Let him know in every way possible that she was happy he was alive. Yes, his harsh words yesterday had wounded her to the core, but she couldn't blame him. Based upon Dr. Lamar's observations, Declan had endured torture most people wouldn't have survived. His distrust of people, including her, was understandable. That didn't mean she intended to let him continue that distrust. She hadn't betrayed him. And today, no matter how he put her off, she was going to find out why the hell he believed that lie.

Last night, his tenderness toward her was the old Declan. He might believe he had completely changed, but she knew different. The man she adored was still in there somewhere.

"Smells good."

She whirled around, startled. Declan had always had a cat-like quietness. Standing only a few feet from her, his hair still damp from the shower and the growth on his face even scruffier than yesterday, he was heart-wrenchingly beautiful. She'd always thought he had the face of a poet. His features angular, with a broad forehead, blade of a nose, and classically high cheekbones, he could have made millions as a model.

Pushing aside the sudden breathlessness, she offered him her best bland smile. "Hope you're hungry."

Ocean-blue eyes scanned the kitchen. "Surprisingly, I'm famished."

"Excellent." She nodded at the kitchen table she'd already set with china and flatware. "Have a seat. I'll have everything ready in a jiffy."

The old Declan would have hauled her into his arms for a hot, hungry kiss and then snagged a biscuit before sitting. Making it clear that the old Declan was gone, he pulled out a chair at the table and sat.

Sabrina returned to her task. Flipping three over-easy eggs onto his plate, she added four slices of bacon and a large serving of potatoes. Slathering three steaming biscuits with butter, she added them to the overflowing plate. Making a smaller one for herself, she turned to carry both plates to the table. And stumbled to a stop. Declan was sitting at the table, calmly holding her SIG Sauer in his hand, pointing directly at her.

Okay. Not exactly the way she preferred to eat her breakfast, but she went with it. Placing his plate on the table before him, she sat down and turned her eyes to the gun. "Looks like you've been snooping."

"Found it in the safe."

"A locked, hidden safe."

His eyes mocked her. "Did you really think you could hide anything from me?"

"I wasn't hiding it from you. It was habit, nothing more."

"You could be right. Using our wedding date for the code was kind of lame."

Sabrina huffed out an exasperated breath. "Are we going to snipe at each other or actually get something accomplished today?"

He placed the gun beside his plate. "You're right. I will, however, hold on to the gun for the time being."

Shrugging as if she could care less what he did, Sabrina forced herself to eat. Though her appetite was now nonexistent, she refused to give him the satisfaction of knowing he'd ruined what she had been looking forward to—breakfast with her husband. Only, he wasn't really her husband anymore, was he? A signature on a marriage license didn't make a marriage. She needed to stop thinking of him as anything other than a wary and distrusting acquaintance. An acquaintance that she happened to be married to.

She dared a quick glance at him and was pleased to see that he'd eaten all but half a biscuit. Silly, but she felt a moment of pride, as if she'd accomplished something major. They might still have a mountain of problems to chisel out, but her success at taking care of him in this elemental way felt like progress.

Leaning back in her chair, she held up her coffee cup. "Want a refill before we get started?"

"Started on what?"

"Going over the events of that day."

"What good will that do?"

"Do you not want to find out who did this to you...to us?"

"What makes you think I'm going to believe anything you say, Sabrina?"

"What do you want me to do, Declan? Take a polygraph? What happened to the trust part of our marriage vows? Or was that just for my benefit, not yours?"

Cold eyes continued to stare at her. She saw nothing of the compassionate man from last night. This was the man who'd faced terrorists without flinching and the man who'd faced his own torturers and survived.

"Okay. Fine. I know you think I set you up. I've already told you I didn't, but you say I'm lying. So let's start with you telling me exactly how you believe I betrayed you."

The blank, emotionless stare gave her his answer. *Dammit!* Sabrina surged to her feet. Declan went for the gun in front of him.

Agony slashed through her, the pain so real that he could have shot her and she swore it would have hurt less. Her heart shattering, Sabrina jerked her head at the gun. "Do it, damn you. If you don't believe me. If you really think I could do something like that, then do it."

"If I'd wanted to kill you that quickly, I would've done it at the cabin."

"Fine. Shoot me in every extremity. Make me bleed. Torture me. Make me tell you the truth. If you really believe I could betray you, the man I swore to love and honor for the rest of my life, then damn you, pull the trigger and force me to tell you the truth. The truth I'm telling you right now." Her voice trembled with rage as she ground out between clenched teeth, "I. Did. Not. Betray. You."

His grip was so tight on the handle, his fingers turned white with the strain. Sabrina braced herself. She was taking a big chance that he wouldn't do it. Somewhere inside this damaged man was her husband, the man she had once trusted more than anyone else in the world.

Minutes passed. Sabrina stayed frozen, barely breathing. The war of emotions on his face would have been fascinating if she had been completely sure he wasn't going to kill her.

At last...finally, he calmly placed the gun on the table and went to his feet. Sabrina forced herself to remain still. Just because he had decided not to kill her didn't mean he believed her. Without a word, he headed to the door leading outside.

"Where are you going?"

"To DC," he growled.

"Why?"

"To get some answers."

She swayed in relief, tears springing to her eyes before she could stop them. Forcing them back, she breathed out shakily, "Let's work together. Please, Declan."

He turned back to her then, and she was disappointed that the distrust in his eyes remained unchanged. He may not hate her enough to kill her, but he still didn't believe her.

"I work alone." He turned back to the door and walked out.

CHAPTER ELEVEN

LCR Headquarters

Noah waited patiently as his operative reviewed the notes he'd made on the Tyndall case. Cole Mathison was a thorough researcher and would want to internalize the smallest of facts before he gave his opinion.

Last Chance Rescue had more than one hundred fifty active operatives, along with ten on the Elite team, each operative as individual as the background that led them to LCR. One of the many things he liked about his people was their diverse approach to an investigation. And something they all had in common was their belief in rescuing the innocent. Noah had endeavored to make that philosophy his life's goal and never regretted it for a second.

Cole looked up from the file in his hand. "Have you talked to Mrs. Tyndall about this?"

"No. I didn't want to get her hopes up."

"And this Declan Steele, you don't think he could be of any help?"

"Actually, I think he would be very valuable. I just don't think he's going to be in the right frame of mind to cooperate."

A glower replaced Cole's calm expression. "Not even to save a life?"

"If there's anyone who might be able to change his mind, it's you."

"You mean because of what Rosemount did to me?"

"Yes. I don't know what was done to Steele, but the briefing I received from Dr. Lamar leads me to believe that he was probably tortured daily."

Cole grunted his sympathy.

"You want to take a crack at him? If so, I'll give Sabrina a call and have her bring him over."

Before Mathison could answer, Sabrina said from the doorway, "Don't bother calling. And Declan won't help."

The deep sorrow in her eyes told the story. She hadn't been able to change her husband's mind.

"I'm sorry to hear that."

She came into the office, gave Cole a tired smile of greeting and then dropped into a chair beside him. "He's gone again. Said he was going in to DC to get some answers."

"Then we'll do the job without him." Noah looked at Mathison again. "I can have Thorne, Ingram, and Kelly here in less than an hour. Angela and Jake Mallory in less time than that. Who else do you want?"

"I want in," Sabrina said.

Noah studied her for a few seconds. She'd been through a lot the past few days. "You're sure?"

"Absolutely. It'll keep my mind off slamming my husband's head into a brick wall and knocking some sense into him."

"It's already been done," Declan said from the doorway. "Several times. None of them had the desired outcome."

Sabrina's head whipped around so fast Declan knew he'd surprised the hell out of her. He also saw the relief in her eyes.

"I thought you were going to DC," Sabrina said.

"Hard to get anywhere around here without money."

Temper replaced the relief in her eyes. "I can give you money for the bus and the Metro or I can get you a car. In fact, I'll even find a way to get you on a helicopter to get you there faster."

A smile threatened at his lips—the first time he'd even felt like smiling since the day he was captured. Sabrina in a snit had always affected him in some way. Either she pissed him off, turned him on, or made him laugh.

Before he could respond, a tall man about Declan's height, stood and gave him a solemn nod in greeting. "Steele, I'm Cole Mathison. I'd like to talk with you, alone, if I could."

"About Barry Tyndall?"

"Among other things." Mathison looked down at his watch. "I missed breakfast and have a hole the size of the federal deficit in my stomach. Let's grab some lunch."

Instead of waiting on Declan's agreement, Mathison glanced over at Sabrina. "I'll return him in a couple of hours in case you're still interested in banging his head against a wall."

A smile lit up her face. "Thanks. That'll give me time to find a wall sturdy enough to take the blow from his hard head."

Mesmerized by that smile, Declan barely registered the insult. Mathison stood beside him. "You feeling okay?"

"Yeah." Declan shook himself out of his stupor. Getting sidetracked by his wife's smile was about as asinine as he could get. Pissed that he could be so easily swayed, he gave her a cold look and walked out of the room.

The popular chain restaurant was busy with the lunchtime crowd. Declan sat across the table from Mathison and unwrapped his burrito. They'd gotten a table in a back corner, but the place was still noisy. Interesting that Mathison would choose a crowded, family-oriented place to discuss an LCR rescue mission.

Mathison's grin told him he'd read Declan's thoughts. "This is my kids' favorite restaurant. I'm missing them like hell and automatically came here for the comfort. Hope you don't mind."

"Not at all. How many kids do you have?"

"Three. Twin girls that are nine going on thirty and a one-year-old son."

"You live close by?"

"No. Upper East Tennessee. LCR's got a branch office there. My wife, Keeley, and I own a farmhouse outside Kingston, Tennessee, that we share with every animal known to North America. Both my daughters have decided they're going to be veterinarians, and it's their responsibility to save as many animals as possible. Keeley is almost as bad."

It wasn't any of his business, but he couldn't help but ask. "So how do you maintain what sounds like a normal home life while being an LCR operative?"

"Takes work, I won't deny that. But Keeley and I knew what we wanted. We love each other enough to make it work."

Declan knew a rare moment of regret. Would that have made a difference? Would Sabrina not have betrayed him if they'd had a more normal marriage? Was that what she had been missing? Some kind of normalcy? She'd gone from a destructive family life to a mental institution and then had become an assassin. Hell, was it any wonder she didn't know the meaning of loyalty and love?

Shoving those grim thoughts aside, Declan addressed the reason they were here. "So I'm assuming you want to know if I saw Tyndall or any other prisoners?"

"Actually, I wanted to talk about your experience."

Suspicion blared like a siren. "Why?"

"Because you need to talk to someone. Believe me, I know. Suppressing all that pain and anger isn't a good thing. It'll end up exploding one day when you least expect it. Talking it out helps."

"And you know this how?"

"I went through something similar a few years back."

"How so?"

In short, precise sentences, Mathison described his abduction and torture. "I was given a drug that made me forget I was even human. Was like a zombie, doing only what I was told to do. I killed people. Watched the abuse of a woman I cared about deeply and did nothing to stop it. When I was rescued, I had no memory. I only knew I was filled with an unending rage."

Rage was a familiar emotion. That, plus the need for vengeance, had sustained Declan, kept him alive.

"Did you go after the people responsible for your abduction?" Declan asked.

"Yes. I managed to kill the main bastard the day I was rescued. Took months to hunt down the doctor who created the drug that almost destroyed me."

"Did that help?"

"Not really. At least not in the way I had hoped. While I was pursuing my own personal vendetta, Keeley and my girls were in danger. The girls were abducted, and Keeley almost died."

"And you rescued them?"

"With LCR's help."

"So you regret pursuing justice?"

"I regret putting my needs first."

He might appreciate Mathison's candor but could see no real relationship between their situations.

"So you think me going after the people responsible for my capture and torture is a selfish act?"

"Hell no. I don't think it's selfish. People need to pay for what happened, but that doesn't mean you can't help others while you're at it."

"You mean by helping LCR find this guy you've been looking for."

"Finding him could lead you to the people responsible for your abduction."

"Or it could send me on a wild-goose chase in the opposite direction."

"I won't deny it's risky, but I will tell you that saving lives is a helluva lot more rewarding than gaining vengeance." Mathison shrugged. "Putting someone else's needs before your own might have been beaten out of you. Might not even be in you anymore. This might be a good chance for you to find out."

After pacing for several minutes, her emotions all over the place, Sabrina dropped into her chair with a sigh. The look Declan had given her before he'd walked out the door had sent ice into her heart. How was she ever going to reach him? "I don't know if Cole can talk him into helping."

"Maybe not, but it'll be good for him to hear Cole's experience."

Perhaps that was true. She'd attended some group counseling sessions to help her deal with the trauma she'd endured at the hands of her family and then later the mental-health workers. She hadn't wanted to go. Had been of the opinion that talking about it did nothing more than keep it fresh in her mind. That was before she'd listened as others had described their own abuse. It hadn't necessarily made her feel any less debased, but at least she had learned she wasn't alone.

"There's a man arriving in a few minutes who wants to see you," Noah said.

"Albert?"

"Yes. I know you're not sure about him, but he wouldn't take no for an answer."

"Doesn't surprise me. It's been my privilege to work for two of the most stubborn men ever born."

Noah's mouth stretched into a grin. "I'll take that as a compliment."

She had meant it as one. Even though she wasn't sure if she could trust Albert, she would concede he was one of the most hardheaded men she'd ever known. "Don't get too cocky. When it comes to hardheadedness, Declan has both of you beaten by a mile."

"No progress last night?"

Telling her boss that she'd had breakfast with Declan while he held a gun on her was probably not a good idea. "I can't get him to listen to reason. Can barely get him to answer a question. He's convinced I lied to him—trapped him in some way so he could be taken. He actually thinks I knew he was alive and being tortured. Yet he won't tell me the reason he believes this. And, for the life of me, I cannot fathom why he would believe something so insane."

"Torture can distort reality. He's apparently a strong man to have withstood what was done to him, but that doesn't mean he wasn't damaged. Did he tell you what the torture entailed?"

"No, but based on what Dr. Lamar said, he shouldn't be alive—much less functioning." She shook her head. "Having worked for EDJE for so long, I'm sure he has a wealth of knowledge inside his head. He wouldn't share secrets with me, so I don't have any real idea what he might know."

"Perhaps I can help you with that."

Sabrina stood at the sound of a dearly familiar voice from her past. She turned and faced Albert Marks, who stood at the door. She hadn't seen him since he'd retired—which was not long after Declan's supposed death.

"Hello, Albert."

He nodded, his face solemn. He recognized the almost formal greeting. "Mr. McCall, might I have a moment alone with Sabrina?"

Noah stood. "Use this office." He gave Sabrina a searching look before saying, "I'll be in the gym if you need me."

She smiled her appreciation, waited until the door closed and then said, "Okay, Albert. It's time to come clean. Just how much do you know about Declan's abduction and torture?"

"I know nothing about that, Sabrina. I'm as shocked as you are. However, if we put our heads together, perhaps we can come up with some answers."

"How could you not know something about it? You were in charge when he was taken. You knew the op he was running." She shook her head, refusing to believe that no one had a clue of who was responsible. "You know the DNA results were tampered with. Either that or the medical examiner you had on staff is part of the cover-up. Several people had to be involved."

He nodded at the sofa. "Let's have a seat."

As Sabrina sat across from him in a chair, she took the time to take in his appearance. He looked tired. Since his retirement, he'd lost a little more hair, a little more weight, added on several new wrinkles. His large nose that'd been broken too many times to set right looked even more crooked.

She fought a rush of affection. If she was to get to the truth, she couldn't allow her feelings for this man to get in the way.

His expression sincere and serious, Albert leaned forward and laid out his investigation. "I've reviewed every piece of evidence we have on Declan's supposed death. Whoever did this was thorough. The DNA results were signed off on by the coroner we have on retainer. I questioned him thoroughly and found no inconsistencies in his story. He swears the remains he was given were Declan's."

"How is that possible?"

"I believe someone, somehow, broke into his lab and skewed the findings."

"That would require more than a passing knowledge of forensics."

"Yes, but as elaborate as this hoax was, it's obvious that there's money behind it."

"What about the man we buried in Scotland? The one we thought was Declan. Let's exhume the body and find—"

"I've already had his grave checked."

His expression said it all. "It was empty, wasn't it?"

"Yes."

She jumped to her feet and paced across the distance of Noah's office. "The last mission Declan was on...he wouldn't tell me about it. He said—" Comprehension came quickly, anger and betrayal soon followed. "That's why he was so secretive. It wasn't just paperwork to finish up some ops."

"We knew we had at least one mole inside the Agency. Some ops had gone bad. A couple of our people had been killed. Declan had been charged with uncovering the traitor. He'd been on the case for almost two years with almost no results."

Sabrina hadn't known about any bad ops, but then she'd already been working for LCR and no longer privy to that kind of information. But Declan should have told her about his assignment. Why hadn't he?

Her confusion mounted. "But Declan was leaving the Agency. Our last night together...he said he had some routine things to clear up and then he was out for good. How could he have ferreted out moles when—" She stopped abruptly and closed her eyes. How very stupid and naïve of her. "It was all a lie, wasn't it? He wasn't leaving."

"That was my idea, not his. We hoped by making everyone believe he was leaving the Agency, the mole wouldn't know we were on to him.

"I can see that you're hurt, my dear, and I'm sorry. Declan wanted to tell you, but I convinced him no one could know. And we both believed you would be safer by not knowing." He paused a moment and then said, "There were bugs."

"That's not possible. I checked the apartment every time I came home. I had a scanner, dammit. There's no way the apartment was bugged."

"The bugs were with Declan."

He'd brought the bugs into their apartment? People had been listening to them? She and Declan had made love against the front door. She remembered being so hot for him...so needy. Then Declan had carried her to bed and had—

The thought came to a screeching halt. "This conversation is over."

"Sabrina, stop. You may be furious with us, even crushed by what you perceive as a betrayal of your marriage. That's something you and Declan will have to work out in your own time. For now, you need to—"

She whirled and for the first time saw real fear in Albert's eyes. He, better than anyone, knew how dangerous she was. "Don't you dare tell me what I need to do. I was not your pawn to play with. That was my marriage, my life, and you screwed with it for your own agenda."

"For the good of the Agency, Sabrina. It was never personal."

Her marriage not personal? Emotions she hadn't allowed herself to feel in years were bubbling to the surface. If she stayed here, she wasn't sure what would happen. She forced herself to walk away.

Declan expected to see Sabrina when he pushed open the door to Noah McCall's office. Albert Marks sitting on the sofa was a distinctly jarring sight.

"What are you doing here?"

"Declan, my boy." Albert stood. The expression on his former boss's face was a curious mixture of both joy and grief.

"I asked you a question."

Albert shook his head and plopped back onto the sofa with a heavy sigh. "You and Sabrina both believe I'm guilty."

"You talked to Sabrina?"

"Yes. I'm afraid she's quite angry with both of us right now."

And Declan could guess why. Albert had no doubt told her about the lies. Damned if he would feel guilty for that. After what she'd done to him, his lies to her that night meant nothing. He'd done it for a good reason. Yeah, he'd felt like shit at the time and had been determined to find a way to make it up to her. Didn't matter now.

"What is it you want, Albert?"

"I want to find out who did this to you."

"You're retired. Out of the game. Hell, for all I know, you and Sabrina cooked up the whole thing."

Albert's eyes narrowed with scorn. "That's ridiculous. And though I can understand your doubts of me—after all, I was the one who assigned you to the mission—but why on earth are you blaming Sabrina, too? She wasn't even involved with Agency business."

"I'm not going to stand here and justify what I know to you or anyone else." He turned toward the door.

"Declan, do you know what she went through?"

"What are you talking about?"

"Come sit down first."

Instead of sitting, Declan stayed where he was and crossed his arms in front of him. Albert gave a loud, abrupt guffaw.

"What's so funny?"

"That's a look I've missed."

"Get to the point, Albert."

"Very well. When you died, Sabrina was a mess. Hell, we all were. But then the rumors started."

"What kind of rumors?"

"All kinds…most were ridiculous, as rumors tend to be. The most prevalent was that you had been involved with another woman."

Of all the things he'd thought Albert might say, this hadn't been one of them. "Why the hell would anyone start that kind of rumor?"

"Why does any rumor start? To discredit a person. The things you had done, your service to the country…your reputation was impeccable. You died a hero. Someone didn't like that."

"And like most rumors," Declan said grimly, "no one knew where they started."

"Exactly."

"Sabrina heard these rumors?"

"Yes. I tried to keep them from her. She didn't exactly stay in touch with anyone at the Agency, so I hoped she hadn't heard. She called me one day and asked if I knew about them. I told her I had heard rumors but didn't believe them for a moment."

"But she did?"

"No, she didn't. That doesn't mean she wasn't hurt by the speculation."

Declan started toward the door, the need to see Sabrina foremost on his mind.

"That's not everything, Declan."

"It's enough."

He ignored the sneering whisper inside him that asked why he even cared she'd been hurt. She was the one who'd lied and betrayed him. Why the hell did any of this bother him? He had no answer.

CHAPTER TWELVE

Declan wasn't surprised to find Sabrina in the LCR gym. Whenever she was angry, he could almost always find her pummeling a boxing bag or running hell-bent for leather on a treadmill.

He stood at the door and watched her pound the boxing bag with relentless and deadly force. She was dressed in a pair of brief navy shorts that showed off her long, well-toned legs. With each forceful punch of her fist, the white, cropped T-shirt she wore gave teasing glimpses of her firm, flat midriff and the occasional underside of a white sports bra. She had worked up a fine sheen of sweat, and her soft, smooth skin glowed with health and vitality. He knew every inch of that gloriously silken flesh, had tasted and teased that beautiful body into submission. And in return he had been conquered, surrendering body, heart, mind, and soul.

The rush of arousal was unsurprising. One certain body part didn't give a damn about her betrayal. It wanted what it wanted. He leaned against the doorjamb and clenched his jaw until he'd gotten control of his entire body.

If she knew he was there, she gave no indication as she continued to pummel the bag. He wondered whose face she saw as she pounded. His or Albert's? Or perhaps she saw her stepbrother and the family who'd almost destroyed her before she had been able to defend herself.

Not bothering to stop the slams of her fists into the bag, she asked, "You here to finish the job?"

"What job?"

"Albert's already ripped open my heart. Are you here to tear it from my chest?"

"No, I'm here to set the record straight."

That brought her to a sudden, abrupt stop. "So I'm supposed to listen to you, but I can barely get a word in before you shut me down. Too bad that time in captivity didn't help with your arrogance."

"You want the truth or not?"

Wariness and doubt glistened in her eyes. He didn't like seeing that. He might not trust her, but having her distrust him was unacceptable. He refused to speculate why.

He threw her a towel from a stack at the door. "Grab some water and cool off. Then let's go back to the apartment."

"Why can't we talk here?"

"Because I envision there will be shouting and cursing. I'm assuming you want some privacy."

"Privacy? You mean you know the meaning of the word? After you allowed people to hear us in our home—having sex, doing the most intimate things a man and woman can do to each other—you're concerned about privacy?"

He had walked right into that one but wouldn't back down. "I was suggesting that for you, not me."

"How sensitive, Declan." The words dripped with bitter sarcasm. Nevertheless, she wiped her face and grabbed her clothes, which had been lying on a bench against the wall. "My car's out front."

There were a lot of things he wanted to say, but would wait until they were completely alone. Despite what she believed, having an audience for anything private with his wife had never appealed to him.

She knew what he had done and believed the worst. And why the hell shouldn't she? From her perspective, his behavior looked staged. He didn't know why he felt the need to clear up her misconceptions. He still believed she sold him out, but for some inexplicable reason, he needed her to understand the reasons for his lies.

And the rumors of his infidelity? Laughable. Since the moment he'd met her, he hadn't wanted another woman. But just because she hadn't believed the rumors didn't mean they hadn't hurt her.

Declan suppressed a harsh laugh as he followed her. Of all the scenarios he had envisioned when he finally saw her again, apologizing sure as hell hadn't been one of them.

Sabrina pushed the apartment door open, several steps ahead of Declan. The thought of taking a hot shower to soothe her aching muscles was tempting, but she wanted answers more than she wanted to be soothed. Settling for a bottle of water from the fridge, she watched Declan pace around the living room. That was one of his tells—something he rarely did when he was on a job, but with her, if he had something on his mind, he had paced around until he formed the words he wanted to say. Where she could spontaneously combust in anger, Declan rarely lost his temper. He was methodical and usually measured his words, choosing them carefully.

He surprised her with his first words. "I never cheated on you."

She shook her head. "I never for an instant believed you did."

"Albert said there were rumors."

"Rumors. Nothing more. I knew that."

"Good. Fine."

"Tell me about the job. Why you told me the lies about leaving the Agency."

"I started looking into a traitor at EDJE about two years before I was taken."

"Yes, Albert told me that."

"I had worked my ass off without any substantive proof that there was a mole. We knew there was at least one, because of some ops that had gone bad and wouldn't have without the leak of vital intel.

"When I found the bugs, I knew I'd been compromised. There was no other explanation. Someone knew I'd been digging. The decision to tell you I was leaving the Agency was impulsive… not well thought-out. Whoever's behind this knew me too well to believe I'd just up and quit."

And she had been so stupidly in love, so willing to believe that whatever he said was the absolute truth, she had never even questioned his words. If she hadn't trusted him so completely, she too would have seen the lie.

A wave of humiliation rolled through her. Had the whole night been a lie? Those last hours together had gotten her through those terrible days when she'd thought Declan had died. They had comforted and consoled her, helped her to grieve. When she'd heard the horrible rumors, she had been able to push them aside, knowing without a doubt they weren't true. That one night had lived in her memory as untainted and perfect. What if it had all been a lie?

"No. It wasn't all a lie, Sabrina."

She had spoken the last words aloud. "What wasn't, Declan? That you weren't leaving the Agency? Yes, it was."

"I wanted to protect you. When I found the bugs, I knew you could easily become a target. I couldn't risk that."

She turned away from him, from the sadness in his eyes. What hurt the most? That he had allowed some of their most intimate moments to be heard by others or that he'd lied about leaving the Agency? She had been so excited, so thrilled that she would be seeing more of him. That he would be out of the dangerous game of covert ops.

She knew the truth and refused to hide it from him. Having people hear their intimate moments wasn't comfortable, but that didn't demean what it had meant. "If you had told me what you were doing, I would have helped. Maybe I could have made it more convincing."

"Your reaction was perfect."

Of course it was. She had trusted him as though his words were sacred. A thought flickered through her mind at his explanation that'd it'd been an impulsive and not well-thought-out plan. "When did you find the bugs?"

"While you were asleep. Stupid, but I hadn't even considered I might've been compromised. I was going through my luggage, looking for my toothbrush. Once I found that one bug, I checked the rest of my stuff. Found three more."

"So you didn't plan it in advance?"

"No. I texted Albert, and we came up with the idea on the fly. Idiotic plan since it definitely didn't work. I intended to tell you the truth as soon as I could."

The fact that he hadn't known about the bugs in advance helped a lot. She'd been in enough tough spots to know that you worked with what you had. Swallowing hard, she nodded. "I believe you. And I forgive you."

"Albert told me there were a lot of rumors."

She flicked her hand in a careless gesture. "They were ridiculous. Others might have believed them. I didn't."

"But they still hurt."

She couldn't deny that. You can't listen to those kinds of words about someone you adored and not be hurt.

"They made me mad." She shrugged. "It was nothing. Don't worry about it."

His mouth opened as if to argue. Yeah, he didn't want her quick understanding or forgiveness. Tough shit.

Proving her thoughts, he took her right hand and folded it into a fist. "I'm glad you were smart enough to know I'd never cheat. But you have every right to be angry about the lies. Instead of the boxing bag you were beating the shit out of, hit me instead."

"What?"

"I deserve it."

She didn't know whether to laugh in his face or kick him for being so infuriating. "I'm not going to hit you, Declan."

"Come on. You know you want to."

His eyes lit with laughter, his grin almost sent her to her knees. That was a Declan grin, charming, sweet, oh so sexy. Oh heavens, how she loved this man.

Telling herself not to say the words, telling herself she was a fool, didn't stop her from saying, "You're right. You do owe me one."

Even though his eyes flared with surprise that she was actually going to take him up on his offer, he tilted his head a little to give her a better shot.

She shook her head. "A hit isn't what I want."

"What then?"

"A kiss. The last time our lips met, people were listening. No one can hear us now. Give me what I should have had that last day—a kiss without an audience."

He was shaking his head before she could finish her request. "No. No way. You think I'm going to kiss you and forget everything you did." He actually backed away from her.

She told herself to let it go. That he would only continue to say hurtful things if she pursued this outrageous request. Instead, she taunted him. "Scared, Declan?"

The icy glare from his eyes could have frozen a forest fire. He stood there for several seconds and then walked toward the door.

Sabrina closed her eyes. She had been stupid to even think that—

Hard hands gently cupped her face. Breath caught in her throat, she opened her eyes to see his searing, heated look. He lowered his head slowly. Even though this was what she'd asked for, she knew he was giving her time to pull away. That wasn't going to happen. She'd dreamed about this for too long.

At last, his lips touched hers. Sabrina whimpered at the first soft stroke of his mouth. Beautifully familiar…delicious, perfect. Better than all her dreams combined.

Declan swallowed a groan at her taste. Hell, what was he doing? He shouldn't want this. Shouldn't want her. Somehow, the rest of his body disagreed with his brain. He drew her closer, yanking her so hard against him, she gasped. He took advantage of her open mouth and thrust his tongue deep inside.

Heat surged, pounded within him. Sabrina's body pressed against his, and every cell inside him said to take her. He wanted her beneath him, taking him deep, screaming his name as she came. He wanted to explode inside her, taking the pleasure denied him for so long. He wanted to feel her pulsing around him, hear her cry in ecstasy as she came, over and over.

He wanted.

With a growl of need, he devoured her lips as his hands slid over her, then under her T-shirt. His fingers touched silken skin, and it was all he could do not to lay her on the floor and taste every inch of that succulent flesh. His hands slid down to her beautiful ass, and then holding her hips still, he pushed deep into her. Soft, warm, giving. Her mound providing the perfect home for his arousal, he ground himself into her, creating a friction and heat that could not be denied. Buzzing, roaring in his brain shut down all rational thought. He had to have her now…wanted her more than anything. He had to—

Declan jerked out of her arms, stumbling backward to get away from her. "Damn you, no."

Beautiful face flushed, eyes dilated, glazed with need, she whispered his name.

He gave an emphatic, angry shake of his head. "No. Just no, Sabrina. You are not going to seduce me into believing you."

"You think that I—" A laughing sob broke from her. "You think this was about some kind of coercion. That I would— You're my husband. I—"

She wrapped her arms tightly around herself, and he could see she was trembling. Then, like a switch had been flipped, blankness washed over her face. The passion in her eyes disappeared, replaced by a cold, contemptuous stare. Her lush mouth flattened into a sneer. "I forgive you for lying to me that night. I even forgive you for allowing those monsters to hear us making love. But I will never forgive you for this, Declan Steele. Never."

She turned and marched out the door.

CHAPTER THIRTEEN

The drone of the plane beneath Noah's feet was a familiar, comforting noise. Other than being with Samara and their kids, there was nothing he enjoyed more than to head out on a rescue mission with a team of operatives. He didn't get a chance to go on as many ops as he wanted. This wasn't one he felt he should miss.

His eyes shifted to the hollow-eyed, silent couple across from him. Whatever had happened between these two wasn't good. Hard to believe they looked worse than they had when LCR had knocked down the doors in Idaho and rescued Sabrina. It was obvious that they hadn't worked anything out. The wariness seemed to be even more heightened. But on both sides this time.

He had broken more rules for Declan Steele than he ever had for anyone. Rarely was a non-LCR operative invited to participate in a mission. And never had he approved an individual for an op who held a personal vendetta. Declan Steele had made it clear he had one goal—to find the men who had tortured him and make them talk. Saving the life of Barry Tyndall wasn't a priority for him. In fact, Noah had grave doubts the man would go out of his way to save the lives of any of the operatives he was working with—even his own wife's.

That kind of emptiness of the soul was worrisome. Even though he could understand and sympathize with how the emptiness came about—torture not only destroyed flesh and bone but the spirit as well—it was hard to know what to expect from the man.

Noah had the utmost confidence in his own operatives. They were highly trained, focused and determined. The mission of rescuing the innocent would always be their number one goal. He could depend on them no matter the circumstances. But what about Steele? If things got hairy, would he run or stay and fight? Would he watch the backs of others or just his own?

Shifting his eyes slightly, he observed the woman for whom he had broken his rules. Without a doubt, Sabrina was one of his most competent operatives. She had come to LCR with more than enough training to head up a mission on day one. She had fully embraced LCR's philosophy and had told him more than once that the adrenaline rush of saving lives instead of taking them kept her sane.

And just like all his operatives, Noah trusted Sabrina's judgment. She had vouched for Steele's competency and skills. The man had once been her trainer at EDJE. She'd said he was ten times better than she was at hand-to-hand.

He'd seen for himself Sabrina's skills. If Declan Steele was better, that was damn impressive.

When Noah had expressed doubts about Steele's motives and agenda, she had made a promise...one that shouldn't have surprised him but did. If push came to shove and Steele betrayed the team, she would put him down herself.

Noah believed her. He just hoped to hell it didn't come to that.

Sabrina relaxed against the soft leather seat of the Gulfstream G650. There were a lot of differences in working for a government agency and working for Last Chance Rescue. The ride was one of them. Working for EDJE, she'd hitched rides on every kind of transport, not one of them this luxurious. Despite their desire to keep their ops low profile, LCR had some grateful and often wealthy donors.

The team on this mission was a larger number than usual—nine total. Two would stay behind, handling communications. When the time came for extraction, every second counted. The other seven would be on the raid, including her husband.

She knew she was taking on a huge responsibility in vouching for Declan. Especially when she'd seen little evidence of the man she had thought she knew better than anyone. A few days ago, she wouldn't have vouched for him and still couldn't say with any certainty that her trust was warranted, but she had to give him this opportunity. She just prayed that she wouldn't be forced to keep her promise to Noah. If it came down to the lives of victims or her fellow operatives over Declan, she would have to live up to her word. She hoped with all her being that she wouldn't have to make that choice.

Their altercation five days ago had left her in a turmoil of seething emotions. Sexual frustration and rage were not a good combination. If she hadn't walked out the door when she had, without a doubt she would have given Declan the punch to his face he'd asked for.

Instead of punching him, she'd returned to the LCR gym and had gone after the punching bag like a lunatic. Days later, her hands were still bruised and aching. And she'd still been hurting.

All of that self-righteous anger had changed two days ago. Albert had called to speak with Declan. When she'd knocked on his bedroom door and hadn't gotten an answer, she'd walked into his room. The sound of the shower running had carried her to his bathroom. Declan was just getting into the shower, with his back to her. She had seen the scars—deep welts, most likely from a whip and cane, were interspersed with burn scars that mottled his skin from his broad shoulders to the backs of his muscled calves. She had known he had been tortured. Had known about the scars—Dr. Lamar had told her they were bad. She had never imagined how bad nor how much hatred would rise within her at their sight. Not at Declan but at the people who had done this to him. Dammit, he did deserve vengeance. And she was going to do everything she could to see that he got it.

She had backed out of the room before he could see her. The need to throw up had warred with the need to sob out her fury and pain. She had done neither. She had simply continued on as if nothing had changed—even though everything had. If she had to leave LCR to do it, if she had to fight her own government, or even her own code of ethics, it didn't matter. Declan would see justice—this she vowed.

Since that day, there had been an uneasy truce between them. His distrust was still there, lying between them like a huge, giant pit, but he'd refrained from accusations. She'd tiptoed around him as if he were a land mine waiting to detonate. It wasn't comfortable, but after all the volatile emotions, the lack of rancor was a peaceful if edgy respite.

In between their prep work of packing for their trip and the daily briefings at LCR headquarters, she saw little of him. They lived together, but that consisted only of occupying the same apartment. They could have been strangers for all the intimacy they had between them.

"You got a minute?"

She turned to Aidan who'd been sitting several seats down from her. He now stood in front of her, and from the look in his eyes, she knew he wanted a private conversation. He'd been amazingly non-vocal about the civilian addition to their team. She had a feeling that was about to change.

Standing, she headed to the plane's private quarters, knowing he followed her.

The sight of his estranged wife going off into a private meeting with another man shouldn't have fazed him. Just because Aidan Thorne looked like some sort of Hollywood actor with his too-perfect face and muscular body should have meant nothing. Having an emotion remotely resembling jealousy should have been laughable. So why then did his gut feel as though he'd guzzled acid?

Sabrina had once told him he had the face of a poet and the body of a Greek god. That had both amused and embarrassed him, but there'd been a small part of him that had been secretly delighted at her words. What man wouldn't want his wife to feel that way?

There was little of the man she had loved left, in looks or anything else.

He had seen her back out of the bathroom the other day. She had seen his scars, what those savages had done to him. His chest and stomach were almost as bad. For some unknown reason, they'd left his face alone, but the rest of his body had been their playground, where they'd played out their sadistic games.

So what if Sabrina had a relationship with another man? Like he gave a damn.

She was still angry about the kiss. It'd been a low blow, but the only thing he'd been able to come up with to draw attention away from his driving need. He had desired her more than he even remembered. She was a great actress, so the hurt on her face could have been feigned, but no way in hell could a person turn ghost-white on command. She'd been devastated by his accusation.

Since that day, since those strong doubts had emerged, he'd been riddled with more, even fiercer, headaches. He didn't know their cause, but if he'd mentioned them, without a doubt Sabrina would have hauled him back to the doctor. He couldn't risk being put on medication that might dull his senses. Nor could he chance being taken off this mission. Over-the-counter pain meds would suffice. Nothing could get in the way of this op.

Other than Sabrina and maybe Mathison, his presence wasn't appreciated or wanted by the other team members. He didn't blame them. They were focused on rescuing—he was focused on vengeance. Even McCall, who'd had a long and frank discussion with him, wasn't sure he'd made the right decision.

That was okay—he understood their reticence. And despite their doubts, he would help where he could. He owed them that. LCR was making it possible for him to hunt down his torturers. Declan would do his best to see that their mission was successful and without casualties.

"How many rescue missions have you been on?"

Declan turned to face Cole Mathison. Of all the operatives he'd met so far, this man seemed to be the most normal. Hard to believe that he had gone through something similar to what Declan had experienced.

"My first few years with EDJE, maybe six or seven. Our primary objectives were to destroy terrorists and prevent future attacks. Rescuing was sometimes a byproduct of our job but never our main focus."

"What changed?"

"How's that?"

"You said your first few years. Did you change jobs?"

"In a roundabout way, yes. I became the trainer for the most-promising recruits. I still worked ops but not as many. Last few years, I coordinated and oversaw missions."

"And that's how you met Sabrina?"

"Yeah." He still remembered that first day when she'd barged in on a meeting he'd been having with Albert. She had been in training for about eight months but had yet to advance to Declan's courses. Instead of apologizing for interrupting, she'd complained to Albert about the treatment of a new recruit by one of the instructors. After several minutes of grousing, she'd stopped and looked directly at Declan as if expecting him to agree with her. Oddly enough, he had. The instructor she'd complained about was an asshole who had a tendency to treat new recruits as if they were the lowest form of humanity.

Declan had always thought it interesting that his first meeting with Sabrina had involved her sticking up for someone. She would fight tooth and nail to defend the underdog. What had made her change?

"I've only worked a few ops with her," Mathison was saying, "but I've been impressed each time with her professionalism and heart."

Interesting observation, Declan thought. Insightful. Sabrina had the courage of a warrior and the heart of a lioness. She could be cold and methodical. Deadly when pitting herself against an opponent. And with her most difficult ops, she decompressed by letting all emotions come to the surface. It was her way, and though sometimes seeing her so raw and hurting had been difficult, he had felt grateful to be the man to soothe her. As far as he knew, he was the only one who knew that about her. He had counted himself fortunate that she allowed him the privilege of being the one to calm and comfort her.

His eyes darted to the closed door where Sabrina and Thorne had disappeared. Was that something her new partner did? Did he hold her, soothe her? Make love to her until she quieted and knew peace?

Apparently reading his thoughts, Mathison directed his gaze at the door, too. "Aidan and Sabrina have a unique relationship."

"What the hell does that mean?"

Though his eyes remained impassive, Mathison's mouth twitched as if he was struggling not to smile. Instead of a direct answer, he gave another enigmatic reply. "You've been gone a long time."

So did that mean their relationship was physical as he had suspected? Is that why they'd gone behind closed doors? They'd wanted privacy for their little tryst? When her husband was sitting on the other side of that door like some kind of a clueless pansy-assed wimp?

Like hell!

"Look, tell me to mind my own business if you like. Just remember, you are my partner, which makes it my business. And you're also my friend."

For the past five minutes, Sabrina had listened to Aidan express his concerns about Declan's involvement. She couldn't exactly argue with him, as she'd had similar thoughts. And he was right—they were partners, which meant they watched each other's backs and didn't pull punches on expressing their opinions.

"He deserves the opportunity to find these savages."

"I agree. I just don't want it to be to your detriment, the team's, or the guy's we're going to rescue. Our goal, like always, is to bring everybody back alive—that includes your husband."

"If it comes down to choosing, I'll go against Declan. And if necessary, I'll take him out myself."

Aidan jerked back as if shocked at the statement. "Hell, I would never ask you to do that."

Even though the thought of having to do such a thing sliced through her insides like a scythe, she almost felt amusement at Aidan's protectiveness. He trusted her to be able to handle any situation with deadly force if necessary, but her partner had a protective streak a mile long, especially toward women. Someday he was going to make some very fortunate woman a wonderful husband.

"No one else should have to handle Declan. He's my responsibility. Here at my request. I should be the one to handle the situation if it goes sour."

"Let's just hope it doesn't. I've seen that look in men's eyes before. Right now he only has one thing on his mind. He's damaged. Caring about others is way down on his priority list."

"After what he's suffered, can you blame him?"

"Hell no, but that doesn't make him a great team player."

She couldn't deny that, either. All she could do was play the hand she'd been dealt. And pray with all her might that she never had to make a decision of that magnitude.

With barely half a rap in warning, the door pushed open, and the subject of their discussion stuck his head in the room. "Is this a private party or can anyone join?"

"Since the door was closed," Aidan drawled, "I'd say that was obvious."

Ignoring Aidan's less-than-friendly answer, Declan turned to Sabrina. "Should I leave?"

For the first time since seeing him again, there was something in Declan's expression other than pain and bitterness. She saw jealousy, temper, possessiveness. She saw life! Call her silly, stupid, or juvenile, but her foolish heart leaped with optimism.

"We were just discussing the mission," Sabrina said.

Declan arched a black brow, and once again her foolish heart pounded at that familiar and lovable trait. "Odd. Seems like the entire team would be in on that kind of discussion."

"We're partners," Aidan growled, "which means we have a lot to say to each other. You got a problem with that, Steele?"

"You and my wife having a work partnership doesn't bother me in the least, Thorne."

"Good." Aidan looked pointedly at the door. "Now if you don't mind, we'll continue our discussion…alone."

His expression going glacial, Declan stepped into the room and headed toward Aidan.

"Oh, for heaven's sake," Sabrina snapped, "would both of you stop acting like thirteen-year-old boys?"

Even though the spark of jealousy in Declan's eyes delighted her, having two grown men snarling over her like two dogs after the same pork chop was infuriating.

Noah appeared at the door, his look taking in all three of them. "Something going on in here I need to know about?" The abrupt question cut into the tense silence.

Instead of backing away, Declan kept a cold, dark stare locked on Aidan. Seconds passed and finally, Aidan said, "No, boss, we were just chatting about the fine weather in Dolisie."

"Then I suggest everyone take their seats and buckle up, because we're about to land and experience that fine weather firsthand."

CHAPTER FOURTEEN

Republic of Congo

Their home base wasn't much. A three-room house with a dirt floor and thin, ragged cloths to cover the open windows. Most everyone had stayed in worse and took it all in stride. They weren't here to enjoy themselves.

They had chosen this location because of its proximity to the prison Steele had been held in. Noah's intel had discovered two other possible locations as well. The plan was to search each one with the hope of finding Tyndall.

Noah stood at the door, eyeing his operatives, as well as Steele. They'd dropped off their heaviest supplies here. Operatives Angela Delvecchio and Jake Mallory would handle communications. The prison was a hard day's trek. If they found Tyndall, they'd hightail it back here and get the hell out, ASAP. If he wasn't located, they'd move on to the next location. If still no Tyndall, the team would make the trek back to the house, restock their supplies, sleep, and then head out again the next day.

The first two locations weren't far apart but were at least twelve miles from the home base. If nothing popped at any of the locations, they'd have no choice but to accept Tyndall wasn't in the area and return home. Noah felt in his gut that the man was close by.

"Okay, team, we know our mission, we know what's at stake. Watch your back, watch each other's. Let's find our target and bring him home."

He turned to Jake and Angela, who stood on the other side of the room. "We'll keep our communication to a minimum unless there's a problem."

With her thick, black hair braided, fatigues covering her long, lithe body, Angela looked nothing like the over-pierced and tattooed receptionist and research assistant she'd once been. Now a full-fledged operative, she had proved herself more than once. Her dark, velvet-brown eyes showed none of the anxiousness he knew she was probably feeling as she said, "Godspeed."

The tall, muscular man standing at her side was Jake Mallory, her fiancé and partner. A former Chicago cop, Jake was fiercely protective of Angela and would fight hell itself to keep her safe.

Noah had a certain fondness for many of his operatives, but Angela was special. She'd been with LCR almost from the beginning and was like a little sister to him. On her very first op, she'd survived a brutal attack and had taken down a serial killer in the process. She was as capable as any operative, but knowing Jake had her back eased Noah's mind.

"Good luck," Jake said. "We'll keep the home fires burning."

They traveled as far as they could in an old, beat-up, canvas-covered truck. Five of them sat in the back. Mathison drove, while McCall navigated. Once they reached the base of the mountain, they'd have to park the truck and head out on foot.

Talk was kept to a minimum. The expression on each person's face was one of determination and resolve. From time to time,

Declan caught glances or smiles passing between Sabrina and Thorne, but for the most part they seemed content to stay silent.

He tried to keep his own focus straight ahead. He had only one reason for being here. A distraction like whether or not Sabrina and Thorne had something going wasn't something he planned to contemplate again.

Okay, yes, maybe he'd experienced some jealousy earlier. Actually, he wouldn't even call it that. He just hadn't liked that she'd gone off alone with a man while she was still legally bound to him. What man wouldn't get pissed about that?

A human trait when he no longer felt human was probably some kind of a breakthrough. But the jealousy had passed. Sabrina was free to pursue other relationships, romantic or otherwise. It was none of his concern.

The truck slowed and then came to a loud, squeaking halt. Gathering their gear, they jumped from the back onto a pathway that had been created by their vehicle. The jungle surrounded them. Sounds he hadn't heard since his rescue pounded incessantly in his ears. Declan swallowed back the bile gathering at the base of his throat. He was no longer a prisoner. This was just another step in taking back his life.

While Mathison moved the truck deeper into the wilderness, McCall joined them. "Let's get to cutting."

With the exception of Declan, all operatives pulled knives from sheaths strapped to their thighs and went about cutting branches to hide the truck from the view of anyone who might pass by. Though it was hard, Declan squelched his resentment. They had given him no weapons. His gun had never been returned. Maybe their distrust was understandable, but it still infuriated him. Reminding himself that he didn't need a weapon to kill did no good. Dammit, he felt naked.

"Here."

Declan looked down at the soft, delicate hand holding a wicked-looking fixed-blade metal knife. Raising his gaze to her face, he looked into fathomless emerald-green eyes. "You trust me with this?"

A soft twist to her mouth and then, "If you wanted any of us dead, we both know you don't require a weapon."

Declan took the knife and joined the men cutting the branches. Though Thorne gave him a hard look, neither he nor anyone else objected to his help. For the first time in a very long while, he felt like he was actually doing something productive.

"Okay. That should be enough," McCall said. "Let's get it hidden and get going."

With the branches they'd cut, it took barely ten minutes to completely hide the vehicle. Unless someone walked right into it, it should be here when they returned.

"Let's move," Mathison called out.

Without conscious thought, Declan slid the knife into his belt. It wasn't until Thorne made a move toward him that he realized he'd done it. Before he could consider his options of either telling the asshole to back off or returning the knife to Sabrina, she grabbed Thorne's arm and said, "It's fine."

Thorne gave him a hard look of warning but backed away. Good thing, that, but Declan knew at some point there would be a reckoning between the two of them. He looked forward to that day.

In silence and an odd but telling formation, they moved forward. Declan had McCall on one side of him, Mathison on the other. The young, solemn-faced Riley Ingram walked behind him, along with her partner, Justin Kelly. Both Ingram and Kelly had been eyeing him with equal parts distrust and hostility. Sabrina and Thorne walked in front. The positioning of each operative was deliberate. If he'd had any illusions that he was a trusted member of the team, they dissolved the moment they'd started their trek.

He told himself they were right to be wary. They'd allowed him to come along to help locate the prison, but he'd made no secret that he had his own agenda. If the two didn't mesh, he wouldn't hesitate to walk away and go off on his own.

Sabrina was the only oddity in their seeming unanimous distrust. Something had happened over the last couple of days, because she'd been treating him as if he was a member of the team. The knife had been a deliberate move to show him that trust. Not that she was playing the wife, but she seemed to have lost that edge of resentment she'd been carrying with her. She actually was acting as if life was almost normal.

If she believed that, she was delusional on top of being a traitor.

Aidan could feel Steele's hostile eyes burrowing into his back. The man didn't trust him, but since the feeling was mutual, he had no issues with that. What did concern Aidan was Steele's purpose in the group. He'd made it clear he was only here for himself. Even if Aidan could identify and understand his need for retribution, it didn't belong on an LCR op. But McCall had made the decision to bring him on. Aidan disagreed with a lot of things in life, but he rarely disagreed with his boss. The man had his priorities straight. If he felt Steele should be on the team, he wasn't going to argue with him. Didn't mean he wouldn't watch his back, though—or the backs of his fellow operatives. A man who'd had his humanity beaten out of him could be damn dangerous.

To be fair, he knew some of his ire was directed toward Sabrina. Why the hell hadn't she told him she was married... and thought she was a widow? He figured the couple of months she'd taken off and then returned looking like a shadow of her former self must've been when she'd thought Steele had been killed. Dammit, he had even teased her about having a hot and heavy love affair. She'd just smiled. And now he felt like an ass.

"I know you're angry at me."

Sabrina's words broke into the silence. She had kept her voice low so only he heard.

"You should've told me."

"You're right, I should have. I actually planned to tell you about him right before we got tapped for the Elite team. But then—"

"That's when you thought he was killed?"

"Yeah." Her voice went even softer. "I couldn't talk about him then. Hurt too much."

"I don't understand why you kept it a secret in the first place. Hell, LCR has a lot of married operatives."

"True." Her shoulders lifted in a defensive shrug. "I just don't like to talk about myself."

He snorted. "You got that right."

Instead of apologizing again, she shot him a hard look. "And you're an open book? You've told me all there is to know about Aidan Thorne, right?"

"I've told you—"

She cut him off with a wave of her hand. "Cut the crap, Aidan. You've told me what you could, just like I told you what I could. Noah doesn't hire people whose lives have been full of sunshine. So either quit giving me your bullshit line of an uncomplicated and happy past or spill all those secrets you hide behind that Prince Charming demeanor."

Aidan slammed his mouth shut. Hell, she was right. He had no right to expect her to reveal her secrets when he had so many dark ones of his own. Acknowledging the well-aimed arrow with a slight nod, he said, "I still trust you more than anyone I know."

Showing him once again that grudges weren't her thing, she shot him a smile. "Right back at you, partner."

Declan heard the soft whispers of the two people in front of him. Their voices were too low to make out their words, but he could tell from their tones that there had been irritation and then an almost amused affection before they'd gone silent. That reinforced his belief that Sabrina and Thorne had more than just a working relationship going on. Why that bothered him, he had no idea. He told himself because it was just damn rude and tried like hell to make that opinion stick.

The sun was high in the sky, and though the foliage above blocked much of the direct heat, it was still hotter than blazes. The only sounds besides their trudging, determined strides were the normal jungle sounds. All-too-familiar noises to Declan. How many nights had he lain awake listening to the roar of predators and the squeal of victims? Life, whether in the wild or in urban cities, was much the same. The strong devoured the weak.

The sounds opened up more memories. The pounding of fists into his gut, the slash of a whip slicing into his skin, the awful, insidious voices telling him things he couldn't bear to hear. *She's responsible. She betrayed you. Hate her, hate her, hate her.*

"You okay?"

He was jerked out of the darkness. *Sabrina.* How could she pull him away from the horror when she was the one who'd put him there? Her concerned, searching expression was one he bitterly resented. "I—"

"Let's take ten, everyone." McCall's voice cut off what would have been Declan's snarl.

Unwilling to admit his weariness, Declan glared at the LCR leader. "You don't need to stop on my account."

Not one to pull punches, McCall snapped back, "Carrying your ass for the next six miles isn't my idea of a good time. It won't hurt any of us to take a break."

Protesting any more would only make him sound petulant. Besides, with sweat dripping down his body and his breathing escalated to pants, it'd be an obvious lie. As much as Declan resented the extra concession, McCall was right. Collapsing at their feet wouldn't do any of them any good.

Declan dropped his gear and sat down on top of it. He noticed that he wasn't the only one who looked ready to drop. Everyone was sweating profusely.

Setting her gear a few feet away from Declan, Sabrina took a long swallow of water from her canteen. She had done her best to glance his way only occasionally. Showing him concern was only going to put his back up. Many things had changed about her husband, but that fierce Scottish pride was still intact. When she had glanced at him that last time, her concern had overridden her need to protect his ego. He'd looked ready to keel over. He was in just as good shape as any of the other team members, so she knew much of his fatigue had to be mental. How difficult it must be to return to the hell you thought you had escaped.

She pulled a pack of moist towelettes from her backpack and slid one out. Giving little thought to how it looked, she handed the pack over to Declan. He took it from her, pulled one out and then handed the pack back. They both wiped their faces, and then Declan held out his hand for her soiled wipe. She handed it to him, and he tucked them both into a vinyl pocket in his backpack.

Then, as if it was just as natural, he pulled an energy bar from another pocket and tossed it to her. She caught the snack with one hand and threw him a smile of thanks. Unwrapping it, she bit off a bite and then froze as she realized that everyone's eyes were on her and Declan. She swallowed her mouthful and said, "What?"

Justin Kelly tilted his head toward Declan. "I take it you two worked ops with each other?"

They had unconsciously reverted back to being partners, their routine as familiar to her as cleaning her gun. She glanced over at Declan to see if he realized what had happened. By the fury in his eyes and the bitter twist to his mouth, he had and obviously didn't like it one bit. Well, tough shit.

"Declan and I were partners for two years before I left the Agency."

"Why'd you leave?"

The question wasn't a surprise, the questioner was. Riley Ingram rarely took a personal interest in anyone beyond what the mission required. Despite her delight that the young operative had done something that showed she was actually more than an emotionless robot, Sabrina found it difficult to answer with any degree of honesty. Her reasons for leaving EDJE were intensely personal.

"She had to stop killing."

Her head whipped around. "Stop it, Declan."

"What?" His voice held a mocking amusement. "Is that something your LCR chums don't know? You think they'll think less of you if they discover that you were an assassin?"

"I'm not ashamed of my former occupation."

"Why should you be? You were born to kill."

Wearing identical expressions of barely concealed fury, both Aidan and Justin went to their feet. Declan arched a dark brow and stayed seated, but the mocking glint of amusement stayed. It was obvious he wanted to fight. So different from Declan, the peacemaker. Her heart ached at the change.

"I know a thing or two about killing," Cole Mathison's deep voice broke into the tenseness. "There are some who kill for entertainment...for pleasure. Sabrina might have been good at her job, but she wasn't born to kill. I'd say each kill took something out of her."

Amazed at his insight, she gave him a nod of appreciation. "No, I never enjoyed killing." And in the still of her mind, she heard Declan's tender, concerned words from long ago. *"Sabrina, you're the best I've ever trained, but I can't stand by and watch you slowly die with each kill you make. It eats at you."*

It had. Even though she had made only sanctioned kills, and the men and women she'd targeted had been monsters, killers who preyed on the weak and helpless, each one had taken something from her.

"One day I fear I'm going to look into your face and see nothing but the hell you feel. And I'll want to die."

So gentle, so protective. So unlike the Declan sitting across from her, the amusement still evident in his soulless blue eyes.

Was she crazy for even thinking that beneath that hard, grim exterior, her wonderful, caring, adoring husband still lived?

Noah stood, catching everyone's attention. "Since I'm assuming everyone has rested, let's move. And you, Mr. Steele." He turned cold black eyes to Declan. "You've made your point, hoping, I'm sure, to lessen Sabrina in the eyes of her fellow operatives. Let me assure you that can't and won't happen. Remember that before you try it again. It won't go as well for you next time."

With that said, everyone gathered their belongings and started back on their trek. Noah's words helped heal the wounds that Declan had deliberately inflicted. Yet the sting lingered. Is that how he saw her and she had never realized? To him, she had been a natural-born killer?

Chapter Fifteen

It had taken four more hours of steady walking to reach the first prison—the one where Declan had been held. Knowing they were getting closer, all unnecessary chatter had ceased. Eyes and ears open for hostiles, they moved stealthily, quietly through the jungle.

Since that small altercation with Declan, Sabrina held on to her self-righteous anger, allowing it to build like a fast-moving wildfire. How dare he try to humiliate and minimize her? *He* was the one who'd taught her everything she knew about killing. *He* was the reason she was so good at it. Not once had she enjoyed the actual act, not even when she'd taken out sick, twisted bastards who had committed hideous, inhumane, vile acts. Not once had she felt joy. She had done a necessary job because it needed to be done, and she had been good at it.

Cole held up his hand to halt their progress. Then, with individual signals for each team duo, he sent them to scout the area. As she moved away, she noticed Declan stood perfectly still, as if frozen. Noah gave her a nod in an unspoken assurance that he would stay with him.

Within ten minutes, they had surrounded the perimeter of the prison, which consisted of three square concrete buildings, a couple of ragged-looking tents and a long, metal trailer. In the distance, she spotted an archaic-looking outhouse.

"I see no activity," Cole murmured. "Everyone, report."

Riley, Justin and Aidan all reported no visible hostiles. With high-powered field binoculars, Sabrina scanned the area and concurred. The place looked abandoned. "I see no one."

"Okay," Cole said. "Let's move in. Extreme caution."

With only a few yards to their destination, Cole, again using hand signals, directed Aidan and Sabrina toward one building, Justin and Riley to another. Cole took the third.

Aidan pushed the door open, Sabrina went in low, and her partner came in behind her. Other than a three-legged upturned table in the corner and a tipped-over metal chair, the room was empty. A few soiled rags covered the blood-stained concrete floor, and she spotted a couple of cigarette packs. A stench that spoke of the violence and death that took place here permeated the room.

"Report," Cole said tersely.

"Empty," Justin answered.

"We got the same," Aidan reported.

"Okay," Cole said, "let's meet outside."

Sabrina stood in the middle of the filthy, vile room and tried to imagine what Declan had suffered here. Was this where he was kept or where he had been tortured? The stains on the floor were most assuredly from blood, as well as other bodily fluids. How could you call yourself human and commit such sickening acts against another human being?

"You okay?" Aidan asked.

She nodded and turned away, swallowing the bile surging up her throat. The fury and resentment she'd been building up at Declan for the last few hours died an instantaneous death.

How could she hold on to her anger after knowing what he had suffered?

Once outside, she took in great gulps of air, hoping to cleanse her lungs of the overwhelming blanket of despair and death that had seeped into her.

Everyone met in the middle of the clearing. She noticed the pale cast to Declan's face, but his eyes remained cold and emotionless. Just how horrific must it be to return to your own hell?

"You sure this is the place?" Noah asked him.

Teeth clenched and every muscle as tight as a bowstring, Declan gave a grim nod. Oh, hell yeah, he was sure. "This is it."

"Where were you kept?" Mathison said.

"Various places." He jerked his head toward what looked like an outhouse. "Over there." He pointed to the metal trailer. "And there."

He took several long strides to the place that still appeared in his nightmares. Vines and branches hid the area. He ripped away a handful of vines and looked down at the hell pit he'd called home for several months. A hole, the space no bigger than four by eight, covered by a steel grate. "This is where I spent a large part of my time."

Footsteps came up behind him. He heard a gasp, knew it was Sabrina's.

"Hell," McCall muttered, "when it rained, the hole would fill up. How'd you survive?"

The first time it rained had been a welcome relief. They'd thrown him in and left. No water or food for days. When the rains started, he had relished the moisture, drinking the life-giving rainwater as if it had been the most expensive of wines. It hadn't been until late that night that he realized the salvation of the rain might well be his death. When the hole had flooded, raising him to the top, he'd held on to the grate, breathing as best he could. Sometimes he'd have to let go and sink to the bottom. Then, when he could no longer hold his breath, he'd swim back to the top. Finally, on the third day, the rains had stopped, the water had receded, and he'd grown thirsty once more.

"I didn't." He strode away from the group. From the prying eyes, the pity. He didn't need it, didn't want it. All he wanted were the bastards who'd put him there.

At the edge of the jungle, he stopped. Listened. How odd to be standing here only yards away from the place of his worst nightmares. Even though his captors had moved on and he hadn't been able to ask questions or seek vengeance, at the very least he should have felt a sense of relief. The knowledge that he was free should have given him some kind of peace. All he felt was emptiness—a barren soul in a desolate land.

"Declan?"

That soft, husky voice—one he'd heard in his dreams and far too often in his waking nightmares.

"Not the plush accommodations you expected, is it, Sabrina? Or did you even think about what would happen to me when you sold me out?"

He couldn't see her, but he felt her flinch, take a small step back. Then, as if steel straightened her spine, she took several steps forward until she faced him. He saw what she wanted him to see. Compassion, caring, sadness. Emotions a guiltless person might exhibit. But they both knew the truth. When would she stop lying?

"I'm not going to defend myself again. It's pointless. You wouldn't believe me anyway."

He turned away from her, refused to watch as she continued her lies.

"I…" She swallowed hard. "I just wanted to tell you how much I admire you for surviving. Most people wouldn't have. I don't know if you'll ever believe in my innocence. If we'll ever have any kind of…peace between us again. I just want you to know that you have my undying admiration."

She turned and walked away.

"Okay. Listen up," Noah said. "I know everyone's exhausted, but we've got about an hour of daylight left. Let's get as far away from this dump as possible. We'll stop close to dusk, set up a cold camp and then get going at sunup." He turned to Mathison. "We've got what, at least a day and a half of travel before we reach the other prison?"

"We've got some tough terrain ahead of us, so it might take a little longer. We should be able to make our destination before dusk tomorrow."

No one spoke, but Noah read their faces. Everyone wanted to get away from the grim aura of death and hopelessness that hung over the small prison. In silence but in one accord, they trudged into the jungle, Mathison and Steele leading the way. Noah figured Steele was having a hell of a time not running. Being confronted with the place of his torture couldn't have been easy.

He glanced back at Sabrina, who was taking up the rear with Thorne. Her face was almost bloodless, her eyes holding a dark pain. Seeing where her husband had been tortured might have been tougher on her than it'd been on Steele. But he knew her well enough to know she'd bounce back. Steele he wasn't so sure of.

Seeing where Steele had been kept reinforced his opinion of the man's iron-willed strength. He had survived hell. Question was, would he be able to overcome it?

It was early morning. Dawn would arrive in about an hour. Other than the occasional screech of a hapless victim or animalistic call for a mate, the jungle was silent. Nighttime predators were winding down, getting ready to take their rest. At daybreak, the daytime predators would wake and search for sustenance. A light mist fell softly around them, making the darkness of their surroundings even more ominous than usual.

They had made their destination at dusk yesterday and, as planned, set up another cold camp. As had been the case the night before, sleep had been almost impossible for Sabrina. Even though Declan had slept on the other side of their makeshift camp, she hadn't been able to take her eyes off him. He had been silent all day, giving the occasional answer when someone asked him a direct question. The dead emptiness in his eyes scared her to death. Yet she didn't fear him. She was afraid for him.

It was time to move. Guards would be sleepy. Defenses would be down. Cole and Aidan had done recon last night, reporting two men with AK-47s guarding the perimeter. And they'd seen at least one more sitting in one of the buildings. With at least three men on duty, how many prisoners were they guarding?

"Okay, listen up," Noah said. "We're here for Tyndall, but if there are more prisoners, then let's get them. Under these conditions, it's doubtful any of them will be able to travel on foot. Angela and Mallory have a helicopter on standby. Remember, just because we're rescuing them, they may not all be friendly. However, they sure as hell don't deserve to stay here."

Sabrina's eyes moved to Declan. He had the same determined look on his face as the rest of the team. Because he intended to help with the rescue? Or was he playing his own game? She understood his need for vengeance. If any of his torturers were here, she would do whatever she could to help him. But the victims came first. Would that be a problem for him?

"Here's how it'll go down." Noah drew a crude drawing of the prison on the ground with a large stick. "Thorne, I want you on the south side, on this hill. Our mission is clear, so we either leave the assholes on the ground, hurting but alive, or dead."

Noah shot a look at Justin and Riley. "You two take the outside building here." He pointed at one of the squares he'd drawn. "Fox, you take this middle building. Mathison, you take this one. Steele and I will take the one on the far right."

"If we get separated, let's plan to meet back here." Noah paused for several seconds then said, "Any questions?"

Silence.

"Okay. Let's move."

They headed out together. The only sounds were the awakening jungle surrounding them and their soft footsteps. Though she was outwardly calm, adrenaline raced through Sabrina's veins. As they neared the prison, everyone went in their assigned direction. The thought of rescuing a man who'd been held almost as long as Declan fueled her blood. If only she had known about Declan. Thank God that Jackson had carried through with his hunch. Otherwise, Declan would still have been suffering.

"We'll go on three," Noah murmured in his mic. "One, two, three."

Gun at the ready, Sabrina broke through the bushes and ran full force toward her target building. She took a moment to listen at the door. Heard nothing. There were no windows. The door was made of weathered wood and looked close to falling apart. Easy enough to break it down, but stealth would work better. She twisted the handle, pleased that it turned. She pushed the door open a small crack and peered inside. Bile shot up her throat as she took in the scene. The killing was recent. A man hung by his arms from the rafters. He was naked, and blood from the thousands of cuts and open wounds on his body still looked wet. Infected, open sores covered his skin. His face wasn't one she recognized, and while she was thankful it wasn't Tyndall, she wished they'd been able to help this poor guy sooner.

Sabrina picked up a chair and carried it over to the hanging man. She stood on the chair and, though she knew it was useless, checked for a pulse. The man's skin was ice cold, no hint of life. Pulling her knife from its sheath, she cut the ropes holding his wrists and, as gently as possible, lowered him to the floor. Before they left, they would take his fingerprints, photograph his remains, and then bury him. Perhaps he had family thinking he had died long ago or wondering where he was. Even though this wasn't a good outcome, at least maybe they'd have some type of closure.

She backed away. Other than the dead man, the room was clear. Was this their torture room? It smelled of death and nightmarish events that few people knew existed.

She could imagine the torturer sitting in relative comfort in that lone chair, asking the man questions and, when they weren't answered to his liking, giving the go-ahead for more pain. And the man hanging from the ceiling…his arms hurting and then going numb. The slices on his skin searing him as he wondered what other hellish acts would be done to him. Was this one of the things Declan had endured? Her eyes blurred with tears as she knew, without a doubt, that he had.

Bile surged again, and Sabrina lost it. Turning away, she threw up the small amount of water and energy bar she'd consumed for breakfast. Then, drawing her emotions back where they belonged, she backed out of the building. This man might be beyond help. That didn't mean she couldn't help someone else.

Declan ran alongside McCall. Before they'd taken off, McCall had handed him his SIG Sauer—the one they'd taken away when LCR captured him. He had accepted the weapon, surprised he'd been allowed to assist with the raid. Considering everyone's feelings, he wouldn't have been surprised if they'd tied him to a tree until this was over. Not that he would have allowed that to happen. Never again would he be held hostage by anything or anyone.

Their steps rapid but silent, both men approached their assigned building. McCall listened at the door, nodded his head. The room was occupied. He gently twisted the knob—locked. McCall said almost soundlessly, "I can knock it down. Can you follow through on your end?"

Declan gave an affirmative nod. For the first time in almost two years, he was doing something worthwhile. Just because his primary goal was to find the bastards who'd tortured him, the thought of actually doing some good made his blood pump with excitement.

Backing up slightly, McCall kicked hard. The door splintered and, with a resounding crash, slammed to the concrete floor. Low to the ground, Declan peered into the room. Gunfire exploded. Declan jerked back. Voices, cursing and yelling in Spanish and English, spewed out. More gunfire followed.

McCall stood on one side of the door, Declan on the other. Knowing there might be victims inside made the job tricky. He'd like nothing better than to lay down a rapid-fire response. He couldn't. He took a chance and peered around the door again. The guy was reloading, giving Declan the chance to get off a few more rounds. The man went down but returned fire as he made a fast crawl to an overturned table. The other man ran through a door on the other side, shooting as he tried to escape.

McCall fired, hitting the running man in the shoulder. The guy dropped and then threw himself behind the same table. The two men, though both now wounded, barricaded themselves behind their cover and continued to fire.

His voice low and urgent, McCall said, "There's a man—prisoner—lying in the corner. I can't see anything but the back of his head. Can't tell if he's still alive. I need to get to him."

"Go," Declan said. "I'll cover you."

Declan didn't wait for McCall's agreement, just laid down steady fire at the two shooters. Staying low, the LCR leader stepped inside and raced to the other side of the room.

Totally focused on keeping the two gunmen busy, he still managed to see out of the corner of his eye that McCall was dragging the man toward the door. Guy was either unconscious or dead. One of the shooters noticed that, too. He rose up to take a shot at McCall. Declan fired, nailing the man in the head.

The instant McCall had the man outside, Declan called to McCall, "I'm out."

"Take this one." McCall pulled a Glock from his thigh holster and threw it toward him. Declan easily caught it and started firing again. The shooter peeked out, and Declan finally got a good look at his face—one he saw in his nightmares.

"Son of a bitch," he muttered.

Whether the bastard recognized him or realized he had little chance of survival, Declan didn't know. Taking advantage of Declan's shock, the man disappeared into another room.

Declan followed.

Sabrina raced toward the building where gunfire had erupted. Declan was in that building. Halfway there, Riley's voice, tense and urgent, came through her earbud. "Need assistance here."

Torn but knowing her obligations, Sabrina switched directions and ran to the building Riley and Justin had been assigned. A few yards from the entry, gunfire exploded, spraying bullets in front of her. Sabrina looked up. A gunman on the roof had her in his sights. An instant later, the man tumbled forward and landed on the dry, packed earth.

Knowing her partner had come through, Sabrina whispered, "Thank you, Aidan," and continued through the door. She spoke into her mic. "Riley, I'm here. Where are you?"

"Basement. We've got a mess down here."

"How many shooters are inside?"

"Thorne just took out the last one."

Reassured but still wary, Sabrina walked into the room. This was apparently where most of the guards had spent their time. It looked like a regular office with desks, chairs, a coffee maker, and a small fridge. What looked like a brand new computer sat on one of the desks. Clean and neat—freakish, considering what these bastards did here. The two dead men lying in the middle of the floor definitely looked out of place.

Spotting an open door and a stairwell, Sabrina ran toward it. She was halfway down the stairs when the stench caught her, almost knocking her down. Gun still at the ready in her right hand, she held her left hand over her nose and mouth and kept running. What the hell was down there?

She stopped at the bottom of the stairs. Her imagination could never have come up with the horror. Five different cells held three to five men, all in the nude, all showing signs of malnutrition and hideous suffering.

"They're all dead," Riley whispered, horror in her voice.

Sabrina glanced over at the young operative standing in the middle of the room. For the first time since she had known her, Sabrina saw something on her face other than her typical cool arrogance. Tears streamed down her cheeks, and her mouth trembled with emotion.

Showing sympathy or compassion would help no one right now. "Where's Justin?" Sabrina snapped.

Riley jerked, and then, as if realizing what she had revealed, that damn mask returned. "He's in the back room."

"You've checked all these bodies? You're sure they're all dead?"

"Yes."

"Okay. Let's go see what Justin found." She headed toward the area Riley had indicated. The young operative's solid, determined steps coming behind her was a reassuring sound. She had herself back together.

Justin had found more men. Sabrina managed to retreat from the horror without losing control of her stomach—but barely. Four men, again all nude, hung from the ceiling. The limp bodies and frozen features revealed their condition even before she checked each one for a pulse—they were dead, had been for a while.

"Hell," Riley muttered.

Sabrina headed to a cell at the end of the hallway. There she found Justin kneeling over a man on the filthy floor.

"What have you got?" Sabrina asked.

Without looking up, he muttered, "Tyndall."

"Is he dead?"

"Not yet."

Sabrina stepped closer and then stopped abruptly, seeing exactly what he meant. His face was so swollen and filthy, he barely looked human. "How'd you ID him?"

"Tattoo of his wife's name on the left wrist."

Setting aside her own pity, she said, "I'll alert Noah. The helicopter can be here in minutes."

Though Justin nodded, she could see the same doubt she was feeling. Would the guy even live long enough for that? Whether he survived or not, his family would want him back.

Sabrina headed out the door...the worry she'd successfully squelched now back in full force. Silence surrounded the entire area. All gunfire had ceased. Neither Declan nor Noah had spoken into their mics since the raid had started.

"Declan? Noah?"

"McCall here. Need you here ASAP, Fox."

Heart pounding with dread, Sabrina raced up the stairway and ran out the door. She was halfway to the building when Noah shouted, "Over here, Fox."

She turned at Noah's voice. He was stooped beside a body. *No. No. No!* She was within a few feet when she realized the man's hair was the wrong color for Declan. It had looked dark because of the blood.

Dark eyes grim, Noah said, "He's alive...barely. I've already called for transport."

"Justin found Tyndall. He's in bad shape but alive for now." She looked toward the building, swallowed hard and asked, "Declan?"

Noah jerked his head toward the jungle. "He ran after one of them."

She took a step and then heard a shot, far off in the distance. Her feet flying, she yelled over her shoulder, "Going after him," and didn't wait to hear her boss's reply.

CHAPTER SIXTEEN

Sweat poured down Declan's face, blood pumped hot and wild through his veins as he ran after his prey. They'd been at it for over an hour, but the bastard was tiring and was now within reach. At last he would get some answers. He told himself it didn't matter if those answers confirmed Sabrina's involvement. He had to know the truth, no matter the cost.

Clomping sounds, ten, maybe twenty yards ahead of him. He imagined he could hear the bastard breathing, gasping for breath. The asshole probably thought he had only minutes to live. Would he be relieved to learn that Declan didn't intend to kill him? Probably not. Death would be much less painful than what he had planned.

Declan increased his speed, plowing down tree branches and bushes like a bulldozer. He wouldn't get away…he wouldn't.

The bullet came from out of nowhere. Declan acknowledged the sting, but nothing, other than death, would slow him down. Adrenaline and the fierce need for vengeance blocked out everything else. At last, soon, he would know the truth.

Footsteps again. Big feet crashing through piles of ground vegetation. Tiny animals squealed, scampering to get away. Breath wheezed from the guy's lungs. Oh, hell yeah, he was close. So… damn…close.

With almost no sound or warning, a giant body flew through the air. Declan turned to dodge a direct hit, landed sideways and was back on his feet in seconds, facing his opponent.

Damn, the guy was massive. He'd almost forgotten how large. At six-foot-five, few people towered over Declan. This creature was close to seven feet tall, well over three hundred pounds. From up close and personal contact, Declan knew the man's fists were the size of hams.

Even though sweat poured down his face and fresh blood stained the front of his shirt, the big idiot was grinning. "Never thought I'd get the chance to have at you again."

"You'll find I fight better when I'm not strung up."

The grin got meaner. "That'll just make the kill sweeter."

The giant threw the first punch, missed Declan's face by inches. Declan had the advantage of being quicker and better trained. Meat-Face, as he'd nicknamed the guy after their first brutal meeting, slammed another fist toward him with less skill than speed. At some point, the guy was going to tire himself out. Declan intended to let him, then he would strike.

As Meat-Face swiped another fist toward him, Declan studied the man—something he'd never had the chance to do before. An American—had a thick Jersey accent, but without the charm. And though accents could be faked, there was no good reason for him to pretend—especially now.

The gleam in Meat-Face's eyes said it all—he planned for this to be a death match. With a couple of exceptions, that suited Declan just fine. First, it'd be Meat-Face's demise, not Declan's. And second, death wouldn't occur until he got the answers he'd come looking for. He'd waited a long time for this day.

Hidden behind a tall, leafy bush, Sabrina watched in silence. After the heart-plunging fear that Declan had gone off alone and she could lose him again, the scene before her was anticlimactic. Actually, it was almost comical. The man—she nicknamed him Brutus for lack of a better name—was oversized in every way. In this case, size didn't necessarily count. Declan's training, skill, and perfectly conditioned body gave him a huge advantage over Brutus.

Relieved, she leaned against a sturdy tree and treated herself to a few minutes of relaxation and enjoyment.

The way Brutus kept swinging, it was obvious that his super-sized body didn't correlate to a larger brain or intellect. At some point, surely he would figure out that a change in attack was in order. But no, he kept swiping like he was swatting at bugs and had yet to make contact with any part of Declan's anatomy.

She knew her husband well. Brutus would eventually wear himself into a breathless, exhausted mess. Declan would pounce like a sleek panther and effortlessly bring down his prey.

A crackling in the bushes across the way caught her attention. Animal or human? Sabrina drew her gun. Declan must've heard it, too, and for a second, he was distracted. Brutus might be lacking in brain cells, but he was no fool. The instant Declan glanced away, Brutus slid a knife from the back of his belt and charged.

Shit! Without any compunction, Sabrina shot him dead center between his eyes. Brutus fell forward like a hacked-down timber. Declan jumped out of the way and watched his opponent perform a face-plant in the underbrush.

Sabrina walked into the clearing. "That was close."

She hadn't expected effusive thanks. As physical as Declan was, he would've wanted to take the man out another way. She never expected him to glare at her and snarl, "You double-crossing bitch. You killed him."

"Excuse me?" Indignant, infuriated, she snarled back, "I saved your ass, you jerk."

"No, you killed the man that had the information I needed. He was one of my captors. Beat the shit out of me almost daily. But that's not news to you, is it, Sabrina? You knew he'd tell me the truth and implicate you."

She wilted like a dead weed. Of all the freaking people to kill… Unexpected tears raced to the surface, and Sabrina closed her eyes to prevent their escape. Damned if she would let him see her vulnerability. Instead, she let her temper loose. "You idiotic, stubborn asshole. I had no idea who the guy was. He was about to plunge a knife into your gut. I saved your life."

Declan took a step toward her, fury in his eyes. Sabrina stepped forward, too. She was tired of mollycoddling the jerk. He wanted to have it out? She was more than up to the task.

"Lay one hand on her, Steele, and you'll wish that dead giant on the ground had finished you off."

Aidan stood a few feet away. His Glock pointed directly at Declan's chest.

"Aidan…don't." Sabrina shook her head. He didn't know Declan the way she did. "He would never touch me in anger."

Aidan snorted. "Now who's being delusional? He kidnapped you, held a gun to your head. Hell, Sabrina, you said yourself that he's not the same man. Are you willing to take the chance he won't hurt you?"

Declan drew in a controlled breath and then blew it out in a giant huff. Instead of assuring them both that he had no intention of striking her, he said, "So your partner's in on it, too? Should've figured."

She rolled her eyes heavenward. "Shut up, Declan. Just shut the hell up."

Sabrina went toward Aidan, believing he would lower his gun. She was wrong. All he did was make a slight shift so the gun was pointed away from her but still at Declan.

She put her hand on his wrist and pushed down. "No, he's not the same man, but he's not going to hurt me. At least not that way."

His eyes remained focused on his target. "You willing to take that chance, that's your business. Right now, I'm your partner and I watch your back. Got that, Steele?"

Sabrina turned to the man she had once believed she knew better than herself. The old Declan would have cut his hand off before ever touching her in anger. Was she being delusional, as Aidan had accused? Twice he'd held a loaded gun on her. This wasn't the old Declan. He had proved that repeatedly.

"Fine, you're right. I don't know that he wouldn't hurt me physically." She turned back to Aidan. "Let's head back."

Aidan shook his head. "Too late. Chopper's already picked up the rest of the team and survivors. McCall is sending the authorities out to take care of the dead. We're to head to the closest village and contact him. He'll send transport to get us out." He jerked his head as if pointing over his shoulder. "I grabbed up yours and Steele's gear and dropped it back there."

Sabrina nodded her thanks. "Let's go then."

Declan followed behind the other two. They acted as if he wasn't around, as if they were alone. They talked to each other as if they'd known each other their entire lives, throwing out insults and jokes, totally comfortable with one another. He felt like a third wheel.

Could she actually have shot Meat-Face to save his life, like she'd claimed? He had been distracted, and most likely the bastard would've gotten a nice slice of him before Declan could've stopped him. Or, as that hideous voice inside his head claimed, she'd shot him because he would've revealed her role. With Meat-Face out of the picture, he had no one else to confirm his suspicions.

And Thorne had made the noise to distract him. Had he been in on it all along or was he just helping out his lover?

They traveled for miles without stopping. Though Sabrina and Thorne were several yards ahead of him, he noticed she kept looking back at him. They could've moved faster without him. He was holding them back. Dammit, why was he so cold? Wasn't he in the middle of a freaking jungle? Had somebody turned on the air conditioner?

He felt his feet move forward, but for some reason he thought he might be flying. Maybe floating. A roaring in his ears. A plane? Someone was here to rescue him. Him? No, them. Them, who? Who else was here?

Black spots danced before his eyes. The roar in his head increased. Like a black, oozing river, darkness flowed over him. He felt himself falling. Thought about catching himself before he hit the ground and changed his mind. What the hell? Why not take a nap till he felt better?

CHAPTER SEVENTEEN

He fought her like a madman. Like she was trying to kill him instead of saving him. Why hadn't she noticed he'd been shot? They'd walked for miles. Self-righteous indignation had given her extra energy. She'd made sure she stayed several yards ahead of him as her mind hurled curses and insults at the stubborn bastard. Let him think she was a killer, that she had been lying to him all along. Let him fend for himself. What the hell did she care?

And where had all that moral indignation gotten her? Nowhere. Now Declan could die because of her stupidity.

"Oh, for the love of all that's good and holy, would you just give it a rest?"

She glared across at Aidan. "It's my fault. If I—"

"No, it's not your fault. It's mostly the fault of the prick who shot him, and some of it is this asshole's fault for getting shot in the first place."

"How can you say that? If not for me, he wouldn't even be on this mission. He'd—"

"If it wasn't for you, he never would've had a chance to find one of the men who tortured him."

"Yes, and I killed him. He could've told Declan who betrayed him. But no, I had to go in like Wyatt Kidd and blast him to hell."

"Wyatt who?"

"You know." She waved a hand. "That gunfighter."

"Wyatt Earp was a sheriff. Billy the Kid was an outlaw."

"Whatever." She shrugged, infuriated with herself and with Aidan, who should have shared her fury. "The thing is, if not for me, he wouldn't be in this predicament." She was getting ready for another dose of guilt when a fist slammed into her face.

"Son of a bitch," Sabrina snapped.

Aidan grabbed the fist that Declan had swung and held him down. When he glanced at Sabrina again, he didn't even bother to hide his amusement. "While I don't endorse hitting a woman unless she's threatening me or mine, I do hope that knocked some sense into you."

A one-eyed glare didn't have as much impact, but she gave her partner one anyway. The delirious man on the ground had no idea what he had done. They'd cleaned and bandaged the wounds on his arm and thigh, given him an antibiotic and mild sedative for pain. His temp was slightly over one hundred two, and they'd taken turns bathing him with their limited supply of bottled water. And now they could do nothing but wait. They were at least one day's hard travel to the nearest village.

Glad to see that Declan's movements had stilled and he seemed to be resting easier, Sabrina leaned back against a tree. Aidan sat on the other side of her and took a long swallow of water from his canteen. "So. Before I decide I completely hate this shithead you married and are obviously still crazy about, tell me what he was like before."

She knew why he was asking. When she had taken Declan's shirt off to treat his wound, her partner had seen the scars. And for the first time Sabrina had seen the ones on his chest and stomach. How had he survived? The irrefutable evidence that Declan had gone through the horrors of hell reinforced her opinion once again of his strength and courage.

Aidan's statement indicated he, having seen the damage, was willing to give Declan another chance.

"He'd been with EDJE several years before I met him. Grew up in Scotland. Started with the Agency in his early twenties."

"Scotland? Really? Where's that Scottish brogue all the girls go crazy over?"

Surprised she still had an ounce of amusement in her, Sabrina laughed softly. "When he wants, he can definitely bring it out." Unbelievably, she found herself blushing. How many times had Declan whispered to her in that beautiful accent while making love to her?

Hoping Aidan hadn't seen her embarrassment, she went on, "Anyway, when I met him, I was greener than a new apple. Had assisted on a few ops, mostly by gathering intel. Was still attending classes. Still had no idea what I'd gotten myself into. Thought I'd already seen everything I needed to see." She shrugged. "Believe it or not, I was slightly cocky."

"You?" Aidan's eyes widened in mock disbelief. "Never."

She grinned and continued. "One day I barged in on a meeting between Albert Marks, the head of the Agency, and Declan. Even that early, I was looking at Albert as family. He'd saved me from..." She swallowed. "Let's just say I didn't have a very good life before I went to the Agency. I'd been there just long enough to feel like I finally had a family, but still had a chip on my shoulder the size of France.

"The first time I saw Declan, I just knew he had to be some kind of a model." She snorted as she remembered her naïveté and stupidity. "Like a secret government agency was going to do recruiting posters. But he was just so gorgeous. Like James Bond and Jason Bourne wrapped up in the most delectable—"

Aidan gave an overloud clearing of his throat.

She threw him an embarrassed grin. "Sorry. Anyway, he fascinated me from the start. Albert introduced me to him. Told me he was going to be my new trainer."

Declan had been rough on her...ruthlessly mean to the point of cruelty. She had gone back to her room almost every night and cried. She'd never intended to let him see what he did to her. And each time she had gone back with the same cocky attitude as the day before. He'd done his best to destroy her, and she had refused to let him.

"We worked a couple of ops together in the middle of my training. During those missions, he treated me as an equal. I guess I expected that to continue, but when we got back to training, he was just as mean, maybe even meaner. This went on for close to a year. I'd go off on an op, come back for more training, and he'd treat me like shit. I'd give it right back to him."

"What changed?"

"I'd walked out the door in a temper and left my weapon. Stupid. I knew from the first day that you never leave your weapon behind. That it was an extension of me. But he had me so frazzled that day I forgot. He came to my room with it, ready to ream me out. I didn't answer the door, and being the arrogant asshole that he was, he came inside. Heard me having my nightly meltdown in the shower."

He had talked with her as an equal, told her about himself, his family.

"And from that moment things were better?"

She snorted. "Are you kidding me? The next day he was tougher than ever." But it had changed her. She had reveled in that toughness, determined to learn all she could and be the best she could be.

She didn't tell Aidan about the other nights he had found her in the shower, picked her up, and just held her while she let all the pain and fury of that day drain from her. Those moments were between her and Declan, precious memories she would hold in her heart forever, no matter what happened in the future.

"When did you guys start your relationship?"

"About a year later, we were on an op together. My first kill. I lost it and almost got myself killed instead. I did the job, but it wasn't pretty or neat. I figured he was going to rail at me and then fire me. Or call Uncle Al and have him take me away. Instead, he told me about his first op, about how messy it was."

She swallowed and remembered how he had held her, comforting her as only Declan could.

"We worked almost every op together after that."

"And he was good to you?"

Her voice was husky and thick. "In a word—amazing. He knew me better than anyone. Treated me like I was precious… valuable." She lifted her shoulder, unable to articulate how wonderful he had been to her. "Like I said, I didn't have the best home life. I'd never been treated as if I was something special."

"If you were such a good team, why'd you leave the Agency?"

It wasn't something she talked about a lot. A part of her was embarrassed about the weakness. Another part was glad she was human enough to care. "Killing became my job. That wasn't their initial plan for me, but when they saw how good I could be, I got called in to do the deed. Up close and personal was my specialty.

"But then it became too much. It was like a piece of my soul left me with each kill. I knew I was saving lives. The people I took out were scum, had murdered, kidnapped, tortured. Done all manner of unspeakable things, so it wasn't as if I thought I was doing wrong. I knew I was in the right. I just…" She trailed off. Hard to articulate something she'd felt so conflicted about.

"You wanted to feel clean."

Her head jerked up at Aidan's bald statement and amazing insight. "That's exactly how I felt. How did you know?"

"Just a guess."

Her eyes narrowed in an accusing glare. "You know, Mr. Thorne, at some point you're going to have to reciprocate. You jumped down my throat for not telling you about Declan, but you've got more than your share of secrets. Someday you're going to have to spill."

"But not today."

He said it with such grim determination that Sabrina didn't push. "But not today," she agreed.

"So you came to LCR for a change of pace?"

She laughed. "The pace is about the same, sometimes a little faster, but the high of saving lives…being right in the thick of the action and actually seeing the difference I've made…"

"Nothing like it," Aidan said softly.

"Nothing."

"Why LCR, though? There are lots of rescue organizations."

"An LCR operative—can't say who—is a former EDJE agent. Declan contacted him. After I talked with him, he arranged for a meeting with Noah."

"Steele wanted you out?"

"He wanted me out of the killing business. He saw what it was doing to me."

"So those words he threw at you the other day…that you were nothing but a killer." Aidan shook his head. "Bastard knows where to stick the knife, doesn't he?"

A lump developed in her throat. Those words still stung.

Apparently not expecting a response, Aidan went on, "I'm surprised Steele didn't come to LCR with you."

"Declan was too valuable."

"You think that's why he was taken?"

"Yes, no doubt. But—"

"But?"

"I still have no idea what they wanted from him. He's been so busy blaming me and not trusting anyone, he won't tell me a damned thing. How the hell is he ever going to find the truth if he doesn't trust anyone enough to help him find it?"

"What was his role at EDJE, other than trainer?"

Her gaze dropped to the man lying on the ground before her. Unable to stop herself, she tenderly brushed a strand of hair off his forehead and was pleased to note his skin was much cooler. "He was a field agent, but he had responsibilities even I wasn't allowed to know." She swallowed hard. "And unless I earn his trust again, prove to him that I had nothing to do with his abduction, I might never know why he was taken."

Instead of giving her trite reassurances, Aidan said, "Guess we'd better get some rest. If he's not better tomorrow, I'll head out on my own and bring help back."

Because she could and Declan would never know, Sabrina stretched out on the ground beside her husband and placed her head on his uninjured shoulder. Many nights she had gone to sleep exactly like this, but with one marked difference. Declan had been holding her. Would she ever feel his arms around her again?

She fell asleep with an ache in her heart.

"You stupid son of a bitch. You think anyone's going to save you? Hell, your so-called brothers-in-arms are the ones who sold

you out. You've been abandoned. No one's looking for you. No one cares about you."

Meat-Face loomed over him—so close Declan could see the large pores in his florid face, smell the onions he'd had with his breakfast. *"Your ass is mine, Steele, and I'm going to smash it into the dirt."*

Declan kept his gaze steady, his face expressionless. They couldn't break him. He had been tortured by the best for months on end. The training he had endured had put him through almost every imaginable scenario. No matter what they did to him, they would never break him.

Agony erupted in his head. His entire body felt as though they were burning him alive. *Breathe through the pain, inhale, exhale, inhale. You're bigger than what they can do to you. Float out of your body, away...far away. See her beautiful face...know she's waiting on you. You can survive anything knowing Sabrina loves you.*

Peace enveloped him. He was floating. There was pain, but it was distant, inconsequential. Then he heard her voice, soft, rich, thick with emotion, "Tell them, Declan. Tell them what they want to know and you can come back to me. Tell them and we'll be with each other again. Tell them, tell them..."

Declan shook his head. No, couldn't be Sabrina. She would never want him to give in. She would tell him to fight. It was a trick. They were using his one weakness to try to break him. They would never succeed.

Pain sliced through him again. Sabrina's voice followed. Then more pain, Sabrina's voice again. Over and over. *Stop, stop, stop. Stop!*

Sabrina mopped Declan's brow again. His fever had risen. Aidan had left just after dawn to go get help. Waiting around for

Declan to be able to travel could take days or might not happen at all. The bullet wound in his arm was just a flesh wound and was healing quickly. It was the deep gash in his thigh that was worrisome and most likely the cause of the fever raging inside his body.

He had been in and out of consciousness since he'd passed out two days ago. When he was conscious, he was lucid, asking direct questions and responding to her queries with clear, concise answers. His attitude was unfailingly polite, cool, letting her know he still believed she was the enemy.

And when he was unconscious, he slept like the dead, never moving. She checked his pulse repeatedly just to reassure herself. The strong, solid rhythm never failed to give her immeasurable relief.

But in between consciousness and sleep, there were moments of sheer terror for her. He screamed, shouted, and muttered, and she knew he was reliving what those bastards had done to him. She despised hearing it, but at least she had some idea of why he believed she had betrayed him. They had used her against him. They may not have succeeded in getting the information they wanted—whatever it had been—but they had succeeded in one thing—convincing Declan of her guilt.

A normal man would have broken, even an extraordinarily strong man might have broken. But Declan hadn't, at least not in the way his captors had wanted. But they had broken the bond between husband and wife, destroying trust.

She wished knowing the truth made it easier. She had thought it would. It didn't. She didn't know how to reach the core of his distrust and destroy it. How do you defend when there's nothing to defend?

"Look very serious."

Declan's slurred, gruff voice broke into her thoughts. She took in his eyes, saw the clarity and reason, and was relieved.

"With good reason. You have two bullet wounds and a raging fever."

His eyes roamed the perimeter. "Where's your other half?"

The words slashed at her. Her other half was lying on the ground before her, distrust back in his eyes. Refusing to address his remark, drawing them into an argument neither of them would win, she said, "Aidan left this morning for—"

"Deserted you, huh?"

"He went to get help, supplies."

"I'm surprised you didn't go with him." Before she could respond with a furious answer, he added, "Oh, wait, you wouldn't abandon me, though, would you? You still don't have the answers you seek."

"May I remind you that you're the one who came after me? I had no idea you were even alive."

"Yeah. Right."

Sabrina stood up and stretched. Damned if she would sit and tend him like some kind of hapless victim while he hurled insults.

"Believe what you want. It's obvious you will anyway. I need some privacy." Without waiting for what she was sure would be another hurtful or sarcastic remark, she walked away.

He told himself the hurt in her eyes was fake. Sabrina was an excellent liar—he had trained her himself. Even so, every time she flinched or those green eyes darkened with hurt, something like guilt sliced through him.

He lifted his head, realized he couldn't and eased it back to the ground. Hell, he hadn't felt this weak since he'd been in prison. Jaw clenched tight, he tried again. Sweating, nausea roiling in his stomach, he managed to sit up on the third try. Damn. His head whirled like somebody had loosened his eyeballs. He could barely focus.

Closing his eyes, he concentrated on breathing, in, then out. Slow and easy. Long minutes later, he opened his eyes. Still felt like shit, but at least he could think more clearly and see halfway straight.

He remembered almost nothing of the last two days, other than voices from time to time, Sabrina's and he supposed Thorne's. Something else he remembered were soft hands that soothed his brow and, though he was sure he dreamed it, soft lips that kissed his forehead, his mouth. Yeah, he'd definitely been hallucinating.

But what he did remember—what he knew to be factual—was the death of the bastard who'd tortured him for months. The one man who could have told him who'd hired him. Why hadn't he tried to taunt the man and get answers? Stupidly, he had thought he had more time. Beat the asshole to a pulp—getting some of his own back—and then he'd make him talk. He hadn't counted on Sabrina stepping in and taking the man down.

She had said she did it to save his life. He supposed there was some validity to that. Meat-Face had been holding a knife in his giant paw of a hand. Declan hadn't seen it, and the man would have no doubt used it. And why hadn't he seen it? Because he'd been distracted by something in the bushes. Aidan Thorne, Sabrina's partner. Had they set that up to make it appear as if Sabrina was saving Declan's life while also getting rid of the only man who could give him answers? Just how damn convenient was that?

He pressed his fingers to his forehead, where an anvil-pounding pain threatened to rip his brain apart. Hell, he wasn't thinking straight. Had he had a rational, coherent thought since his capture? Wearily, he admitted that he didn't know.

The snap of a twig brought his head up. Sabrina was coming toward him, holding the bottom of her T-shirt out. He saw that she had gathered a variety of exotic-looking fruits. "Okay, I've got some kind of berries, I'm fairly sure they're edible. Here're a couple of banana-looking things. And I'm almost positive this is some kind of grape."

Everything within Declan froze. For the first time since his return, he looked at Sabrina without suspicion and hate coloring his perception. Her brilliant auburn hair hung in a long braid down her back, her face, though naturally creamy, looked almost translucent, as if she were exhausted. Heavy shadows circled her eyes. Her generous mouth had lines on each side of it, as if she hadn't smiled for years. Her camouflage pants were covered in mud and muck, and her tan, sleeveless T-shirt was spotted with his blood.

He remembered so much in those long seconds of staring. Her laughter, delightful sense of humor, the implacable belief she'd had in him. He remembered her heart, her soul, and her humanity. Her love.

Oh God.

And he remembered other, more recent things. Things he had denied before. Soft, cool hands working to lower his fever, a voice, thick with tears, telling him he was going to be all right. A warm, womanly body lying beside him, kissing his cheek, whispering soothing words of love. Why would she do those things when—

In that moment, he saw her clearly, the woman he had loved and lost. And he knew the truth.

"You really had nothing to do with it, did you?"

She jerked as if he'd slapped her. The gleaming relief in her eyes couldn't be mistaken. He heard her swallow hard and then in a shaky voice, she said, "No, Declan. I swear on my life, I didn't."

He wanted to be angry all over again. Wanted to howl at the injustice of what had been done to him. To them. Instead, he pushed all of that aside and said, "I'm so damn sorry, Sabrina."

She wanted to throw herself into his arms. For the first time since learning he was alive, there was no distrust or hatred in his eyes. What she did see stopped her cold and tore her heart to shreds. Yes, there was remorse and sadness, bitterness at what had been done to them. The one thing she didn't see, and needed with unrivaled desperation, was love. Not even affection or even the slightest degree of warmth was revealed in his expression.

She told herself the lack of hatred was a start. He'd been through too much to expect a complete reversal. But deep within him was the core of Declan Steele—the man who had loved her, adored her. Dammit, that love couldn't be destroyed. No matter what he'd been through, those feelings still existed. She knew they did.

With a tentative smile, she dropped the food she'd collected onto her backpack. "How are you feeling?"

"Like a fool."

"Declan, don't. What happened to you wasn't your fault." She handed him the last bottle of water. "Take a few swigs and eat something. Aidan probably won't be back until tomorrow."

He took several sips and then handed it back to her. "That's enough for now." Reaching forward gingerly, he snagged one of the bananas and peeled it.

"Can you talk about it yet or are you still processing?"

"There's not much to say."

Not much to say? Like hell. "Why were you taken? What did they want from you? Who do you think is responsible?"

"Just because I no longer believe you were involved doesn't mean I'm going to share those things with you."

"You know it wasn't just you they hurt, Declan Steele."

The expressions of contrition, remorse were gone. In their place was the flat, hard look of an EDJE agent. One who would show no weakness or mercy. When they'd worked ops together, she'd seen that look many times and had been reassured by it. But that's because it had never been directed toward her.

"You still don't trust me, do you?"

"Trust isn't the issue. This is an Agency matter. One I'll have to handle on my own."

"You can't expect me to just sit back like some kind of—"

"You're not even involved in this kind of life anymore. You're—"

"I know what the hell I am, Declan. I also know my life was turned upside down. I thought I lost you." She didn't add what she knew in her heart—that in a way, she had still lost him. "Don't for a minute think you're going to do this on your own. We—"

"There is no we. Get that out of your head."

Knocking some sense into his stubborn head was tempting, but since she'd just spent two days trying to make him better, it would have been self-defeating. She was good at blocking unpleasant things out to get the job done. This would be one more. She would ignore his ridiculous statement and do what needed to be done.

"Eat what you can of the fruit. It's good for you."

He eyed her warily but didn't argue. Exhaustion and pain shadowed his eyes, and the mouth she loved so much drooped with fatigue. There would be plenty of time for him to argue with her when he was feeling better.

She was relieved to see him consume the banana and some berries. After he drank more water, she said softly, "You're safe here, Declan. Get some sleep."

Surprising them both—and showing her just how unwell he was—he lay down again and in seconds was asleep.

As he slept, Sabrina made her plans. Someone had sold them out. There was no other answer for it. Delving into the Agency's secrets would be difficult, if not impossible. But perhaps an enterprising and talented LCR Elite operative who also happened to be a research expert might be able to do just that?

She might not be in the game any longer, as Declan had said, but she had an offer of assistance from one of the savviest leaders of undercover operations in the business. One she would gladly accept.

CHAPTER EIGHTEEN

Virginia

"When are you going to tell me where we're going?" Declan asked.

A small smile tilted at her mouth, her eyes brimming with excitement, Sabrina shook her head. "Stop badgering me. I'll tell you when we get there. Sit back, relax, and enjoy the scenery."

Scenery? Well, he supposed there was a certain kind of peacefulness to the landscape. For almost an hour, they'd been driving toward an unknown destination. Unknown to him, but Sabrina knew exactly where she was going.

They'd returned to Virginia five days ago. LCR and, yes, Aidan Thorne had come through. Rescue had occurred just a day after Thorne had left them.

Since Declan had refused to go to the hospital, he'd been treated at the LCR clinic and then released. Had been told to rest, recuperate. He had done what he'd been ordered to do. Surprising Sabrina and himself, he had slept, taken his meds, and eaten nutritious food.

Sabrina had told him that the two men they'd rescued were being treated in a private hospital in Germany and were expected to survive. She'd said that Barry Tyndall had been easy enough to identify, but the other man was still unconscious and so far had no name.

Even though he hadn't gotten the information he needed, Declan felt a sense of accomplishment in being able to assist in the rescues.

He'd woken this morning, all set to start unraveling the mystery of his abductors. Even though he was still weaker than he liked, spending another day in bed or hobbling around the apartment wasn't something he'd been willing to do. He had to have answers.

Instead of arguing with him when he'd told Sabrina, she had just told him to grab his clothes and toiletries and come with her. Stupid, but at first he'd been hurt, figuring she was throwing him out of the apartment. Not that he would have blamed her. He'd been nothing but an ass to her since his return.

The minute they'd gotten into her car and pulled out of the parking lot, she'd thrown him an inscrutable look and said, "I've been dying to show you this."

When he'd asked what, she shrugged and said it was a surprise.

So here he was, enjoying the rural scenery of northern Virginia without any idea where he was headed. Allowing this to happen was a major breakthrough for him. For a man who had to be in control at all times, giving someone else this much power wasn't easy. But he owed her that trust. Hell, he owed her a lot more than that.

"Okay, almost there."

Declan sat up in his seat. They were on a winding, two-lane road that desperately needed some work. Sabrina maneuvered around potholes with the ease of familiarity. She'd obviously been down this road many times before.

"Close your eyes."

"You're kidding, right?"

"Nope. I want you to see it all at once."

Hell, when she gave him that sweet, pleading look, Declan knew without a doubt he'd do almost anything for her.

Closing his eyes obediently, he heard her curse slightly as she made a sharp turn.

"Sorry. That's a new pothole I didn't know about."

Seconds later, the car stopped moving, and she said in a breathless, excited voice, "Okay. You can look."

His eyes opened, and all he could do was stare. "What the hell is it?"

Laughter bubbled from her, a sound he hadn't heard in forever. "Isn't it gorgeously awful? Hideously beautiful?"

Without comment, he opened the car door and got out, his eyes never leaving the giant structure in front of him.

She came to stand beside him and gazed adoringly up at one of the ugliest monstrosities he'd ever seen. "I think they started off with a Victorian house, decided they'd go all castle-like, changed their minds in the middle of the renovation and chose a farmhouse instead. I just call it home."

He tore his eyes away to look at her. "You live here?"

"Yes. What do you think?"

What did he think? He thought she was crazy. Ridiculously insane. Possibly blind. But he could see by the gleam in her eyes that she loved it. No matter how ugly this thing was, she had fallen in love with it and was calling it home.

Not wanting to hurt her feelings, he chose a diplomatic response. "It's certainly unique."

More laughter erupted. "I know it's awful, but once I'm through with it, it will be spectacular."

No, it would still be ugly. They'd have to tear down two-thirds of it before it could even resemble attractive. She was probably right about what the builders had done. One part of the house was artistically Victorian, with all the angles and charm from that era. The addition of the rock turrets and tower might have actually worked, but when the wraparound porch, tin roof and the rooster weathervane were added, it had become something else.

"Come on. Let me show you around." She held out her hand.

The moment Declan put his hand in hers, she knew everything would be okay. She had worried that bringing him here would make him uncomfortable. The last thing she wanted to do was make him feel like he was being forced to live here. She felt as though she'd been walking on eggshells around him since their return. Since he knew she hadn't betrayed him, she worried that he'd just up and say he was going off on his own.

Knowing she was living on borrowed time, she'd spent all day yesterday preparing a place for him to work. She wasn't going to give him an opportunity to disappear again. If he had what he needed to get the job done, and if he trusted her, then there was no reason he couldn't do that work from her home.

His remarks about the house didn't bother her in the least. No, the house would never grace the cover of a magazine, but that was okay with her. It had character and was definitely one of a kind. It was perfect to her.

Still holding hands, they stepped up on the wood porch, and she unlocked the door. As soon as it swung open, she let his hand go and said, "After you."

The moment he stepped inside, her tense muscles relaxed. Declan was here, in their home. The only thing stopping her from dancing a little jig was the worry that he'd think she was crazy.

Since she'd purchased a house that no one in their right mind would want, he probably already thought that anyway.

"Foyer is nice."

"Thanks." She'd spent a full day sanding the floor before she'd decided that she'd rather spend her time on other endeavors. "I had some professionals come in. They had it sanded and stained within a day.

"I'm taking it a little at a time. There are twelve rooms, plus a giant attic. I've only managed to finish a few rooms."

"When did you buy the place? And, more importantly, why did you buy it? You never wanted a house before."

"I bought it about six months after you... After I thought you died."

Still feeling like a fool for believing his obvious lie, she lifted her shoulder in an offhand shrug. "When you told me you were leaving the Agency and wanted to get a house, I started looking at real estate. When you came back, I wanted to have a list of places we could look at together. Of course, the houses I was looking at were in France, since that's where I was based at the time."

"And when I didn't come back?"

"I realized I still wanted a house. Guess I'd caught the bug. So when McCall moved the main LCR office to Virginia, I started looking around here." She turned her face away from those too-piercing blue eyes. "Somehow concentrating on it, thinking you had wanted the house, made me feel closer to you."

He was silent for a long time. She knew he still felt bad about lying to her. She didn't want to get into that. She understood his reasons and had forgiven the deception.

Instead of apologizing to her again, he said, "Show me around."

She blew out a silent, relieved sigh. "Delighted to."

Declan couldn't believe she had done this. And all because he'd told her he wanted a house.

He followed along behind her as she showed him room after room, most of them badly needing work. Hideous wallpaper and migraine-inducing colors covered the walls. Though all the floors were hardwood, they needed sanding and staining. Some of them needed to be replaced.

The finished rooms included a refurbished kitchen with sparkling new appliances, a master bedroom that had both masculine and feminine touches, as if it belonged to a married couple, and a remodeled bathroom that included a giant antique claw-foot bathtub.

With each room, whether finished or not, she exuded enthusiasm and her special brand of humor. When she stopped at a door at the back of the house on the first floor, her demeanor changed. He detected a hint of both nervousness and excitement. Giving him a small, enigmatic smile, she pushed the door open.

Declan took one step inside and stopped, his breath catching in his chest. It was most decidedly a room designed and decorated for a man. Not just any man. She had created the room for him.

One entire wall was floor-to-ceiling bookshelves filled with his books. Even without walking closer to look at the spines, he recognized his first editions, along with the poetry, thrillers, and history books he'd collected over the years.

On the other side of the room was a giant fireplace. He recognized the reading chair and lamp he'd had in his apartment. Beside the chair was a small table that held his reading glasses, a bottle of his favorite brandy and a book. He drew closer. Hell, that was the book he'd been reading the day before he'd been taken.

His chest so tight he could barely breathe, he took in the rest of the room. A dark brown leather sofa, a chess table holding his chessboard already set up to play, the stereo system he'd spent a fortune on, with the old albums he'd collected through the years.

He was about to speak, ask her why she'd done all this, when he caught a glimpse of a photo and froze. Speechless, he walked slowly to a small alcove in a far corner. It was filled with photographs. Not of him and Sabrina, but of his family. His mother, father and sister. The photos showed a family who loved each other. A mother who adored her husband and children. A father who was proud of his family and fiercely devoted to them. And two happy, well-adjusted kids who had known from the moment of birth that they were loved.

"Where did you—" His voice was so thick and garbled with emotion he had to stop.

"Remember those old videos you had of your family? I had still shots made of some of them."

She couldn't have done all of this since he'd been back. Not only would she not have had time, there was a faint mustiness in the air, as if the room had been closed off for a while.

The room had been decorated by a wife for her husband, by a woman for her man. By the beautiful, warm-hearted, courageous woman in front of him. "Why didn't you show me this before? This would have proven your innocence."

"I wanted you to believe me without physical proof, Declan." She lifted one shoulder in a small shrug. "I guess I wanted you to trust my word."

"Come here."

She stood in front of him, and the heart that he swore no longer existed swelled beyond his ability to accommodate it in his chest. Emotions he hadn't allowed himself to have flooded through him like a rushing river.

"Thank you, Sabrina." Bending his head, he pressed a kiss to both of her creamy cheeks, her forehead and then a tender one to her soft lips.

As though she'd been holding her breath for a long time, she blew out a gusty sigh and gave him a brilliant smile. "You're welcome."

He wanted to say something else. Give her something more. He couldn't.

She drew away from him and said, "That's not all, though. Follow me."

She crossed the room to the bookcase and pulled out a book. Before he could ask her what she was doing, he heard the squeak of a hinge. He whirled around. The wall behind him had moved, and a door stood open.

"It's a hidden room. I never really knew what to do with it, but I—" She shrugged and said, "Take a look."

Throwing her an incredulous smile, he went into the secret room and stopped, once again stunned.

She spoke from behind him. "I came here yesterday and set this up. If you need more equipment, I can get it."

He could only shake his head in wonder. The room, though small, held everything he would need to work his investigation. One wall had a board for writing or hanging photos. The opposite wall held a world map. There was a desk in the middle with a new computer.

"I know it's not much, but we can add whatever you need."

"It's perfect." He glanced over his shoulder. "You're perfect."

Silky brows arched, her full mouth curved in a delightful smile. "I'd better check your temperature…make sure that fever isn't back and giving you delusions."

"Seriously." His eyes roamed the area again. "Thank you."

Her smile so bright it hurt his eyes, she whispered, "You're welcome."

Days later, Declan stood before the wall charts he had created and cursed in frustration. He'd listed all operations he'd handled since his first with EDJE. Organizations and terrorist cells he'd had a hand in destroying. Names of all men and women he'd been responsible for killing were listed, as well as all known family members of those people. Arrows shot, swirled, arched, pointed at connections. And still he had no real clue.

He got to his feet and hobbled back and forth in the small room. He'd been in this space for three days, and other than creating lists, he'd done jack shit.

He had seen little of Sabrina. Once she had shown him the house, the rooms she'd prepared for him, including a bedroom she'd obviously rushed to get ready for him, she had left him on his own.

He had treated her terribly. He felt shame for the things he'd said, what he had done. And for allowing himself to be brainwashed. They had not only almost killed him, but they had destroyed his marriage, had hurt his wife. He had a lot of reasons to make these people pay, and he intended to collect each and every debt.

A knock on the door, and Sabrina walked in. "Wow, you've been busy."

He looked up at the wall again. "Suspect list is bigger than I thought it would be. Seems like most of the creeps I've put down had plenty of family and friends."

She came and stood beside him. He told himself the fresh fragrance of apples would make anyone's mouth water. Just because it happened to be coming from the alluring woman he was still married to had no bearing. Even he wasn't a good enough liar to believe that.

She reached up and pulled down a photo of a short, thin, bald man with a hooknose and beady eyes. "You can eliminate this guy's family."

"Hans Gerlach? Why?"

"His widow gathered the entire family together for a reunion in their vacation home in Switzerland. Once everyone arrived, she set off a bomb. Blew them all to hell."

"When?"

"About eight months after you disappeared."

Declan couldn't say he was surprised. "Hans always claimed his wife was the meaner of the two. Guess he was right." He threw out a hand. "You see anyone else that needs to be eliminated?"

She didn't answer right away, taking the time to study each one, along with the notes he'd scribbled beside each photo. "I don't know this one." She nodded toward one of the men. "Must've been before my time."

"Yeah. I hesitated putting that up there. I took Joseph Bosch out about a year after I joined the Agency. He was one of my first kills. Messy job. I should've been killed, too. He had a wife and a couple of kids. Wife swore she knew nothing about his activities. I believed her, but who the hell knows anymore?"

"Doubting yourself isn't going to help. Whoever did this fooled more than just you."

"Maybe…still pisses me off."

She touched another photo. "Haven't thought about this asshole in a while."

"Gerald Ronan," Declan muttered. Just the thought of the creep brought rage. "If there was one kill I could go back and relive, he's the one."

"Reports are that his son, Darius, is even meaner."

"I've barely gotten beyond making these lists. What's Gerald's little boy been up to?"

Her hand touched his arm with a gentle caress. "Dinner's ready. Come eat, and we'll talk about it."

Sabrina sat quietly, waiting for Declan to finish his first plate. His color was much better and his movements less stiff. He was well on his way to mending. And seeing him load up his plate with the colorful stir-fry made her breathe even easier. His appetite had returned.

And because she wanted him to regain his health, she forced herself to wait until he'd eaten at least one full plate of food. She picked at her own small helping. Even though she was sure of her course of action, it didn't mean she looked forward to the coming confrontation. The man could teach stubborn to a mule. His personality might have changed in many ways, but his stubbornness seemed to have survived intact.

The clanging of his fork hitting his empty plate was her signal. Before she could speak, he said, "Okay. I'm finished with my requisite one plate. You ready to talk?"

"What do you mean?"

"Every time we have a meal together, you're completely silent until I finish at least one serving."

She shrugged. No use denying what was true. "So? I just want you to get better."

"And I appreciate it, Sabrina, but I'm not your responsibility."

She wasn't even going to respond to that, because it would start an argument neither of them would win. Best to stick to the mission—one that, for the first time in a long time, they were both involved in, whether he wanted to admit that or not.

"Okay. Back to Darius Ronan. He's got a sizable following. His father's legacy left him with a lot of lost followers. They eagerly joined with him. And he's collected quite a few on his own."

"And their cause? Is it the same as Gerald's? Take out as many innocents as possible just because they can?"

"Hard to say what his agenda is. He changes it frequently. From what I can tell, money is his motivator. He's made a boatload in the last few years."

"He takes contracts?"

"Oh yeah. Whatever pays him the big bucks."

"His father was scum, but at least he had some kind of belief system."

"From what I can tell, the only thing Darius Ronan believes in is money."

He nodded his thanks. "I appreciate you telling me this. Having your expertise and knowledge will make my job easier."

"I'm glad you feel that way, because there's someone else I'd like for you to work with, too."

"Who?"

"Hear me out before you make a decision."

"I—"

"You owe me that, Declan."

The dark flicker of regret told her she'd scored a point. Didn't mean she was proud of it, but she had to get through to him. If using his guilt worked, then that's what she'd damn well do.

"You're right."

She started with facts. "First of all, you didn't have to help with Tyndall's rescue. You could have gone to the prison on your own, and you didn't need LCR to do that. You have thousands of dollars and a dozen or more passports stashed throughout the world—that includes the US. You could have found a way to access those funds and been on your way. But you didn't. You assisted because, despite what was done to you and how you say you've changed, there's still that core of decency inside you. You wanted to help.

"However, other than funds and fake IDs, you have almost no resources. You won't allow EDJE to help you because you trust no one there. You're totally alone. Even with help, finding the person who betrayed you will be almost impossible. Without help, you won't succeed."

A small twitch at his mouth gave her the idea he was trying not to smile. "Hope that wasn't intended to be a motivational speech because, frankly, you suck at it."

"You know I'm not one to pull punches. You need to hear the truth."

"And how do you presume to help with that?"

"I've got the resources to dig deep."

"Hacking into EDJE records? No way can you do that. I've got a lot of faith in your talents, Sabrina, but hacking isn't one of them."

"You're right, it's not. But I know one of the best hackers in the business."

"Who?"

"Angela Delvecchio."

"The LCR operative? No way will McCall allow his—"

"Noah has offered her services."

"Why would he do this?"

"Because I asked him to."

"This isn't a rescue."

"No, but it involves rescuers, and that's a concern for Noah. Hell, it should be a concern for everyone. You were taken and tortured for information. If Jackson hadn't gone off on his own to investigate, you'd still be there, maybe dead."

"How does that concern McCall?"

"Our lives were destroyed. They tortured you. You might not have given them anything to use, but that doesn't mean they won't do it again. They might get someone who can't survive what was done to you."

Before he could throw up a roadblock, she continued, "Look, all I'm asking is that you come with me to LCR and talk to Noah. Let him show you what they can do. After that, if you still think you'd do better on your own, I'll agree, and we'll stick to just the two of us."

"There isn't a 'just the two of us' any longer, Sabrina."

She wouldn't let his words hurt her. He could lie to himself all day long. There was still a "we" whether he was ready to admit it or not. "I'm not saying we're together as a married couple. I'm saying that I refuse to sit back and not try to find the people who did this. I was hurt, too, Declan."

"Look, I know it destroyed our marriage, but other than that—"

Okay, forget the "he can't hurt me with his words" mantra she'd been practicing for the last few days. He'd said it like their marriage had been a small, insignificant thing. It had been the most important thing in the world to her. Much more important than her job, though she loved her job. More important than her life, and she'd loved her life.

"I told you before, but I'm not sure you were listening. I got that text, asking me to meet you in Florence, at a little café. Fortunately, I got there late since it saved my life."

He nodded. "I remember. You said you saw the explosion. Saw a man who looked like me die."

"That's true. But if I'd gotten there a minute sooner, I would have died with him."

"Were you hurt?"

"It was nothing."

"Tell me," he growled.

"Cuts and bruises. Nothing serious." What was the point in detailing her injuries? Or revealing that she woke up screaming his name for months after?

"I didn't know."

"Thing is, even though you don't think our marriage was that big of a deal, I do owe them for making me think my husband was dead, as well as almost killing me. Surely that's worth something."

"I never said our marriage wasn't important."

Yes, he had, but arguing would do no good. He had spoken the truth as he saw it. She pushed away from the table and stood. "Will you talk to Noah?"

"I'll hear him out."

"Thank you." She turned to walk away.

"Sabrina?"

She stopped but kept her back to him. He didn't need to see the hurt in her eyes.

"Thanks for dinner."

Stupid, stupid Sabrina. How silly to think he had been going to apologize, tell her their marriage had meant something to him. She gave a short, curt nod and left the room before she threw the empty dishes at his stubborn head.

CHAPTER NINETEEN

LCR Headquarters

As Sabrina and Steele came into his office, Noah stood and gestured for them to sit at the conference table, where Angela had already set up for the meeting.

Even though LCR was his organization, using company resources on a non-rescue wasn't something Noah took lightly. However, he had made a commitment to his operatives to help them in times of need. Sabrina needed his help. And whether Steele wanted to admit it, he was one of LCR's now. He'd helped with a rescue and had saved Noah's life. He owed the man.

Noah waited until everyone was seated and then began. "As discussed, I've agreed to use LCR resources to assist in determining who abducted Steele. That assistance will involve new territory for us and will be dangerous. We'll be delving into a government agency that only a handful of people know about."

Noah took in both Sabrina's and Steele's gazes. "With the understanding that whatever information is revealed here never leaves this room, I'd like for each of you to share as much as you can about EDJE. Angela's skills are incomparable, but having as much information as possible to start with will help her get the job done much faster."

"First, I'd like to thank you, McCall and Angela, for agreeing to help," Steele said. "I didn't want to involve anyone else for a lot of reasons. One being that this is risky for both of you, personally and professionally. However, Sabrina convinced me that getting the information I need as soon as possible is better for all of us."

Few things surprised Noah anymore, but Steele's expression of thanks had. For the first time, he saw a glimmer of the man Declan Steele had been before his capture. Noah figured the woman at Steele's side was one of the biggest reasons he was coming back to life.

"As you probably know by now, EDJE stands for Eagle Defense Justice Enforcers. Albert Marks formed it about thirty years ago. Albert is former CIA. Had the brains and the balls to pull off the creation of one of the most secretive and elite agencies in the world. He, along with a couple of other former CIA agents, were the first operatives. The president and his most trusted advisers are the only ones aware of its existence. No one else.

"The Agency began as a small group of men and women dedicated to infiltrating organizations and terrorist cells to destroy them. They grew as the threats against our country increased. When I was taken, we had twenty-two field agents, eighteen support staff, five commanders and then Albert, who ran the Agency."

Picking up where Steele left off, Sabrina said, "Unless we were on a special assignment, we either worked alone or in pairs."

"And your main focus was on taking out the people who'd attacked the US?" Noah asked.

"About half of the Agency was dedicated to this task," Steele said. "The other half infiltrated to gather intel."

"And these people you worked with," Angela said, "they were fully vetted?"

"Yes."

"And you believe at least one of them sold you out?" Noah asked.

"At least one. Probably more."

"Declan's right," Sabrina said. "Setting everything up had to take considerable resources and involve numerous people. The bombing in Florence, with the guy who looked similar to Declan, took some doing to pull off. Fooling me into believing the man I saw die was my husband was a feat in itself.

"On top of that, Declan's DNA somehow got switched. Uncle Al...I mean, Albert Marks said the medical examiner swears that the DNA he tested was Declan's."

"So it's someone with plenty of money," Noah said.

"Yes," Steele agreed.

"You're worth that much?" Noah asked.

"Yes," Steele answered.

"Sabrina told me that you were working on uncovering a mole in the Agency. Do you think he or she is the reason you were taken?"

"Yes, I do. Albert and I were the only ones who knew my mission. I found bugs on my clothing and in my luggage. I knew I'd been found out." Steele shot Sabrina an odd, uncomfortable look. "I gave out false information, hoping to get them off my trail. It didn't work."

"And did you have any main suspects before you were taken?"

"No. The mole is good. He or she continued to successfully do their job, but was also working on the side to circumvent a few missions."

"That's a good start." Noah glanced over at Angela, "You're on."

Giving a quick smile to Noah, Angela clicked a couple of keys on her laptop and then turned to the large screen behind her. "As you can see, I've already hacked into the mainframe of the Agency. It's not giving me a lot yet, because everyone has an encrypted password. However, I think this will give us a start."

The screen revealed photos and short biographies of every EDJE employee since it began. The details for the most part were sketchy.

"Damn," Steele breathed. "How long have you been working on this?"

Angela shrugged. "A day…day and a half."

Steele shot a look at Noah. "She is good."

"Yes, she is."

Acknowledging the compliment with a nod, Angela then gave Steele a look that had Noah fighting a smile. It was an expression that Jake, her fiancé, called her "down and dirty look." Meaning, if her opponent didn't go down, it was going to get dirty.

"Okay, Mr. Steele, I've shown you mine," Angela said. "Now it's time for you to show me yours. I've gotten this far. Help me get deeper inside, and let's find out who did this to you and Sabrina."

"Very well. Ask me anything."

"Let's start with your abduction. When did it happen and how?"

"Three days after I found the bugs, I was taken."

A gasp came Sabrina. "I always assumed you were taken around the time of the explosion. Why did they wait almost two months before staging the explosion?"

"I don't know." He named his greatest fear. "Unless the plan was to kill you just to get you out of the way."

"And they almost succeeded," McCall said.

That, among other things, tore at Declan. Not only had he treated her like shit since his return, but she had been injured, almost killed, and he hadn't known about it.

"You were tortured for information," McCall said. "About your mission to find the mole inside the Agency or something else?"

"No, the mole was never mentioned. The information they wanted pertained to the Agency. They wanted everything I knew."

"When did they start using me against you?" Sabrina asked.

"Hard to say." He rubbed his forehead as that damn headache returned. Something that happened every time they discussed her involvement. "The months kind of ran together."

Thankfully changing directions, Angela asked, "How were you taken?"

"I got a text from Sabrina, asking to meet me in front of the church where we were married."

"No wonder you believed it was me," Sabrina said.

"Wait," Angela said. "Why would her request to meet at the church where you married be a red flag?"

Despite the seriousness of the discussion, Sabrina had to smile. Angela and Jake were getting married in a few months, and from the sound of it, the attendance would rival that of a royal family wedding.

"Declan and I were married alone. The minister and his wife were the only people present. No one even knew we were married for months."

Sabrina turned back to Declan. "So you showed up at the church, and they nabbed you."

"Yeah. A taxi dropped me off in front of the church. I think I made it to the first step, and they jumped me."

"Suspecting me right off seems strange. Did they—"

"No, I didn't think that right off." He rubbed his head again. "I remember fearing that someone had taken you, too."

Even though she wanted to pursue how they had persuaded him of her guilt, she didn't like seeing that pain in his eyes. "So what happened next?"

"I woke up in a cell, hanging from a chain. Stripped."

She swallowed hard. Maybe she didn't want to know this. She chastised herself for the thought. He had gone through hell. The very least she could do was listen to what happened and give him as much comfort as she could.

"They began with the usual fare. 'No one knows you're here. No one will rescue you. Tell us what we want, and we'll make your death easy.' Shit like that. I trained for that. Hell, I taught that. I wasn't worried. The beatings, whippings, sleep deprivation, starving, waterboarding. Not pleasant, but it was nothing I hadn't been preparing for most of my life."

"They must've been so angry that they couldn't break you."

"Yeah. They were. The brutality got worse. I figured I'd just die at some point. But my death would have worked against their plan. They got me better. Fed me, treated my wounds. Then they started over again."

"Did they ask anything that surprised you?"

"No, not really. With my clearance and knowledge, which they were more than aware of, they were specific in their requests. Names of agents, locations of missions, past, present and future. Locations of past agents."

"But why would these people want that from you? You were—" Seeing the guilt in his eyes, she cut off her question. "You weren't working ops and training anymore, were you, Declan?"

He expelled a long, harsh breath. "No. With Albert's retirement, I was taking over the reins of the entire organization. I knew what Albert knew…more, actually. I was actively involved in assignments. Albert was phasing himself out of the day-to-day details. Every mission came through me for review or approval."

"So you had all the intel to not only destroy all missions, but to destroy the Agency as well."

Noah had asked the question, and Sabrina knew he had done it to give her a chance to recover. She'd felt the blood drain from her face, and there'd been a tremor in her voice. Hard to hide your feelings when you've been kicked in the stomach by the mule of truth. Declan had kept this from her. Why?

"Yes," Declan was saying. "They knew about my new position. There's no way they would've asked those questions if they'd thought I was still just an agent. The stuff I have in my head could bring in enough money to buy a small country."

"And did you give them anything?"

Noah had asked the question. It needed to be asked, but it would be a sore point. Declan's eyes flashed hot and then went back to that emotionless blandness that infuriated her.

"No, I told them nothing."

"They're not finished with you," Noah said.

"I know that. But if I can find another of the bastards who tortured me, I can make them talk."

Before she could apologize again for killing the man who might have been able to give them that information, Declan said, "You saved my life, Sabrina. I was too stubborn to acknowledge it before."

She managed a stiff nod.

"So, if you don't mind me summing up, Steele, your mole caught on to your op, had you abducted to gain information from you to sell. If he had just wanted you eliminated, sounds like that would have been easy enough to do."

"True enough."

"The way I see it," Noah went on, "you've got three choices. Accept what happened to you and walk away, use what resources we can provide to find your mole, or go it alone. Your choice."

"Walking away isn't an option. They won't stop until they get what they want."

"I agree." Noah pushed his chair back and stood. "I'll leave you to mull over your other options." He turned to Sabrina. "I need to speak with you."

Sabrina followed her boss, well aware that Declan stared after her.

Apparently deeming they were far enough away that they wouldn't be overheard, Noah stopped in the middle of the reception area. "This may not be a good time for you, but I need you on a job. Is your mind clear enough to handle it?"

"Yes. I can be worried and upset on an op just as well as I can be here."

"I don't want you distracted."

"I can do the job. Don't worry."

"Good. Be back here at ten o'clock tomorrow morning for a briefing. Have your go-bag ready. You'll leave right after."

Sabrina returned to the conference room. Angela was packing up her laptop and paper. Declan was standing at the window looking out. Apparently, the meeting was over. Had he made a decision?

He turned as if he'd heard her ask the question. "Looks like Angela and I will be working together."

Relief flooded through her. At least he wasn't going to try to do this on his own. Anxiety quickly followed. His captors had almost destroyed him the first time. If they caught him again, they wouldn't take any chances—they would kill him.

After what she'd just learned, would her fears mean anything to him? Probably not. "I'm glad. You ready to head back?"

He followed her out the door in silence. Knowing Declan, he was feeling powerless. A man who had relied only on himself for so many years would find it difficult to accept help from others.

The instant they were in the car, Declan broke the silence. "I'm sorry, Sabrina. I should have told you I was taking over for Albert."

"Yes, you should have. I've been trying to figure out why you didn't and can come up with only two explanations. Neither one of them makes me happy."

Instead of offering her an explanation, he asked, "Why do you think I didn't?"

Not answering immediately, she drove out of the parking lot and pulled out onto the road.

"Sabrina?"

Her tone cool and flat, she said, "You either didn't trust me or I wasn't important enough for you to share that kind of information with me."

"That's bullshit, and you know it." Declan's voice, usually even-keeled and smooth, held a seething anger. "It had nothing to do with trust and everything to do with trying to protect you."

"Protect me how? By lying to me?"

"It wasn't a lie. Yes, I was changing jobs, but I still did a lot of the same things, too." He turned to look out the window. It was going on dusk, and things were getting dark and obscured. Much like her perfect marriage had been.

His voice low and reflective, he asked, "Do you know what it did to me, seeing you suffer from what we put you through?"

"What do you mean?"

"I could literally see life draining from you with every kill. After you left the Agency, I swore I would do everything in my power not to involve you in any of that shit again."

She held on to her temper, barely. "I had a right to know what kind of job my husband was doing."

"You're right, you did. I screwed up. But I promise on my life, it had nothing to do with not trusting you. And your remark about you not being important enough pisses me off too much to even comment on it. I did what I thought was right to protect you. I was wrong. I'm sorry."

The wind now completely taken from her sails, Sabrina found herself flailing to hold on to her anger. She didn't hold grudges, finding them useless and draining. She either believed him or not.

"I understand why you did it, Declan. Don't do it again."

"I won't." He turned his attention back to the side mirror he'd been eyeing since they'd gotten in the car.

"No one's following us."

"Just making sure." He shot her a searching glance. "The house. It's hidden…right? No one knows about it?"

"Of course not. A woman named Eloise Sweetwater from Kansas City, Kansas, owns it. There's not a soul who can trace it back to me."

"We're going to keep it that way. I want you safe."

"I want us both safe, Declan. The bastards are after you, not me."

"And they know my one weakness. If they found you, they'd use you against me."

For long seconds, there was silence. Was she still a weakness to him? Almost afraid to ponder the question, she asked the one thing that had been pounding in her brain. "How did they manage to convince you that I betrayed you?"

"I don't have an answer for that. Stupid, I know. All I can remember is waking up one day and being one hundred percent certain that you had sold me out."

The pain in his eyes, both from real pain and for believing a lie, tore into her.

The lights from the house were a warm, welcoming sight. Sabrina drove into the garage. She tilted her head to the Jeep Laredo she'd parked beside. "Forgot to mention that you're welcome to use that. Keys are on a hook in the laundry room."

"Thanks. Haven't had a chance to go car shopping yet."

She knew he was trying to make a slight joke. Unfortunately smiling would have taken too much effort.

The instant they were inside, she said, "There're some leftovers in the fridge if you want them. I've got some packing to do, so I'll say good night."

"You're going on a mission?"

"Yeah. Briefing in the morning. I'll leave right after."

"Where?"

She tried not to resent his questions. It might be a natural thing to ask, but it rankled. How many times had she asked the same questions? His answers had been either vague or he had just refused outright. She had tried to understand. And based upon his earlier explanation, she knew he'd done it out of concern for her. Still, it galled that he was asking.

"I don't know yet." At least that much was true.

"You said that you're in a different kind of job than when you first started with LCR."

"Yes. Noah created LCR Elite right after you disappeared."

"What's the difference from the other LCR ops?"

"High-value targets. Volatile locations. We go places most people have been told to get out of."

"Just for the US?"

"No. Since we don't work for any government, several countries have called on us. There's an edgier element to Elite missions that aren't always part of the regular LCR jobs." She smiled and added, "Either way, it's good because I get to save lives."

"You saved lives at EDJE. Saved a lot more than you took."

"I know I did." She headed to the stairs. "I'm glad you agreed to work with Angela. She's the best researcher I know. Hopefully, Jake will offer his expertise, too. He's a great strategist. He was once a cop and is former military."

"You don't want to be in on it? Like you said, they destroyed our marriage. You got injured in the blast. I'm surprised you don't want to help bring them down, too."

She looked at him over her shoulder. For the first time, she saw a hint of hurt in his expression. He wanted her to help, but instead of asking outright, he was going to try to guilt her into helping.

"I have faith that the three of you will figure it out. When I get back, you can catch me up."

She put her foot on the first step. If she stayed, she'd brush that dark strand of hair off his forehead and try to bring light back into his eyes. He didn't want that. He didn't want her.

"I'm sure McCall would understand."

She whirled around, suddenly irritated. "Yes, he would understand, but I have a job to do, Declan. If you don't understand that—"

"I understand plenty. I had a job to do, too, when I told you I was leaving the Agency. But you're still pissed that I lied to you."

"I can't believe you're bringing that up again. I told you I forgave you for that."

"I had no choice."

She huffed out an exasperated breath. "Who are you trying to convince? Me or yourself?"

"I should have found a way to tell you the truth."

Fine. He wanted to wallow in his guilt, who was she to deprive him of it? "Yes, you should have. I was your wife. I deserved the truth."

"You're still my wife."

Seriously? She could only gawk at him. How many times had he made it clear he didn't want to be married to her anymore? Even after acknowledging she was innocent, he still maintained that they weren't married. "No, I'm not."

Declan saw red. Even as he stalked toward her, a little voice in the back of his mind told him to stop, that this was a mistake. He had nothing to give her anymore, and what he wanted wouldn't be good for either of them. He ignored the warning and went for what his body said it needed. Jerking her to him, he slammed his mouth over hers. She fought him at first. Not hard. Sabrina was trained well enough to get away from him, and do some serious injury while she was at it. But he could feel the resistance in her body. He murmured against her lips, "Don't fight me, Little Fox."

With a whimper of need, she pressed her body deep into his. At her acquiescence, Declan gentled his touch. How many times had he dreamed of this? Before the day he'd woken believing she had betrayed him, he had spent much of his waking hours remembering Sabrina, their connection. And even when he believed she had sold him out, there had been many times he had allowed himself the weakness of forgetting her perfidy so he could relive the moments in her arms. Those memories had kept him human.

They ate at each other's lips as their hands shoved and ripped at clothing. The instant he felt the soft silkiness of her skin, he caught his breath and slowed down to savor. She felt even more magnificent than he remembered.

His hands and his mouth trailed kisses from her neck and downward. Sabrina was equally as busy. When he felt her hands touch and then hesitate on the scars on his back, he whispered, "Please."

The thought of her not wanting to touch him because of how he looked did something to him. Instead, he heard a soft, "I just don't want to hurt you."

"They don't hurt anymore. I know they're ugly, but—"

"No. They're marks of your bravery. Only the people who did this to you can make them ugly."

As if to match her deeds to her words, she gently kissed the scars on his chest as she caressed the web of scars on his back. "My brave warrior."

Undone by her words, by the sheer beauty that was Sabrina, he lifted her into his arms. "Declan… Your arm and leg."

"The day I can't carry my wife to bed and ravish her is the day I don't want to see."

He went up the stairs, pushed open the door to the bedroom he'd been using, and dropped her on the bed. Yes, his healing injuries ached, but the rest of him felt too damn good to care. For the first time in forever, his entire body felt alive with fire and hope.

She lay before him, even lovelier than he remembered. Her body, always beautiful and sexy, glowed with good health. For an instant, the expression in her eyes matched his earlier concern. She was wondering if this was a mistake. "Don't think about anything but this moment, Sabrina. Okay?"

She nodded and opened her arms in welcome. He lay beside her and gathered her close, cherishing the feel of her body next to his. They held each other tightly. Finally, he pulled away from her and with an unhurried deliberateness that belied the arousal pounding through him, Declan began to make love to his wife.

Emotion clogged Sabrina's throat. Declan had always been passionate, occasionally rough when excitement reached its highest peak. She had thought that would be the case today. But now he was tender and giving. His lips trailing kisses down her body were both passionate and gentle. How many nights had she lain awake and fantasized about this? How many nights had she woken screaming his name, her body on fire for the only man who had ever been able to meet her desires, quench her thirst?

Thoughts disappeared as fire and heat took over. His mouth drew on her nipple, suckling and tasting. Sabrina panted, breathless and wanting. Her eyes closed as the delicious feel of him drawing on her caused the deep, familiar throbbing in her core. It felt too good, too wonderful. She couldn't take much more.

"Declan, please. I need you inside me now."

"That's where I need to be, too." Rolling her to her back, he hovered over her and growled. "Hold me in your hand and put me inside you."

Closing her hands around his hard, thick penis, she positioned him at her entrance. "Take me."

And he did. Thrusting deep, he pushed all the way into her. Even though there was a slight discomfort at his entry, she relished even that. He filled her completely. No one had ever been able to make her feel this way.

He held himself still inside her, allowing her to adjust, to ease and soften around him. "You okay?"

"Perfect."

"Ready?"

"Always."

He began to thrust, slow and steady. Sabrina wrapped her long legs around him and gloried in the ride. Every thought, every emotion, every feeling centered on the deepest part of her being, where she was possessed, taken. Her body felt as though it was flying, soaring. She wanted, needed nothing other than this delicious, wonderful need driving her. She felt her release coming and fought it. Not yet, not yet. She didn't want to let go. She couldn't. It felt too good to climb to those heights, to fly. But Declan, her wicked, beautiful lover, refused to let her hold back. His hand came between their bodies, and those devilish fingers flicked delicately, deliberately where they were joined. With a scream of sheer, incredible, carnal delight, she came hard.

Under the roaring in her head, she heard his muttered, "Let's see if we can go for another."

Giving her no time to recover, Declan pulled out, threw her legs over his shoulders and covered her sex in a hot, open-mouthed kiss. Sabrina zipped back to full arousal. Arching her body, offering herself freely, totally, she soared toward the heavens and then fell off a steep cliff into ecstasy.

And still he wanted more.

How could he have forgotten how delicious she tasted? Delicate and salty, musky and sweet, Sabrina throbbed around his tongue as he lashed at her, licking inside and out, and then nibbling lightly on the knot of nerves at the top of her sex.

She put her hands in his hair, and fearing she planned to push him away, he grabbed her hands and placed them on her knees, spreading her even more. "Stay just like that." He pressed a kiss to the inside of each thigh and said, "Don't move."

Her eyes, dark pools of green, were dazed with heat and arousal. "Declan, what are you doing?"

"Pleasuring both of us once more." She was open to him. Swollen, wet with arousal, with need. He lowered his head and openmouthed kissed her center again.

She arched and screamed his name.

"Not yet," he growled. Her entire body was shaking with need. He knew she wanted to let go, but he wanted to bring her back up slowly. He tongued her delicately, licking, enjoying himself. When he felt her body loosen, surrendering once more, he took her hips, held them still, and then began a hard thrust and retreat of his tongue. The soft tissue of her folds gave, moistening his way. When he felt the tension in her increase, he backed away.

"Declan, please. I can't wait much longer."

"Almost there," he murmured, and went back to licking her. Then, using his fingers, he penetrated her as he suckled her hard. She screamed hoarsely and came, her body arching into his mouth.

Giving her no time for recovery, he rose over her and buried himself as deep as he could go. The pull of her orgasm squeezing him like a fist, he pounded hard, relentlessly into her tight softness. Her eyes locked with his, and he felt the connection he never thought to have again. Never losing eye contact, he plunged, retreated, plunged again. His impending release zipped like an electrical charge up his spine. With a shout for his own surrender, Declan let go, emptying himself into her beauty.

Breath shuddered from Sabrina. Declan lay beside her, his own breath labored and deep. They were still and quiet for several long minutes, simply holding each other.

"It was even better than I remember." she whispered.

"You haven't been with anyone in a long time."

"Not since our last time together."

He raised himself on his elbow to frown down at her. "Why, Sabrina? You thought I was dead. Why didn't you move on?"

How could she explain that she'd intended to never let anyone touch her again? "Before you, sex was either painful or degrading. I knew whatever came after you would never be you."

"And Thorne?"

"He's my partner, my friend. Never my lover." She swallowed and opened her vulnerable heart. "Only you, Declan. Always, only you."

If she was waiting for a declaration of devotion, she knew it wasn't coming when he dropped his head back to his pillow and remained silent.

Disappointed but not surprised, she let a shaky breath shudder from her as she dealt with the blow. Yet she refused to give up, refused to believe he would let all of this go.

"Tell me this is a turning point for us, Declan. That you won't just up and disappear on me again."

Instead of answering, he drew her back into his arms and began loving her again. This time, he was all tenderness, as if giving her physical pleasure was all he had left.

Sabrina took everything he offered, knowing that someday soon this might be all she had again—memories. They might still have the physical chemistry to burn up the sheets, but without love, they wouldn't survive.

CHAPTER TWENTY

Declan woke to an empty bed. She was gone. Even though he hadn't heard her leave, he recognized the lack of life, the emptiness in the house.

Making love to her last night had been a mistake. He'd known that the moment he'd walked toward her with the intent to devour. But the instant he'd touched her, all those feelings and emotions came rushing to the forefront. How he had loved her.

Knowing it would do no good to continue to regret something that had already happened, he rolled out of bed and got dressed. He was meeting with Angela and Jake early this afternoon to go step by step through all of the Agency's employees. At least one of them, maybe more, had sold him out.

He grabbed the Jeep keys from the hook in the laundry room and then stopped in the kitchen for a slug of coffee before heading out the door. He found the note on the counter from Sabrina:

I hope to be home in about a week. If you need to get in touch with me, let Noah know. SS

The simple note clutched at his heart. Instead of giving him access to her, she'd made McCall their go-between. A deliberate move to keep the distance between them. Her signature said something else. It had been the way she'd signed her notes from the moment they married. She hadn't taken his name—that would have been too complicated with their clandestine lifestyle—but for him, she had always referred to herself as Sabrina Steele, or SS.

Something about the note snagged at his memory. His subconscious grasped for meaning, insight. He shook his head. Dammit, it had felt like an important thread and now it was gone. What the hell was it?

Shaking it off, hoping it would come back to him at some point, Declan headed out the door. He would meet with Angela and Jake at LCR as planned, but he had a detour he needed to make first. It was time for Declan Steele to announce his presence and return to the land of the living.

Caracas, Venezuela

Riley Ingram sat on the hard, tiled floor, her expression one of both dejection and fear. Shifting slightly, she tried to ease the numbness from her body. They'd been sitting here for what seemed like hours, waiting for "the boss" to arrive. When and if that happened, she'd have to move fast. She needed everything in good working order.

She'd certainly been in much more uncomfortable positions. Compared to the life she had escaped from, this was nothing. She'd take a numb butt or human stink over a luxurious prison any day. Despite that assertion, her nose did take exception to the two sweaty fellows by the door. They had the manners of swine. Between one guy's constant belches and the other one's unfortunate flatulence, her sense of smell might never be the same.

Without moving her head, she cut her eyes over at Sabrina. The scrunching of her fellow operative's nose said she was having the same thoughts. No wonder these creeps felt they had to steal women. No woman in her right mind would ever willingly be in the same room with them.

Getting kidnapped had been more difficult than anticipated. Two young, female tourists flashing obscene amounts of money while cluelessly shopping in a high-crime area should've been easy pickings. Instead, it had taken two days before she and Sabrina had attracted their target.

Once taken, though, things had worked out as planned. After being bound and gagged, they'd traveled in the back of a van for over an hour. During that hour, while acting suitably terrified, she and Sabrina had learned what they needed. These were the same men who had kidnapped the Dentons.

Andrew Denton was an American businessman living with his family in Caracas. Four days ago, his wife, three children, and their nanny hadn't returned from a shopping trip. Only hours after their disappearance, a ransom demand had been made. Venezuelan authorities had recommended paying the ransom.

Denton had contacted LCR with a request for assistance.

Though kidnapping for ransom had become almost too commonplace worldwide, the most well-known and organized group in Caracas was the Bracho family. Known for kidnapping and ransoming wealthy tourists, they had a reputation of returning the victims but not always in the best shape. Though Denton had indicated he would pay whatever was necessary, he had wanted LCR's assistance and expertise. Understandably, he didn't want his family injured in any way.

The mission was clear: recover Denton's family and protect them from harm.

Riley twisted her head slightly and took in the other captives in the room. Three children in one corner, two women in another. The Denton children, two girls and a boy, sat huddled together, quiet except for the occasional sniffle. The women in the corner were Marsha Denton, Andrew's wife, and the family's nanny, Cecile Poole. Marsha sat with her back to the wall and, despite the horrid bruise on her face and a puffy lip, maintained a cool arrogance. She had sneered more than once at the human pigs who had kidnapped her family, clearly showing them she would not be intimidated. Riley already liked her.

The nanny was a different story. In the hours since Riley and Sabrina had arrived, Cecile had been statue still. Riley got the feeling she saw everything. She had no emotion on her face, and Riley hadn't decided if that was a good thing or not. Could be she was in shock.

So far, other than a few shoves and some groping, the kidnappers had been surprisingly hands-off with her and Sabrina. Hopefully, they would remain that way, but if they didn't, both of them were more than capable of teaching the creeps some manners.

Sometimes, it amazed her that she was doing this kind of work. Having been born to do nothing other than look pretty and do what she was told, who would have thought she could actually be of use in this world? One thing her old life had trained her for was to show absolutely nothing of what was going on inside her. If the world had been able to see behind her facade, they'd have been shocked, appalled, and possibly entertained. She would take being able to make decisions for herself—choose her own clothes, food, friends, and who she married—over that kind of luxury any day.

Justin and Aidan were on their way. While everything had gone seamlessly with her and Sabrina's abduction, their backup had encountered a minor glitch. The two operatives had been trailing the van when the vehicle they'd been traveling in suddenly stalled and refused to restart. It had taken them almost two hours to find a replacement ride. During that time, she and Sabrina had arrived at the house. Their earbuds were well hidden and hadn't been detected by the kidnappers, so she and Sabrina had been treated to creative and colorful language as the guys worked to catch up to them.

When they arrived, the fun would begin. Hopefully, that would happen before "the boss" showed up. Even though it'd be nice to take down a few more of the creeps, LCR always put the victims first. They were here to rescue the Dentons. Catching the bad guys would always come second.

"We're finally here," Aidan growled. "Ingram, clear your throat if you're okay. Then, Sabrina, you sigh."

In response, Riley cleared her throat, catching the eye of one of the creeps in the corner. Uh oh.

A long, sorrowful sigh came from Sabrina, so loud that the guy whose attention Riley had gotten was distracted. She knew the other operative had done that on purpose.

"Heard you both loud and clear," Aidan said. "We're about—"

Another growl, this one from Justin. "Ah shit. You've got company. Black SUV is parking in front of the house. Three guys, one armed to the teeth. Other two look like they're headed to the Ritz for a tea party."

Justin's voice, even with an irritated edge, soothed Riley. Not that she would ever let him know that. After that one huge blowup their first year as partners, he rarely spoke to her unless it was regarding an op. But that was okay. As long as they could work together, he didn't have to "like" her. She could choke that feminine part of her that wanted a different kind of attention from him. He never needed to know the truth.

"Hmm. The two suits," Aidan mused. "Dressed damn nice for this kind of job.

"They're coming toward the house, front entrance. As soon as everyone's inside, we'll join the party," Aidan said. "Sabrina, if you get the chance, take down the guy with the gun. The other two might be armed, but looks like he's the muscle."

"Ingram, once Fox moves," Aidan continued, "gather all the hostages in one corner. Kelly and I will handle the other five."

She shot another quick glance at Sabrina, wondering what the supremely confident operative was thinking. If there was one woman she could have emulated, it would have been Sabrina Fox. As if certain of every decision, the self-possessed operative never appeared to worry or hesitate. Did she ever question herself? If so, it never showed.

Riley knew nothing about Sabrina's background. She must have had some incredible training before she'd arrived at LCR, since almost from the day she'd started, she had been on the most dangerous ops. It had taken Riley almost three years before Noah had put her on anything but the most-routine rescues. Admittedly, she had been untrained—probably the most untrained operative he'd ever taken on. But Noah being Noah hadn't hesitated. Once he'd heard her story, did research on her background, he had become her champion. He had promised that no one would ever find her.

Without Noah's support and Samara McCall's counseling, Riley knew without a doubt that she would have been dead.

Sabrina adjusted her body slightly...Riley recognized that she was preparing for battle. Taking an inner breath, Riley did the same thing. Hopefully within the next few minutes, these scumbags would be lying unconscious and hurting on the floor, and this family would be headed home.

That is, if nothing else went wrong.

Sabrina mentally braced herself for what was about to happen. The hostages were acting suitably terrified and cowed. As long as they stayed out of the way, no one should get hurt.

Even though she was prepared for the takedown, her mind kept veering to what had happened three nights ago in her apartment. She and Declan had made love. She still found that hard to comprehend. He'd gone out of his way to convince her that their marriage was over. But he had been insatiable. Tender, passionate... like the old Declan. As if nothing had changed between them.

No, one thing had definitely changed. The words hadn't been there. No declarations of love, no assurances of forever.

She'd left without waking him. Probably a cowardly act, but a part of her had feared that if he'd woken, he'd have been back to his coldness. After having spent a passionate night in his arms, she couldn't have taken that detached attitude of his again. When she returned would be soon enough to find out if anything had changed.

A movement to her left brought her eyes around. Finally, this thing was about to go down. Three men entered the house. Hmm. Aidan and Justin were right. Two of the men were snappy dressers—Brioni suits and ties, Berluti shoes, Patek wristwatches.

No. Wait. Alarms clanged in her head. Something was off. The Bracho family didn't get involved in the day-to-day activities of kidnapping. Their business model was to hire the muscle, then sit back and reap the rewards. So why would two men wearing six-thousand-dollar suits come along on a routine job?

The guys they'd been expecting should have been only a level or two above the creeps who had nabbed them. These guys were far above that. Why would the Brachos risk coming here for a routine kidnapping? Had they been wrong? Were the culprits not the Brachos after all?

She swung her gaze to Riley again. The operative had the same confusion on her face that Sabrina felt. This was just not right.

On the surface, the Rambo wannabe was the one to watch. Armed with an AK-47 strapped to his shoulder, a pistol in a side holster, and a long, evil-looking knife in a sheath attached to his left thigh, he was a big fellow, nasty sneer on his lips, cold eyes.

Still, the other two might be even more dangerous.

Sabrina let things settle in her mind. All they could do was play out the scenario as planned and adjust if necessary.

"Which one's the wife?" one of the suits asked.

"Dark-haired one in the corner."

The suited men went over to the corner where Marsha Denton and her companion sat. "Your husband better come through with the money or you'll all be killed."

Instead of looking terrified, Marsha stared up at him with disdain gleaming in her eyes. The look of hatred was fine and understandable, but hopefully the woman would stay put and allow her rescue to take place.

The other suited man turned to Riley, tugged at her hair. "I heard about you. You and your friend will make a nice profit for us on the open market."

So instead of trying to ransom them, she and Riley were to be sold? Another oddity. The Brachos kept their business dealings simple and streamlined. Kidnap and ransom only. Human trafficking was not in their evil bag of tricks.

Riley had some of the best acting skills Sabrina had seen—she was a chameleon. "Please, sir, I...I don't know why we're here, but if you let us go, we won't tell nobody. Will we, Dina?"

Sabrina shook her head. "We promise, mister. Just let us go."

Instead of answering, he yanked Riley up by her hair and slammed his mouth over hers.

Son of a bitch. Sabrina jumped up to go after the guy. A gun pressed against the back of her neck. "Move, and you get it."

Sabrina froze. Fury and hatred gathering into a storm, she watched helplessly as the man groped her fellow operative. Dammit, until she could get behind the bastard holding the gun on her, she could do nothing but watch. Where the hell were Aidan and Justin?

At that thought, it happened. The door burst open, and the two LCR operatives entered. Sabrina saw Justin's eyes target Riley, who was still enclosed within the man's arms. With a growl, he flew at the man, and as if they'd synchronized it, Riley slipped from the man's arms, rolled away.

Sabrina whirled, knocked the gun from the big man's hand, then threw a kick to his stomach. While he teetered on his feet, she followed it with an uppercut to his nose. He staggered back and reached for his other gun. Sabrina caught his arm, twisted quickly until she heard a satisfying crack. He yelled a vicious curse and punched her face. Ignoring the pain, she jabbed her elbow into his stomach and followed that up with a hard, targeted kick to his groin. Then, for good measure, as he teetered unsteadily on his feet, she sent a hard, fast fist into his groin again. His eyes rolled back into his head, and he went down.

She whirled to see who might need help and was pleased to see that both suits were lying flat-out on the floor, and the three smelly beasts who had abducted them were now huddled in their own corner, looking dazed and whipped. The children and women had found refuge with each other. Mrs. Denton had her arms wrapped around all three children. Her companion, Cecile Poole, stood outside the small group with an odd look on her face.

Sabrina checked again just to make sure that all threats had been contained. Pleased that it had gone down so well and her uneasiness had been unfounded, she turned back to the family, noting out of the corner of her eye that Riley reached over to place her hand on the nanny, probably to reassure her.

No one saw it coming. Cecile turned, a large knife gripped in her hand. With a roar of outrage, she slashed toward Riley, and then, her eyes wild and glazed with fury, she targeted Marsha Denton.

Aidan tackled the woman before she could reach Marsha, slamming her to the floor. Justin made a grab for Riley. Sabrina threw herself toward Cecile, who was fighting Aidan like a maniac.

What the hell?

Riley blinked up at Justin. He had the strangest expression on his face. He rarely looked at her with any kind of emotion anymore. That was for the best. Can't afford to get attached to what you can't have.

"Well, now," Justin said in the low, slow drawl that she loved. "That was a close call. Looks like you're going to need a little more training."

His tone was insulting as always, but his expression said something else. She frowned up at him, surprised at the effort it took to keep her eyes focused. "Justin?"

"Don't quit on me now, Riley. You hear me?"

Riley. He never called her by her first name.

She heard a growling curse and felt him pressing his hands against her stomach. An odd ache thudded in her gut. Not pain exactly. Just odd. Coldness seeped through her bones. She'd felt like this once before. When she had misbehaved and had been punished. But no, *he* wasn't anywhere around. *He* couldn't find her…couldn't hurt her anymore. So why this feeling of cold fear?

"Dammit, Riley. Did you hear me?"

That's right. Justin was here. He couldn't know how she felt about him. *Gotta keep stuff like that to yourself, Riley.* If he knew, he wouldn't want her as his partner. He couldn't find out.

So sleepy. Her eyes drooped closed.

"No, dammit, Riley, no. Keep your eyes open and on me. You hear me?"

Feeling loopy and a little silly, she raised her hand to caress his cheek, vaguely wondering why her fingers were wet. "Such a tyrant," she mumbled. "Can't figure out why I like you so much."

She heard him say her name again…this time even more urgently. With a sigh of longing, she carried the sound of his voice into the darkness.

CHAPTER
TWENTY-ONE

LCR Headquarters

Declan sat in the conference room with Angela and Jake. What the young hacker had been able to uncover in just a few days astounded him. He now had access to all old records going back to when the Agency first began. Much of it was encrypted, and Angela was working on breaking the code, but what he had seen so far was nothing short of phenomenal.

Angela had also uncovered the file of every EDJE employee from the lowest clerk to Albert Marks himself. So far he'd gone through a quarter of them and as of yet, not one red flag.

"Do you think anyone at EDJE would be willing to work with us?" Angela asked.

"Probably not. I can probably get a couple of guys who used to work there. They might be able to help."

"You trust them?" Mallory asked.

"Within limits."

"Why don't you contact one of them, meet him in a neutral place?"

He could do that. Maybe use the apartment that he and Sabrina had stayed in before they'd gone to her house. No way would he take anyone, trust or no trust, to her home. She'd been smart to keep it off the books with no one knowing about it. Endangering her was the last thing he wanted.

Angela pointed to an employee record on her display. "These areas here have been redacted. If I can find their code for redactions, I can reveal the full record. Anything—passwords, code words—would be helpful. I can—"

Both Jake's and Angela's cell phones chimed alarms. The two operatives looked at each other and in unison rose to their feet. "We have to go," Angela said.

An ominous feeling zipped up Declan's spine. "What's wrong?"

"One of our operatives is down."

He hadn't heard from Sabrina since she'd left. He told himself that there were probably dozens of ops going on at one time. The chances of the operative who was down being Sabrina were low.

"What's the protocol?"

"We'll wait to hear from Noah, but for now we're on alert. We'll head into his office and wait until—"

McCall shoved open the door. "I'm headed to Caracas. We've got two injured, one serious. I'll alert you as soon as I know something." He gave Declan a hard look. "Steele, you're with me."

Feeling as though he was wading through quicksand, Declan followed McCall out of the room. The LCR leader wanted him to come along? That could mean only one thing—Sabrina had been hurt.

Caracas

Sabrina sat in the uncomfortable chair in the waiting room. The pain in her side throbbed like a bad toothache, but compared to Riley's injury, it was barely a scratch. Why oh why hadn't they seen it coming? Cecile Poole, the nanny, had apparently helped set up the entire scenario. Marsha Denton was supposed to die. Once the ransom was paid, the children and Cecile would be saved...returned. The kidnapping had been inspired by nothing more than old-fashioned jealousy. The nanny had wanted Andrew Denton and his children for herself. With Marsha out of the way, Cecile had believed her path would have been clear.

Because of an evil, jealous woman, Riley might die.

Aidan and Justin had handled their worry in different ways. Aidan acted calm and confident, as if he didn't for a moment believe Riley would die. She imagined his attitude would be helpful in any situation. Believing the worst wasn't helpful.

Justin, on the other hand, had an almost opposite reaction. He had been gentle and careful with Riley. They'd been miles away from any kind of medical facility. While Aidan notified the authorities and arranged for the hostages to be returned to their home, Sabrina had driven like a crazed lunatic to the closest hospital. And Justin had worked to save his partner's life. Talking to her, urging her to stay awake, promising her she was fine, and telling her he was going to kick her ass as soon as she was well enough to take him on. He had tried to bandage the deep wound in Riley's stomach, but there'd been so much blood it had been useless.

Sabrina had actually thought Riley would die on the way to the hospital. No one could stay alive after losing that much blood. Somehow, Riley had. But for how long?

Once Justin had relinquished his partner to the doctors and nurses who'd met them at the door, he had lost it. One broken chair, a shattered window, and two bloodied fists later, he had managed to calm down.

For the past five hours, Justin had been standing as close to the surgery doors as possible. She had a feeling he was trying to stare through those doors and will Riley to stay alive.

Sabrina had always been intrigued by how the two operatives worked so well together yet didn't seem to like each other. Compared to her and Aidan, who teased each other mercilessly, these two acted as if they barely knew the other existed. But when they were on an op, they moved as if they shared the same thought processes. If nothing else, this event had shown that feelings definitely existed.

The sound of running feet caught her attention, drawing her to her feet. Noah and Declan burst through the doors. Noah gave her a sweeping glance as if to reassure himself she was fine.

"I'm okay."

He acknowledged her words with a nod and went straight to Justin.

"Are you all right?" Declan asked.

She saw the concern on his face and, despite the circumstances, relished that it was there. What would he do if she threw herself into his arms? She made herself stand still. "I'm fine."

"You have blood on your shirt."

She glanced down. "Most of it is Riley's."

"Some of it's yours?"

"I tried to get the knife away from the woman. Aidan had her pinned down, and I thought she was contained. She got a slice of me."

"How bad?"

"A few stitches. No biggie."

She could tell he wanted to say more but instead asked, "How's Riley?"

"We don't know yet. She's been in surgery for over five hours." And then because she knew he would understand, she blew out a shaky breath. "I've never seen that much blood, Declan. She had to have lost more than half her blood before we could get her here."

"Come here."

The gruff gentleness in his voice was dearly familiar. Even though she told herself she didn't need this and it certainly meant nothing to him, she went into his arms anyway. As they closed around her, Sabrina closed her eyes with a sigh. Okay, she had lied to herself. She did need this.

A door squeaked open, and all eyes went to a short, thin man in green scrubs with a tired and serious look on his face. Noah and Justin met him at the door. Sabrina, Declan, and Aidan gathered behind them.

"You're Ms. Ingram's family?"

"Yes, we are," Noah answered. "How is she?"

"She's no longer bleeding internally but she's lost a tremendous amount of blood. We should know within the next forty-eight hours. She's young, in excellent health, so that's in her favor."

"Can we see her?" Justin asked.

"She's in recovery, then she'll head to ICU. If she wakes, it won't be for several more hours. It would be best if you wait until tomorrow to see her."

The doctor turned and walked away, leaving the ominous words "if she wakes" hanging in the air.

CHAPTER TWENTY-TWO

Alexandria, Virginia

Declan took a long draw off his beer and eyed the man who sat on the sofa across from him. Jackson Sands had once been a trusted friend and co-worker. To be sitting in a living room in a civilized manner having a cold one together felt surreal. The normal, everyday stuff still seemed off-kilter and strange.

Since Declan's rescue, Jackson had checked in with him two or three times a week. The man's concern had been appreciated but hard to take. Having no one interested in his wellbeing for so long, Declan had been resistant to his interest.

He'd invited Jackson to the LCR apartment. He and Sabrina had yet to return to her house. He had wanted her to be close to those she trusted while she healed. And Sabrina had wanted to stay nearby for Riley's sake. The young operative had been transferred to the LCR medical facility and was making great strides in her recovery. Still, probably because of all the uncertainty in her own life, Sabrina had said she wanted to be completely sure of Riley's good prognosis before she went home.

"So, are you ready to let me help you find the bastards who did this to you?"

One thing Declan always appreciated about Jackson—he didn't beat around the bush.

When Jackson and his team had rescued him, Declan hadn't taken much notice of the man, but now that he had, he swore the guy hadn't aged a bit from the first time they'd met almost fifteen years before. A little over six feet tall, skin bronzed from the sun, dark brown hair with a few glints of gold, and a face that Declan had been told made women fall at his feet.

"You have any ideas?" Declan asked.

"Several. You've made a lot of enemies along the way. Assassinating evil men has a way of pissing off other evil men."

"True. Having enemies within my own agency is a little disconcerting."

"But not unexpected. The Agency doesn't exactly hire choirboys."

"No, but we try to bring in those who are loyal, with a strong sense of patriotism. Selling out one of your own isn't exactly the type of behavior I'd expect."

"You've grown soft. Takes all kinds of assholes."

Soft wasn't the description Declan would give himself. Before his capture, he had been as jaded as any covert ops agent. And now, after what he'd been through, he had about as much faith in his fellow man as he had in the Easter Bunny.

"I'm glad you found Sabrina," Jackson went on. "Bet she was as surprised as hell."

Declan gave a noncommittal grunt but inwardly winced. He hadn't told his friend what an ass he'd been, not relishing the idea of confessing that he'd abducted Sabrina with the intent of killing her. Not exactly his finest hour.

"Never seen two people more in love than you two."

Again, Declan made no comment. At one time, there had been no doubt of his feelings. But that was then—when he'd had something still inside him. With only bitterness remaining, he had nothing left to give. What woman, especially someone as warm and caring as Sabrina, would want a hollow shell for a husband?

"She had a rough time of it," Jackson said.

"Were you around when it happened?"

Regret darkened his eyes. "No. I was on an op in Yemen. Didn't hear about it until I got back a week later. I only heard it secondhand. Didn't even know what hospital she was in."

"Hospital?"

"She didn't tell you she was hurt in the blast?"

"She told me cuts and bruises. Made it sound like it wasn't a big deal."

Jackson shrugged. "Again, this is only secondhand, but I heard she was unconscious for a few days. Severe concussion, broke some bones."

A cement-like weight settled in Declan's gut. Why had Sabrina downplayed her injuries? Why hadn't she told him how badly she'd been hurt? *Because, asshole, you acted as if you didn't give a damn.*

"I finally got to talk to her a couple of weeks later. Just a phone call, but damn…never heard her sound so lifeless. She took what was left of your body…well, the body she thought was yours, to Scotland for burial. I got the impression she wished she had died, too."

"Why do you say that?" He didn't need to ask that question but, perhaps as self-punishment, did it anyway.

"She was searching through the remains, trying to find you." Jackson swallowed and continued, "Found an arm. Thought it was yours. Had a wedding ring just like yours. No one had any doubts that you were dead."

Unable to just sit and listen, Declan stood and wandered over to the window. Pushing aside the horror Sabrina had endured, he said, "Somebody went to a lot of trouble to make everyone believe I was."

"Yeah, they did. I worried about her...told her she needed to be careful since they tried to kill her, too."

Jackson was right. Ever since Declan had gotten back, it'd been all about him. He had wanted to find the traitor. Sabrina had kept insisting they'd both been hurt, and he had assumed it was because their relationship had been destroyed. But it was a helluva lot more than that.

"I haven't seen her since she left the Agency," Jackson was saying. "Hell, I don't even know who she works for."

Though LCR was a known organization, the identities of its operatives weren't public knowledge. That, along with Sabrina's natural reticence to share personal information, ensured that no one outside a few knew of her activities or whereabouts.

The other man had paused, most likely thinking that Declan was going to reveal Sabrina's occupation. Since that wasn't going to happen, Declan changed the subject. "You have any issues... close calls of your own?"

Jackson snorted. "I've always got a couple of people gunning for me, but it has more to do with pissed-off small-time criminals these days."

"So what does your security company do besides rescue wayward EDJE agents?"

"Almost anything we can get our hands on. Bodyguard, security services for celebs, and high-target businessmen. I've got four full-time employees, two part-time. If you hire us, I'll guarantee we'll do everything we can to find the assholes."

"Thanks. But I don't—"

The apartment door swung open, and Sabrina walked in. The instant she saw Jackson, her eyes lit up. They met in the middle of the room and gave each other a warm hug.

Seeing the delight in her eyes and the smile curving her beautiful mouth helped dissolve some of the heaviness inside Declan. There was just something about Sabrina's smile that made life seem better.

"I was thrilled when Declan told me you were coming over," she said. "I wanted to thank you personally for what you did. If you hadn't gotten the tip on his whereabouts and followed your instincts, he'd still be there."

"It was my pleasure. I wished I could have let you know, but I couldn't find you."

She grimaced. "You know me. Staying in touch is not one of my strong points."

Jackson glanced over at Declan. "Guess it was a shock to see his ugly mug again."

She laughed as Jackson had intended. It didn't surprise Declan that she didn't tell his friend the circumstances of their reunion. That wasn't her way.

She went over to the sofa and dropped onto it. "Declan tells me you have your own security business now. I was surprised when I heard you left the Agency."

"Without Declan making it interesting and fun, things got boring." He shrugged, and his eyes shadowed slightly. "Agency just wasn't the same anymore. Too much politics. Got to the point you had to fill out a requisition before you could get a flipping toothpick."

"And now you're your own boss?"

He grinned. "Now I get to buy my own flipping toothpicks."

Sabrina laughed and stood. "I'm starving. You guys had dinner?"

"Yeah. We ordered pizza. There's some in the kitchen for you," Declan said.

Throwing him a grateful glance, she headed that way. "Thanks. I didn't have lunch. Be right back."

"She's even more beautiful than I remember."

Sabrina halted just inside the kitchen door. Neither man could see her as she listened shamelessly for Declan's reply. His response was a grunt—not the least bit flattering or encouraging. How stupid and juvenile was she? Eavesdropping like some anxious teenager hoping to hear a compliment from the hottest guy in school. Stupid, because this particular hot guy, who also happened to be her husband, continued to act as if she meant nothing to him.

They hadn't yet talked about what happened the night before she had left for Caracas. At some point they had to address it, but she wanted to delay the inevitable as long as possible. She already knew what he would say.

Her mood more somber than when she'd entered the apartment, Sabrina went about reheating a couple of slices of pizza. She stayed in the kitchen and ate what she could, wanting to give herself a few minutes of peace before returning to the living room. Being in Declan's presence for very long always set up an ache in her chest. Trying to consume a meal when he was around had become somewhat difficult, as swallowing was almost impossible with a lump in her throat.

One good thing she had learned today was that Riley should make a full and complete recovery. The young operative was now at the LCR medical facility but still had several more weeks of recuperation and rehab before she would be able to return to work in any kind of capacity. Sabrina had managed to see her for a few minutes earlier today. The small, pale woman lying on the bed had looked nothing like the energetic and focused Riley Ingram. She had looked as harmless and innocent as a child.

Justin had been by his partner's side almost from the moment he'd been allowed in to see her in Caracas. He had been there today, too. The worry etched on the man's face made Sabrina wonder if his and Riley's relationship would change once she was back on the job. It would be interesting to watch.

Sabrina's own injury was still a little inconvenient, and Noah had pulled her off ops for a couple more weeks. She would have protested, but she had been too grateful. Since Declan had returned, she hadn't had much downtime and was running on fumes. Also, despite his insistence that he didn't need her help, Sabrina planned to assist him in finding out who had betrayed them.

She was glad he had called Jackson for input. She hadn't worked with the man on many ops but she did remember that he had a tendency to see things from a different perspective. His help could be essential.

And unless Declan put his foot down, there was another man she wanted to ask for assistance. Since Declan's return, Albert had called several times to check on him. Each time she had talked with him, her doubts about his betrayal increased. But would Declan agree?

Throwing away the remains of her pizza, Sabrina took her beer and returned to the living room.

Settling back on the sofa, she was ready to plan their strategy. She and Declan had talked this morning before she'd headed off to her meeting with Noah, and he had agreed with her that the fact that LCR was providing help needed to stay with them. Noah, Angela, and Jake were taking a huge risk by hacking into a government agency. It could come back and bite them in the ass. The last thing she wanted to do was cause problems for LCR and the people she had come to love and respect.

"So did you guys discuss the most likely suspects?" Sabrina asked.

"Not yet," Declan said.

"Between the three of us, we know most of the players from our time with the Agency," Jackson said. "I can run background checks and—"

Declan shook his head. "That's already being done."

A dark frown furrowed Jackson's brow. "Man, you don't have the resources I do. I can get it done a lot faster and—"

"We've got it covered," Sabrina said. She grinned, hoping to take the sting out of Declan's gruffness. "I've got friends, too."

"So you don't want my help?"

"Of course we do," Sabrina assured him. "I left the Agency over four years ago, and with Declan's job, he didn't get to work out in the field with as many agents as he once did."

Jackson lifted a shoulder. "Sure. Whatever I can do to help, you know I will."

She appreciated his attitude. Even though he might be offended that they weren't sharing more information with him, his willingness to help in any way he could showed his loyalty and maturity.

"So who's on your short list?" Jackson asked.

Declan named his top five, with Darius Ronan being his top pick.

Jackson gave a slow, considering nod. "Yeah. I could see all of them wanting a go at you. But are you sure it's not just someone inside the Agency? You had a tendency to ruffle feathers."

"You mean Jason Starling," Declan said.

"You have to admit, the guy didn't like you."

That was an understatement. Professional jealousy was never pretty, but Starling had gone out of his way to vilify Declan's name by claiming that he was too much of a risk taker. He was one of the few who knew Declan had been up for Albert's job. Starling was aware of it only because his own name had been bandied about for the position as well. The man had wanted the job and didn't mind telling others he'd do a better job than Declan.

"He's on my list, but...I don't know. This seems too lowlife for him."

"Lower than going straight to the president and telling him you were a loose cannon?"

Yeah, that'd pissed him off, but in a way Declan had understood. He and Starling were polar opposites when it came to running an op. The man trusted intel more than his gut. Declan had a healthy respect for intel but would always go with his instincts.

"The man seemed genuinely surprised to see me the other day. Almost like he was glad I was alive."

"You've seen Starling?" Sabrina asked.

Declan didn't know who looked the most horrified and surprised, Sabrina or Jackson.

"What the hell?" Jackson said. "Where? How?"

"I went to the Agency, walked around a bit."

"Declan? What were you thinking?" The horror in Sabrina's voice almost made him smile.

"That whoever did this might still be there...probably *is* still there. He or she needed to see I'm alive, healthy, and royally pissed."

In his opinion, the entire event had been anticlimactic. He'd called a secure number, got transferred to Jason Starling. The man had agreed to let him come inside but was surprisingly absent when Declan arrived. A serious looking young man Declan had never seen before had been waiting on him and other than saying, "Hello, Mr. Steele" no words had been spoken inside the building.

The Agency was small, employing less than fifty people, both field agents and support staff. All eyes had been on him as he'd leisurely made his way through the maze of desks. Nodding at a few people he recognized, he hadn't stopped to chat. The visit had lasted less than three minutes.

He'd been outside, standing on the sidewalk of the Washington Monument when Starling had called out his name.

"What did Jason say to you?" Sabrina asked.

"Just that he was damn glad to see me alive. Said they were doing an internal investigation, trying to determine who sold me out. Said the mole had been silent for over a year."

Temper flashed in her eyes. "He wasn't accusing you, was he?"

"No. He actually apologized for being such an asshole before."

"That's kind of easy for him, since he got the job he wanted." The dry irony in Jackson's voice indicated he wasn't ready to believe in Starling's innocence.

"I'm not saying the guy is innocent. Hell, he may have set it all up and is doing a masterful snow job."

"How did you leave it with him?" Sabrina asked.

"We agreed to share significant intel when we got it." Declan lifted a shoulder. "Then I walked away."

Jackson shook his head as he gave an admiring whistle. "You always did have balls of steel."

Declan grinned. "Hence the name."

Jackson leaned forward in his seat. "You know, you've got someone on your side who knows more about the Agency than the three of us combined. A helluva lot more than Jason Starling will ever know. Any reason you're not involving him?"

"You're talking about Albert, I assume," Declan said.

"The man knows everything. He even remembered my nephew Stuart's name. Asked me about him the last time I saw him. He's got a memory almost as good as yours."

Before Declan could respond, either positively or negatively, Sabrina jumped in. "I agree, Declan. Al would be of great benefit."

Confused, he shot her a narrow-eyed look. "I thought you suspected him, too."

Her grimace was a mixture of guilt and uncertainty. "I did. But I'm wondering if my suspicions were colored by my anger at him. He was in charge when all this went down. I know he feels a grave responsibility for what happened to you."

"Maybe because he had something to do with it," Declan countered.

"That's pure bullshit, man," Jackson snapped. "He treated you like the son he never had."

Declan pulled in a silent breath. Jackson was right. Albert Marks had taken him under his wing when he'd first gone to the Agency. Everything he had learned about covert operations and intel gathering, he had gotten from his mentor.

"After what you've been through, I understand why you trust so few people, but is there a specific reason you think Albert might be involved?" Sabrina asked.

Was there? Had his torturers tried to make him believe Albert was guilty, too? He rubbed his temple where an insistent throb was pounding. For so long he had believed Sabrina had betrayed him, but when he'd allowed himself some rational thought, he had realized that was downright crazy. Was that the same reason he thought Albert had something to do with it, too? Or was it an instinctive reaction to something he didn't want to be true?

"Declan, you're going to have to trust him," Sabrina said. "I finally had to realize that the man isn't invincible. He made a mistake and let a traitor in. That doesn't mean he is the traitor."

"I'll give it more thought." He took in both their gazes and said, "But for now, let's start naming names."

They worked late into the night, each recalling what they could about every individual they'd worked with in their time at the Agency. When Sabrina stifled her third yawn in as many minutes, Declan called it quits.

"Let's call it a night. We've got the names and most of the data we'll get from memory."

Jackson gathered his notes. "I'll run these and see what—"

"No need," Sabrina said. "Like I said, I've got them covered."

"So when are you going to fill me in on this mysterious job you have? Declan won't tell me anything about it."

Declan wasn't surprised to hear Sabrina laugh off the question with a, "Let's just say I don't have to wear those damn stilettos nearly as often as I used to."

Sadness flickered in Jackson's eyes, and he knew his friend was hurt by her brush-off. There was no reason for anyone to know she worked for LCR, even the man who'd rescued him.

Jackson stopped at the open door and turned back around. As if things weren't uncomfortable enough, he said, "It's so damned good to see you two together again."

The door closed behind him before either of them could think of a suitable response.

Sabrina shot Declan a grimacing smile. "Well, that was awkward."

"Yeah." He shoved his hand through his hair and blew out a sigh. Hell, it had to be said. "About the other night."

Her body went limp like a deflated tire. "I don't think I'm up for that discussion tonight."

"We have to have it sometime."

"Okay, fine. Say what you have to say."

Now that the time had come, he was at a loss for words. Even as tired as he could see she was, Sabrina was still as lovely to him as the day he'd met her. It wasn't just her physical beauty that appealed to him, it was who she was on the inside. A place she allowed few people to see. She had a beautiful heart. A gentle spirit that had almost been completely decimated before she'd gone to EDJE, but there had been a small flame still inside her. The care, attention, and training she had received had made that flame brighter.

"Declan?"

He gave himself a mental shake. Dwelling on the past would get him nowhere. Better get to it and get it over with. "You're one of the most beautiful people I know, inside and out."

"That wasn't what you thought a couple of weeks ago."

"No, and I'm sorry about that. I said some stupid, asinine things. Things I didn't mean." Pain seared his head again. "I still don't know what happened to make me believe you betrayed me. I just—"

A warm hand gripped his wrist. "I'm sorry. I shouldn't have brought it up. You've apologized already."

Declan nodded. What more could he do other than move on from here and be as honest as he could? "Thinking that just shows how screwed up my brain is. What I went through—I was trained for that. I didn't give up any information. I can be sure of that. But they didn't leave me with a lot, Sabrina. I'm not the same man I once was."

"I see some changes in you. Not as many as you seem to think, but the ones I do see…I'm sorry for them. It hurts me to know what you endured." She swallowed hard. "The irony isn't lost on me. While you were held captive, going through hell, I was rescuing strangers. I'm proud of those rescues, but the thought of you out there somewhere while I was rescuing others… It's hard… very hard to take. I'm just glad Jackson followed his instincts."

"Yeah, I owe him a lot." He shook his head. Hell, he still hadn't said what he needed to say. "Here's the thing. I can't be your husband anymore."

Sabrina pulled in a breath before she could release it in a gasp. Even though she had known that's what he was going to say, or some version of it, the words hurt worse than the knife she'd taken in her side last week.

"I…" She stopped, tried again "We haven't…you haven't…" She pressed a shaking hand to the top of her nose where the burn of tears had developed. "Let's not make any major decisions until this is over. Okay? We've got more than enough to keep us busy without getting involved in any kind of legal separation or divorce." She winced when her voice trembled over the D-word.

"I just didn't want you to misinterpret what happened the other night."

Fury replaced the hurt. "Don't worry. Just because you screwed me senseless gave me no illusion that I was anything more to you than a willing body."

"You know that's not what I meant."

"Do I? Ever since you returned you've treated me with disdain, distrust. You've gone out of your way to let me know that you don't want me as your wife. That you don't see yourself as my husband. Why the hell would I even begin to misinterpret sex between us? It'd been a long time for both of us. We let off a lot of built-up steam." She headed to her bedroom. "I'll see you tomorrow."

"Sabrina... I—"

She didn't bother to see if he could come up with anything else. Whatever came out of his mouth was sure to either be the same thing or hurt her even more. She was too tired to deal with it tonight.

CHAPTER TWENTY-THREE

Angela Delvecchio was a godsend. What would have taken Declan months to uncover, she'd found in a matter of days.

In some ways, investigating his former boss made him feel guilty. Albert Marks had been his friend and mentor. Had hired him, trained him. Had brought Sabrina into his life. He owed the man more than he could ever repay. But that didn't mean he wasn't keeping secrets. If Albert was the one who'd set him up and sold him out, Declan had to know. And if he was innocent, then Sabrina and Jackson were right. The man would be an invaluable resource.

On paper, the man who had killed evil men and ordered the destruction of terrorist cells and mad dictators was almost boringly normal. The EDJE founder was financially comfortable but not wealthy. His withdrawals, deposits, and indebtedness showed nothing suspicious. His family consisted of a wife, three grown children, five grandchildren, a Maltese named Maximilian and a cat named Star.

Odd to just now be learning these things about a man he had known for over fifteen years. Sharing personal information wasn't something you did inside the Agency, even with people you trusted.

Damn amazing that he and Sabrina had ever gotten together. He rubbed at the persistent pain in his head at the thought of Sabrina. Their conversation the other night had been as awkward and gut-wrenching as he had feared. And he had, once again, hurt her. Every time he thought about that painful conversation, he wanted to smash something. He had always had a gift for words. He credited his father for introducing him to the written word long before he could even walk. He'd grown up reading the classics, devoured every word of poetry Robert Burns had penned and used to quote him often.

As a younger man, Declan had used words to seduce women into his bed, and once he'd started working ops for the Agency, he had used them to pluck secrets from people without them knowing it. With Sabrina, he had been much less poetic. Raw was the only word he could come up with. His feelings for her were so basic and gut-level strong that poetry had often escaped him, and it was just pure emotion that came through. She had never seemed to mind.

Why hadn't he been kinder to her when he told her he could no longer be married to her? She'd gone three shades paler than her normal creamy complexion, and her eyes had darkened to a dull green. He had wanted to take the words back as soon as they'd escaped his mouth. Even though he had meant them, something tore inside him to be saying that to her. She had been the love of his life, his everything. Even though he no longer had those emotions, it didn't mean he wanted her hurt.

She had gone through her own hell. And he'd acted as if what had happened to her was unimportant. Just because every good thing had been beaten out of him, leaving him only an empty shell, that didn't mean he had a right to inflict his bitter dregs on to others.

The knock on the apartment door broke him out of his self-indulgent pity. What the hell good did any of that do? Best thing that could happen was for him to find the shithead who'd sold them out, deal with him, and then get out of her life for good.

It was with that grim, nasty thought that he opened the door.

"I must say you don't look any happier than you did the last time I saw you."

"Thank you for coming, Albert."

"Anything I can do to help, Declan, you know I will. I appreciate you giving me the opportunity to try."

"I wanted to talk with you before Sabrina arrived."

"Of course." Though pushing seventy, Albert still had that keen look of intelligence in his eyes. Most people who met him probably thought of him as just a somewhat absentminded elderly man. But if they looked beneath the facade, they would see a man who'd had more kills and captures in the Agency than anyone else since its existence.

Declan waited until Albert sat down before he said, "I need your input...your ideas on who did this to me."

Albert opened his mouth to reply, but Declan held up his hand. "There's something else, though. It's been chewing at me since I got back."

Knowing Albert would wait patiently, Declan took a few moments to put his thoughts together. Even though he still had some doubts about Albert, this man had trained him to take any kind of torture or coercion possible. Albert would know.

"My captivity...I was tortured—beaten, whipped, the works. Almost every shitty thing one human can do to another...I got the royal treatment."

He appreciated that Albert didn't express his regret or spout platitudes. What was done was done. "Thing is, I survived them.

Not only did I survive them, I never gave anything up. What I learned from you saved my life."

"I'm glad, my boy...very glad."

"But they did something else to me, and for the life of me, I don't know what it was."

Again, Albert waited for Declan to continue.

"I believed...had no doubt that Sabrina set me up, sold me out. I don't know how they put that in my head or when it happened. I just remember waking up one day and knowing for certain that she was the one. Hating her, wanting to make her pay was the only thing that kept me alive. When I took her..." He swallowed hard, the horror of his words sticking in his throat. "I planned to kill her."

"I see." Though there was no real shock on Albert's face, sorrow darkened his eyes.

"I don't know how they made me believe that. Every time I get to the point of thinking of it, questioning it, I get this fierce headache." Talking about it now had made that headache start pounding again.

"And you came to believe it was only Sabrina who did this to you? No one else?"

"Yes." He had wondered if they'd used Albert against him, too. But the pounding, insidious headache only occurred when he questioned himself about Sabrina's involvement.

"Were you able to form an opinion on why she did it? Did you wonder if she planned this for months? Had the plan from the beginning when you first started training her? What was her motivation? Money? Revenge? Did you think she'd been playing you all along? That everything had been a lie?"

"Hell, I don't know. I've asked myself the same questions thousands of times. I. Just. Don't. Know." Declan pressed his fingers to the agony now pounding at his temples.

Albert was quiet for several moments, his eyes assessing. Even though the pain had become more intense, Declan forced patience. He saw something in Albert's expression that gave him hope.

"There's a new drug. Experimental for right now. Probably won't be approved by the FDA for years, if ever. Of course, it's already out on the black market. Its purpose is to help people overcome drug and alcohol addictions. Supposed to help people with severe OCD problems, too. But anything good will always have its downside. It can be used, in conjunction with extreme coercion, to make a person believe the pain is coming from a specific person."

No, that didn't sound right. "I never believed Sabrina was actually doling out my torture. I believed she sold me out...was responsible for my abduction and torture."

"The drugs, used in conjunction with brainwashing techniques, sleep deprivation, and severe pain, could convince you of her guilt. It doesn't work the same way on everyone. They could have altered the drug. Possibly blended it with a hallucinogen. You and Sabrina have an unusual bond, and she is your one vulnerable area. They could have used that to create the illusion that she was the cause of everything." Albert lifted a shoulder. "Controlling the mind is still a mystery."

"And mankind has found a way to screw it up in every conceivable way possible."

"Sadly, that is often the case."

"So could the drug still be in my system?"

"You no longer believe she had anything to do with it?"

"I have residual thoughts that she did, but I can fight them now, knowing the truth. But that's usually when the pain intensifies."

"I have a suggestion...you may not like it."

"If it'll help me figure out what they did to me...help me find the pricks responsible, I'm all for it."

"I'd like to have a psychiatrist put you under hypnosis."

Shit. Somebody digging around in his psyche sounded about as much fun as lying in a bed of fire ants. But he'd been through worse shit. "Let's do it."

"I'll set it up. We can—"

The door opened, and Sabrina rushed in like a whirlwind. "Sorry I'm late. Hi, Uncle Al."

"Sabrina, my dear. Don't you look lovely."

"Thank you. It's good to see you. Thanks for agreeing to help us out."

"It's my pleasure, dear."

Concerned with the dark look on Declan's face, she asked, "Everything all right? Did I interrupt something?"

"Not at all," Declan said. "In fact, Albert was just giving me some insight into what might have happened to make me believe their lies."

"That's great. What do you think happened, Al?"

"I believe, in conjunction with his torture, he was given a drug to make him believe you were the traitor."

"But what would be the point in making him believe that?""

"That's something I can't explain."

"Albert made a suggestion of hypnosis to help me try to remember what they did."

"Is that safe? Won't that bring you more pain?"

"Can't be worse than what the SOBs did to me."

"The doctor would monitor you," Al said. "If it becomes too painful, he can pull you out immediately."

"Let's do it then," Declan said. His eyes locked with Sabrina's. "I'd like you to be there."

"Me? Why?"

"Since you're the one I blamed, seems only fair."

Before she could reassure him that there were no hard feelings, he added, "And because there's no one in the world I trust more than you."

When he said stuff like that, she wanted so very much to tell him that his words sounded like the old Declan. Since she knew he'd just deny that, she gave a small nod and said, "I'll be happy to be there with you."

CHAPTER TWENTY-FOUR

Sitting in the doctor's office three days later, Declan wasn't so sure of his decision. In theory, finding out how he'd been brainwashed would be helpful, but going through that shit again sent nausea roiling through him.

Sabrina, who sat in a chair across the room from him, looked about as happy to be here as he was. Would he be hurting her further by allowing her to hear this? It seemed only fair that she be present. After all, she was the one he'd almost killed because of what he had been forced to believe. He owed her.

And he'd told her the truth. She was the only one he trusted completely. Crazy, since every time he thought about her innocence, his head wanted to explode. This shit had to stop.

What about Albert? Just because the man acted as if he were on the up-and-up, Declan could no longer take chances. Albert had arranged for this session. How did Declan know this wasn't just another way to get information?

"Declan?"

He jerked his head around. Sabrina stood before him. Hell, he hadn't heard her move...hadn't seen anything but the doubts clouding his pain-dulled mind.

She sat on the arm of his chair, put her hand over his. "You don't have to do this. Finding out what they did to you probably won't reveal the real traitor."

"Maybe not, but I damn well need to know how it happened. I would think you'd want to know, too."

"Not if it's going to hurt you more."

"After everything I've done, why do you still care?"

A riot of emotions, including anger, showed in her eyes before she concealed them. "We have a history, Declan. Just because you don't feel the way you once did doesn't erase my feelings."

"Everyone ready?"

Declan turned to Dr. Desmond Horatio. Tall, thin, with a shock of brilliant white hair and a long thin nose, the doctor looked exactly how he envisioned a psychiatrist should look. Angela had checked the doctor out and uncovered nothing but glowing credentials and excellent references.

If he and Sabrina had still been as they once were, they would've been laughing their asses off about the guy's pretentious-sounding name. Unfortunately, nothing about this was funny.

Albert stood at the door. "Declan, I'm going to step out. We'll talk after your session is over, if you like."

The man knew of Declan's distrust. A part of him felt guilty for that, especially if Albert was innocent. But that didn't mean he wanted him in the room.

With Declan's quick nod, Albert gave Sabrina an encouraging smile and then left the room.

"Okay, Declan," Dr. Horatio said, "I'd like you to recline back in the chair, get as comfortable as possible. We're going to go deep into your memories. However, you will be an observer only. It will be like you're watching a movie."

Declan frowned. "So I won't know it's me? How? Why not?"

"You want to find out what they did to you. However, you don't need to relive the pain and the trauma of those events. There's no reason to put yourself through that again."

Okay. That sounded a helluva lot easier than he had anticipated.

He gave the doctor a grim nod. "Let's do it."

"Very well. Empty your mind of everything and concentrate on being at peace. Beautiful puffy clouds in a sea of light blue skies float overhead, you're lying on the beach, and all you hear is the peaceful rhythm of the ocean waves hitting the shore. It's warm, the sun is on your face, and peace surrounds you."

As he spoke, Dr. Horatio's voice went softer, lower. With his eyes closed, Declan felt as if he were floating with the clouds, the warmth of the sun gently heating his face...he drifted.

"Declan, you're going to go back and witness what happened in that prison. This man is not you. You can't feel the things he feels. You're watching this but you're not personally involved. Nothing can hurt you. Those men cannot get to you. You are perfectly safe. Repeat after me. This man is not me. I am safe."

Declan mumbled, "This man is not me. I am safe."

"Now, count backward from one hundred. At ninety-six, you will be back in that prison, but remember, you will be observing only."

Following the doctor's suggestions, Declan began: "One hundred, ninety-nine, ninety-eight, ninety-seven, ninety..."

He opened his eyes to horror.

It was as if he were levitating above the room but still part of it. He could smell the sour odor of unwashed bodies. The ripe and pungent stink assaulted his nostrils. Two beefy men, wearing dark pants and filthy-looking T-shirts, stood looking up at something.

Declan moved his gaze and swallowed hard. A man hung from the rafters. His face was swollen from bruises, but he looked familiar. Who was he? The brutes on the ground shouted up at the man, speaking various languages, cursing him, calling him names. The hanging man, dripping with blood and sweat, stared them down. Declan couldn't see his eyes but could tell the man's expression was cold, emotionless.

Snap! Declan jerked at the sound, and the hanging man winced as his body swayed violently. That was when he realized another man stood behind him holding a cane. Another snap sounded. The man's body swayed again, but this time he made no grimace, no expression. The blows continued, the man continued to sway. The taunts, name-calling, and curses went on. Yet the man stayed staunch. The only movements were from the beat of the cane as it ripped into his skin and the sway of his tortured body.

Finally, a male voice shouted, "Release him."

The man dropped to the ground and lay there. Was he unconscious? What did these people want with him? Why were they doing this? Why did this guy look so familiar? One of the men, giant-like, jerked the tortured man up and threw him over his shoulders. He carried him down a filthy, dark hallway and threw him onto the floor of a cell. The door clanged shut.

Declan was torn. For some reason, he wanted to stay with the man, find out who he was. But he also wanted to follow the big brute back, find out who these people were and why they were torturing someone.

Another male voice, this one kind but insistent and coming from somewhere above him, said, "Okay, Declan. Let's go to another day. Same location. Tell me what you see."

As if he were watching the same program but on a different channel, Declan saw a deep pit covered by a giant grate. The same man was inside. Face dry and cracked, lips swollen, his body was rail-thin, emaciated. He barely looked like the same man, but somehow Declan knew he was—the one he'd seen beaten before. Declan could almost feel his thirst...his pain. A roar of thunder exploded, and a torrential rain beat down on the man. For a few minutes, he didn't think the man even knew he was being rained on. Then, he looked up and blinked. His lips were so swollen it was hard to tell, but Declan thought he smiled.

Rain gushed down over the man, and Declan could almost feel the poor guy's relief. The man opened his mouth and allowed the rain to slide down his throat. He took great gulps of it and then used his hands to wash his face, then his body. What horrible thing had this man done to be treated so horrifically? Someone needed to stop this.

As Declan continued to watch, he saw something the man had yet to notice. Water was filling the pit. The depth was knee level now, but what would happen if the rains continued? Would the man drown? Maybe the bastards who'd beaten him would return before then and get him out. It was obvious they wanted some kind of information from him. Surely they wouldn't let him die.

Hours or days later, Declan didn't know how long he had been hovering over the guy who was now even more miserable than when he'd been dying of thirst. The water had risen to his neck. No one had come to check on him. The man had yelled until he was hoarse, but no one came. Suddenly, the pit was filled to overflowing, and the man's head was buried beneath the water. Declan felt his own heart thud in panic...or was that the man's heart? It was almost like he was in the pit with him. He felt the cool water on his skin. It seeped into his bones. Cold permeated his entire being. Where was the man? Was he dead?

Declan struggled to maintain his objectivity. This wasn't real. The man wasn't dying. Just a movie.

A face appeared at the grate. The man was still alive. He was breathing through one of the grate's openings. Trying to keep himself from sinking, his fingers held tight to the steel frame.

Declan was relieved for the guy but wondered how long he could hold on. Then the man disappeared. Had he given up? Was he allowing himself to let go? Declan held his breath, fearing the worst. Then the face reappeared again as the man took in more breaths.

Was it hours or days that Declan watched him, wondering each time he submerged if this would be the last time? A deep, violent hatred seethed inside Declan. How dare anyone do this to another human being?

"Remember, you're just an observer. This man didn't die...he did not die. Regulate your breathing...take slow, even breaths. You're all right, Declan. You're safe." That voice, kind but firm, pulled him away from his fury.

"Okay, I think that's enough for the day. Let's—"

Declan jerked away from the voice. No, he wasn't leaving. He didn't know why, but he couldn't leave yet. He had come here to learn something. He hadn't learned it yet. He would not leave until he had.

Somehow, despite the voice's insistence, he was back in the prison cell. The man had apparently survived, because he was seated in a chair, bound by rope and duct tape. He looked even worse than he had in the pit. Murky blue eyes dilated and glazed. Drool oozed from his mouth. His hair had grown well past his shoulders. Someone had put it in a ponytail and then tied it to the chair, effectively keeping him from being able to drop his head.

A voice—familiar, feminine, husky, sexy—sounded through the room. He knew that voice. Sabrina...it was his lovely Sabrina. Her voice was filled with life and vitality. He saw the man try to shake his head. Heard him mumble, "No, no, no." Why? What was...

And then he finally paid attention to Sabrina's words. Her confession, telling him she had sold him out, that she didn't love him, had made millions by selling him to his captors. She told him he had nothing to live for. That he should reveal everything, and then they would let him die in peace. She said the same words, over and over and over.

Declan didn't know how much time had passed, but the man continued to sit there and listen as Sabrina's voice revealed she was a traitor, a betrayer.

Bile surged up his throat. Declan didn't want to hear those words any more than the man in the chair. Why were they doing this? He forced himself to listen carefully and finally realized there was something off about the sound, the quality of the recording. The pitches were wrong, all over the place. Various words and sentences sounded as if they were said at different octaves, different intonations.

The answer came swiftly. Someone had recorded several conversations of Sabrina and then used only the words they wanted to create a certain type of message. But why would they do that? What did Sabrina have to do with them, or this man? And, surely, if the man knew Sabrina, he would know she would never sell anyone out. She wasn't capable of that kind of treachery.

But the man listened and then did something extraordinary. Tears poured down his face, and he screamed Sabrina's name.

He jerked on the rope, ignoring the pain as the rope cut into his arms and his hair was pulled from his head. He stopped, shouted, cursed. And still Sabrina's voice continued, on and on.

"Declan, come back. Now, dammit. Come back to me, now!"

He shook his head. That was Sabrina again. She sounded different than she did in the recording. Her voice was thick with emotion, as if she were on the verge of crying. He wanted to see what happened to the man, but he could never deny Sabrina anything. With a sad sigh for the poor bastard who continued to swear and jerk in his chair, Declan felt himself floating away again.

He opened his eyes, blinked several times. Sabrina was kneeling before him. Her eyes were dry, but the hell in them spoke volumes. Her face was death pale, her breathing erratic.

"Declan, you back with us?"

Dr. Horatio's voice jerked him back into full reality. It had been him. He had been that poor, abused bastard. He remembered what they'd done to him. And he wanted to kill them.

"They gave me an injection. I barely remember it...was so out of it. And then they played that sound bite over and over. Your voice, Sabrina. They took bits and pieces of your voice from different recordings and made you say the things they wanted. And for days, they made me sit and listen. When I fell asleep or lost consciousness, they'd whip me until I woke, splash water on my face, and then turn up the volume. They tortured me into believing a lie."

It took every bit of willpower for Sabrina not to throw herself into Declan's arms. And irrationally, she wanted to apologize. Even though she had done nothing, she still felt the need to say she was sorry. Someone had used her voice, her words. But what hurt more than anything was the knowledge that in the other two torture scenes he had described, Declan had never said anything, never made a sound. But when they'd convinced him she had betrayed him, he had cried, sobbed.

"It's my opinion," Dr. Horatio said, "that with the use of psychotropic drugs, the recording of your wife's voice, as well as the torture you'd already endured and your weakened condition, they were able to create the mind-set that Sabrina and no one else betrayed you."

"That's what it sounds like." Declan's voice was now matter-of-fact, calm.

Sabrina battled surging emotions. She felt as if she could erupt at any moment. "How can you sit there so calmly and act as if you're not furious?"

"Watching it like it was a movie was a helluva lot easier than going through it."

Dr. Horatio stood. "I believe I'll step out for a while and let you two talk. Feel free to stay as long as you need. I'll be in my private office if you need me."

"Wait. What about his headaches? Will they go away?"

"I don't have a lot of experience with the type of drug he was given. My advice would be to talk with your personal physician."

"Give us your opinion, then," Sabrina said.

"Very well." He turned to Declan. "Your headaches were caused by your denial of what you knew couldn't be true— that your wife had betrayed you. Now that you know the truth…know what happened to you, I would think the headaches would go away on their own." He gave them a kind smile and said again, "Feel free to stay as long as you need."

Sabrina waited until the door closed behind the doctor and then said, "I'm so very sorry, Declan. I knew you went through hell. I just never realized how very much worse than hell it was."

"There's nothing for you to apologize about. You were as much of a victim as I was. If I hadn't been so strung out on whatever they gave me and so damned weak, I would have recognized the wrongness of that recording."

"Did you see any faces you recognized? Hear any familiar voices or names mentioned?"

"No. They were strangers. My big question is, why did they want me to believe that lie? What purpose did it serve?"

"Maybe they thought you'd give up all hope and tell them what they wanted."

"Perhaps."

"So where do we go from here?"

"We're going to find the prick who did this to us, and we're going to send him to hell."

CHAPTER
TWENTY-FIVE

Declan lay on the bed in the guestroom, fighting his instincts. Instead of returning to the LCR apartment they'd been using, they had come back to Sabrina's house. He hadn't even considered arguing. Even though it was an hour's drive and Sabrina had looked ready to drop, he had realized she needed the familiarity of home to help her deal.

Why hadn't he considered how hard this would be on her? Though he had initially dreaded the hypnosis, he'd found it much easier to endure than he had expected. Watching it like a movie had been bearable. But to Sabrina, it had been fresh and new... and she had suffered. Her expressive eyes had been dark green pools of despair. His heart ached for her.

The drive to her house had been silent and grim. The instant they'd walked inside the foyer, she'd thrown him a wan smile. "I'm beat. It's a little early for bed, but I don't think I can keep my eyes open any longer. There's plenty of food in the fridge if you want to make yourself a sandwich."

She hadn't allowed him to respond. Just went upstairs and then he'd heard her bedroom door click closed. He knew exactly what was going on behind those closed doors. Not once had he ever seen Sabrina cry in public. One of the many cruel things her stepbrother had enjoyed was mocking her pain. If she cried, he'd made fun of her as he raped her. She said the hard things were easier if she remained stoic and detached. Only when she was alone did she allow the powerful emotions to overtake her, overwhelm her.

And only with Declan had she ever allowed her vulnerable emotions to be revealed—a gift he had never taken for granted.

After all he'd done to her, didn't he owe her the comfort of his arms? He surged up from the bed and opened the bedroom door. And there she was, standing before him, her hand raised to knock. She had never sought him out before. His conscience reminded him she had never needed to seek him out. He had always gone to her.

"Hold me?" she asked softly.

Pulling her into his arms, he gave her the only comfort he could. Turning back into the bedroom was too damn tempting. Instead, he swept her up in his arms and headed down the hallway to the small sitting room she had refurbished. He settled into an oversized chair and held her close.

She pressed her face into his chest, and Declan, just as he had so many times in the past, smoothed his hand down her hair and shoulders, kissed the top of her head gently, and waited for the dam to break. It didn't happen.

"No tears tonight?" His voice was gruff, thick with his own emotions.

"Some things…" Her voice broke. She swallowed hard, tried again. "I think I've just discovered that some things hurt too much for tears."

He continued to stroke her hair, hoping that either the tears would come or she would fall asleep in his arms. Either way, he wanted to continue to hold her, offering what comfort he could.

How many nights, at the beginning of his imprisonment, had he lain awake and relived their last night together? He had replayed every tender kiss, every soft sigh. Envisioned her lovely, expressive face, the long, silky length of her body. Those memories had sustained him for months.

"Tell me," she whispered.

He drew a breath. He knew what she meant…knew that he owed her this. Didn't mean it'd be easy.

"It was so stupid of me. I got that text from you and knew it must've been important for you to be contacting me so soon. I was distracted, worried. The fact that it didn't come from your private phone didn't cross my mind. Wasn't the first time you'd texted me from a burner."

He huffed out a disgusted sound at his own ignorance and carelessness. "Still…I should've known something was off. The minute I got out of the car, I knew it was a setup. You know how it is. Air's different. That odd, cold zip up your spine. I went for my weapon. Got Tasered. Went down. Tried to fight. Got a kick or two in before they shot me up with something.

"I woke up, hogtied and as helpless as a babe. Whatever they'd given me knocked me on my ass. I barely knew my name. By the time we got to the prison, I was cognizant but still tied so tight I couldn't twitch a finger, much less get loose."

"And you didn't recognize any voices? Accents, dialects? They didn't talk about anything familiar?"

"No. Nothing. They rarely spoke. When they did, it was in English…occasionally Spanish and French. The only one with a distinctive accent was that giant jackass you took down. The others had none. They kept me blindfolded for a few days. Threw me into a cell and left me there."

"When did the questions start?"

"Hard to say. Days slid into nights, and I was out for long periods. The minute I started coming out of it, I'd get another needle."

"You think they were waiting on instructions? Or waiting for someone?"

"I thought about that but decided the purpose was to just make me wait, dwell on what was coming. I'm sure they thought I'd feel helpless—I did, but it was buried beneath a ton of anger. I was too pissed to be too worried."

"And the questions? Were they specific or general in nature?"

He knew what she was doing. She was trying to find a clue, that one thread that would tell them who was behind everything. It was something he'd done himself already, but Sabrina was an intelligent, savvy woman. Hell, maybe they could learn something new.

"Questions were general at first. Almost like they didn't want me to know the real reason I'd been taken. And they were the fairly generic ones for an enemy combatant—name, who did I work for, what were my superiors' names…shit like that. They got pissed when I said nothing."

"I've seen you in interrogation." He heard the smile in her voice. "You can make silence sound like a scream."

"Yeah, well. That's when they decided to have some fun."

Sabrina winced at those words. Declan was a warrior through and through. His capture would have infuriated him and made him want to fight with every fiber of his being. That kind of anger gave a captive strength. Maintain the anger, they couldn't bring you down. But strength from anger would last only so long. Once the pain penetrated the consciousness and couldn't be blocked, a new psychological battle took place. One where the brain fought to deny the agony, battled to reinforce the anger. A push-pull of opposing forces.

She cleared her throat. "I guess it was SOP on the torture tactics?"

"Yeah, nothing new. Typical standard operating procedures that I'd been through dozens of times before—training and teaching. Sleep deprivation, waterboarding, electrical shocks, plenty of beatings."

"When did the questions get specific?"

"Probably about a month or so into my captivity. Guess they figured I'd be broken down enough to tell something. They offered all sorts of shit to entice me—food, water, medical care. Didn't work any better than the physical torture."

"What did they ask?"

"No surprises. Wanted to know the undercover names of agents, locations of upcoming ops, locations of retired agents, code names, aliases."

"And there was no one specific question that made you think—oh, this could be the guy behind it?"

"I thought that would happen, so I tried to stay as focused on the questions as possible. Eventually concluded that even if one particular question would specify the bastard's identity, he planned to get as much out of me as possible."

"When you didn't talk…it got worse?"

"After a few weeks of…let's just say stringent questioning, they backed off. Maybe they were giving me time to think about things. Or maybe they were waiting for instructions."

"And then they came at you in a different way?"

"No. Started all over again. Probably thought I'd healed up too much to start with the other stuff, so the same shit happened. Another few weeks to break down my resistance."

"They threw you in that pit a lot?"

"Yeah. That wasn't fun."

She pressed her face against his neck, partly in sympathy and partly because she just wanted to feel his warmth...feel the beat of his pulse against her mouth. "Did they talk to you before you heard the recording of my voice?"

"Yeah. It didn't really dawn on me at first. I'd gotten in the mind-set to endure, so the words were just a buzz...a noise. But then they showed me your picture."

"Where did they get a photo of me?"

"Must've been taken when you were new to the Agency. Your hair was a lot longer, and you were wearing that ball cap I ended up throwing away."

"That was my favorite cap," she grumbled. She felt him shift, knew he was smiling. They'd had a blowout of an argument over that silly little cap.

"What did they say when they showed you my photo?"

"Taunted me...lot of vulgar innuendoes. Unfortunately, I was tied up or I would have defended your honor."

She pressed a kiss to his beard-stubbled cheek. "I'll forgive you this time."

"Then they started talking about how you had set me up. Reminded me you'd sent me a text. They told me you were in on the plan all along. Of course, I knew they were full of shit, but I maintained silence."

"And then came the recording?"

"Yeah. I vaguely remember the first time. I think I smiled at hearing your voice. It sounded so damn good. It took two or three tries before the words penetrated. I laughed in their faces."

She closed her eyes against the tears she'd sworn she wouldn't shed. She could picture him in her mind—bruised, bleeding, starving, but still so very strong, so very brave. Of course he wouldn't believe she had set him up, no matter how much they tried beating it into him. But then, with the recording playing 24/7, along with the drugs, it was no wonder he became convinced of her guilt.

"I don't know how many days or weeks they played that damn recording. Every time I passed out, they'd either throw cold water on me or shock me back to consciousness. I'd wake, and the recording would still be running." His arms tightened around her. "They hit at the weakest, most vulnerable part of me—my love for you. Crafty bastards."

"I was surprised you didn't try to kill me right away, instead of abducting me."

"I guess I wanted to watch you suffer."

"No. You knew LCR would come for me."

He drew away slightly to look down at her. "What?"

"The tracker in my arm. You knew about it. Knew the protocol I'd told Noah to follow if I was ever taken. That Noah would contact Albert." She shook her head. "With all the craziness of these last few weeks, that fact didn't occur to me until the other day. That's why you didn't kill me. You knew I would be rescued.

"A part of you remembered how much you loved me...could never physically hurt me." She lifted her head from his shoulder to press her forehead against his cheek. "You're still the same heroic, noble man I fell in love with."

His entire body stiff with denial, he pushed her off his lap, his face an expressionless mask.

She stood before him, wanting him so much she literally ached with pain. "I still love you, Declan."

In a swift move, he stood, probably expecting she would back up. She didn't, and she wouldn't back down. This was too important.

"Deny it all you want. It's not going away, and neither am I."

Instead of arguing, which she really preferred since it would have been a good catharsis for the anger she knew still bubbled inside him, he unexpectedly grabbed hold of her shoulders, dropped a hard kiss on the top of her head, then said with a resoluteness she knew he meant, "Give it up, Sabrina, and move on, because as soon as this is over, we are, too."

She watched helplessly as he walked away from her, and seconds later, she heard the click of his bedroom door shutting.

Her feet were moving before she even knew it. She made herself stop in front of his bedroom, but the glare she gave the closed door could've melted a hole in the wood. "Give up? Like hell, Declan Steele. Like hell."

Chapter Twenty-Six

"How's it going?"

Pulling his eyes away from the computer screen, Declan relaxed back in the chair. Sabrina stood at the office door. Dressed in faded jeans that lovingly hugged her long, lean legs and a long-sleeved black T-shirt that, for some insane reason, showed an almost indecent amount of cleavage, she was healthy, beautiful, and so damned sexy his mouth went dry.

Concentrating on her question and not on how much he wanted to get up from the desk and take advantage of the invitation lurking in her eyes took discipline. He cleared his throat, refocused. "Let's just say there are a helluva lot of Agency employees who have too much debt, lots of vices, and have had more affairs than I ever thought possible."

Her grimace was one of sympathy. "Still no real leads?"

"Not yet. By the time we're finished, we'll know the shoe size of their great-great-grandmothers."

"Not exactly helpful in determining a traitor."

"No, but somewhere in all this shit, something's going to pop. I feel it."

"Angela still helpful?"

"She's amazing."

"Good. She's saved LCR's ass plenty of times. Last year, she—" The phone in her pocket chimed. Holding up a finger, she grabbed the phone and held it to her ear.

As she talked, apparently to McCall, Declan studied her. The long, lean lines of her body, the generous, lovely breasts that he had caressed, kissed, and suckled with endless delight, the intelligence gleaming in her eyes, the beauty of her fair, clear complexion. Her thick, auburn hair that he had grasped in his hands and held as he pounded into her. The well-toned legs that had wrapped around his waist while he— Ah hell, what was he doing?

Declan pulled himself away from the lustful thoughts about his wife and instead thought about the deceptively delicate-looking package that made up Sabrina Fox. In no way, shape, or form did she look like a woman who could bring down a man twice her size without a weapon. Since he had trained her, seen her in action, he knew what she was capable of, what she could do.

She had amazed and enthralled him when he had been training her, and deep in his soul, he acknowledged she still did.

Unbelievable as it seemed, life had become routine and easier after their discussion. Declan gave Sabrina full credit. She had every right to kick him out on his ass. And, actually, he should have moved out. He didn't need to be living in her house. He could get his own place. But he hadn't mentioned moving out, and neither had she.

The memories of his life before his capture were constant companions. He could never forget the days and weeks of falling in love with Sabrina, their ops together, the laughter, the tears, the amazing camaraderie of being with the one person who totally understood him and loved him in spite of knowing everything— the good, bad, and downright ugly. That kind of love came along only once in a lifetime.

She'd gone on several more assignments while he continued to work with Angela to uncover every strand and thread of information regarding all EDJE employees, former and current. Within this mass of mostly dry but sometimes salacious information was the key.

"Hey." Sabrina stood in front of him, snapping her fingers. "Where's your mind? You okay?"

"Sorry. Yeah, I'm fine." Noticing the excitement on her face, he said, "What's up?"

"You remember Reuben Pierce?"

"Rotten Reuben? The asshole that sold a truckload of stolen military equipment to some militants in Egypt. Took out an entire elementary school. Hell yeah, I remember the scumbag. Don't tell me he's started taking hostages along with his other slimy deeds."

"Kind of. He's now doing double duty as a human trafficker—mostly kids. Selling them for a tidy profit."

"And the scum just gets scummier."

"Yep. Anyway, we almost got him right before you, um... found me."

"You mean before I kidnapped you and tried to kill you?"

She grinned. "Potato, po-tah-to." She shrugged and continued, "Anyway, we rescued the kids and most of his goon squad, but Reuben got away."

"Bet that riled you."

"You have no idea. But that was Noah on the phone. He's resurfaced in Italy. We've got someone on the inside already. We're setting up an ambush so we can finally nail the bastard."

Sabrina's excitement was contagious. Her eyes gleamed, and waves of energy seemed to bounce off her body. She was born to this kind of life.

"So I'm assuming you're in on the op?" Declan asked.

"Oh yeah. He's not getting away from me again."

"When are you leaving?"

Her expression brightened even more. "You mean, when are *we* leaving, don't you?"

"What are you talking about?"

"We're short a team member. Riley's still out of commission, recovering. Noah asked if you'd like to join us."

The very idea fired his blood. See Rotten Reuben get his just deserts? Hell to the yeah. "I'm in."

"I'll call Noah back." And before he knew what she was going to do, she strode over to the desk, grabbed his face in her hands and kissed him hard on the mouth. "It'll be like old times."

Torn between telling her he'd changed his mind and grabbing her for a harder, deeper kiss on that soft, luscious mouth, he instead did nothing but watch as she placed a call to the LCR leader.

Like old times? No. Those days would never be again.

Teramo, Italy

The takedown should be simple and straightforward. Dylan Savage, one of LCR's top deep-cover operatives, had infiltrated Reuben's band of sleazy thugs last year. Dylan had been within days of springing the surprise that would have brought down the man's entire operation. Something had spooked Reuben, and instead of a successful op, the mission had fizzled into nothing. Reuben had moved on to another city, leaving more than half his employees behind, including Dylan.

Intel had revealed that Reuben had gotten wind that he was being actively hunted and took only the men he'd worked with for years.

Then, the opportunity to utilize Sabrina's deep-cover personality of Lucia St. Martine had come along. But, once again, Reuben had evaded them.

LCR was determined that the third time would be the charm. Reuben Pierce was going down.

Dylan had bided his time, and when Reuben had surfaced in Italy, the operative had reconnected with the creep. To prove his loyalty and usefulness, Dylan was bringing in a truckload of stolen military-grade weapons—among Reuben's favorite contraband. Unlike many of these kinds of deals, Reuben had insisted on inspecting the merchandise himself—perhaps as a test for Dylan, or maybe a show of his arrogance. Whatever the reason, this might be their last chance to apprehend the bastard. Things had to go off without a hitch.

Sabrina took in the faces of her team. Aidan sat in the back, the expression on his face one she'd seen dozens of times—determination. She knew he'd been just as pissed as she was when Reuben had escaped in Honduras.

Her eyes shifted to Justin Kelly. Since his partner's injury, the man had become even grimmer. As young and fit as Riley was, the prognosis for a full and speedy recovery was excellent. Still, the shadows in Justin's slate-gray eyes revealed a darker-than-usual sadness. It was apparent that he missed his partner. She'd never seen two people who were more in tune with one another during an op.

Moving her gaze again, she amended that thought. Yes, she had seen two people more in tune with each other than Riley and Justin. She and Declan. Since they'd had a strong bond even before they'd started working ops together, their partnership had been seamless. She could read every nuance of his body language, every expression on his face as easily as she could read her own thoughts. And he had been able to do the same.

Removing all the hurt and volatile emotions she'd been feeling over the past few weeks, Sabrina studied her husband. Still the most handsome man she'd ever seen. The thick black hair might have a few strands of silver, but that only added to his allure. She had once thought he had a poet's face, elegant, refined, and still totally masculine. That wasn't the case anymore. Maybe most people wouldn't notice the changes, but having loved him for so long, she saw distinct differences. Declan now had the face of a hardened warrior—tough, ruthless, uncompromising.

She had loved him when he had been so harsh in her training she hadn't believed she would survive. She had loved him when he'd made love to her with a passion so intense and unequaled that her body still trembled at the memories. And she loved him still.

He had told her they were over. That once they'd identified and apprehended those responsible for his capture, he would no longer be her husband. Declan had apparently forgotten an important characteristic of her personality—she was a fighter. As a kid who'd been through multiple rapes and beatings, imprisoned in a psychiatric hospital for the criminally insane, so drugged she hadn't even known her own name, she had never stopped fighting. EDJE had honed her fighting skills, but at her core, she was a rebel.

No one, not even her beloved Declan, was going to keep her from what she knew to be right. And what she wanted most. They were meant to be together. He wouldn't agree with her thought process, but she didn't give a damn. No way was she letting him go.

"Okay, listen up." Noah's voice came through the speakerphone she'd set on the small table of the camper. "Savage is making his way inside the warehouse. He's been frisked, so we were correct with our decision on no mics or weapons. Infrared is working well. Ten men have come in so far. None of them Pierce. This needs to go down clean and simple. I'll let you know the minute our target arrives. Angela and Mallory are with me, set to go. The minute I give the word, we all go in as planned. Any questions?"

When no one spoke, Noah continued, "Fox, you and Thorne have the show."

"Roger that," Aidan said. "You give the word, we're a go."

"Stand by," Noah came back.

While they waited, she and Aidan would give one more quick review. Sabrina rolled out the blueprints of the large warehouse. "Aidan and I will enter through the front. Justin and Declan, you've each got an entrance in the back. Noah will take the south side door. Angela and Jake have the north."

"The instant McCall gives the signal," Aidan followed up, "we go in quiet. Kelly and Steele, the instant you've unlocked your entry, alert us. Then it's radio silence till we make our presence known. If we can do this without bullets, we will. If not, just make sure you're the one shooting."

Each operative doubled-checked their weapons one more time. When she finished checking hers, she glanced over at Declan. His eyes held resolve, but the relaxed set to his mouth told her he was looking forward to the action. Even though they weren't rescuing anyone tonight, her heart lifted that he could be involved in her work.

"Okay, it's a go." Noah's voice came through low and calm. And with that, the four of them exited the camper and headed toward their designated areas.

Blood pumped through Declan, and he felt alive and purposeful. Damn, he loved the excitement of an op. That spine-tingling knowledge that anything could happen but also the assurance that he'd trained for years for everything to go as planned. Out of the corner of his eye, before he headed to the back of the warehouse, he spotted Sabrina and Thorne running to the front. No one would move until everyone was in position.

When he and Sabrina had worked ops together, he'd always taken the lead. Felt a little odd to see her under the command of someone else. Felt even odder to see her team up with another partner.

Declan arrived at the back of the warehouse. He stooped down at the door and double-checked the lock. Never seen one he couldn't pick. In less than a minute, he had released the lock, then spoke into his mic. "This is Steele, all set to go."

Less than thirty seconds later, Justin Kelly responded with the same words.

Declan held his breath. Any second now... Sabrina's voice came through, soft and calm, "Go, go, go."

Opening the door, he went low, his favorite SIG Sauer gripped in his hand. The room he entered was empty other than a couple of folding chairs, cigarette butts, and a few candy wrappers. He crossed the room, put his ear to the door, and listened. No sounds. He cracked open the door enough to peer in and spotted the main part of the warehouse, where the deal was going down. A large semitrailer truck sat in the middle of the cavernous room... several men surrounded the truck. He searched for Pierce. Didn't see him. Where... Then he heard the man's hyena-type laughter and knew the creep was on the other side of the truck. Dylan Savage's gruff voice responded to whatever Pierce had said.

Declan waited. When the time was right, either Sabrina or Thorne would give the signal, and they were to swarm the area. He heard the wheedling voice of Pierce, and then Dylan said in an overly loud voice, "Open the doors and let me show you what we've got."

With all attention on the doors, Declan knew the time was now. Thorne's deep voice said, "Go."

Declan took off.

Staying low, he ran toward the truck. It took several seconds for the ten goons and Pierce to realize what was happening. The men turned in unison. Declan targeted two men closest to him. "Okay. Real slow, drop your guns and kick them toward me."

One guy quickly complied. "Hey, I just teamed up with these guys. I don't know nothing."

"Bad luck for you then, mate."

Keeping his eye on the other man, who had frozen in place, Declan quickly secured the compliant man and pushed him to his knees. "Stay there."

He addressed the other man, "Now, why not be as good as your partner and drop your gun?"

"He ain't my partner," the man sneered.

"Do it anyway."

The guy was obliging enough to lower his gun, but instead of dropping it, he aimed it at Declan. Reading his expression correctly, Declan kicked the man's hand, knocking the gun to the floor. The guy went to one knee for his secondary weapon at his ankle. Declan put his gun to the man's head. "Maybe you misunderstood me the first time. Now, with your left hand, take the gun from your ankle holster and put it on the ground. If I even see you flinch, you're going to have a neat little hole going straight through the middle of your brain."

Cursing fluently in both Italian and English, the man did what he was told. The gun slid several feet away from him. "Good job. Now, stay down there and put your hands behind your head."

As soon as the man complied, Declan secured his hands with a plastic zip tie. Pulling both men up by their elbows, he led them over to the wall. "Sit. Stay."

Declan turned and surveyed the rest of the team. Seven other men were either sitting or kneeling, all secured and ready for transport. Reuben Pierce was in a chair. Though his hands were secured behind his back, he looked as arrogant and unconcerned as if he were getting a speeding ticket. Declan hoped like hell that McCall had the clout to keep this bastard behind bars.

Searching for Sabrina, he felt his heartbeat tick up when he didn't see her. Noticing Aidan struggling with one of his captives, he shouted, "Where's Fox?"

Thorne jerked his head toward the door. "One of them got loose."

Without waiting for more information, Declan took off. Trees, bushes, and giant weeds surrounded the perimeter of the warehouse. Declan stood and listened for a few seconds. Not hearing anything, he spoke into the mic, "Fox, where are you?"

"Chasing this asshole through a briar patch. I'm about five hundred feet north of the warehouse."

He grinned at the breathless aggravation in her tone. She was pissed. "Right behind you."

Declan ran northward, wondering if he should figure out a way to head the guy off. Before he could ask for an update, he heard Sabrina's scathing voice. "Listen, jerk, it'll be easier on both of us if you just come on in quietly."

"Come and get me, bitch."

Declan headed toward the voices. He stopped abruptly and watched Sabrina facing a man. He was a few inches taller with a whole lot more meat and muscle than Sabrina. Didn't matter. Declan would bet his last magazine cartridge that the guy had never come up against anyone like Sabrina.

Leaning back against a tree, Declan crossed his arms and settled in to enjoy the show.

Eyes narrowed, Sabrina circled the man. The jerk had gotten away from her and led her on a chase through a briar patch. Her favorite camo pants were ripped, and she had a scratch on the side of her neck that stung like a bee. She was angry and hot, not a good combination. Bastard had managed to get the drop on her, and she'd lost her gun. Fortunately, he had also been disarmed. She could go for the gun at her ankle or the knife in a sheath at her waist, but she was too furious to take the easy way out. Guy wanted a fight? She was more than happy to oblige.

The man swung a fist toward her fast. She ducked, pleased that he appeared to have had some training. Maybe this would be a worthy opponent after all. She spun on her left foot, brought her right leg out, and caught the guy with a good one on the chin. He spat out a curse, along with some blood.

He circled her a couple more times and then rushed her, ready to throw himself on her in a full-body tackle. Deciding to prolong it a little longer, Sabrina leaped out of his way at the last second. The man thudded to the ground, but she was pleased to see him get back on his feet. They danced around each other for several seconds.

She knew Declan was watching her, most likely enjoying himself. Out of the corner of her eye, she spotted Aidan take a position beside Declan.

"What's going on?" Aidan asked.

"Idiot doesn't want to come quietly."

"Hell, Sabrina," Aidan said, "he's surrounded. We can easily take him."

"And miss the fun?" she asked.

Declan smiled fondly at his wife. They used to have sparring matches all the time. Neither of them had given any quarter. It had kept them both well trained and ready for anything. He was pleased that she hadn't let her training slip. In fact, he thought as he watched her deliver a roundhouse kick and then pivot for a left-right punch to her opponent's nose and then his stomach, she had picked up a few new moves.

"I've missed this," Declan admitted.

"She do this a lot when you were working together?"

"Not as much as she liked," Declan said. "Hand-to-hand combat is one of her specialties, but most of the men she took down were the power men. Fighting them was never her intent."

"Killing them was her goal?"

Not taking his eyes off Sabrina, he said, "You got a problem with that?"

"Hell no. I know her well enough to know she would never kill someone if there'd been another way."

"Some people believe there's always another way besides killing."

"Those people are usually never faced with the consequences if the scumbag ends up living and doing even eviler things."

"Sounds like you know something about making those kinds of decisions."

"I might."

Recognizing in the other man's voice the reluctance to share, Declan didn't push. Seemed damned odd for him to be having a civil conversation with Thorne when he was quite sure they didn't like each other.

"Hate to bust this up, Little Fox, but the man seems to be breathing quite heavy. Mightn't you want to finish this up soon?"

"Gee, you guys know how to spoil a girl's fun."

Still, he was happy to see her give the man a sturdy kick in the groin and follow it up with a blow to his chin. The man fell backward and then tried to rise again.

"Oh, for heaven's sake. Stay down, will you," she snapped. Throwing herself on her opponent, she worked to pin him in place. He wasn't having it. They scrambled around for several more moments. Declan winced as he saw her take a hit to her shoulder.

When the guy grabbed her knife, Declan stepped up, placed a heavy, booted foot on the man's hand, then reached down and grabbed the knife from his fingers. "Now that would be very unsportsmanlike."

Throwing him a grin, Sabrina said, "Thanks." And then proceeded to wiggle around in the correct position. Wrapping her legs around the man's neck, she tightened her thighs and waited him out. It took a good minute before his body went limp. When he was done for, she released the unconscious man and rolled away from him.

Jumping to her feet, she dusted the dirt from her pants, and then examined a tear at her knee. "Crap, I'll never be able to sew this back up."

Declan's heart turned over. Damn, he had missed this.

CHAPTER
TWENTY-SEVEN

"I'm going to set up a meeting with them." Declan made the announcement as calmly as if he'd ask her to pass the salt at the dinner table.

Sabrina jerked back as if she'd been punched in the face. "Are you crazy? No, absolutely not."

"You know it's the only way."

Her spirits crashed. All good feelings from taking down the skeevy scumbag Reuben Pierce went up in flames. Hell, they'd only been back one day...hadn't even unpacked.

"No, it's not the only way. We can still—"

"We can search and research till doomsday, and it's not going to give us the information we need. Hell, whoever set this up had enough money and influence to create an elaborate hoax. If they can do that, then they can hide so we can't find them through normal means."

"Everyone leaves a trail, Declan. We just haven't found it yet."

"Sabrina. Think this through. They falsified DNA results inside a government agency. Killed innocent civilians. Stole a body from his grave to hide the identity. Pulled the wool over the eyes of some of the smartest and savviest people in covert ops. These bastards have proven they can and will do whatever they have to do to get the information they want."

"Then why haven't they come for you again? I know you're not exactly living high profile, but you haven't been underground, either. If they're so damn smart, then why haven't they already found you and taken you? Hell, you walked through the freaking Agency, making yourself an open target."

"I don't know. What I do know is I'm not going to wait around and let them call the shots. When they try for me again, they're not going to find the same man they did before."

"They'll know it's a setup."

"Of course they will. With their arrogance, they'll still think they can win."

"This is insane. I won't let you do this."

"You have no say or input. I'm telling you out of courtesy. It's already a done deal. I sent the message out this morning."

The pain was massive. Swept through her like a tidal wave. And it shouldn't have. They were no longer partners, and he'd gone out of his way to make sure she knew they weren't partners in marriage, either. "I guess I should be grateful you thought to mention it to me at all. Thanks for putting me in my place."

"Stop it. This is about bringing down the bastards who did this to me. Nothing more."

White-hot fury incinerated the hurt. She stalked toward him, anger vibrating in every muscle. "You listen to me. I'm sick and tired of you saying they did this to you. Yes, I know you suffered, but damn you, Declan Steele, they took my husband away. Destroyed my marriage. Almost killed me. They damn well did this to both of us."

Though regret dimmed his eyes, she saw no softening in his expression. "I misspoke. That's not what I meant. I'm just saying that these people are trying to destroy more than an EDJE agent and a former agent. They want to destroy hundreds, perhaps thousands, of lives. Even bring down the entire Agency. This is bigger than you and me."

And now she felt like a selfish bitch, because, of course, he was right. She drew in a ragged breath. "Okay. Where and when do we do this?"

His jaw took on that implacable tilt that she hated. "I told you...you're not involved. As I said, I advised you out of courtesy, nothing more."

"Tough shit, macho man. I will be involved, and you can't stop me."

"Oh yes, I can." He grabbed her shoulders and shook her. "Think, Sabrina. If they can use you against me, they will."

"They won't be able to."

"If they got you, they could."

"You've made it perfectly clear that our marriage is over. That you feel nothing for me anymore. Using me would be pointless."

"They don't know that."

Ha! And she hadn't thought the pain could get any worse. She swallowed hard. "Okay. Who are you going to use?"

"McCall has offered LCR's help. I turned him down. He—"

"Of course you did. You're the great and powerful Declan Steele, able to leap over tall buildings, see through walls and outrun bullets. Oh, no, wait, that's a superhero. And damn you, that's not you. They will fucking kill you this time, Declan. Does that even matter to you?"

Hot anger glittered in his eyes. "They won't get me, Sabrina."

She turned her back to him and forced her legs to walk away. For the first time in years, she feared the violence inside her. She had fought like hell to overcome that depth of anger.

A hard hand landed on her arm and pulled her around. With rage and deep hurt as the impetus, she threw a hard punch at his face. He caught her fist. Undeterred, she threw a punch with her left fist, which he caught, too.

She wanted to howl her fury, to cry at the hurt he'd dealt her, and she wanted to apologize for striking out at him.

Instead of retaliating or responding with anger, he did something so very Declan. Holding both wrists in one hand, he lifted them above her head and then pushed her backward a few steps until she was pressed against the wall. He moved in closer, melding his body against hers. Even though he held her, she could have easily gotten away, and he gave her plenty of time to do so. Instead, she whispered his name.

He lowered his mouth to hers, and she prepared herself for an assault. It should have been a brutal kiss. She could feel the violence vibrating through him. Instead, when his mouth touched hers, it was tender, soft. This was a kiss a man gives a woman he cherishes. It was a kiss of love.

She could have fought an angry kiss. She couldn't fight this one. Didn't want to fight.

With her hands trapped above her, the only way she could show him what she wanted was with her lips and body. Her mouth open to receive his tongue, she sucked gently and then tangled and dueled with him. Her body heated, flushed with arousal, softened, preparing itself to be taken, conquered, loved.

"Declan," she murmured softly.

"Little Fox," he answered back.

They rubbed against each other, creating a friction, increasing their heat, their need. Then he stepped back and, amazingly, even with one hand occupied holding her wrists, managed to undress her. Of course, her wiggling and stepping out of clothes when he instructed her helped a lot.

Sabrina felt like a sacrifice. Arms over her head, pressed up against the wall, offering herself up to be taken, devoured. The sapphire flame in his eyes had never burned brighter as they roamed over her naked, trembling body. And every place his gaze landed pulsed with needy excitement. Her nipples ached for his mouth, his hands. Her sex throbbed, wet with arousal, her body readying itself for her lover.

"You are so damn beautiful," he growled.

Breath hitching in her throat, she whispered a sultry invitation, "And I'm yours for the taking."

He lowered his mouth, and she opened hers to accept him. Instead of kissing her lips, he pressed a kiss to her forehead. "Sabrina. Lass." His voice held an achingly husky tone, the slight hint of his Scottish heritage sending another rush of need throughout her being.

She wasn't above begging, and she opened her mouth to do just that. "Don't stop, Declan. Let's at least have this one last time together."

He answered her in the best way possible. Covering her aching nipple with his hot mouth, he sucked on her so unexpectedly deep and hard, she rocketed past full arousal and teetered on the edge of orgasm. Still holding her wrists, he used his other hand to leisurely explore her body. All the while, his mouth drew deeply on her nipple. The throb between her legs began to match the rhythm of his mouth. His fingertips lightly grazed her clit, and just like that…just as he had always been able to make her do, she soared over the edge and into an explosive, body-clenching climax.

As she drifted back to reality, she heard his soft, reassuring words. Nonsensical and pitched in an even thicker brogue.

"Declan. I need to touch you."

He released her wrists, allowing her arms to drop, but before she could glide her hands over the hard body she so loved, he went to his knees before her, opened her folds and pressed his lips to her in an openmouthed kiss. Sabrina cried out, unable to control the new climax washing over her. Her fingers wove into his thick hair as she held him to her center and rode out the waves. His tongue thrust gently into her, allowing her to once again settle softly, quietly.

Declan drew in a breath. He would never get enough of her taste. No matter how far he went away from her, how badly he wanted to deny it, Sabrina owned him—his heart, his mind, his body.

"Declan," she whispered softly above him. "I want you inside me."

His smile one of wicked mischief, he said, "My pleasure, Little Fox." Holding her hips steady against the wall, his big hands spread across her lower abdomen, while his thumbs parted her again. He heard her soft protest, knew she'd meant another body part, but he couldn't resist. "Once more, my darling."

His tongue went deep, retreated, swirled around the outer edges, licked, went deep again. He could feel the tenseness in her body as it tightened, heading toward another release. Wanting to hold off just a little while longer, he drew back and blew softly all over her exposed sex. The whimper she gave made him smile.

Knowing he wouldn't be able to delay her much longer and on the verge of explosion himself, he put his mouth to her again and lashed at her with his tongue, inside and out, and then he sucked…hard. Her entire body went taut as a violin string, and she came hard.

Unable to wait a second longer, he stood, gathered her in his arms and carried her upstairs. When he would have gone to his bedroom, she said in a breathless, husky voice, "No. Let's use mine. It's bigger."

Barely able to speak, since his jaw felt it might break from the strain, he headed to her bedroom. Pushing open the half-closed door, he strode to the bed, dropped her onto the crimson-red comforter and stepped back. Her eyes reflected a look of panic, and he knew she feared he would leave her. He said nothing. Just stripped down to nothing and joined her.

The instant his knee touched the bed, she opened her arms. His eyes stung. The love and acceptance on her face, the open way she welcomed his body, was like coming home. Refusing to dwell on whether this was a massive mistake or not, Declan settled between her open legs, pushed her knees to her chest and thrust deep.

Sabrina gasped, and Declan stilled within her, allowing her to adjust, accept. When he felt the give, her breath shuddering out softly, he began to move. Keeping her legs up and spread, he controlled his movements and hers. Their gazes locked, her eyes telling him of her love, her acceptance, her total faith in them, in him. He could only imagine what his eyes were telling her, but no way could he look away. No way would he allow himself to miss the beauty before him. Face flushed with excitement, eyes glazed with passion, lush breasts swollen and ripe with arousal.

His thrusts became harder, less controlled. Release coming quicker than he wanted, determined that she would come with him, he reached between their bodies and pressed his thumb at the top of her sex. Her eyes widened as her body spasmed, and that was Declan's signal. Pounding hard, deep, the intensity almost more than he could bear, he came with a roar, shouting her name in surrender.

Sabrina woke to an empty bed. Her body felt sore and deliciously used. She wanted to snuggle back into her pillow and relive the last few hours. The entire room smelled of passion, sex, and Declan. She wanted to savor, remember. She couldn't.

Declan was getting ready to leave. She could hear him rummaging around in his bedroom. She squinted at the clock, surprised that it was almost dawn. She knew he had only left her about half an hour ago, which meant he'd held her all night. She didn't know whether to rejoice in that or sob her heart out. Had he done it because he'd finally acknowledged what he still felt for her, or had he stayed because he was determined that this was their last time together? She greatly feared she knew the answer to that.

How could he deny their love? No man could make love to a woman the way Declan had and not have an intense love for her. No, she wasn't being a silly, romantic fool. She was his wife. She knew this man backward and forward. Yes, he had changed, but not in the way he believed.

Hearing him stomping down the stairs, Sabrina threw the covers back and leaped out of bed. Snagging her robe at the foot of the bed on the way out of the room, she ran down the stairway and caught him in the foyer just as he was about to open the front door. He was going to leave without even saying good-bye.

"Where are you going?"

He froze, didn't turn. "Got a few things to do to set this up."

"When does it go down?"

"Day after tomorrow."

"Declan, I—"

He turned to face her. "Don't say it, Sabrina. I'll be all right. It'll work out." He took one last look at her face and then put his hand on the doorknob.

"Wait. You need to hear this."

"I don't have time."

"Make time."

"We can talk after everything's over."

"And if it's never over? What then?"

"One way or other, it will be over."

"Okay, fine. It will be over, but I need to tell you something, and you need to listen." When she saw he would argue again, she added, "You owe me this, Declan."

Damned if he could argue with that.

"Fine. Say it."

Her full, mobile mouth curved in a rueful smile. "Not exactly the atmosphere I wanted, but I'll take what I can get." She went to him, stood within inches of him, and cupped his face in her hands. "I love you, Declan. I have for years. Our marriage vows of till death do us part never worked for me. Even when I thought you were dead, you owned my heart. I will always love you."

"Sabrina...don't."

"You say you're not the same man. I disagree. They might have done a lot of things to you...to your body and your mind, but they couldn't touch the core of the man you are. Strong, resilient, heroic, and good. That's still inside you."

"I've told you—"

"Yes, I know. You've made yourself perfectly clear. You've told me those things are gone for good. That you're just an empty shell. Let me be just as clear. Empty shell or the same man as before, or somewhere in between, I love you, Declan Steele. No matter what the future holds, no matter where you go, what you do. That will never change. You will have my love forever. Whether you want it or not. Our forever after got interrupted, but it doesn't have to stay that way. We can still be together."

Grinding his teeth, refusing to give in to his need to touch her, he said, "Is that all?"

"No, there's one more thing."

"And that is?"

"You still love me, too. Deny it all you want, but I know the truth."

He kissed her. That was his only way to protect himself, to get her to stop talking. His only weapon against words he couldn't defend or argue. Pulling away, he whispered softly, "Good-bye, Little Fox," and walked out the door.

CHAPTER TWENTY-EIGHT

Sitting in a van a block from the meeting place wasn't her idea of being involved. However, it was a concession from Declan, and one she had decided to accept. Especially since she wouldn't put it past him to knock her out and tie her up to keep her from being involved. This way, at least, she'd be able to get there in a relatively short amount of time when things went sour. And she didn't for a moment believe that this wouldn't go sour. It was as stupid a plan as any she'd ever heard. What pissed her off was the fact that she couldn't come up with a better one.

Declan was right. They weren't going to give up trying to extract information from him and could strike anytime. Waiting around for that to happen would be counterproductive. Facing the bastards and playing them was the only way. Still sucked lemons, though.

"Can't believe he's doing this without our backup," Jackson grumbled.

She pulled her gaze away from the three monitors in front of her. She knew Declan had agreed to his friend's involvement as another concession. Jackson wanted to help, and even though he wasn't in the thick of things, the man had been kind enough to agree.

Sabrina was glad to have him here for another reason. When things went to shit, he'd be able to help.

Playing the helpless female didn't sit well with her, and she was sure Declan saw through the thin veneer she'd adopted. It didn't matter. Keeping Declan safe was the only concern she had. Ego went out the back door when it came to protecting the man she loved.

Wanting to ease Jackson's worry without revealing anything, Sabrina threw him a reassuring smile. "I've seen the guys he's hired to help out. Looks like they can do the job."

"Not like a trained agent."

Sabrina didn't respond to that complaint. What could she say? Noah, Aidan, Justin, and Jake were close to Declan, behind closed doors, ready to assist. Since they couldn't tell Jackson about LCR and their involvement, Declan had claimed he'd hired some former Special Forces guys to help out. There was actually quite a bit of truth in that.

Thankfully, Jackson had bought the story, even if he didn't like it.

"You really think they'll show?" he asked.

"Yes. They know it's a setup, but Declan's right. They'll be arrogant enough to think they can win."

"Risky as hell."

"It is, but pulling them out from underground is our only hope to capture them."

"As elaborate a setup as they had, they've got some big money backing them. They bring an army in, Declan doesn't have a prayer."

She winced at the image but couldn't deny the truth. Maybe that's why their lovemaking had held felt so desperate. It had been as if they were saying good-bye to one another. For the past two days, they'd hardly spoken to each other. Whenever she'd had something to say, she had used as few words as possible. Declan, not to be outdone, had used mostly grunts and body language to get his message across.

"He's better trained than they are."

"You trying to convince me or yourself?"

She lifted her shoulder in a halfhearted shrug. Saying that Declan was better trained than anyone else was all she could come up with to reassure herself that he wouldn't die tonight. She simply didn't know what he would face.

"So you and Declan are back together, right? His being gone didn't mess you guys up?"

Even though he was their friend, Sabrina didn't feel comfortable spilling her guts to him. She gave him a vague, "We're working through things."

"Seems as protective of you as ever."

Yes, Declan had always had that protective streak. Even in their early years, when he'd been her trainer and so incredibly tough on her, she'd always been safe with him. He would always do everything within his power to take care of her.

Her gaze riveted to the screen, Sabrina sat up in her seat. "We've got some activity."

She and Jackson watched as Declan strode into the building. No one in his right mind would assume he would come in unarmed, so he didn't bother to conceal the SIG Sauer in his right hand. If they checked, they'd find at least five more weapons on him. She hoped like hell that no one got close enough to try.

The expression on his face was grim, implacable, and determined. She knew that look...had seen it on his face many times in the past. His intentions were clear. He would end this thing tonight, no matter what.

A movement in the corner of another screen caught her attention. Her breath caught and held. She shook her head in denial. *No. Just no.*

"What the hell?" Jackson snarled. "No. No way in hell. This has got to be a mistake."

She didn't want to believe it, either, but the ugly proof was on the screen in front of them. They now knew who the traitor was. But, oh, sweet heavens...why?

Declan stood in the middle of the room and waited. He wasn't alone. McCall and three LCR Elite team members were out of sight, ready to assist. No one would expect him to show up alone, but revealing his backup would do him no favors. He would pretend this wasn't a setup until it became necessary to stop pretending.

Knowing that Sabrina was a block away was both reassuring and worried the hell out of him. She would come running, guns a'blazing if this thing went to shit, which she definitely believed it would. And because the possibility was all too real, he felt fear for her. He didn't want her involved, but didn't have the heart to trick her into staying completely out of it.

Jackson would see to her safety—no matter what went down.

He heard footsteps and turned immediately to his right. When he made out the person coming toward him, a mule kick to the chest couldn't have surprised him more.

"Declan? I'm here."

"So you are."

"You said you wanted to talk. But why here? I could've come to Sabrina's apartment again."

And because he had to know, he said, "Why, Albert?"

"Why what?"

"Don't play games with me. Why did you betray your country? Betray me and Sabrina?"

"What are you talking about?"

He wanted to play games? Then Declan would oblige. "I sent a message, underground. Set up the meeting to talk. You're here."

"What the hell? I got a phone call from you. Said you wanted to meet me. You gave me this address. Said you had an idea of the traitor's identity."

Could that be true? Was this just another hoax? Or was this a setup to try to grab Albert, too. Or was the old man lying?

Unable to take the chance, he held his gun steady and said, "Why don't we wait and see if anyone else comes, then we'll decide if you're telling the truth?"

His expression one of both anger and resignation, Albert nodded. "Fine. But when this is over, we're damn well going to have a long talk."

They waited ten, then fifteen minutes. Deciding no one else was coming, he called out, "Okay, guys. Looks like this is over. Come on out."

Appearing out of the darkness were McCall, Thorne, Kelly, and Mallory. Even though he hadn't needed them, LCR's backup had been much appreciated.

Knowing he wouldn't be able to keep her away from the questions he had for Albert, Declan spoke into his mic. "Sabrina, you and Jackson want to join us?"

No answer.

"Sabrina? Jackson?"

Shit! Declan took off. Running from the building, he raced down the street. The black van was still there. But why wasn't she answering?

"Sabrina, dammit, check in." Then, "Jackson, can you hear me?"

Silence.

His gun at the ready, he reached the van and then jerked to a halt. The back doors lay on the street. Jackson was on the van's floor. Blood trickled from his forehead—he was either unconscious or dead. And Sabrina? She wasn't there.

Declan knew his worst fears had been realized.

CHAPTER
TWENTY-NINE

Sabrina listened carefully. She'd woken several minutes ago and, realizing immediately what had happened, quickly regulated her breathing. If they thought she was still unconscious, she might be able to pick up something.

Other than a dull headache and a wrenching in her shoulders from her wrists being cuffed and tied to her ankles, she felt reasonably good.

So far, she'd heard nothing substantial or helpful from the men who surrounded her. She had yet to see them, but there appeared to be five distinct voices. Three were American and two French. Unless someone else showed up, language would not be a barrier. Now if she could just figure out the identity of the traitor, the moneyman calling the shots and, oh yeah, a way to escape.

Declan must be going crazy. And he was sure to be blaming himself. He wouldn't agree, but this was all on her. She had insisted on being involved. And Jackson? He had to be okay. There was no reason for them to want him. She was the prize—she would be what they wanted so they could get at Declan again.

She remembered little of what had happened. Someone had knocked on the van's back door. Jackson had stood and gone to look out the window. There'd been a small pop. Before she could react, the doors had dropped away, and two masked men were there. She remembered electrified agony rushing through her body, knew she had been Tasered. Then nothing.

How would they use her to lure Declan? She had no doubt that he would comply with their demands. He might deny his love to her face, but she knew his heart. Declan would give himself up to save her.

No! She wouldn't allow it. She still had her locator device in her arm. LCR would track her down, just as they had before. They would—

The memory returned of what had happened right before the attack. Albert had appeared. He was the traitor. How could that be? How could he have done this to her and Declan?

Her mind was scrambling to fight back despair when footsteps approached. She continued to breathe in easy, regular breaths. Damned if they would know that—

"Okay. Up and at 'em," a gruff voice shouted. He pulled at the rope locking her hands and her ankles together. What was happening?

She heard it before she felt the tug on her restraints—the squeak of a pulley. Wrenched from the ground, she was hefted up and found herself hanging several feet in the air, facing downward. Her hands locked behind her and bound to her ankles, she swung back and forth like a pendulum. The pressure on her shoulders and back was immense. An unwilling screech of agony shrieked from her mouth.

Someone gave her braided hair a nasty tug. "That's a good girl. Give us a good show."

Fighting the pain with all her might, Sabrina raised her head and faced a camera. They were filming her. No. She refused to give them the entertainment they wanted. Biting the inside of her mouth until she tasted blood, she lowered her head, determined not to utter another sound.

The laughter of several men erupted, but before she could raise her head to get a look at them, something struck her in the stomach. Took her breath. *Shit, that hurt.* Another hit, then another.

Her chin tucked against her chest, she drew in a breath as she absorbed each blow. They wouldn't hear a peep from her.

More laughter. Then their fun really began. Unable to stop, the pain immense and overwhelming, her screams erupted. Minutes, hours later, her voice hoarse from the strain of her cries, a hard hit landed on her head. The blessed relief of darkness descended.

LCR Headquarters

Declan sat across a table from Albert. Even while everything was screaming inside him to run out the door and try to find Sabrina, he had no choice but to do the work. Sabrina's tracker had stopped working within an hour of her disappearance. They'd traced the signal to an old airstrip outside of Fairfax, Virginia. And then it disappeared.

"I love Sabrina like a daughter, Declan. And you like a son. I'd never betray either of you, much less the Agency or my country. You need to stop focusing on me and look for someone else."

"You're the only other person who knew about the tracker in her arm."

"Maybe she told someone. Noah McCall knew about it. Maybe he—"

"No," a cold voice said.

Declan didn't bother glancing over his shoulder as the LCR leader entered. If there was anyone almost as motivated to find Sabrina, it was McCall.

"Then I don't know what to tell you. As I've said a hundred times already, I got a call from you, from your cell phone. You asked me to meet you at the warehouse. You said you believed you had targeted the traitor and wanted my input. I talked to you." Albert took off his glasses and rubbed his bloodshot eyes. "I even asked you if you'd caught any of Friday's Nationals game."

"And what did I say?" Declan asked.

"That you'd been too busy trying to catch a fucking traitor." Albert lifted a shoulder in a halfhearted shrug and gave him an apologetic smile. "I reprimanded you for your language. Sorry."

Dammit, that sounded exactly how one of their conversations might have gone. "McCall, what about the phone?"

The LCR leader placed Albert's cell phone on the table. "The block on the phone that prevents calls from being logged is a damn good program. Took our techs a few hours, but we found a back door in. A phone call came from your cell phone, Steele. Yesterday morning. The call lasted less than a minute."

Unable to sit still any longer, Declan surged to his feet and began to pace. Someone had been close enough to clone his phone? Several people qualified, including Albert.

He eyed the man who'd been his friend and mentor for almost half his life. Albert had trained him, taught him everything he knew about lying, deceit, and taking advantage of another person to get the job done. Declan knew what the man was capable of. Question was, was he capable of betraying his country for financial gain? His heart said no. His brain told him it was possible.

"I can't take the chance with you, Albert."

"If you're telling the truth, Marks," McCall said, "you'll be released after Sabrina's rescue. Until then, feel free to enjoy LCR's hospitality. If you're not, I'll leave it to Steele to decide your fate."

As if he'd known what the answer would be all along, Albert leaned back in his chair. "If you would be good enough to let me know when she's safe, I would appreciate it."

Declan nodded and walked out the door. He couldn't worry about Albert's disappointment. Even though his instincts said the man was telling the truth, he could take no chances. Not when it came to Sabrina's survival.

So far, Jackson had been unable to tell them anything. He was in the hospital, still unconscious from the blow to his head. The doctors believed he would be fine but had admitted that his continued unconsciousness had them worried.

Feeling as helpless and desperate as he ever had as a prisoner, Declan went into a small office that McCall had lent him. Fat lot of good the office was doing him, though. They had nothing. The tracker had been their only hope, but by the time they'd made it to the airstrip, the plane had been long gone, and the signal had stopped.

He turned to leave the room when a ping on his laptop told him he had an email. Stomach roiling, Declan had to force himself to go to the desk and click on his email icon. He had known they would be contacting him. There was no email message, only an attachment. Why use words when a graphic image said so much more?

Jaw clenched, he clicked the attachment and watched the video. A small sound, like the whimper of a wounded animal, escaped him. The image before him would be engraved in his brain forever. Nausea forged upward, clogged his throat. Declan swallowed it back. Getting Sabrina back alive meant staying strong for her.

Grabbing the laptop, he stormed out the door and into McCall's office.

Noah watched Steele come into his office like a warrior on a mission. The stark whiteness of his features, the burning hell in his eyes told Noah that he'd received the contact they'd been waiting on.

"Got a video," Steele growled.

Noah jerked his head at the conference table. "Put the laptop down and let's see what we've got."

Within seconds of plugging in the laptop, the video appeared on the large screen on the wall.

"Shit," Noah said softly.

The video lasted less than two minutes, but that didn't mean the torture hadn't continued for hours. Seeing Sabrina, his operative and someone he liked and admired, treated in such a manner sent both fury and sickness through him. Just what was it doing to the man beside him?

"I'll get Angela to trace the IP address."

"It won't do any good. They're too smart for that."

"Maybe. But we explore all possibilities."

While Noah placed the call to Angela, he watched Steele stalk out the door. In the midst of his instructions to Angela, he heard a massive crash. Having dealt with tough operatives and volatile tempers for many years, Noah figured he knew what the noise had been.

A minute later, Steele returned and said simply, "I owe you a vending machine, McCall."

Her body trembling with shock and pain, Sabrina worked to gather her wits and fight against the agony. She was alone. All voices were in another part of the building. There was no telling when the bastards might return and do something much worse.

She would never look at a piñata the same way again. She had been used as a human one. Four men had beaten her with sticks, another had filmed it. By now, Declan had seen the footage. Worrying about him would do no good. He and LCR would be here soon. She was sure of it. They'd found her before. They would find her again.

She moved gingerly as she evaluated her health. Starting from the top down, she mentally listed and acknowledged each injury. Contusions to her head, probable concussion. Her head ached with a pounding consistency, but that could be a physical reaction to the stress and her other injuries. The broken nose she was sure she had could produce a blinding headache. Three, maybe four, cracked ribs, broken left wrist, severely bruised abdomen that she could only pray didn't include internal bleeding, possible fractured pelvis. In short, she was a mess.

On the bright side, when she had woken, she had found herself untied, alone, and still alive.

Gritting her teeth, she worked to sit up and managed only part of the way before she collapsed. Not giving up, she used her right arm as leverage and crawled toward the wall. Sitting up would go a long way to making her feel less vulnerable. Agony screamed through her at every inch of progress, but finally she made it to the wall. Dizziness swamped her, and she bit the inside of her mouth as hard as she could to keep herself conscious. When it finally passed, she dragged her body the last few inches and then rolled over onto her back. Now came the tricky part. Sitting up was going to hurt like a son of a bitch. She couldn't let that stop her. She had to get off her back.

Though black dots danced before her eyes and tears spilled down her face, she finally managed to prop herself against the wall. Breathless, she forced herself to take shallow breaths and did her best to ignore the protest of her damaged ribs screaming with each breath she took.

Exhausted but finally able to concentrate on something other than her discomfort, she took in her dismal surroundings and made more assessments. Dirt floor, square room, one door, tiny windows. Musty, dank odor. A basement or cellar?

She listened to the sounds around her. No traffic outside. Another prison like where they'd held Declan?

Eyes closed, she listened harder. Birds squawked loudly. Was that a monkey chattering? So she was in a forest or a jungle? But where?

The question of her location flew out of her mind when the door opened. She tensed, held her breath. What would they do to her now?

CHAPTER THIRTY

LCR Headquarters

It was standing room only in the small LCR conference room. Grim and silent, five LCR operatives, along with McCall and Declan, stared at still shots of Sabrina's torture. Declan had been able to do so only by keeping his eyes off Sabrina. When this was over and he had her back safe, then he'd allow himself to combust again. McCall's lack of response to the vending machine Declan had destroyed was a testament to the man's understanding. He could see why Sabrina had such respect for her boss.

Since the camera was jostled and moved around a lot, they were studying the stills of each frame. If the cameraman was as inexperienced as he seemed, there was the hope they'd be able to see something they weren't supposed to see.

"Can we zero in on photo twenty-three?"

Declan glanced at the woman who'd asked the question. Above-average height, white-blond hair, stunningly beautiful. McCall had introduced her as Eden St. Claire. The tall, grim man beside her was her husband, Jordan Montgomery. Declan had never worked an op with Montgomery when the man had been at the Agency. He knew of his reputation, though. Tough as shit and hard as nails. Declan was glad to have him here.

Angela clicked on photo twenty-three and enlarged it. The entire room leaned forward and focused on the photo.

"Yes," Eden said, "I see it, Jordan. There's an opening in the door…just a crack, but something's there."

"Zoom in closer on the door," Declan said.

For a second, the photo went out of focus and then became clearer. That "something" was someone. A tall, broad-shouldered man stood at the door, watching. Unfortunately, other than that one indistinct, large blur, Declan couldn't make out any of his features.

A chime sounded. McCall grabbed his phone, held up his hand to ask for silence, and began to speak in rapid Portuguese. Declan was able to understand only a few words, but by the expression on the LCR leader's face, the caller had some significant information.

Knowing McCall would share as soon as he could, Declan turned his attention back to the photos. "Angela, will you enlarge photo three?"

Photo twenty-three shrank down, and number three enlarged on the screen.

"Zoom in on that white speck in the corner."

Once again, the photo went blurry, and then the zoom became vivid and clear.

"What is that?" Montgomery leaned forward. "A food wrapper of some sort? Candy wrapper?"

Before any conclusions could be made, McCall ended the call. "Okay, one of our watchers in Brazil got a call about a small plane landing yesterday. Four tough-looking guys and one long, tarp-wrapped bundle."

"What part of Brazil?" Montgomery asked.

"Right outside Rio."

"Your source is good?" Declan asked.

"Very."

"Then I know where she might be," Montgomery said.

Declan twisted round. "How? Where?"

Montgomery jerked his head toward the screen. "The wrapper. It's from a mom-and-pop restaurant in São Paulo. There's a small, abandoned village on the outskirts of the city. Perfect place to take a prisoner."

Declan studied the photo again, then all of the photos combined. Forcing the grief and despair down to the pit of his stomach, he made himself click on the video again. This time, instead of watching the surroundings for a clue or Sabrina's torture, he took in the expertise of the cameraman, along with the lighting. His gut confirmed his thoughts.

"No. It's a trick."

"What do you mean?" McCall asked.

"I think the cameraman's doing a poor job on purpose. They're too careful to have allowed these glimpses. Too professional. After all the shit they've been able to get away with, no way are they going to be so careless. They're trying to lead us away from where she is."

"My source in Brazil is as reliable as they come," McCall said.

"I'm not saying she's not in Brazil. I'm saying she's just not in the area they're trying to lead us to."

"Then how the hell are we going to find her?" Thorne asked. "This is our only lead."

"It's me they want, not Sabrina."

"Maybe so," Thorne said, "but in the meantime, they're torturing Sabrina."

"I'm well aware of that, Thorne. Don't bloody well tell me what I already know. She's my wife."

"Is she?" Thorne said softly.

Declan took a step toward the asshole. McCall placed a hand on his shoulder. "Back off, both of you. Steele, I have an LCR team in Rio. They'll check out the village Montgomery referenced. If there's any activity, they'll let us know, and we'll go there. In the meantime, let's get in the air and head toward Rio. When those assholes contact you again, I want us as close as possible."

"Hello, Mrs. Steele."

Sabrina remained silent as she took in the man who sat before her. Instead of more torture, apparently it was time to talk. An interrogation or just a chance to taunt her? He was only slightly taller than she was—maybe six feet. He had an American accent, but she knew her languages. It was fake. Was he disguising his voice because she knew him or for another reason?

The only good thing about this whole ordeal was the fact that she'd yet to see anyone's face. Everyone wore dark cloth bags over their heads with holes cut out for eyes and a small slit for their mouth. If they weren't allowing her to see them, they didn't plan to kill her. At least that was her thinking. Of course, that didn't mean she wouldn't die from her injuries. They weren't fatal yet, but what else was coming?

"I see you're going to maintain your silence. Perhaps a wise choice, as I've been told you have a volatile temper. I'd hate for you to offend me and have to punish you again."

He waited once again. His politeness was meant to lower her guard and put her off-balance. Whoever this man was, he knew she'd been through every type of training as an EDJE agent. Nothing he said or did would unbalance her.

As if he'd read her mind, he said, "I'm aware that you've been trained to endure much. I also know that when you're in good physical condition, you could easily kill me. However, I'm sure you're in considerable pain. Just so you know, my men were instructed to go easy on you. Other than the unfortunate bump to your nose, your face has been left virtually untouched. If you survive this ordeal, you should have no lasting scars or impairments."

Going against everything she had been trained, Sabrina couldn't help herself, she had to get some answers. "If you think this is the way to get Declan to talk, why torture him first? Why didn't you just use me at the beginning?"

"You were our backup plan." His laughter was rich and deep, as if he were sharing a joke. "You have any idea what we did to that poor bastard? No one should be able to withstand that kind of pain or psychological bullshit. The man is a machine."

"Then you must know that whatever you do to me won't stir him. He's even asked me for a divorce." It hurt to admit that, and the fact that she could well be signing her death warrant with that confession hadn't escaped her, either. But she'd be damned if she'd let Declan back into their clutches again.

"You'd better hope that's not true, for your sake."

"You tortured him to make him hate me. Made him believe I was the one who betrayed him. Seems damn stupid to use me now."

Another deep and hearty laugh erupted from him. Did she know that laugh, or in her pain-filled mind was she hearing things that weren't there?

"I have to admit, that plan backfired on us. But he's fallen for you again." And then, probably because he knew it would freak her out, he said, "Isn't that right, Little Fox?" In Declan's voice.

Her heart clutched, and despite her best intentions, she was sure the agony of hearing those words in Declan's voice was on her face. Cursing her weakness, she clenched her teeth and ground out, "You called Albert and told him about the meeting, using Declan's voice. Albert isn't the traitor."

"You think?"

The fact that he wasn't willing to reveal the name of the traitor was a puzzle but also slightly reassuring. Did he not tell her because he wasn't sure of his plan, or because he intended to let her live?

"How do you know so much about Declan and me?"

"Now, that would be cheating, wouldn't it?" He went to his feet. "Ready for round two?"

The door burst open. Her four hooded torturers came for her again. Sabrina tried to shrink back into the wall, but that didn't deter them.

"Make sure we get enough convincing footage this time," the man said.

Refusing to give in without a fight, she managed a punch, recognized the soft give of a throat and the collapse of cartilage. Hands grabbed her, but before they could restrain her, she got off a hard kick to a groin. The bellow that followed was gratifying.

She felt her feet leave the ground, and a new, fresh hell began.

CHAPTER THIRTY-ONE

Declan was thirty thousand feet in the air when the next email came. As much as he didn't want to open it, he had no choice. This time, there were words to go along with the attachment. The message wasn't long but was crushingly meaningful.

"She's not holding up as well as we had hoped."

Drawing in a breath, he braced himself and clicked on the image. The video wasn't as long as the first one. Probably only thirty seconds, but it had been enough.

Nausea once again surged into his throat. This time, he couldn't fight it.

Doing what he needed to do, he forwarded the email to McCall. On the way to the head in the back of the plane, he stopped at McCall's seat. "Just sent you another email. Be back in a minute."

Not waiting for a response, Declan made it to the toilet with seconds to spare.

Noah spared a pitying glance for Steele. Five years ago, he had been in his place. When Samara had been taken and tortured. He knew that feeling of desperate helplessness and a rage so intense it threatened to implode your insides.

Clicking on the email, he grimly took in the terse note and then viewed the video. Four men, he assumed the same ones as before, surrounded a nude Sabrina, who hung from the ceiling by her wrists. Before looking for clues or hidden meanings, Noah took the time to evaluate her injuries. Dried blood covered her face, most likely from her busted nose. Her eyes were already half-swollen shut. Her skin was pale, so the purple bruising on her rib cage stood out in vivid color. He was guessing they were cracked. Those sticks they'd beaten her with would have had no problem breaking bones. The rest of her body was a mass of cuts and bruises. Hard to tell if anything else was broken.

Noah lifted his eyes to her face again and was heartened to see the fierce gleam in her eyes. This was the LCR operative he knew. She still had a lot of fight in her and was not giving up. He had expected nothing less.

Steele dropped into the chair beside him. The man's face was bleached white, but the wrath blazing in his eyes said it all. He'd do what he had to do to get his wife back.

"Did you pick up any clues?" Steele asked.

"No. The camera never moved away. From what I can tell, she has a broken nose, possible concussion, cracked ribs."

"Her left wrist is broken."

Noah peered closer. Yeah, he'd missed that. Bruising and a protrusion of a bone. Hell, and she was hanging from her wrists. "Bloody bastards."

"They're not finished with her."

"No," Noah agreed softly, "they're not."

"I need you to make me a promise."

Noah waited, already figuring he knew the request.

"Once we find the location, all I'm asking is that you get her out alive. I don't care what else happens. Just get her out."

Arguing would do no good. Noah didn't plan on losing anyone to these SOBs, but he knew Steele needed the assurance. "You have my word."

"Aw, shit."

Noah looked over his shoulder at Thorne. The man's eyes held a similar hell. She was his partner and his friend, but that wouldn't get in his way of doing his job.

"No real clues with this one. Just a taunt."

Though looking as though he wanted to let loose a string of vitriol, Thorne's admirable control took over. He allowed himself one sentence: "I'm going to enjoy taking these assholes down."

"We're all looking forward to that."

The cell phone on the table in front of him chimed. Noah checked the readout. "Excuse me, I need to take this." Standing, he held the phone to his ear and relished the sound of his wife's voice.

"Noah, any news yet?"

Declan couldn't take his eyes off Sabrina. Would this be the last time he saw her alive? How the hell could he have let this happen?

Cole Mathison's words of warning came back to haunt him, and he knew exactly how he'd let this happen. While he had been focused on his own vengeance, concentrating on his own agenda, the one person in the world he would literally lie down and die for had been taken.

"Before you embark on a journey of revenge, dig two graves."

Confucius's statement fit this scenario too damn well. But if two graves were indeed needed, neither of them would be Sabrina's. This, Declan swore on his life.

What was going through her head as she endured this torment? Did she know he would find her? That he would tear the world apart to save her? Yes, she did. More than anyone else in the world, she believed in him. She knew him inside and out... knew his heart. She had so much more faith in him than he did in himself. When confronted with vicious rumors that he had been unfaithful, she hadn't believed them. When he had told her he couldn't love her anymore, had nothing left inside him, she had proudly stood before him and told him he was wrong.

So, yes, Sabrina knew without a doubt he would come for her.

He was aware that Thorne dropped into the seat vacated by McCall, but still Declan couldn't move his gaze from the brutal image before him.

"She's tougher than any person I know, man or woman."

Declan appreciated the man's reassuring words, but he wasn't telling him anything he didn't already know. Sabrina was tough—he had trained her. He knew everything about her. But he also knew, despite all that toughness and bravado, she was as fragile as any human. Her body could endure a lot, but at some point, it would fail her.

"She ever tell you I made a pass at her once?"

Declan tore his eyes away from the screen to give Thorne a crooked half smile. "No. She wouldn't, though. That's not Sabrina's way."

"Yeah, you're right. She turned me down, of course. Didn't take long for me to realize that her heart was locked up with someone else. And it's still locked up." Thorne leaned forward in his chair. "She's going to survive, Steele, I don't doubt that for a minute. And when this is over, don't let her go. If you do, you'll regret it for the rest of your life. Take it from someone who knows."

Declan swallowed hard, trying to push down the giant clog in his throat. "Thanks for the pep talk. You're not as big of an asshole as I pegged you."

Thorne stood and slapped him on the back. "Back at ya, man."

Declan slumped back into his seat and closed his eyes. Why hadn't he died in that hellish prison? If he had, Sabrina would never have known what happened to him. He never would have gone after her. She would have eventually gone on with her life. Found another man to love and appreciate her.

For the first time since his rescue, he wished with all his heart that Jackson had never found him.

His cell phone chimed. Declan checked the caller ID and was surprised to see Angela's name pop up.

"Angela, you got something?"

"Yes, but you're not going to like it."

As Declan listened, he surged to his feet as a seething hatred emerged. How stupid he'd been. How very fucking stupid.

Thanking her for the information, he ended the call and turned to reveal what he had learned.

McCall was making rapid strides his way. "Got another call. I've got some info."

"Yeah, I do, too," Declan said grimly.

"Listen." McCall placed his cell phone on the table and said, "Hey, Dixie, you have something?"

"Hey, sugar." The soft, female voice dripped with Southern charm. "We sure do. We've found our girl." A hard edge entered her voice. "I hope you make those assholes suffer."

"We will. No worries about that."

"Good." Then the charming, syrupy sweet voice returned, "She's in Colombia, right outside San Felipe. Here're the coordinates."

As McCall jotted down the location, Declan drew in a settling breath. Sabrina would survive. They would arrive in time to save her, and she would live. Then, when she was out of danger, and he'd held her one last time, he would hunt down the traitor and ensure that at least one of those graves would be needed.

Outside San Felipe, Colombia

The pain wasn't bad as long as she didn't move and barely breathed. Her wrist had stopped throbbing, and other than the strain on her shoulders and neck, she felt almost normal. Well, as normal as anyone could who was hanging from a hook in the ceiling.

They weren't through with her yet. She had pissed them off, and the next time they'd want retribution. She had been surprised at their naïveté. Did they have no idea who they'd captured? She didn't need both arms and legs to maim or kill. One of those men had discovered that when she slammed a well-placed fist into his throat. She'd heard his gurgle of agony before he'd fallen to the ground. They'd dragged him out the door, and she knew he would never get up again.

The other one she'd caught in the groin would live, but his equipment might take years and multiple surgeries to repair. She doubted he'd be back to torture her. His friends, however, would make sure she paid. How long before Declan and LCR reached her? She refused to consider that they wouldn't. She knew Declan, and she knew Noah. Working together, those two could find a penny in the ocean.

The tracking device in her arm was gone. She'd discovered that soon after they'd strung her up. Someone had dug it out, leaving a small, open wound. They hadn't bothered to treat it, but compared to the rest of her injuries, she supposed it was just a slight inconvenience.

LCR had contacts all over the world. Some were paid. Others informed out of gratitude for LCR's help. These assholes believed they had her hidden away from the world. They'd soon learn differently.

The door creaked open, and the man who had talked to her earlier stood there, studying her. She was surprised he was still wearing the head covering. She had already accepted the truth. No way did they plan to let her live.

Once they got hold of Declan, she had little doubt that she would be used as a torture device for him. If he didn't talk, they'd use her in whatever way they could to make him do whatever they wanted. Not that she would allow that. If it came to allowing herself to be tortured in front of Declan, she would take herself out of the equation. Forcing Declan to watch them torture her would be worse than letting him see her die at her own hand. She'd rather go out on her own terms anyway. Declan would understand that.

"You're more trouble than we anticipated."

Even though she was smiling inside, she didn't allow him to see her triumph. Why make her retribution more painful?

"You temporarily disabled two of my men."

That was a lie. She had killed one of them, and the other wouldn't be able to walk upright for at least a couple of weeks and would probably be peeing through a straw for months.

"How did you know about the tracker in my arm?"

"Standard procedure to scan a prisoner before transport." He held up his fingers in a mocking gesture. "Scouts honor."

He drew closer. "So, here's the thing, Mrs. Steele. We hadn't planned on doing anything more to you. Our last message to Mr. Steele should have been sufficient. However, my men have made a special request. And who am I, their employer, to deny them their entertainment?"

Two men entered. Despite the knowledge that she could and would survive any pain they inflicted, her body tensed, and panic roared through her bloodstream. Still, she knew she could take it. She had been trained by the best to endure everything, anything. She would endure this, too.

Hard hands twisted her body around and slammed her against the wall. One man wrapped a leather strap around her waist and then secured it to hooks embedded in the wall. If she'd been able to get some leverage, she might've taken out at least one of them by swinging both her feet up. With her broken wrist, she didn't have the strength.

Knowing she had no choice but to endure, her mind prepared itself for what came next.

"Too bad we don't have room for a bullwhip, as we did for Mr. Steele. His bare back made an appealing landscape. Yours is smaller but truly exquisite. All that pale, smooth skin. We do have the next best thing, though."

She heard a whir, as if something flew through the air, and then a sting across her back revealed what it was. A cane.

Gripping her hands on the chains, Sabrina went to that place she'd taught herself to go when things became too much. She and Declan were on a sailboat. He was at the helm. She stood in front of him. His arms were around her, and they guided the boat together. The wind whipped through her hair, the sun blazed above them, and his arms held her, strong yet tender. She leaned back against his hard, masculine strength and rejoiced in his love. She chanted softly in her mind, *Declan. Declan. Declan.*

Odd. The sounds behind her had stopped. Her entire back-side, from shoulders to ankles, burned as though she had been licked by fire. But they had stopped before she lost consciousness. Why? Even though she knew her skin was most likely bloody and raw, she was surprised they hadn't beaten her until even her fantasy had been penetrated.

She took in a shallow breath, fully expecting the pain to begin again. When she heard running feet, she smiled. Ah yes. Her torturers were now otherwise occupied.

CHAPTER
THIRTY-TWO

It was an abandoned house—quite large, almost a mansion. According to McCall's source, it had once been owned by a drug lord who'd left it behind when things got too hot. Weeds and bushes had grown around the exterior, hiding much of it from view. Declan's high-powered binoculars revealed broken windows and scraps of curtains blowing in the breeze. He saw no activity.

According to the blueprints they'd obtained, the house had both a basement and an attic. The attic was small. From the video they'd seen, Sabrina's torture area looked larger, the walls red brick and damp, slightly moldy. They were betting on the basement.

McCall stood about fifty feet to his right side. Thorne was about fifty feet to his left. Kelly, Montgomery, St. Claire, and Mallory were coming in from the back.

"We're in place." Kelly's voice came through Declan's earbud. "No activity here. Place looks abandoned."

St. Claire broke in, "I'm closest to the garage. I see two SUVs. House is definitely occupied."

"Mallory, anything?" McCall asked.

"Sorry. Almost there," Jake Mallory answered. "Had to stop for an unfriendly python that got in my way."

A good reminder that brutal kidnappers weren't the only dangers in the jungle.

"Okay. I'm stationed in a tree about thirty yards from the house. From this vantage point, I see a couple of duffle bags on the second floor, along with sleeping bags. No movement, though."

"Let's assume the place is guarded," McCall said. "We go in low, fast, and as one. Wait till I give the go-ahead before entering."

"Roger that," they said in unison.

"Now."

Crouched low, Declan raced toward the front entrance. Wearing camouflage pants and an olive-green T-shirt, he blended with the jungle like a hidden predator. Forcing himself to think of this as just a job wasn't easy. Sabrina was in that house, severely injured. He refused to believe it was even worse than that. Allowing his mind to go there would do her no good.

"Go," McCall said quietly.

Declan pushed open the door. McCall went in low, his weapon sweeping the room. Declan came in behind him. Thorne followed. The jungle had entered the home. Vines covered the walls. Grass, weeds, and even a couple of small trees sprang up from under the floorboards. Some kind of vine curled around a ceiling fan and then spread across the ceiling. Hell, they'd probably find as much wildlife in here as they would outside.

Using hand signals, McCall directed Thorne to the left side of the house, then he went right. Declan went looking for an entrance to the basement. He found a padlocked door off a hallway. No reason for a padlock unless you had something you wanted to keep hidden.

Pulling out pliers, he clipped the lock. The sound echoed in the too-silent house, and he held his breath. No movement. He opened the door, quiet and quick. A tickling on the back of his neck was a warning he never ignored. He dropped low and twisted. The butt of a gun swung at his head. Declan dodged right, surged to his feet, and slammed a fist into a man's hooded face. He then followed with a kick to the man's stomach, and then two punches, fast and hard, to his head. The man fell to the floor with a loud thud.

"Major, what was that?" A voice sounded from a room down the hallway. Declan looked up, spotted McCall. The man nodded and then pointed to a doorway, where the voice had sounded. He got the message. McCall would take care of the owner of that voice. Declan's priority was getting to Sabrina.

He pulled the door open and peered into darkness. Pulling his flashlight from his tool belt, he clicked it on and headed downstairs. He stopped at the bottom of the stairway and swept the light around the basement. Three doors, all closed. Footsteps silent, Declan moved toward the first one, opened it, and peered inside. Old furniture, and sounds of small, frightened animals scurrying to get away. Closing the door, he went to another one. Locked.

His hands delved into his pocket for tools. He put his hand on the door and then felt a gun pressed to the back of his head. "Well, well, well. I was just about to send you an update and photo, but being here to see it in person is so much better. Hands on top of your head, spread your legs."

Declan didn't bother to fight. The man would take him to Sabrina. That's all he cared about right now. He had five LCR operatives backing him up.

Allowing the man to take his weapon, Declan submitted to a one-handed search and was surprised at the man's naïveté. The idiot seriously didn't know that Declan could kill him in half

a dozen ways before he got off a shot? This wasn't the traitor...
just one of his flunkies.

"Head on inside."

Hands in the air, he followed the man's orders and walked
through the door. He stopped abruptly. Sabrina was still hanging
from the ceiling, facing and strapped to the wall. Her entire
back, from shoulders to her ankles, bore red welts, vicious cuts,
and bruises. They'd beaten her again. He recognized the mark-
ings—they'd used a cane this time. Fury pushed the horror aside.

"Hey, Red, you got company."

A pale face, covered in blood and bruises, twisted around.
There was only the slightest reaction in her swollen eyes.
Considering what she had endured, he was surprised she was
still conscious.

"She's tougher than she looks. I look forward to breaking
her further."

"You got what you wanted...I'm here. Let her go."

"Oh no. You've misunderstood the situation totally. Do you
think that's the only reason I took her? Surely you're not that
dense."

No, he knew exactly what they wanted her for, but stalling
for time until everyone was in place was imperative. Where the
hell was—

The soft sound of a shoe scuffing the floor was the man's first
notice that Declan had brought backup. Whirling around, the
man faced a very pissed-off and heavily armed Aidan Thorne.

Taking advantage of the hooded man's distraction, Declan
slammed his fist into his face with a satisfying crunch. Before the
guy even reached the ground, Declan had Sabrina in his arms.

"I've got you, darling."

As gently as possible, he unhooked the strap at her waist. Holding her with one arm, he tried to unhook her from the ceiling.

"Let us help," Eden St. Claire said. The compassion and anger in her voice were obvious.

While Eden and Jordan Montgomery worked on the hook, Declan held Sabrina upright. The moment she was loose, she collapsed into his arms.

"Here, I brought something for her. It'll make her feel more comfortable."

With a nod of gratitude, he took the short cotton slipover dress from Eden. He hadn't given any thought to the fact that she would want to be covered. His only intent had been to rescue her.

As Declan tended her, McCall's voice came through. "Let's get out of here. I'm getting some bad vibes."

Declan lifted Sabrina in his arms and headed toward the door. He stopped briefly to eye the man who'd tortured his wife. He didn't know him, but he swore with everything within him that before it was over, he would know what the inside of his tonsils looked like.

Holding the love of his life close in his arms, he whispered, "Let's go home, Little Fox."

Sabrina breathed through the pain. Her relief at seeing Declan...of knowing he and her fellow operatives were all right, made the suffering infinitely easier. Declan was trying to be as gentle as possible, and she refused to release the slightest whimper. He had suffered much worse treatment for a longer period of time. How could she complain?

Not wanting to lose consciousness in case she was needed, she ignored her discomfort and took in everything that was going on around her. She'd been in an abandoned house. Overgrown with weeds, it'd probably been a perfect hiding spot. She looked forward to finding out how LCR had found her.

Finally outside, she saw Noah looking down at an unconscious man on the ground. He raised his head and gave her a smile. "Good to see you, Fox."

"You, too, boss."

"Okay, let's get out of here," Noah said.

"You sure you got everyone?" Sabrina asked.

No sooner had she said that than bullets pinged past. Holding her close, Declan raced for the cover of the jungle. She heard him grunt and jerk and knew he'd been hit.

"Let me down, Declan."

"When you're safe," he growled.

He finally lowered her to the ground, and while she was trying to find his injury, he was looking around.

"Where is everyone?"

Holding her hand on the bleeding wound in his upper shoulder, Sabrina said, "They must've gone in the other direction."

"McCall, can you hear me?"

"Yeah," Noah answered. "We're trapped on the other side of the house. Looks like they called in reinforcements."

"Where's Thorne and Mallory?" Declan asked.

"I'm on the south side," Mallory answered. "Got tied up with a couple of assholes."

"Thorne, check in," Noah said.

No answer.

"I'm headed your way, McCall," Mallory said.

Declan held Sabrina's face in his hands. "You stay here. Understand?"

"But I—"

"I'll get Thorne. It'll be a lot easier if I don't have to worry about you." He handed her a weapon, her SIG Sauer, and then pulled something from his pocket. "Here's an extra earbud. You hear anything bad...anything at all, you scram. You hear me?"

She knew exactly what he meant, and no way would she take the time to tell him that he was crazy if he thought she'd leave him. Instead, she grabbed the back of his neck with her good hand and pulled him to her for a quick kiss. "Get back safe or I'll kick your ass."

He grinned. "But I'd much rather kiss yours, sweetheart."

"Come back safely, and I'll consider it."

Giving her his own hard kiss, he disappeared into the bushes, heading back to the house.

How many were out there now? Gunfire popped around her. She tried not to think about what was happening. Declan and Aidan would be okay. She—

"Aw, shit."

Declan's voice sounded pained, stressed. No, she damn well would not lose him again.

Ignoring the pain in every part of her body, along with the knowledge that running barefoot through the jungle wasn't exactly a brilliant idea, Sabrina headed back toward the house. They needed help.

She got to the edge of the overgrown yard and stopped. Declan was running toward her, carrying Aidan over his shoulder. Her breath hitched. Movement at the side showed a gun emerging from the bushes. Taking careful aim, she pressed the trigger. A yelp and then silence.

Declan made it halfway across the yard when another shot rang out. He jerked, stumbled. Racing toward him, Sabrina grabbed him right before he fell. Gunfire erupted. She took the time to look around...saw Jordan, Noah, and Eden shooting at the house. Jake ran toward her and pulled an unconscious Aidan away from Declan.

Knowing she had no choice if she wanted to save him, Sabrina grabbed Declan under his arms and pulled with all her might.

She managed to reach the edge of the jungle. Painful breaths rasped from her lungs, and no matter how she cursed her body for letting her down, she could not force it forward one more inch. Massive gunfire, like an explosion of fireworks, erupted. Unable to do anything else, she threw herself on top of Declan and held tight.

CHAPTER THIRTY-THREE

She was floating on a cloud, cocooned and free of pain. Occasionally, she'd hear a grumble, growl, or bark and wondered vaguely who the big dog was that was making all that noise. Then she'd fall back into that soft, puffy nothingness where pain didn't exist.

Eventually, that growling voice started to get on her nerves. It kept saying her name, over and over. Finally, she got irritated enough to open her mouth and say, "Enough already."

A bark of laughter and then a kiss on her lips. She had no idea why she smiled but could feel her lips curve up.

"Okay, Little Fox, I know you're in there. Open those pretty eyes and glare at me."

Never able to resist that beautiful, masculine voice, she forced her eyes open. Declan sat beside her. "Declan? You look like crap."

Another burst of laughter. "Your charm is the first thing I fell in love with."

"Liar. You told me it was my ass."

"It was your charming ass, as I recall."

She lifted a hand to touch him and then winced. Her arm was in a cast up to her elbow. He took her hand and held it to his mouth. "You gave me quite the scare."

"Back at you, Ace. Are you okay?"

"Yeah. Couple of flesh wounds."

She knew that wasn't the truth. She'd seen at least one bullet hole in him. But other than a too-pale face and a noticeable stiffness in one shoulder, he seemed to be healthy.

Memory returned, and grief quickly followed. "Aidan?"

"He's going to be fine. Got a nasty hole in his shoulder and arm, but the man's got the hide of an elephant. Doctor said he'll be up and around in no time."

She closed her eyes in relief. "Thank God. And everyone else. They're okay?"

"Yeah. The good guys won this time."

"No survivors?"

"No." His face went grim, hard.

"What are—"

He pressed his fingers to her mouth. "You're going to rest and recover. No worrying. Got that?"

"Declan, tell me."

"I'm headed out tomorrow."

"You know?"

"Yes."

She saw the sorrow in his eyes, and it confirmed her suspicions as well. After all those years working together, how could he have betrayed Declan? Betrayed her?

She took a breath, and they said his name together.

"How'd you figure it out?" Declan asked.

"As hard as it was to come to terms with, it was the only thing that made sense."

"I'm sorry. I know how you feel about him."

"You've known him even longer. It'll be harder on you." And then, even though she knew he had no choice, she had to add, "He won't be taken alive."

"I know that. But I have to do this, Sabrina. You know that...right?"

"Yes."

"When I get back, we're going to have a long, serious talk."

"Just make sure you come back to me."

"No worries about that. I've got too much to live for to let this end badly."

He stood, leaned down, and kissed her mouth, lingering, sipping, moving gently, slowly savoring.

"Promise me, Declan. Swear to me you will come back."

Leaning over the bed, he whispered softly, *"And fare-thee-weel, my only Luve. And fare-thee-weel, a while. And I will come again, my Luve, Tho' 'twere ten thousand mile."*

And with Robert Burns's beautiful words lingering in the air, he walked out the door.

Declan made it out of the hospital before he exploded. Damn them all. What they had done to her was unforgivable. He didn't care what the man had meant to him, and he no longer gave a damn about the hellish torture he'd been put through. The bastard would, however, pay for what he had done to Sabrina.

She had been beaten, her bones broken, her beautiful skin marred and scarred. And to add insult to serious injury, she'd saved his ass. Throwing herself over his body and taking a bullet for him. The bullet had narrowly missed her spine. It'd been a through-and-through but had nipped one of her lungs. He'd thought they were going to lose her on the way to the hospital.

He'd kept his hand over her chest to stop the bleeding, pleading and shouting at her until he was hoarse. Screaming at her to live.

He would kill them all. He didn't care who they were, how much money they had, or how much power they had behind them. He would fucking kill them all.

McCall met him in the hospital parking lot. The man was wearing that grim, resolute expression that Declan had gotten used to and totally identified with. He owed McCall and LCR the world. Without them, Sabrina would have died.

"You're going after him?" McCall asked.

"Yeah."

"Want some backup?"

"No. Thank you for everything. You've done more than I could ever repay. But I've got what I need."

"He won't come quietly."

"I know that. He won't have to."

"Do you know who else was involved?"

"Not yet. I intend to before it's over."

"She'll never forgive you if you don't come back."

"And I'll never forgive myself for what I've put her through."

"I'd say the best way you can make it up to her is to come back in one piece."

"That's the plan." And then because there were no guarantees and it had to be said, he added, "Take care of her for me."

"She's part of the family. She'll be taken care of."

Nodding his thanks, he went to the edge of the parking lot where a black SUV with tinted windows waited for him. He got into the backseat, nodded once, and the driver sped down the highway.

This was his destiny. Whether it ended in hours, or he was blessed with another chance with Sabrina, Declan would not shirk this duty. The man had betrayed his country, the Agency, and his friends. He had to pay.

Juarez, Mexico

The bar looked even seedier than the last time he'd been here. Built in the 1960s, it had supposedly been a refuge to some of the most-notorious criminals in Mexico. Declan figured most of that was made up to appeal to a certain clientele. And Lupe's Cantina definitely drew in some of the slimiest worms. It'd been one of his favorite places to pick up intel or throw back a few after a successful mission.

Declan stood at the doorway and took in the familiar fragrances of grease, spice, beer, and a few other smells he'd just as soon do without. Lupe still ran the place with an iron fist, although when he spotted her in the corner, sipping a beer, that fist looked a little more wrinkled and her face older and sourer.

Place was half-empty this time of day. A few men stood around a worn-out pool table shooting balls with a desultory languidness. Three others sat at the bar, all turned halfway, as if expecting trouble anytime. Since most everyone here either had a record or was running from someone, turning your back was a good way to get a knife in it. However, Declan had no doubt these men had another agenda. The bastard wouldn't have come alone.

Declan zeroed in on the man sitting at a table with his back to the wall. Finding him hadn't been a problem. How many nights had they ended up at Lupe's to play pool…chug down some beers, and blow off steam? What the hell had happened to make him turn his back on everything he had vowed to uphold and protect?

"Figured you'd be here sooner or later."

Jerking his head over to the bar, Declan said, "Some of yours?"

"No. Too sleazy. I came alone."

And he was full of shit.

Declan pulled out a chair at the table and sat where he could see both the men at the bar and the front door. When a worn-out-looking waitress headed his way, he shook his head to let her know he wouldn't need a drink.

"Believe it or not, I'm glad you survived...both times."

One last glance around the bar, then he targeted the man he'd once called friend. "Why, Jackson?"

"Why does a man do anything? Money."

"That wasn't the way you used to feel."

"You mean when I was new and stupid. Thought making a difference in the world really counted. That was a long time ago, my friend."

Declan could see it in his eyes. Disillusionment, anger.

"Why not just quit and go into the private sector earlier? You had a lot of marketable skills."

"Yeah. And when I finally took that last bullet that would put me down for good, just what would I have? I decided I wanted a life before it ended."

"And selling out your friends was the kind of life you wanted?"

"I'm used to doing things I don't particularly like to do." He eased back into his chair as if he were just hanging out with an old friend. "Mind telling me how you figured it out?"

"I didn't for a long time. I never would have let you get within a mile of Sabrina if I had."

"Then how'd I tip you off? I was so damn careful."

"A few things. When you wouldn't wake up in the hospital, the doctors ran some blood tests."

"I figured with the knock-out drug I took, they'd just let me sleep. That I'd wake up, and no one would ever know." His mouth tilted in a rueful grin. "I'll have to remember that for next time."

Declan didn't bother to tell him there would never be a next time.

"But that can't be all. I mean, that alone wasn't enough, was it?"

"You said Albert remembered your nephew Stuart's name. You don't have any family, including a nephew. There is a Stuart Sands, however, who has deposited a million-plus dollars into his bank account over the last two years. Of course, that Stuart Sands with that Social Security number died over forty years ago at the age of three."

"Shit. I knew that'd come back and bite me in the ass." Jackson's face held both wonder and admiration. "But that had to take some serious research to dig that info out."

"I have a serious researcher." *Thank you, Angela Delvecchio.*

Apparently, more upset about making such an obvious mistake than being a traitor, he shook his head and muttered, "Damn rookie mistake. Should've known better."

"And then there's the text."

The cocky glint was back in his eyes. "Which one?"

Declan refused to be baited. "The one to me that looked like it came from Sabrina. I knew that note bothered me for some reason, but for the life of me I couldn't figure out why. Then I remembered I once mentioned to you that Sabrina liked to sign her notes to me with SS. I'd never told anyone else that."

"Can't believe you didn't catch that before."

"Yeah. Stupid of me, trusting my friend and all."

Jackson lifted a shoulder. "You always did take things too personal."

"Why'd you rescue me? Or should I say, fake rescue me?"

"We couldn't get you to talk, no matter what we did. I figured the only way was to bring Sabrina to you. Problem was, we couldn't find her."

"And you knew I'd be able to find her."

"Yeah. If only to try to kill her."

"If you couldn't get me to talk, why not have me killed and go after Albert or even Jason Starling?"

Jackson snorted his disgust. "Starling doesn't know his ass from a hole in the ground. And Albert? Hell, the old fool probably wouldn't have lived to tell us anything useful. Besides, the moneyman insisted it had to be you. Had a score to settle."

That confirmed Declan's theory. He had pissed someone off. And that someone had wanted revenge.

"Then why make me hate Sabrina first? Seems risky that I wouldn't find her and kill her immediately."

"I knew, no matter what you believed she did, you wouldn't be able to go through with it. You loved her too much. But I knew you would find her, and that's what we needed."

"Then why the hell make me hate her?"

"Truth is, I really thought we could break you without getting Sabrina involved. I know we went through extensive training, but shit, man, you were a tough nut to crack. The money people were getting tired of no results. I had to do something."

"So you watched while they tortured and almost killed Sabrina, tortured me, all because of money?"

An ugly gleam glinted in his eyes. "Get this, Declan. Not everybody likes to live like a pauper. I saved thousands of lives in my time with the Agency, and what did I get when I left? A measly stipend I can't touch until I'm in my fifties and a phone call from the president—one I can't even tell anyone about because I'm sworn to secrecy. I deserved more."

"You knew that going in. Things like that didn't used to matter to you."

"Yeah, well, they matter to me now. The whole system sucks. Politicians sit on their fat asses and make millions in secret liaisons or book deals. I saved lives and get squat. It's not fair."

"And what happened to Sabrina? You think that's fair?"

"She wasn't supposed to get hurt in that blast. She was only supposed to witness it so she would believe you were dead."

"What about the people who died in the building? What was their crime?"

"I made sure the place was empty except for the owner, his wife, mother-in-law. Made sure as few people as possible were hurt." He lifted a careless shoulder. "Innocent civilians get killed all the time in war, and nobody blinks an eye."

"This wasn't a war," Declan ground out.

"It was my war."

Arguing with a narcissistic sociopath was pointless. "The guy who resembled me. Who was he?"

Amused satisfaction gleamed in Jackson's eyes. "A desperate, out-of-work actor. Schmuck thought he was auditioning for a television pilot. Guy had no family, so it was easy enough to have him just disappear."

"And the DNA results showing it was me?"

"My people have deep pockets."

"Who else was involved at the Agency?"

"It was just me."

Stupid to ask a liar a question and expect the truth. But he'd deal with that later. "You wanted us to think it was Albert who sold us out."

"That seemed like a good plan. Took everything I had not to laugh out loud when Albert showed up at the meeting. Not sure who looked the most horrified, you or Sabrina."

"So you used Sabrina, had her tortured, almost killed her."

"Not my fault. You're the reason Sabrina had to get involved. If you'd just told us what we wanted to know, she wouldn't have had to go through the torture."

"No, of course not. None of this is your fault, is it, Jackson?"

"If you think I wanted Sabrina tortured, you would be wrong. She didn't deserve what happened to her. If you'd only done what you were supposed to do."

"Sorry I couldn't accommodate you by selling out my country and my fellow agents."

"You may have the American flag up your butt. I'm smarter. I look out for number one these days."

Declan had thought this job would be more difficult. Jackson was making it incredibly easy.

"So what are you going to do?"

"I'm taking you back home and letting someone else deal with you."

"I'm not going back."

Even though he had known that would be the answer, he had hoped for a different one. He gave him one more chance. "Go back willingly or go back in a box. Your choice."

"You think I didn't plan for this? That I didn't know you'd figure it out? How stupid do you think I am?"

"I don't think you want me to answer that question." He leaned forward and spoke in a deadly voice few still-living men had ever heard. "You think I didn't plan for this, too?"

Jackson shoved the table forward, catching Declan in the chest. In one swift move, Declan pushed the table back toward

Jackson and pulled the gun from his ankle holster. Squeezing the trigger, he got off a shot before Jackson disappeared into a back room.

The three men at the bar whirled as one and started shooting. Declan dropped to the floor and rolled. He shot toward the men, heard a grunt of pain. Before the other two could move on him, bullets started flying as reinforcements poured through the door.

Knowing his fellow EDJE agents had things well in hand, Declan headed out to find Jackson. Blood drops left a trail, letting him know he'd at least winged the man.

The dimly lit hallway stank of urine and fast, rough sex. Declan had three doors to choose from. One led to a bathroom, one to a storage room, the other to an alleyway.

Speaking into the mic on his watch, he said, "I'm headed into the alley. Just in case I'm wrong, check the bathroom and storage room."

"Roger that," came an abrupt reply.

Declan pushed open the door and then stepped back. Bullets pinged, and holes appeared in the door. He threw himself outside, shooting as he dove for cover behind a large garbage bin. Springing back to his feet, Declan saw a surprised and pained expression on Jackson's face. Bloody hands clutched his belly as he slid down the wall and landed in filth.

Seeing death in the other man's face gave Declan no satisfaction. "Tell me who the moneyman is, Jackson. At least let me make him pay."

"Ronan. Darius Ronan. Tell Sabrina...sorry." His eyes glazing, Jackson gave one last, rattling breath and then slumped into death.

CHAPTER
THIRTY-FOUR

Paris, France

Would he come? Should she have made her note more clear? Like maybe given directions or a street address?

Sabrina sat on the bench outside the small church where three years ago today, she and Declan had exchanged wedding vows.

She knew he was all right, at least physically. Other than that, she had no details.

Would he understand the message she'd left him? Was *Come to the place where our forever began* too vague? No, of course not Declan would know what she meant. And the platinum wedding band she'd left on the note had been better than a road map.

Question was, would he come with the intent to move forward with her or tell her again it was over?

She knew he loved her. And she had never stopped loving him. But sometimes love wasn't enough. Could they get beyond their jobs, their need to make a difference in the world, and be a happily married couple?

Could they have a normal marriage? Admittedly, most married couples didn't have people constantly trying to kill them, arrange assassinations of evil dictators, or willingly go into the most dangerous places in the world. But lots of people put their lives on the line on a daily basis. A lot of them were married and some happily. Why couldn't she and Declan do it, too?

As she waited, hoping against hope that he would appear, she thought about everything they'd been through and what he meant to her. No matter the outcome of this meeting, she owed Declan a wealth of gratitude. He'd given her so much. Love, acceptance, understanding. He was the only man to teach her that sex could be pleasurable. That physical desire was normal and healthy. That she could have that kind of relationship after what she had been through was a testament not only to his patience but to his love for her.

"I can't decide if I should spank you for leaving the hospital too soon, traveling thousands of miles when you should still be in bed, or kiss you because you are undoubtedly the most beautiful creature on the planet."

At the first sound of that gravelly, rich voice, she turned. He looked wonderful. Even though he had an air of sadness about him, she saw the glint of peace in his eyes.

He moved toward her, and she scooted over to make room on the bench. He sat beside her, lifted her uninjured hand, and carried it to his mouth. "How are you feeling?"

"Not all that bad. Stitches itch a little. My ribs only ache when I take too deep a breath. My wrist really doesn't hurt."

He gently touched her nose with his fingertip. "And this?"

She winced slightly. "Still a little sore."

"And the rest of you?"

Out of all the injuries she had sustained, she knew the beatings had probably hurt Declan the most. In her time at the Agency, she'd sustained broken bones and bullet wounds. And having endured torture training, she had known what to expect. But for Declan, there had been no training on how to handle his wife being tortured. Maybe that was something EDJE should add to their training schedule.

"Still have some colorful bruises, but they don't really hurt anymore."

"I wish I could have stayed with you."

"You had to do what you did. Is it over?"

"Yes."

"Jackson?"

"He's dead."

She had figured that would be the outcome. Even though Jackson had been cowardly in many ways, she had figured he'd rather die than be taken. Government agencies, secret or not, didn't deal kindly with those who betrayed them.

"I'm sorry it had to be that way."

"He made his choice."

"Are you okay?"

"I will be."

"And the moneyman? You got his name?"

"Yeah. Darius Ronan, like we thought."

"Are you going after him?"

"The search is already on. His father evaded us for years before I caught up with him. Doubt his son will make himself any easier to find."

"Did you get other names?"

"Not yet. The two men who accompanied Jackson on my fake rescue, Erickson and Ames, are in custody. With their assistance, along with Jason Starling's internal investigation, I'm optimistic we can get the names we need."

His gaze moved to the peaceful scenery of the church gardens. "McCall offered me a job."

She had known he would. The last conversation she'd had with Noah, he'd asked her what she thought of Declan working for LCR. She loved the idea, but she knew her husband well.

He turned back to look at her. "You know I can't take it, don't you, Sabrina?"

"Yes, I know. I told him you probably wouldn't."

"I greatly admire him and LCR's cause. I'm glad you've found a place there, but it's not for me."

"I know that, Declan. What you do is just as important."

He grinned, and for the first time in way too long, she saw the Declan she adored. "I talked to Albert. He was understandably pissed at me. I apologized and suggested he come back to EDJE as a consultant. He got as excited as a schoolboy at Christmas."

Her heart lifted. She knew that their distrust of the man who'd meant so much to them had hurt him. "I'm glad."

She straightened her spine. They'd been talking around it too long, and she could no longer wait. "So where does that leave us?"

Instead of giving her a direct answer, he said, "Before we go any further, I need to tell you how sorry I am for what happened."

His fingers pressed against her mouth, stopping her protest. "Let me finish. I thought by not telling you things I was protecting you. I was wrong. Not telling you put you in serious jeopardy, almost got you killed, and very nearly destroyed us both.

"I put the job before you, Sabrina. Something I never believed I would be stupid enough to do. And my need for vengeance came first, too. I was so damned wrong. Nothing and no one is more important than you. You are my everything, Little Fox, and I swear on my life I will never put anything before you again."

He shifted from the bench and knelt before her. Still holding her hand, he said quietly, "Three years ago I promised to love and cherish you. Even when I thought I hated you, I never stopped loving you. But I never cherished you as I should have. If you'll agree to be my wife again, I'll spend the rest of my life making that up to you."

"I never stopped being your wife, Declan. Even when I thought you were dead."

He turned her hand and placed something in it. Sabrina looked down to see his wedding band. "If you would, *A ghrá geal?*"

Beloved.

Her heart so full she felt it might burst, Sabrina slid the ring onto Declan's finger, then looked into his wonderful face. The adoration shining in his beautiful eyes was a reflection of her own love. This time nothing would tear them apart.

Cupping her face in his hands, he pulled her forward, kissed her tenderly. "Like you said, our forever after got interrupted. I don't intend for anything to ever interfere with that again."

Sabrina whispered softly, "Forever is a good start."

Thank you for reading Running On Empty, An LCR Elite Novel. I hope you enjoyed it. If you did, please help other readers find this book:

1. This book is lendable. Share it with a friend who would enjoy a dark and steamy romantic suspense.
2. Help other people find this book by writing a review.
3. Sign up for my newsletter at http://christyreece.com to learn about upcoming books.
4. Come like my Facebook page at https://www.facebook.com/AuthorChristyReece

Acknowledgements

Special thanks to the following people for helping make this book possible:

My husband for his loving support and numerous moments of comic relief.

My mom who housed me during the hair-pulling parts of writing this story. And to Billie and Marlin for once again opening their home on the river for me to finish the book.

Joyce Lamb for her copyediting, great advice and input.

Marie Force's eBook Formatting Fairies, who answered my endless questions with endless patience.

Marie Campbell for her medical advice. Any mistakes are entirely my own.

Tricia Schmitt (Pickyme) for her beautiful cover art.

Reece's Readers, my incredibly supportive and fun loving street team.

My beta readers for reading so many versions of this book, even I lost count.

And a very special thank you to all my readers. Without you, this book and all the others, past and future, would not be possible. You make my dreams come true!

ABOUT THE AUTHOR

Christy Reece is the award winning and New York Times Bestselling author of dark and sexy romantic suspense. She lives in Alabama with her husband, three precocious canines, an incredibly curious cat, two very shy turtles, and a super cute flying squirrel named Elliott.

Christy also writes steamy, southern suspense under the pen name Ella Grace.

You can contact her at Christy@christyreece.com

Praise for Christy Reece novels:

"The type of book you will pick up and NEVER want to put down again." *Coffee Time Romance and More*

"Romantic suspense has a major new star!" *Romantic Times Magazine*